simple

enroulée avec ironie
                    ou
            le mystère
                        précipité
                                hurlé

tourbillon d'hilarité et d'horreur

autour du gouffre
                sans le joncher
                            ni fuir

            et en berce le vierge indice

                        COMME SI

Poetry
in
France

Metamorphoses of a Muse

edited by
KEITH ASPLEY and PETER FRANCE

EDINBURGH UNIVERSITY PRESS

© Edinburgh University Press 1992

Edinburgh University Press
22 George Square, Edinburgh

Typeset in Linotron Galliard
by Nene Phototypesetters Ltd,
Northampton, and
printed in Great Britain at
The Alden Press, Oxford

A CIP record for this book is
available from the British Library

ISBN 0 7486 0335 2

11695

Contents

Acknowledgements

Thanks are due to the publishers for permission to reprint the following poems in whole or in part:

Yves Bonnefoy, 'L'Ecume, le récif', from *Pierre écrite* © Mercure de France (1965)

Alain Bosquet, 'Portrait d'un peuple heureux', from *Sonnets pour une fin de siècle* © Editions Gallimard, Collection Poésie (1980)

Robert Desnos, 'Idéal Maîtresse', from *Corps et biens*, © Editions Gallimard, Collection Poésie (1968)

Paul Eluard, 'La Terre est bleue comme une orange', from *Capitale de la douleur* © Editions Gallimard, Collection Poésie (1966)

Jean Follain, 'Les Siècles', from *Territoires* © Editions Gallimard (1969)

Pierre-Jean Jouve, 'Rêve du livre', from *Diadème* © Mercure de France (1966)

Henri Michaux, 'Projection', from *Mes propriétés* © Seghers (1967)

Raymond Queneau, 'Pour un art poétique', from *Bucoliques* © Editions Gallimard (1947)

Jacques Réda, 'Le Prix de l'heure dans l'île St Germain', from *Retour du calme* © Editions Gallimard (1989)

Introduction

This is not a history of French poetry. It is a collection of individual responses to questions raised in and by poetry in France from the early Middle Ages to the present. The contributors, all colleagues at Edinburgh University, have been concerned not just to describe and analyse poems, but to explore the different meanings and functions given to poetry in a changing society, from the courts of twelfth-century Provence to the complex and fractured world of twentieth-century Paris. Our aim is as much to stimulate thought and debate as to survey the history of a genre. What we are offering readers is not primarily a textbook, therefore, and we hope that it will have something to say not just to students but to all readers and lovers of French poetry, experts and beginners alike.

Many discussions of poetry assume that it possesses some unchanging essence. This may be defined more or less formally, as a peculiar way of using language. More commonly though, in the last two centuries, poetry has been seen rather in some essential quality of an utterance – illuminating, transfiguring, giving access to a different (higher?) plane of reality. Even by a writer as unpoetic as Sartre, it is allowed a special status which distinguishes it utterly from normal verbal communication.

Given this tendency to imagine poetry as a universal, it is not surprising if modern readers are often blind to other and older notions of the subject. It is only natural that poets in particular should subscribe to what one might call a Whig view of poetry, in which earlier ages are seen as coming close to, or falling away from, the creation of 'true' poetry. On such a view, poetry is born, decays, dies and is reborn. Famously, then, the poetry of sixteenth-century France was despised by the critics and poets of the classical period, only to be resurrected by the Romantics, who wrote off the intervening centuries as a poetic wasteland. In the same way, medieval lyric poetry was – and in some quarters still is – read through modern spectacles, with a quite misplaced focus on notions of sincerity and originality, whereas more recent developments in literary fashion have allowed for the rehabilitation of even the once despised 'Grands Rhétoriqueurs'.

We have tried to avoid any such teleological view of French poetry. The different contributors have their own beliefs about poetic value, no doubt, but these do not converge on any common orthodoxy, any more than all the different faces of this protean art can be said to merge into a common thing called 'French poetry'. This is not to deny the existence of tradition. No poet writes without an awareness of previous poetry, an awareness that can take the form of the 'anxiety of influence'. But rather than speak of a tradition – a great tradition leading majestically from the *Chanson de Roland* and the troubadour poets, through the triumphs of the Renaissance and Romanticism to the achievements of Baudelaire and modern poetry – we should do better to speak of traditions in the plural, of discontinuities, conflicts, ruptures and returns. So while the chapters of this volume are arranged in roughly chronological order, they do not offer a continuous narrative.

Rather than continuity, we witness a dialectic of old and new which is nicely captured in Du Bellay's idea of 'une nouvelle, ou plustot ancienne renouvelée poësie'. At various times, the new has been exalted over the old; revolutions have been proclaimed. Hugo believed that he had put the red bonnet of the First Republic on the old dictionary. But the First Republic itself had its eyes on antiquity. Absolute novelty is a delusion. Often the rejection of one ancestry implies the choice of another. Those engaged in the making of poetry, however different their cultural situation, find themselves confronting similar dilemmas. The same returns, but in a different form. The reader of this volume will be able to trace the threads of a number of recurrent concerns.

One of these pivotal questions is the extent to which poetry should be seen as what classical theorists call 'the language of the gods', a distinguished, exalted form of speech, radically different from the prose of ordinary communication. Or should it not rather be a form of verbal art open to the idiom of Everyman, the language of the streets, clichés, slang and the specialized jargons of different trades and professions, of science and technology? There have been many attempts to widen the scope and the vocabulary of poetry, from the scientific poetry of the sixteenth century to the collages of Apollinaire and Cendrars. Sometimes this means raising all language and all subjects to the dignity of high poetry, but it may equally imply a kind of democratization of the art, the desire to set real life and speech against a beauty or nobility perceived as hollow. Chapters 13 and 15 suggest that a version of the 'language of the gods' has maintained its commanding position in the accepted canon of modern French poetry.

As the language of the streets has been set against the language of the gods, so too has the poet as outcast against the poet as priest. If the poet as teacher, preacher or 'unacknowledged legislator' occurs in different guises in the work of a Ronsard, of a Chénier or of a Hugo, Chapter 3 shows the persistence of what one might call a 'counter-poet' tradition in the Middle Ages, and a modern version of this appears in the outsider or nomad poets of Chapter 12. Often, of course, the figures of poet and counter-poet meet in the same individual – in the ironies of La Fontaine, for instance. A related tension inhabits the 'poète maudit' of the Romantic period, a ridiculous outcast, whose very absurdity is a sign of his value in a prosaic world – a prophet rather than a priest. The discussion of Lautréamont in Chapter 11 poses the essential modern question, taken up again in Chapter 15, of a poetry whose subject is the failure of poetry and the derision of the poetic stance.

The high ambitions of poetry have often been associated with notions of inspiration or divine afflatus. Chapter 5 concerns the paradoxes of imagination in the Renaissance period, Chapters 9 and 11 discuss the ideal ambitions of Romantic poets (always doomed to a failure that is a kind of success) and Chapters 10 and 14 explore the claims of poets from Lamartine to the Surrealists to see visions, hear voices and communicate these to the public. Against this, though not in necessary contradiction with it (as Valéry's example makes clear) is the etymological notion of poetry as 'making', fabrication, the product of a difficult craft. This is perhaps proclaimed most clearly by the lyric poets of the Middle Ages (see Chapter 2); it surfaces again at many points, from the poets of 'la difficulté vaincue' in Chapter 7 to the aleatory craftsmanship of OULIPO mentioned in the final chapter. It is probably fair to say, however, that the tradition of poet as maker has remained subordinate to more exalted conceptions.

A related issue is that of sincerity of expression, of the possibility of a poetry of the self, of originality (that great modern value) in an art where words, forms, images and structures belong to the community (the tribe, as Mallarmé put it). Clearly, the idea of poetry as the 'spontaneous overflow of powerful feeling' is at odds with the practices of the medieval lyric poet described in Chapter 2. This does not mean that formulaic poetry is devoid of real feeling – far from it – but it may suggest that sincerity is too blunt an instrument for dealing with this question. It is above all in love-poetry that this question arises; in Chapters 4 and 6 the coexistence of self, persona and tradition is explored in poems of the sixteenth and seventeenth centuries.

Poetry is most often opposed to prose; Chapter 1 shows how in the early Middle Ages the opposition between the truth of prose and the fiction, or lies, of verse was to some extent overcome. Nevertheless, as Chapter 7 suggests, the suspicion of verse did not go away. Rhyme appeared to many to be incompatible with adult reason. At the same time, theorists began to challenge the identification of poetry with verse. Perhaps its true essence was actually hampered by the demands of prosody? And so, after being contained for eight or nine hundred years within relatively fixed forms of varying shapes and sizes, poetry has in the last century or so broken free from shackles of all kinds. As Mallarmé said, 'on a touché au vers', and this has arguably been the greatest single rupture in the story of French poetry, which has been able to take on such forms – not all of them entirely new, to be sure – as the prose poem, the various kinds of free verse, the *verset*, the *calligramme*, the musical or mathematical notation. At the limit, poetry becomes identified simply with a poet's way of living.

Nevertheless, even the poetry of recent decades retains a relationship (combining opposition and filiation) with the old verse forms, the alexandrine (often present as an unexpressed point of reference in free verse), the sonnet, the ode, and so on. Allusions to music and song (including popular song) in a number of the essays in this volume suggest the interest of the relations between these arts and canonic poetry from the Middle Ages to the present day. From the beginning, verse is closely linked to music, song and dance (a *ballade* is etymologically a dancing song). However, while formal questions are constantly present here, we have not tried to set out the traditional system or the evolution of French versification, or indeed to offer much technical discussion of the relation of verse to music. There are excellent books on this, and we refer to them in the Bibliography, which also lists a selection of general surveys, anthologies and important critical works which will supplement the necessarily partial discussions offered in our own volume.

There are, inevitably, several important areas which we did not have space to explore. Giving ourselves the task of writing about French poetry in France, we could not do more than mention in passing the development of French-language poetry in other parts of the world, notably Africa, the Caribbean and Canada. This is an immensely important field; although it is often closely related to poetry in France, it needs to be studied in its own right rather than as an appendage to metropolitan France. By the same token, we have not attempted, except to a certain extent in Chapter 1–4, to discuss the poetry written inside France in languages other than French – Latin, Provençal, Breton and others.

There is an unfortunate tendency (since Edgar Allen Poe?) to think of poetry almost exclusively in terms of the lyric, the short poem. Such a view is desperately at odds with the poetic practice of many centuries. The earlier chapters here show how poetry (verse) served as a medium for story-telling, and for conveying all kinds of truths and beliefs about the world. In France, as in most European countries, verse was also the language of serious theatre, and some of the great poets of France (Racine, Hugo, Claudel) have been poetic dramatists. This too is a huge subject in its own right; it is treated briefly in Chapter 7 and touched on in Chapter 10; limitations of space prevented a fuller discussion.

We have not been able either to explore as fully as we should have liked the sociology and the politics of French poetry, which concern both poets and their audience. The different chapters here show great variations in the social status of poets, their connections with power and privilege, their integration or non-integration into established society, and their popularity. In the nineteenth century, for instance, one can set the immense public figure of Victor Hugo, whose funeral was attended by many thousands of people, against the 'poètes maudits', a Nerval or a Rimbaud, whose poems at first reached only a handful. A long tradition, going back to classical antiquity, represents the poet as outsider, eccentric, madman, and this tradition remains a powerful one in post-Romantic France. On the other hand, from the *Chanson de Roland* to the poetry of the Resistance, poetic voices have been placed at the service of the nation, or of constituted groups within the nation. Poetry played its part in the religious struggles of the sixteenth century and the political strife of the Revolution. Under Louis XIV, some poets (by no means all) formed a chorus of praise to the monarch, but under the Bourbon restoration, and during the Second Empire, the voices of Béranger and Hugo respectively incarnated protest against the powers that be. Today, poetry no longer occupies the public position which it has held at many periods in French history, and it might seem that the developments traced in the later chapters of this volume have had the effect of cutting it off from a wide readership – except in time of war. And yet poetry is very present in contemporary France, in the great success of the Gallimard collection 'Poésie' for instance, or in the activities of the 'Maison de la Poésie' at the Forum des Halles, Paris. One could say also that the performance of poetry at public readings, on the radio and by singers has reasserted the oral dimension that was so central to it in earlier periods.

All this may lead one to reflect on the constitution of the poetic canon, the body of poems and poets which at any particular time goes under the name of 'French poetry'. The canon changes; it takes in new names, drops old ones, and resurrects the forgotten. At present, for instance, it gives a greater place to Théophile or Lautréamont than was once customary, whereas Vigny or Lecomte de Lisle seem less important. Over the centuries, and even in recent years, women poets have been given only a small corner of this space. Nor have popular song and poetry ever won a significant place in the canon, even though at times poets of the elite culture have stretched out arms of welcome to forms outside the pale – Nerval to the popular songs of the Valois, certain surrealists to children's rhymes. It would be surprising, however, to find a French history of French literature which would devote a chapter to the author of the 'Marseillaise' – as happened fairly recently in the Soviet Union.

One may well question this process of selection, elimination and canonization. Graham Martin asks at the end of his final chapter: who are the people, and what are the institutions who influence the formation and modification of the poetic canon? Can there be any adequate criterion of poetic value which is not vulnerable to the acerbic analyses of sociologists such as Pierre Bourdieu? One must accept that 'poetry' is a construct rather than a given.

Be that as it may, this volume works more or less within the canon as currently constituted. Our ambition has not been to reveal any neglected genius, nor to propose substantial modifications to the order accepted by the majority of scholars and critics. Nevertheless, some of our emphases may surprise some readers. The contributors have been guided in their selection of material partly by their personal preferences, which may or may not coincide with the currently prevalent valuations. Nor have we felt it necessary to ensure that all well-known poets are discussed here; the chapters are structured by the questions asked, rather than by a concern to cover the field. Particularly in the more recent period, some important figures (e.g. Claudel, Verlaine, Vigny) are mentioned only in passing. Other poets (Baudelaire, Rimbaud, La Fontaine, Ronsard and others) appear in more than one chapter, different aspects of their writings being highlighted in different contexts. The discussions of individual poets only rarely claim to be fully balanced treatments. Our subject is poetry, not poets.

The following pages contain many discussions of individual poems, which are often quoted in full. Quotations are given in the original spelling for all texts up to the mid-seventeenth century. To help readers who might have difficulty with the originals, translations are printed underneath all poetic texts (most prose texts being given in translation only, unless the particular quality of the prose appeared to warrant quotation in the original). Needless to say, these translations make no claim to being poems in their own right, they aim simply to give a clear idea of the meaning and – where possible – the form of the original.

Not long ago, those studying French in the higher classes of British schools usually studied some poetry – *Nine French Poets, Twelve French Poets* and the like. Times have changed, and even in university French courses poetry has learned to be content with a very modest place. At the same time, paradoxically, poetic production and the reading and love of poetry remain buoyant, both in France and in Britain. Working in a British university, we offer this book as an act of continuing faith in the richness of French poetry and its value for English-speaking readers.

KEITH ASPLEY
PETER FRANCE
Edinburgh, June 1991

I

Legends Told in Song and Story

PHILIP BENNETT

The literary generation which came to maturity in France around the year 1200 underwent a considerable crisis in the way it considered literary texts. The nub of the matter concerned the truth claims of literature, as authors began asserting that texts in verse were incapable of telling the truth and that only prose could provide a suitable vehicle for veracity.[1] The problem was linked to certain specific formal features of verse: the need to maintain the measure and find a rhyme. For us this appears a non-problem; the underlying truth of a text does not necessarily depend on superficial formal characteristics. The seriousness of the problem for French speakers in the Middle Ages (and in this category I include speakers of the *langue d'oc*) can be gauged from the fact that a century and a half later Froissart still felt the need to preface his *Chronicles* with a statement that he could only tell the truth about the great events that had occurred in France and England if he abandoned the verse of his sources and wrote in prose.

Like many problems that appear trivial to outsiders, and which appear to be posed in a trivial way, this one is highly complex and delicate, affecting as it does the tap root of the vernacular literary tradition as it has been preserved from the period up to the end of the twelfth century. All contemporary attempts to define literature in the vernacular, and significantly these are few before 1200, take as their starting point the truthfulness of the material conveyed. Jean Bodel's definition of narrative kinds is based on just such a perception; he identified three 'matters' (subjects) of differing levels and types of truth. His classifications are epic ('Matter of France') and what we would consider as two sub-divisions of romance ('Matter of Rome' – adaptations of Virgil, Ovid etc. – and 'Matter of Britain' – Arthurian romance). The last of these is considered 'vain et plaisant' (idle and amusing), the other two contain historical and moral truth respectively.[2] The exclusion of hagiography from Bodel's list may simply reflect a rhetorical preference for ternary structures, or it may indicate that, even within a society that considered literature as essentially didactic, the truth of saints' lives was held to exist on a totally different plane from that of what we would consider imaginative literature, even when that literature is underwritten by the authority of the Ancients or by collective memory.

A second point to note is that while prose as a literary vehicle was beginning to emerge in French in the late twelfth century, it had previously been reserved for juridical and similar purposes. Prose also existed in Latin writings accessible to the 'literate' in the medieval sense (educated in Latin). Thus for the bulk of the population one of the essential markers of an utterance as 'vernacular literature' was that it was composed of a series of discrete rhythmic units bounded by rhyme or assonance.

A third important feature of all vernacular literature before at least the middle of the twelfth century, and indeed perhaps for some time afterwards, is that it was oral. This does not necessarily mean that it was composed orally by an improvising 'singer of tales', to use Albert Lord's terminology.[3] Such a means of production is not to be ruled out, but from the earliest texts the signs of an interplay between the poem being recited or sung and its 'written version' are such as to suggest the possibility that none of the surviving examples was actually produced by illiterate poets, in either the modern or the medieval sense. However, it is certain that all literature up to and beyond the end of the twelfth century was perceived aurally by the majority of its audience. This may also help to explain the prevalence of verse in vernacular literature in France, although it can only be a partial explanation, since the examples of Anglo-Saxon, Scandinavian and Irish literatures are there from a very early period to illustrate the use of prose in oral cultures. Whatever the link to oral–aural transmission, it is notable that all narrative in France up to the late twelfth century is organized in tightly cohesive units of four and six syllables. These can be combined variously to produce octosyllables, decasyllables and dodecasyllables (the alexandrine, which will come to be so characteristic of French poetry). Additionally the hexasyllabic unit may stand alone, although its autonomous use is rare in narrative.

The impetus, within a traditionally oral culture, to produce and conserve written vernacular literary texts seems to have come predominantly from the learned influences of the Church. These manifested themselves in the nascent humanism of the 'Twelfth Century Renaissance', which was in fact well under way in the eleventh century. As a result secular magnates felt the need to have access to the authority of the written word in their own language. Given the Church's role in sponsoring this change it is not surprising that the earliest texts to survive, whether from north or south of the Loire, are hagiographic.

The mid eleventh-century Occitanian *Chanson de Ste Foy*[4] already illustrates most of the features I have been referring to. It is written in monorhymed *laisses* (groups of lines of varying number, linked by metre and by a common rhyme or assonance), which will also be the standard form of the *chanson de geste* (the epic poetry of northern France), except that at least until the end of the twelfth century the northern poets prefer assonance to full rhyme. In the *Ste Foy* the lines are octosyllabic, with a caesura (pause) which can fall after syllables three, four or five, or which can be suppressed giving an unbroken flow of eight syllables. Since the text was meant for singing, this flexibility suggests non-mensural music, with the text providing the rhythm.

The story of Ste Foy is that of a martyrdom during the late Roman persecutions. Fire has no effect on the saint, indicating that Hell has no claim over her, and the martyrdom is achieved by decapitation. The saint's death occurs approximately two-thirds of the way through the text, the last third being taken up with the deaths of the three tyrants responsible for the persecution and the extinction of their families in civil war. Throughout the text the author insists on the interplay between reading and singing. His sources are 'an old Latin book' (l. 2) and a Spanish song (ll. 14–15). The inextricable symbiosis of book and song comes out in *laisse* 3:

> Totas Basconn' et Aragons
> E l'encontrada delz Gascons
> Sabon quals es aqist canczons
> E s'es ben vera'sta razons;
> Eu l'audi legir a clerczons
> Et a gramadis, a molt bons [...]
> E si vos plaz est nostre sons,
> Aisi con.l guida.l primers tons,
> Eu la vos cantarei en dons. (ll. 23–33)

> (The whole Basque country and Aragon
> As well as Gascony
> Know which this song is
> And how true is its subject;
> I heard it read by clerks
> And very learned grammarians [...]
> And if this tune of ours pleases you,
> In its initial mode,
> I shall sing it for you *gratis*.)

As happens elsewhere in this early literature, the sung text and the one
for reading have become indistinguishable in the poet's mind. Other cat-
egories that we would keep separate are also indifferently run together here.
Thus, although the evil trinity of Dacien, Diocletien and Maximinien are
carefully designated as a provincial governor and two Roman Emperors,
their idols are covered in Cordoban gold, a clear reference to Saracen
'paganism' as depicted in Old French epics. Similarly in the final battles
classical, Old Testament and contemporary elements are freely mingled.

The martyr, although female, is painted in heroic terms, being aristo-
cratic and quite imperturbable. The simple, even simplistic contrasts and
garish colours of the portraiture can be gauged from this confrontation
between the saint and Dacien, who has just lost the first round of
disputation:

> Com au lo mendix pudolenz
> Qe lei.s non cambia sos talenz,
> Irasc tan fort con fa serpenz,
> Trastorna.ls oilz, lima las denz,
> E dunc jured sos sagramentz:
> 'Czo vostre cabs n'er totz sanglentz,
> O.us cremera la flamm'ardentz,
> Con audistz qe fez saint Laurentz.'
> Ella non.n pres nulz espaventz,
> E dissen motz ben covinentz:
> 'Fell sias tu, si mot m'en mentz!'.   (ll. 283–93)

> (When the stinking liar heard
> That she would not change her mind
> He became more angry than a snake,
> Rolled his eyes and ground his teeth,
> And swore his oath:
> 'Your head will be all bloody for this,
> Or the fiery flame will burn you up,
> As you heard it did to St Lawrence.'
> She was in no way terrified by this
> And replied becomingly:
> 'You're a knave, if one word of what you told me is a lie!')

The stark juxtapositions of ideas are reflected in the unarticulated
paratactic[5] structure of the language, which gives the saint's reply the force
of a closing *sententia*, or moral saying. Such chorus effects, in which a
character or the poet-reciter addresses the audience are common here as in
the epic, and differentiate this sort of writing from the romance, in which
authorial interventions, although they do occur, are more subtly woven
into the fabric of the work's rhetoric. The song ends because the narrator
does not care to celebrate even the deaths of villains, illustrating clearly

that the poem is perceived as a segment extracted from continuous tradition and overtly manipulated by the poet in complicity with his audience:

> E, si.s sun mort, vos nunqua'n calla,
> Q'eu noc'o prez una medalla.
> De.llor cantar jam pren nualla.   (ll. 591–3)

> (And if they are dead, you shouldn't care,
> For I don't give a fig about it.
> I feel sick just singing about them.)

We shall find the same open-endedness with the epic, and to some extent with the romance, but that does not characterize the first major hagiographic text from north of the Loire.

La Vie de Saint Alexis[6] was translated from Latin into French around the mid eleventh century, at about the same date as the *Ste Foy* was being composed in the south. The truth of this text is equally vouched for by a piece of writing, but one which exists within the text, not as an external witness: the saint writes his own story to enlighten his parents, in whose house he has been living as an unrecognized beggar for seventeen years. Angelic voices also announce within the text the status of the 'Man of God'. Like *Ste Foy*, the *Alexis* is composed in a form akin to the epic. Its lines are assonanced decasyllabics, with a caesura falling consistently after the fourth syllable, grouped in regular five-line stanzas. The entire poem is constructed with an eye to mathematical proportioning, so that numerical symbolism gives a learned underpinning to its whole structure.[7]

Rather than overtly invoking the book–song nexus, the *Alexis*-poet opens his work with an appeal to the myth of the Golden Age, which, by an appeal to the Ancestors (realized on one level as Patriarchs), raises the whole poem to the level of instructive myth in a way which intersects with the Christian message:

> Bons fut li secles al tens ancïenur,
> Quer feit i ert e justise ed amur;
> S'i ert creance, dunt or n'i at nul prut.
> Tut est müez, perdut ad sa colur:
> Ja mais n'iert tel cum fut as anceisurs.

> Al tens Noé ed al tens Abraham
> Ed al David, qui Deus par amat tant,
> Bons fut li secles; ja mais n'ert si vaillant.
> Velz est e frailes, tut s'en vat declinant:
> Si'st ampairét, tut bien vait remanant.   (ll. 1–10)

(The world was good in ancient days,
For there was faith and justice and love;
And there was belief, which has no worth now.
All is changed, it has lost its colour:
Things will never be again what they were for our ancestors.

In the days of Noah and Abraham
And of David, who loved God so much,
The world was good; it will never have such worth again.
It is old and frail, everything is in decline:
It goes from bad to worse, all goodness is abandoned.)

In this scheme Alexis, the subject of the following poem, is not just an example of early sainthood but very particularly a founder of our society, in the way that the epic hero is also the founder/preserver of the community celebrating him.

The link to epic poetry exists on the formal as well as on the thematic plane, but shows the same type of remove as well. The regularity of the lines and the rigid formalism of the stanzas reveal a controlling mind such as is rarely found in epic, while repetitions, listings and the paratactic juxtaposition of ideas organized into discrete metrical units all reveal the relationship between the *Alexis* and French epic. A striking example of the tendency is the triple series of laments over Alexis by his father, mother and bride of one day. Not only do we note again the urge to ternary construction but the nature of the laments links them to those of heroic poetry. With the mother's and the bride's laments we may feel that we are hearing the first women's voices in Northern French literature, but this is illusory:

'O kiers amis, de ta juvente bela!
Ço peiset mai que purirat [en] terre.
E! gentils hom, cum dolente puis estra!
Jo atendeie de tei bones noveles,
Mais or les vei si dures e si pesmes!

'O bele buce, bel vis, bele faiture,
Cum est mudede vostra bela figure!
Plus vos amai que nule creature.
Si grant dolur or m'est apare[ü]de!
Melz me venist, amis, que morte fusse.'   (ll. 476–85)

('O dear lover, how beautiful your youth!
I grieve that it will rot in earth.
Ah! noble man, how grief stricken can I be!
I awaited good news of you,
But now I see them harsh and evil!

'O beautiful mouth, beautiful face, beautiful build,
How your beautiful form is transformed!
I loved you more than any creature.
Such great grief has now risen before me!
It were better, my love, if I were dead.')

We may feel the opening of each stanza as 'women's' lines, but they differ hardly at all from ideas expressed in *La Chanson de Roland* by Charlemagne in his lament over the fallen Roland, or by Roland lamenting his companion Oliver. The beauty lamented is not the reflection of sexual attraction, but a mirror of the dead man's heroic (saintly) status. The death-wish expressed by the survivor also recurs regularly, as does the disappointment of hopes aroused. This style of *planctus*, although principally associated with epic in the vernacular, originates in late Latin elegies and funeral eulogies.[8] The emphasis placed in these laments on earthly loss is a mark of their affiliation with the heroic poetry to which I shall now turn.

At the centre of considerations of epic in Old French for us as for its contemporaries lies *La Chanson de Roland*.[9] The most famous extant version of this poem dates from around 1100, and is among the earliest such poems in French to survive. Like the *Alexis* it is composed in decasyllables, but its mono-assonanced *laisses* are variable in length like those of the *Ste Foy*. We should also observe that it contains a fair number of alexandrines and some octosyllables. Moreover the caesura, while falling predominantly after the fourth syllable, is also found after the sixth, and in some lines it is very hard to place a caesura. This suggests that we are dealing with a song produced in the 'popular improvisatory' tradition. As in the case of the *Ste Foy* (but not of the more rigidly composed *Alexis*) we are led to the conclusion that the musical line supporting the text must have been a very flexible psalmody if it was to be singable at all.

The story of the *Roland*, the massacre of the rearguard of Charlemagne's army as it recrossed the Pyrenees after unsuccessfully besieging Saragossa in August 778, is known from near-contemporary chronicles. The avenging of this initial defeat, the trial and execution of the traitor, Ganelon, responsible for the ambush, the crushing of Islamic power represented by the mighty Emir Baligant, and indeed the very presence of heroes called Roland, Oliver and Turpin on the battlefield are all 'fictional' accretions. 'Fiction', however, is a category unknown in this period, which does not distinguish imaginative non-truth from mendacious untruth. The whole is thus treated as legend, in the medieval, etymological, sense of 'things valid for reading', and the veracity of the story is guaranteed by the *geste*,[10] by eyewitnesses and most explicitly by a vision of St Giles, which is transformed into a written record as a 'basis' for the poem:

Ço dit la geste e cil ki el camp fut –
Li ber Gilie, por qui Deus fait vertuz –
E fist la chartre el muster de Loüm.
Ki tant ne set ne l'ad prod entendut.   (ll. 2095–8)

(The *geste* says as does he who was on the field –
The noble Giles, for whom God works miracles –
And who made the written text preserved in the monastery at Laon.
Whoever does not know this has no proper understanding of the matter.)

The paratactic construction of these lines leaves only suggestions of sense in the hearer's mind (as was also the case for many of the isolated hemistichs of the lament in *Alexis* quoted above). What does emerge though is the idea of a tight nexus of tribal and imperial memory, and of ecclesiastical ideology implying the conviction noted in the last line quoted that the text carries a meaning beyond that of the surface narrative, accessible only to those who appreciate its origins, and akin to the higher truths of scripture.

This assimilation is best seen in the treatment of the hero, Roland. On the one hand he is a pre-Christian Germanic epic warrior, who boasts repeatedly and ritualistically of how he will fight, and if necessary die, for his lord (Charlemagne), his family and land and above all for his reputation; his main concern being that no one shall sing a scurrilous song about him. On the other hand he is quite explicitly given Christological attributes, most notably in the way his death is announced:

En France en ad mult merveillus turment,
Orez i ad de tuneire e de vent,
Pluies e gresilz desmesureement,
Chiedent i fuildre e menut e suvent,
E terremoete ço i ad veirement.
De Seint Michel del Peril jusqu'as Seinz,
Des Besençun tresqu'as [porz] de Guitsand
Nen ad recét dunt li mur ne cravent.
Cuntre midi tenebres i ad granz,
N'i ad clartét, si li ciels nen i fent;
Hume ne.l veit ki mult ne s'espaent.
Dient plusor: 'Ço est li definement,
La fin del secle ki nus est en present.'
Il ne.l sevent, ne dient veir nïent:
Ço est li granz dolurs por la mort de Rollant.   (ll. 1423–37)

(In France there is a most marvellous tempest
There are storms of thunder and wind
Lashing rain and hail
Frequent fierce lightning strikes,

There truly was an earthquake.
From Mont St Michel to Saintes,
From Besançon to the roads of Wissant
There is no dwelling whose walls do not collapse.
At midday there is a great darkness,
There is no light unless the heavens split open;
No man sees it without being terrified.
Several people say: 'This is the Last Judgement
The end of the world is upon us.'
They do not know, and do not speak the truth at all:
It is the great grieving for the death of Roland.)

The mixture of borrowings from St Matthew's Gospel and from the Apocalypse, signalled in the reference to the Last Judgement, leave us in no doubt as to how to read these signs, even if 'Roland's contemporaries' in their blindness cannot. The purely warrior hero is subject to a spiritual promotion which places him in the same relationship to his society as was Alexis. It is not surprising then that the actual death of Roland (ll. 2259–396) takes place in perfect peace, in idyllic surroundings on a hill top blending reminiscences of Calvary and the Heavenly Jerusalem, or that, following a series of heroic laments and celebrations of his victories, he is translated directly to heaven, a warrior-martyr.

As with Alexis and Foy, Roland's death occurs about half way through the poem. The second half is taken up with vengeance and ultimate Christian victory. It may, therefore, surprise us that the poet's attitude appears to become increasingly pessimistic. After the grand evocation of the emperor in l. 1 of the poem,

Carles li reis nostre emperere magnes

(Charles the king our great Emperor)

with its classical tmesis[11] giving emphasis, grandeur and hieratic stability to the name, we find a steady decline hardly halted by Roland's great victory-in-death. Victories have to be repeated, militarily (defeats of Marsile and Baligant), spiritually (the conversion of the Saracen queen Bramimonde) and judicially (the executions of the traitor, Ganelon, and his supporters). After all of which the last image we have of Charlemagne is his weeping at the thought that all must begin again, as he is called by an angel to rescue another Christian king:

'Deus', dist li reis, 'si penuse est ma vie!'
Pluret des oilz, sa blanche barbe tiret.
Ci falt la geste que Turoldus declinet.   (ll. 4000–2)

('God,' said the king, 'how burdensome is my life!'
He weeps and tugs at his white beard.
Here ends the *geste* that Turold recites.)

The optimism is replaced by a sense of endurance more akin to ancestral Germanic heroic modes than to hagiography. Again though, as with *Ste Foy*, and with the *Alexis* which ends with an appeal to the audience to sing the *Te Deum*, the *Roland* closes by bringing the audience into contact with a reciting voice (the exact status of Turold as poet, singer or scribe is controversial and ultimately irrelevant) making the poem a living part of collective experience.

The celebration of a community and its founding values which we observe in epic and hagiography are absent from romance. Not that writers of romance see themselves as lacking serious purpose. Jean Bodel may have considered Arthurian material as 'idle and amusing', and the hagiographer Denis Piramus might dismiss the *Lais* of 'Dame Marie' as 'lying',[12] but these positions merely reflect the problems the Middles Ages had in coming to terms with the notion of fiction. Marie de France herself had no doubt about the 'truthfulness' of her *Lais*, whether placing them under the aegis of the Britons who composed the originals she claims to translate, or appealing to the scholastic tradition of exegesis and glossing to invite the reader to find an allegorical meaning behind the story. Her twelve tales told in octosyllabic verse, with an art that gives the lines the unobtrusive-ness of elegant prose, explore many aspects of human psychology (es-pecially in the realms of love and sexuality), exploiting Celtic myth and folk-tale as well as Ovid to provide material for the discussion of problems generated by contemporary courtly society. Chrétien de Troyes likewise appeals to the notion of the *translatio studii et imperii* (transfer of learning and power [from Rome to France]) to justify his text in *Cligés*, which deals precisely with the interplay between 'Classical' (Byzantine) and Arthurian worlds, where the Arthurian renews and saves the Classical. The opening of *Le Conte du Graal*[13] for its part appeals to a biblical exemplar:

> Ki petit semme petit quelt,
> Et qui auques requeillir velt,
> En tel liu sa semence espande
> Que Dieux a cent doubles li rande;
> Car en terre qui riens ne valt,
> Bone semence seche et faut.
> CRESTIENS semme et fait semence
> d'un romans que il encomence [...]   (ll. 1–8)

> (Who little sows little reaps,
> And whoever wants to reap

> Must spread his seed on such land
> As God will twice a hundredfold render;
> For in land of little worth
> Good seed dries up and fails.
> CRESTIENS spreads and sows the seed
> Of a vernacular book which he begins [...])

Not only has the verse form changed here, octosyllabic couplets carrying flexible hypotactic sentences, marked only by rhyme with no caesura, but the fundamental outlook has too. Instead of the collective celebration of a founder/saviour mediated through a reciting voice which represents the community, we have an author justifying his composition as something not self-evidently valuable. Like Marie, Chrétien appeals to outside authority for the truth of his writings (a book given him by Count Philip of Flanders), but the intrinsic justification comes from the subtly presented rhetorical appeal to the twin Gospel notions of the multiplication of the talents and the sowing of seed on good ground. This good ground may refer to the receptivity of the hearers or to the quality of the subject-matter chosen. In his *Yvain*[14] (ll. 150–72) he also insists that stories, which are not lies, have to be understood with the heart as well as heard with the ears, again introducing a biblical allusion as he describes words coming to the ears 'ausi come li vanz qui vole' (as the wind that flies – l. 158).

This amount of self-justification is doubtless all the more necessary as Chrétien's texts are problem texts. Of all his surviving works only the *Erec et Enide* closes on an unequivocal reintegration of hero and society. *Yvain*, *Le Chevalier de la Charette (Lancelot)*, *Le Conte du Graal*, and even *Cligés* are profoundly critical of the courtly and chivalric society they depict, and their endings, even when they appear to be closed (and leaving aside the fragmentary *Graal*) are unsatisfactory in many ways. Despite the conventional happy-ever-after ending of *Yvain*, the hero actually bullies his way back into his wife's graces in defiance of all that he has apparently learned in the rest of the romance, and the endings of *Cligés* (the melodramatic death of a husband) and *Lancelot* (the hero's victory in a judicial duel negating his adultery with the queen) are equally factitious, as though Chrétien having posed the problems of his texts is challenging his audience to seek their own solutions by defying them to accept the apparent facility of what he offers.

The generation which followed Chrétien was already more at home in its romance writing. It moved away from the Arthurian setting and began to develop stories about contemporary society. It also had before it the example of literary prose. So when Jean Renart chose in the 1220s to write his tales in verse he was making a conscious choice in the light of the verse–prose controversy, and poetic form becomes an integral part of his message. This may be seen in his *Guillaume de Dole*, in which characters 'sing' songs from the contemporary lyric repertoire as part of their characterization and to illustrate developments in the plot, or in his *Lai de l'ombre*, in which literary categories are conflated and the traditional truth claim is flouted in the interests of 'realism':[15]

> Ci dit que uns chevaliers iere
> En cele marche de l'Empire
> De Loheraigne et d'Alemaigne;
> Je ne cuit pas que tex en maigne
> De Chaalons jusqu'en Perchois
> Qui eüst toutes a son chois
> Bones teches conme cil ot.
> De maintes ressemble au fil Lot,
> Gauvain, si conme nos dison;
> Mes je n'oï onques son non,
> Ne je ne sai se point en ot.   (ll. 53–63)

> (Here it says there was a knight
> On the March of the Empire
> Between Lorraine and Germany;
> I think none such exists from Châlons to Perche
> Who had quite at his disposal
> As many good traits as he had.
> By many of them he resembles Lot's son,
> Gawain, as we say.
> But I never heard his name,
> And I don't know if he had one.)

The opening words of this passage ('Ci dit ...') appeal to traditions of moralizing rather than romance texts. It then advances by a series of puns produced by rhyme and overflows which defy translation but which link external contemporary reality to the legendary (literary) past of the Arthurian world, to the astounding assertion that the narrator is not only ignorant of his hero's name, but that the hero is literally anonymous.

The ending of this tale of the successful forging of an amorous relationship in a courtly context is equally insouciant. Having got his couple into each other's arms the author re-enters his text:

> N'i covient mes penser de rien
> JEHAN RENART a lor afere;
> S'il a nule autre chose a fere,
> Bien puet metre son penser aillors.
> Que puisque lor sens et Amors
> Ont mis andeus lor cuers ensemble,
> Du geu qui remaint, a ce me semble,
> Venront il bien a chief andui;
> Et or s'en taise a tant meshui!

> Ici fenist li Lais de l'Ombre:
> Contez, vos qui savez de nombre!   (ll. 952–62)

> (It is not seemly for Jehan Renart to think
> Any more of their affairs;
> If he has something else to do
> He can easily put his mind to other things.
> For now that their understanding and Love
> Have brought both their hearts together
> I think they will get round successfully
> To the sport that remains outstanding;
> Now let him say no more of it today!
> Here ends the Lay of the Reflection:
> Take up the tale, if you know the score!)

The last line is really untranslatable containing as it does the notions of counting and telling, of mathematical and intellectual acuteness and above all of poetic (metrical) ability.

In this complex coda to a deceptively simple tale the two categories of fiction and poetry begin to find their own voice. We are no longer concerned with the simple categories of lies and truth or with the simple opposition of verse and prose. A new category is being born: imaginative poetic fiction, the 'truth' of which actually resides in language and its manipulation.[16]

2

Troubadours, Trouvères, Poëtes

PHILIP BENNETT

> L'idée de poésie comme art, comme artisanat et comme passion, comme
> jeu, comme ironie, comme recherche, comme savoir, comme violence,
> comme activité autonome, comme forme de vie, idée qui fut celle de bien
> des poètes [...] dans la tradition européenne, et tout récemment encore
> celle de Raymond Queneau [...] j'en vois l'exemple premier chez les
> troubadours.   (Jacques Roubaud, *La Fleur inverse*)

> (I find in the troubadours the initial example of the idea that poetry is art,
> craftsmanship and passion, game, irony, quest, knowledge, violence,
> an autonomous activity and way of life; it is an idea expressed by many
> poets [...] in the European tradition, and most recently by Raymond
> Queneau.)

The lyric poetry that sprang up in what is now southern France at the end
of the eleventh century, mixing popular folk and learned liturgical forms
and themes, and influenced by Islamic poetry from Moorish Spain,
displays from its earliest surviving manifestations a self-awareness and self-
confidence unrivalled in the Western tradition.[1] It was part of that same
Renaissance that had seen the flowering of narrative forms discussed in the
first chapter, and was destined to have an enduring influence as great as if
not greater than them. From the 150-year period during which Provençal
culture was at its peak some 2,542 poems survive composed by 460 poets,[2]
including 'Spaniards' like Cerveri de Girona, 'Italians' like Folquet, Bishop
of Marseille, and Sordello, and the 'English' king Richard Lionheart and
his brother Geoffrey, Count of Brittany. Directly or indirectly they
generated imitators and adaptors in northern France, Germany, Portugal
and England. Through Dante and Petrarch, both admirers of their poetry,

they bore heavily on the Italian and French Renaissances of the fourteenth to sixteenth centuries, and thus on the whole of modern European literary culture. The basic form they invented, the *canso* or *chanson*, with its subtly interlocked bipartite and tripartite structures, remains to this day an essential part of our musical language. Their predominant theme, that at least which was most avidly taken up in other traditions, was love in the refined form they called *fin'amor* (noble love) and which has been known since the nineteenth century as 'courtly love'. Its basic conventions, love at first sight, the exalted and remote position of the loved one, love as deliberately unfulfilled desire generating a manichean dichotomy of joy and pain within the lover requiring as one of its conditions a quasi-religious asceticism and self-discipline, have coloured the representation of relationships between the sexes in poetry, novels, plays and films down to the present day. Among the 460 known poets there are also some 20 female poets, or *trobairitz*. It has been argued that they offer an original female voice within the corpus, but this position is debatable, since in general they use the same repertoire of formulaic motifs as the men. What is remarkable in an almost totally male-dominated society is that these female poets were accepted as equals in poetic debate by their male contemporaries and that they did contribute significantly to the corpus of what remains the almost unremittingly male-oriented ideology of *fin'amor*.

We tend to refer to all these writers as poets, and when the word 'troubadour' is used, at least in popular parlance, like 'minstrel' it conjures up the image of a wandering musician, a 'thing of rags and patches', carrying his lute from castle to castle or fair to fair. In fact the Latinate word 'poet' only came into use to denote composers of vernacular verse late in the Middle Ages. The itinerant entertainer was a *jongleur* (cf. English 'juggler') and contemporaries referred to the Provençal 'poets' as *trobadors*, from the verb *trobar*, 'to invent', with strong musical overtones of 'composing tropes on liturgical texts'. Within their poems the troubadours frequently refer to themselves as *chantadors* (singers), as in this example from Bernart de Ventadorn (active *c.* 1150–80):

> Non es meravelha s'eu chan
> melhs de nul autre chantador,
> que plus me tra.l cors vas amor
> E melhs sui faihz a so coman.[3]

> (It is no wonder if I sing
> Better than any other singer,
> For my heart [and/or body or personality] draws me
> more forcefully towards love
> And I am better fashioned to its command.)

The double implication of these lines is that 'singing' is the product of inspiration (synonymous with love) and sincerity (the emotion is integral to the poet's personality). This also produces an entirely enclosed and self-referential scheme, as Paul Zumthor has pointed out, in which singing is loving is living.[4] Furthermore, singing implies that this experience is an essentially musical one. Indeed, the musical structure is integral to the poems, which comprise one phrase covering the first two lines of text, repeated with variation in the second two lines, leading to a second, autonomous, musical phrase which develops freely over the remainder of the stanza. The importance of this symbiosis is recorded in the closing lines of a poem in which Guillaume IX (Duke of Aquitaine, 1071–1126), asserts his pride in both aspects of his composition:

> Del vers vos dic que mais en vau,
> Qui ben l'enten e.n a plus lau,
> Que'ls motz son fag tug per egau
> Comunalmens,
> E.l sonetz, ieu mezeis m'en lau,
> Bos e valens.[5]

> (I tell you this about the *vers*: the person who understands it properly
> Increases in worth and is made more praiseworthy by it,
> Because all the words are made in even proportion
> With each other,
> And the tune, I myself am proud of it,
> Is good and precious.)

This introduces us to two new facets of troubadour poetry. Firstly it is intended for a self-defining elite who can approach it with sympathetic, even empathetic, understanding. For this is social poetry. Although the poem regularly addresses a Lady (lover/mistress), who frequently appears to be no more than a philosophic realization of the poet's own self-contemplating emotions, the poem as an artefact is often addressed to a third party, patron or fellow poet. Thus Guillaume IX sends his most enigmatic poem 'farai un vers de dreit nien', (I shall compose a *vers* about nothing at all) to Anjou to have the riddle solved; Jaufré Rudel (active 1125–48) sends one of his poems, 'Quan lo rius de la fontana', (When the stream from the spring) to Lord Hugo Brown (N'Hugo Bru), and Sordello (active *c.* 1220–65), playing the courtly game to the full, ends his poem 'Atretan deu ben chantar finamen/D'invern com fatz d'estiu' (I must sing in just as refined a manner/Of winter as I do of summer)[6] with these highly ambiguous verses:

> Si col soleill(z) esfassa, quan resplan,
> Autras clardatz, vai de pretz esfassan
> Autras dompnas la contess'am cors quar,
> Sil de Rodes, (s)es ma domn'esfassar.

> La comtessa nom deu ges asirar,
> S'ieu am ni pretz lei don sui hom sens par.

> (As the sun eclipses all other lights when it shines,
> So the countess with the precious body
> Eclipses all other ladies,
> I mean the one from Rodez, without eclipsing my lady.

> I must not lay siege to the countess,
> If I love and prize her whose unchallenged vassal I am.)

The multiple cross-references here make it impossible to tell whether or not the Countess of Rodez, who is ostensibly addressed as patron, is or is not the same lady as the poem purports to address as subject.

The second theme introduced in Guillaume's poem is that of craftsmanship. In his poem there is no notion of 'sincere inspiration', such as can be inferred from Bernart's; just of words carefully chosen and fitted to an appropriate melody. This theme of craftsmanship is expounded more explicitly in the work of Arnaut Daniel (active 1180–95) who begins one poem:

> En cest sonet coind'e leri
> Fas motz e capuz e doli,
> E seran verai e cert
> Quan n'aurai passat la lima;
> Q'amors marves plan'e daura
> Mon chantar qe de lei muou,
> Cui pretz mante e governa.[7]

> (In this elegant and delicate little song
> I compose the words and rasp and plane them smooth,
> And they will be true and right
> When I have passed the file over them;
> For love at once planes and gilds
> My singing since it derives from her
> Who maintains worthiness and is its governor.)

The last one and a half lines are actually totally ambiguous, since they could also read '... which depends on it [i.e. love] which maintains and rules valour'. This ambiguity is central to Arnaut's writing, and indeed to much troubadour poetry. The debate over whether poetry should be immediately accessible to a wide public or require the application of hard intellectual effort by an initiated elite raged in the second half of the twelfth century, and Arnaut was definitely of the esoteric school. The interchanges between plastic and verbal arts, the insistence on combining compositional skill with inspiration, the mirage of an outer world which immediately closes in on itself, and the rather ironic reference to this very dense set of meanings and suggestions as a 'pretty little ditty' all underline for us the self-awareness of this poetry as construct.

The first generation of northern French *trouvères* (the word is a simple calque of the Provençal) imitated the troubadours very closely. However if we consider two songs, one by Bernart de Ventadorn, one by Thibaut IV, Count of Champagne and King of Navarre (1201–57), we can see at a glance the essential differences of outlook between the two 'schools' of poets.

One of Bernart's most famous songs is that which opens with an evocation of the song of the skylark:

> Can vei la lauzeta mover
> de joi sas alas contra.l rai,
> Que s'oblid'e.s laissa chazer
> Per la dossor c'al cor li vai,
> Ai! tan grans enveya m'en ve
> De cui qu'eu veya jauzion,
> Meravilhas ai, car desse
> Lo cor de dezirer no.m fon.[8]

> (When I see the skylark moving
> Its wings for joy in the sunlight,
> Until it forgets itself and lets itself fall
> For the sweetness that goes to its heart,
> Oh! such great longing invades me
> For the joyfulness I see it experience
> That I marvel that at once
> My heart does not melt within me out of desire.)

Thibaut's poem presents us with the more frequently encountered image of the nightingale but his opening lines suggest that Bernart's poem was not far from his mind when he wrote it:

> Li rossignous chante tant
> Que morz chiet de l'arbre jus;
> Si bele mort ne vit nus,
> Tant douce ne si plaisant.
> Autresi muir en chantant a hauz criz,
> Que je ne puis de ma dame estre oïz,
> N'ele de moi pitié avoir ne daigne.[9]

> (The nightingale sings until
> It falls dead from the tree;
> Such a fine death no one ever saw,
> Nor so sweet, nor so pleasing.

> Likewise I die singing with loud cries
> Since I cannot be heard by my lady,
> And she does not deign to have pity on me.)

On the purely formal plane we see that Bernart's song links the first four lines (the *frons*) with their repeated musical phrase to the last four (the *cauda*) with their freely developing phrase by phonic echoes (assonances: *mover : chazer ~ ve : desse*; alliterations: *lauzeta – chazer – jauzion – dezirier*) and semantic or thematic ones (*joi – jauzion*; *dossor – enveya – dezirier*). Thibaut on the other hand makes a sharp break between the two parts of the stanza signalling it by a change of line length, by dividing it into two propositions and, despite the thematic continuity of the notions 'sing' and 'die', by making the two halves of the stanza the two parts of an explicit comparison ('as the nightingale so I').

On the thematic level, whereas Thibaut offers us a series of explicit statements linking love, singing and death and launches immediately into a complaint against his lady, Bernart shows himself as totally wrapped up, like the bird which represents him as both poet and lover, in his song and his joy (a key mystical experience for the troubadours, akin to the highest level of religious contemplative exaltation) and its negative pole (longing), providing a paradoxical statement of fulfilled unfulfilment. It is not until his second stanza that Bernart introduces his love and his lady: 'Car eu d'amar no.m posc tener/Celeis don ja pro non aurai' (For I cannot help loving/Her from whom I will have no profit). Death does not appear until the third stanza:

> Anc non agui de me poder
> Ni no fui meus, de l'or'en sai
> Que.m laisset en sos olhs vezer
> En un miralh que mout me plai.
> Miralhs, pus me mirei en te,
> M'an mort li sospir de preon,
> C'aissi.m perdei com perdet se
> Lo bels Narcissus en la fon.

> (I never had power over myself
> Nor was my own since the time
> She let me look into her eyes
> Into a mirror which gives me much pleasure.
> Mirror, since I looked into you,
> Sighs from the depths have killed me,
> For I lost myself just as
> Beautiful Narcissus lost himself in the fountain.)

Again we note that the whole process is internalized. It is not the lady who had killed him, not even love in a strict sense, but his own sighs, rising from what depths? From the eyes that are at once a mirror and a pool, but equally from the depths of his own being, to which the eyes–mirror–pool are merely a gateway. Although Bernart spends the next two stanzas on a diatribe against the fickleness of women, there is really no genuinely external stimulus to his condition. The lady is a passive instrument on which the narrating 'I' reacts, generating his own condition. Thibaut's development is in stark contrast to this. Everyone, says Thibaut, claims to love more intensely than anyone else ever has; ladies should be able to spot the charlatans. He then launches into his own historical comparisons:

> Onques fierté n'eut si grant
> Vers Pompee Julius
> Que ma dame n'en ait plus
> Vers moi, qui muir desirant.
> Devant li est touz jorz mes esperiz
> Et nuit et jor li crie mil merciz,
> Baisant ses piez, que de moi li souviegne [...]
>
> Je ne cuit pas que serpent
> N'autre beste poigne plus
> Que fait Amors au desus;
> Trop par sont si coup pesant.
> Plus trait souvent que Turs ne Arrabiz,
> N'onques encor Salomons ne Daviz
> Ne s'i tindrent ne qu'uns fous d'Alemaigne.
>
> (Never had such fierceness
> Julius Caesar for Pompey
> That my lady does not have more
> For me, who die of desire.
> My spirit is before her day and night begging a thousand times mercy
> Kissing her feet, that she should remember me [...]
>
> I do not think that a serpent
> Or other beast stings more
> Than Love, which stings most;
> Its blows are excessively heavy.
> It shoots more arrows than a Turk or Arab
> Neither Solomon nor David ever held out against it
> Any more than a German fool.)

The lady as well as love is explicitly compared to Julius Caesar hounding an (innocent?) enemy, and to that most archetypal of sexual beasts, the serpent. The interlarded references to Solomon and David and to Turks and Arabs conjure up between them a whole tradition of anti-feminist, and anti-love, tracts, as well as the world of the crusades, with death and defeat inflicted on chivalrous Christian knights, by 'unsporting' enemies

who fire arrows at them, like Cupid, but also like despised foot soldiers
(the only archers in European armies of the time, which makes the allusion
totally negative). In this context the German fool could be either a *jongleur*
or a warrior from beyond the Rhine with more bravado than sense. What
really matters in Thibaut's poem, though, is that all these references are
to concrete external experience, classical, biblical, or drawn from current
affairs. The lady and love are consequentially autonomous phenomena to
be written about, not an integral part of the poet's persona.

This externalizing tendency of the *trouvères* leads them into a much
more anecdotal stance than the troubadours generally exhibited. One
manifestation of this is the development of the *chanson de croisade* (song of
a knight leaving for the crusades, or of a lady remembering her lover
absent on crusade). Its origins may lie in a blend of the Provençal notion
of *amor de lonh* (distant love) with the political *sirventes* or 'partisan's
poem', which clothed polemical material in the garb of the courtly *chanson*.
Many *chansons de croisade* are fairly obvious, tacking a conventional love-
poem on to an exordium relating to the crusades, or vice versa. One
example, by the Chastelain de Coucy (possibly Gui, Chastelain de Coucy
who died in 1203 during the Fourth Crusade), provides a much more
subtle blend.[10] It begins:

> A vous amant, plus k'a nul autre gent,
> Est bien raisons que ma douleur conplaigne,
> Quar il m'estuet partir outreement
> Et dessevrer de ma loial conpaigne;
> Et quant li pert, n'est rienz qui me remaigne;
> Et sachiez bien, Amours, seürement,
> S'ainc nuls morut pour avoir cuer dolent,
> Donc n'iert par moi maiz meüs vers ne laiz.

> (To you, lovers, more than to any others,
> It is right that I should complain,
> For I must go without fail
> And part from my loyal companion;
> And when I lose her, nothing is left me;
> And, Love, you can know for a fact
> That if ever anyone died of a sorrowing heart,
> No verse or lay will ever be composed by me again.)

Stanzas 2 and 3 develop the themes of leave-taking and voyage into a
strange land (where the poet will not have the comfort of his lover's
presence), of memory of the joys of love experienced and amazement at the
poet's surviving the parting. In stanzas 4 and 5, God, rather blasphemously
we might think, is aligned with all boors (*vilainz*) who disrupt love affairs,
and Christ's injunction to 'love your enemies' is recalled ruefully as the

poet thinks of *losengiers* (scandalmongers) who would cause his voyage (crusade-pilgrimage) to be deprived of its spiritual benefit by their evil deeds. The poem ends:

> Je m'en voiz, dame! A Dieu le Creatour
> Conmant vo cors, en quel lieu que je soie;
> Ne sai se ja verroiz maiz mon retour:
> Aventure est que jamaiz vous revoie.
> Pour Dieu vos pri, en quel lieu que je soie,
> Que noz convens tenez, viegne u demour,
> Et je pri Dieu qu'ensi me doint honour
> Con je vous ai esté amis verais.

> (I am going away, lady! To God the Creator
> I commend your person, wherever I might be;
> I do not know if you will ever see my return:
> It is doubtful if I ever will see you again.
> For God's sake I beg you, wherever I might be,
> To keep our agreement, whether I come back or remain,
> And I pray God that He grants me honour
> As I have been a faithful lover to you.)

One way in which this poem differs from others we have considered is that the poet has clearly had a satisfactory and reciprocal relationship with his lady. The words *conpaigne* and *amie* used to refer to her, and the repeated notion of *solaz* (used to evoke emotional if not strictly sexual fulfilment) and a whole series of positive indicators reveal this. It rejoins the main-stream by referring to love remembered and now lost, but the cause of the loss is the poet's departure on pilgrimage (we would say 'crusade') into a threatening land. It is not the *losengiers*, an intrinsic element of the poem's thematics, but the call to save the Holy Places, which is extrinsic to the poetics of *fin'amor*, that enables Coucy to assimilate his poem to the *amor de lonh* tradition. Nevertheless, the *losengiers* do exist within the poem as part of a series of negative symbols that cast the poem into a familiar melancholy mould.

The themes invented by the troubadours survived the great cultural divide of the late thirteenth century and were revived in the works of the fourteenth-century master, Guillaume de Machaut (*c.* 1300–70). The vehicle for the poetry was, however, no longer the *chanson*, but a series of forms based on dance structures. The foundation of the three major forms (*rondeau*, *virelai* and *ballade*) is a simple bipartite structure based on alternating musical phrases and reflected, at its simplest, in the *rondeau* which is built on just two rhyme-sounds. Because these dance forms also contain a chorus element a refrain recurs at regular intervals throughout the poem. The *virelai* comprised three stanzas and a refrain of stanza length repeated at the beginning, middle and end of the piece. The *ballade* provided the fullest blend of the old *chanson* with the dance form, offering three stanzas, each terminating in a refrain; each stanza has the typical *chanson* structure. Although the two parts of the stanza could be treated autonomously it became traditional for the second rhyme of the first section to be repeated as the first rhyme of the second to unite the whole. This structure became more rigid as the text became dissociated from music, an increasing tendency after the death of Machaut, as the great poets of the fifteenth century, Christine de Pizan, Alain Chartier, Charles d'Orléans, François Villon, took as their model Machaut's disciple, Eustache Deschamps, for whom the essential music lay in the words themselves, not in an added 'artificial' melody.[11] The tendency was to write in 'square' stanzas (eight lines of eight syllables or ten lines of ten syllables) which had their own numerological significance, and formed part of the rhetoric which became more and more basic to poetic expression as the fifteenth century advanced.[12]

This move towards viewing poetry as a branch of rhetoric belongs essentially to the renewed Classicism of the fourteenth and fifteenth centuries, which, in France as in Italy, saw the first manifestations of the Renaissance. In France, however, the movement was held in check by the sense of the vigour of native culture (even poets of part Italian blood such as Christine de Pizan and Charles d'Orléans saw no need to import Italianate forms into their writing) and eventually snuffed out, as far as evolving Humanism was concerned, in the bloodbath of the civil wars which led to the English invasion of 1415.

It was also the renewal of the sense of traditional continuity from antiquity, last felt most strongly by late twelfth-century writers like Chrétien de Troyes, which led, in the later thirteenth century, to the application of the word *poëte*, previously reserved for Latin writers, to vernacular poets. It is indeed to imply his master's parity with such 'authorities' that Eustache Deschamps (1346–1407) in his lament on Machaut's death in 1370 wrote:

> La fons Circé et la fonteine Helie
> Dont vous estiez le ruissel et les dois
> Ou poëtes mirent leur estudie
> Convient tarir, dont je suis moult destrois.
> Las! C'est par vous qui mort gisez tous frois
> Qui de tous chans avez esté cantique.
> Plourez, harpes et cors sarrazinois,
> La mort Machaut, le noble rhetorique![13]

(The spring of Circe and the fountain of Helios of
Which you were the rivulet and streams
In which poets studied
Are perforce dried up, which causes me much distress.
Alas! It is because you lie cold and dead
Who were the cantor of all songs.
Weep, harps and Saracen horns,
The death of Machaut, the noble rhetorician!)

It is significant that Deschamps considered Machaut a rhetorician (but
then in his lament for Chaucer, Deschamps labelled the great English poet
a 'translator'!) rather than a musician or poet, either of which terms would
have suited the older man better. The placing of the word *poëte*, however,
does totally blur categories, so that Machaut becomes inseparable from the
classical sources of wisdom and inspiration referred to in the first line
of the stanza, a poet in his own right, as well as a necessary means of
transmission of ancient culture and wisdom to the Moderns. This stanza is
heavy with its own self-conscious rhetoric, as is the entire six-stanza *double
ballade* which begins:

Armes, Amours, Dames, Chevalerie,
Clers, musiciens, faititres en françois,
Tous sophistes, toute poëterie,
Tous ceuls qui ont melodieuse voix,
Ceuls qui chante en orgue aucune fois
Et qui ont chier le doux art de musique,
Demenez dueil, plourez, car c'est bien drois,
La mort Machaut, le noble rhetorique.

(Arms, Love, Ladies, Chivalry,
Clerks, musicians, writers in French,
All sophists, all poetry,
All those who have a melodious voice,
Those who play the organ from time to time
And who love the sweet art of music,
Mourn, weep, it is only right,
The death of Machaut, the noble rhetorician!)

This opening has a distant echo of Virgil ('Arma virumque cano ...', the
first line of the *Aeneid*), and with its protracted list mixing personifications
and persons parades its own classical pretensions in a way Machaut never
did.

Certainly rhetoric was important to Machaut, as it was to all poetic
composition up to the Romantic period, but his exercise of 'subtlety', that
is compositional ingenuity, was far defter than that of his disciple.[14] Even
when writing one of his rare poems not on the theme of love, and

effectively giving a versified exposition of the political and military situation in France after the battle of Poitiers, his use of rhythm and rhyme saves Machaut from the worst excesses of rhetorical versifying:

> On ne doit pas croire en augure,
> Car c'est pechiez contre la foy,
> Car c'est sorcerie et laidure
> Et grant deshonneur; car je croy,
>   Quant homs voit ses annemis
> Qui destruisent sa gent et son païs,
> Qu'il ne se puet escuser de combatre,
> *S'il a pooir de leur orgueuil abatre.*[15]

> (One must not believe in auguries,
> For it is a sin against the faith,
> For it is sorcery, an outrage
> And great dishonour; for I believe,
>   When a man sees his enemies
> Destroying his people and country
> That he cannot excuse himself from fighting them
> *If he has power to beat down their pride.*)

The poem opens with a very 'prosy' statement and its syntax runs in an apparently straight line through its remaining two stanzas. Yet the constant shifting of the justificatory 'car' to different parts of the line, the use of overflow and varying line lengths, the placing of rhymes which underscore the intricate interplay of faith and practicality, the juxtaposed paradoxes and antitheses on which the *ballade* is constructed, producing an ironic tone, and the shifting of the refrain into and out of a rhetorical question, all combine to produce a poem of great complexity. This is echoed metrically in the structure ($a8b8a8b8c7c10d10D10$), in which the *cauda* is separated from the *frons* by a double change of line length as well as by a change of rhyme to underscore the musical development. However, the text, by careful use of syntax, unites the two halves of the stanza adding an extra dimension of rhythmic tension which binds the whole together.

It is in his love-poetry, however, which represents the bulk of his output, that Machaut appears most clearly as the successor to the troubadours and *trouvères*. These poems, still intended to be set to music, also possess a distinct musicality of their own. The following is a typical example also taken from *La Louange des dames*:

> Onques mes cueurs ne senti
>   Si dure dolour,
> Com quant je me departi
>   De ma douce amour;

Mais ce me rendi vigour
    Qu'elle vis a vis
Me dit par tres grant douçour:
    '*A Dieu, dous amis!*'

De ce mot quant je l'oÿ
    La douce savour
Fut emprainte et fit en mi
    Mon cuer son sejour.
Lors ma dame a cointe atour
    Escript, ce [m'est] vis
De sa bele bouche entour:
    '*A Dieu, dous amis!*'

Si ne quier autre merci
    De mon dous labour;
Car j'ay cent joies en mi
    Pour une tristour,
Quant la souveraine [flour]
    Dou monde et le pris
Vuet que je porte en s'onnour:
    '*A Dieu, dous amis!*'[16]

(Never did my heart feel
    Such harsh pain
As when I departed
    From my sweet love;
But my strength returned
    When face to face
She said very sweetly:
    '*Goodbye, sweet love!*'

When I heard this word,
    Its sweet savour
Was printed right through
    My heart where it stayed.
Then my lady by a deft stroke
    Wrote, as I think,
All around [my heart?] with her sweet mouth:
    '*Goodbye, sweet love!*'

So I seek no other mercy
    From my sweet labour;
For I have a hundred joys
    For one sadness,
When the sovereign flower
    In the world and its prize

Wants me to wear in her honour:
'Goodbye, sweet love!')

The themes of pleasurable pain, parting, mercy (the granting of the lady's
favours in one form or other), the heart as seat of love, the lady's
unequalled worth, the honour implicit in serving a lady are all inherited
from the twelfth century. Machaut's handling of the themes is not tragic;
he does not, as Alain Chartier will in the early years of the fifteenth
century, labour the desolate image of the martyr to love. So we can note
that love is fully requited, as it also appeared to be for the Chastelain de
Coucy (although a veil is drawn over the exact nature of the relationship
beyond words and an implied kiss). The hallmark of the later poet's work
is the lightness of touch caused by the mixed metres, the vocalic echoes
and alliterations and the *concetti* of the last two uses of the refrain, where
the lady's loving farewell is seen first as a piece of writing (a reflex of the
poem itself) and then as a favour (an emblem carried by a knight to
represent his lady in a tournament). The atmosphere, then, is one of sweet
melancholy, and a rather precious elegance. As with the first troubadours,
so with Machaut and his school, the sheer craftsmanship of the composi-
tion is one of the features of the poem which the audience is expected to
admire the most.

This sense of writing as craft, with a heavy reliance on rhetorical forms
and self-conscious classical reference, becomes highly developed in the
later fifteenth- and early sixteenth-century movement, which we know
as that of the 'Grands Rhétoriqueurs'.[17] It was against their intensely
convoluted style of writing with its alliterations, internal and punning
rhymes that the Pléiade reacted so strongly. The fifteenth century did see
another current develop, however, in which the inherited traditions mixed
with a more personal voice. This is evident in the work of Christine de
Pizan, the first known female lyric poet of northern France. Although she
was a powerful writer and an independent woman's voice in much of her
prose writings, the bulk of her lyrics conform closely to the expectations
of the school of Machaut and Deschamps. However, particularly in her
poems dealing with her own widowhood, she did turn the inherited
conventions to very striking individual effect as in the following *rondeau*,
in which certain conventions associated with the 'amant martyr' and the
cyclic return of the refrain imposed by the medium are used to create a
very personal world of obsessive grief:

Je suis vesve, seulete, et noir vestue:
A triste vis, simplement affullée,
En grand courrous et maniere adoulée
Porte le dueil tres amer qui me tue.

Et bien est droit que soye rabatue,
Plaine de plour et petit emparlée –
Je suis vesve, seulete, et noir vestue.

Puis qu'ay perdu cil par qui ramenteue
M'est la doulour, dont je suis affollée,
Tous mes bons jours et ma joye est alée;
En dur estat m'a Fortune embatue –
Je suis vesve, seulete, et noir vestue.[18]

(I am a widow, alone, and dressed in black;
Sad-faced, dressed simply,
With broken heart and doleful demeanour
I bear the very bitter mourning that kills me.

And it is right that I should be cast down,
Full of tears, with nothing to say for myself –
I am a widow, alone, and dressed in black.

Since I lost him by whom is borne in on me
The grief which drives me mad,
All my good days and my joy have departed;
Fortune has cast me down into a harsh estate –
I am a widow, alone, and dressed in black.)

A similarly desolate personal tone is achieved by Charles d'Orléans in the same medium. Charles was a pupil in poetic composition of both Deschamps and Christine, and like the latter knew the very real tragedies of bereavement and personal disaster, in his case on the battlefield at Agincourt. Like Christine, Charles turned the received conventional topoi of love-poetry to individual expression:

Esse tout ce que m'apportez
A vostre jour, Saint Valentin?
N'auray je que d'Espoir butin,
L'actente des desconfortez?

Petitement vous m'enhortez
D'estre joyeux ad ce matin.
Esse tout [ce que m'aportez,
A vostre jour, Saint Valentin?]

Nulle rien ne me rapportez,
Fors *bona dies* en latin,
Vielle relique en viel satin;
De tels presens vous deportez.
Esse tout [ce que m'apportez?][19]

(Is that all you bring me
On your day, Saint Valentine?
Is all I get something plundered from Hope,
The expectation of the comfortless?

You give me little encouragement
To be joyful this morning.
Is that all [you bring me
On your day, Saint Valentine?]

You bring me back nothing
But *bona dies*, in Latin,
An old relic in old satin;
You make merry with such presents.
Is that all [you bring me?]

The links with the tradition are obvious, in both form and vocabulary, and the reliance on a universe dominated by the notion of love is integral to the poem. Yet the poem is not about love, but about isolation and depression; as such it reaches forward over the centuries, anticipates Baudelaire and the late Romantics, and puts the poet's psyche at the heart of the poetic experience.

3

Clowns and Chroniclers

PHILIP BENNETT

De moy, povre, je vueil parler:
J'en fus batu comme a ru telles,
Tout nu, ja ne le quier celer.
Qui me feist maschier ces groselles
Fors Katherine de Vausselles?
Noel le tiers ot, qui fut la,
Mitaines a ces nopces telles.
Bien eureux est qui riens n'y a![1]

(Of myself, a poor man, I wish to speak:
I was beaten for it like cloths at a stream,
Quite naked, never will I try to hide it.
Who made me eat this humble pie
Except Katherine de Vausselles?
Noel, the third who was there,
Had such mittens at the wedding.
Happy the man who has nothing to do with it!)

With these words François Villon (1431–after 1463) suddenly inserts himself into the *double ballade* which, immediately before the line which falls one third of the way through his long poetic text *Le Testament* (The Will, 1461–2), deals with the otherwise conventional subject of those who have been made fools of by love. The insertion seems startlingly daring, placing the poet-narrator into the line of descent of Solomon, Samson, Orpheus, Narcissus, Sardanapalus, David, Ammon, Herod (and his victim John the Baptist). The mixture of Old Testament and classical figures, with the small admixture from the New Testament, reveals the very stereotyped nature of what has been presented up to this point. It is effectively a versified *exemplum* or illustrative anecdote to give authority to the equally hackneyed opinion that love leads mankind to disaster.

The stanza is designed to shock and does so in two ways. Firstly the poet-narrator, who constantly presents himself as poor, equates himself with great characters of the scholastic tradition of the Middle Ages. These figures, some historical, some legendary, were held to have universal significance, existing on a plane superior to that of common mortals. Hence their appearance in works carrying a moral message. The promotion of the speaker's self into this company makes a very strong claim for the value of that self. The second way in which the passage shocks is by its formulation and the change of tone implied. From formal 'preaching–teaching' to intimate avowal. We have in fact moved from a plane of impersonal discourse, in which the exemplary characters 'present themselves', the narrator refusing to use 'presentative' verbs, to one of purely personal discourse in which 'I' as a character very explicitly presents himself using the verb 'parler'. There are two subsidiary ways in which this changed perspective impinges on the reader–hearer of *Le Testament*. Firstly the linear presentation of the previous four stanzas (one example per half-stanza with comparatively straightforward syntax) suddenly gives way to a syntax which is anything but linear as the narrator lapses into the 'incoherences' of casual, intimate conversation. Secondly, a point noted by Peter Dale, there is a perturbation in the poem's rhyme scheme in this stanza, since the rhyme in 'ete' is suddenly replaced here by a rhyme in 'ele', with the new, intrusive rhyme underscoring the most blatantly anecdotal features of the text with their popular and comic expressions.[2]

This presentation of the poet-narrator as autobiographer, and as comic victim, is a highly complex and sophisticated manifestation of a tendency that has often led Villon to be presented as the first modern poet, a habit that has survived Italo Siciliano's careful cataloguing of all that Villon owed to medieval tradition.[3] It is indeed the apparent immediacy of his voice that continues to appeal and to give the feeling of modernity to post-Romantic readers. That impression is, however, an illusion, and itself belongs to a tradition that is virtually born with the vernacular poetry of France. It is to that four-centuries-long tradition that I now wish to turn.

Even in courtly love-lyric there was a tendency to read the I-persona as a 'real' protagonist identified with the poet, which led to the construction of biographies, and incidental anecdotes out of what were essentially conventional poetic data. Such a tendency is a misreading of the earlier poems, but the clues which may have pushed thirteenth-century compilers of songbooks and writers of romance to read them in this way lie within the tradition itself.

Alongside the *chanson* proper (understood as a poem of determined form dealing with *fin'amor* and addressed or relating to an anonymous or pseudonymous lady) there existed other types of poem which adopted the external form of the *chanson*, but varied the subject-matter. Among these is the debate poem (known in Provençal as a *tenso* or *partimen* and in French as a *tenson* or *jeu parti*). This kind of text deals in points of love casuistry, and takes as its premises the essential data of *fin'amor*. However, it presents dramatically two poets whose names figure, in the vocative, at the head of each stanza as the poetic voice shifts from one disputant to the other. A third name may also appear; that of an authority appealed to by the disputants to resolve their argument. This not only provides an apparent autobiographical reference for the love problem, on the part of at least one of the contributors, but also furnishes a 'historical' extra-textual context for the debate by the reference to the arbiter, where that exists. An extreme case of such a poem, in the French tradition, is the debate between Colin Muset, a *jongleur* and minstrel as well as a *trouvère* (active *c.* 1230–50), and Jacques d'Amiens. The debate concerns loyalty in love, the difference between *fin'amor* and *druerie* (mercenary flirtation in this context) and how to tell a noble lady, worthy to be loved, from a 'gold-digging' bourgeoise, This could be the subject of a conventional *chanson*, but it is tricked out with personal references:

> 'Biaus Colins Musés, je me plaing d'une amor
> > Ke longuement ai servie
> De loial cuer, n'ains pitiet ne retor
> > N'i pou troveir nen aïe,
> S'i truis je mult semblant de grant dousor,
> Maix se m'est vis ke il sont traïtor,
> Ke bouche et cuers ne s'i acordent mie.
>
> – Jakes d'Amiens, laissiés ceste folor!
> > Fueis fauce druerie,
> N'en biaul semblant ne vos fieis nul jor:
> > Cil est musairs ke s'i fie!
> Pues ke trouveis son cuer a menteor,
> Se plux l'ameis, sovant duel et irour
> En avereis et pix ke je ne die.'[4]

> ('Dear Colin Muset, I complain of a love
> > Which I have long served
> With a loyal heart, yet never could I find pity, reciprocation
> > Nor any help,
> Still I find a vast show of great sweetness,
> But I think they are traitors,
> For mouth and heart are not in accord,'

'Jacques d'Amiens, abandon this madness!
  Flee false flirtation,
And never put trust in fair expressions:
  It's a fool who trusts them!
Since you find her heart a liar,
If you love her any longer, often will you have
Grief and wrath and worse than I can say.')

The first stanza opens with a traditional shift of category, confusing the lady and love, which pivots around the relative *ke* of line 2. This is reinforced in the last two lines of the stanza, in which the plural pronoun *il* is expanded as 'heart' and 'mouth'. The lady, and hence sexuality, are banished from the poem in this 'platonic' view of love. Colin Muset's reply reveals a jarring de-idealizing attitude by referring to 'flirtation' and 'lying'. The register of the language becomes more vulgar, a tendency exaggerated as the poem proceeds and Colin Muset retreats into his preferred poetic persona, based on what Paul Zumthor calls the 'Register of the Good Life'.[5] While Jacques d'Amiens will continue his quest for the perfect blond lady, a symbol of courtliness and worth, Colin will devote himself

'As grais chappons et a la jancellie
Et as gastiauls ki sont blanc come flor.'

('To fat capons and garlic sauce,
And to lily-white little cakes.')

In contrast Jacques d'Amiens asserts:

'Et je kerrai d'amors joie et baudor
Car consireir d'amors ne me puis mie.'

('Yet I shall seek the joy and fun of love,
For I cannot do without love.')

allowing the poem to end on an artificial and totally undermined celebration of the spirituality of *fin'amor*.

Apart from such quasi-anecdotal poems, genuinely anecdotal verse also existed from the earliest period. Alongside his courtly poems Guillaume IX wrote others, mostly addressed to his comrades in arms, whose subject-matter tends to be the sexual boast. One such, 'Faray un vers pos mi sonelh' (I shall compose a poem because I am asleep) presents a figure who will reappear frequently in 'personal' verse throughout the Middle Ages, a ragged wanderer. In Guillaume's case his disguise as a pilgrim is intended to gain him access to the two women who are the objects of his journey. He also pretends to be dumb, that is not totally mute, but incapable of coherent speech:

Ar auziretz qu'ai respondut:
Anc no li diz ni 'bat' ni 'but',
Ni fer ni fust no ai mentangut,
Mas sol aitan:
'Barbariol, barbariol,
Barbarian.'[6]

(Now you shall hear what I replied:
I said neither 'hit' nor 'prod',
I maintained neither iron nor shaft,
But just this:
'Babariol, babariol,
Babarian.')

Behind the nonsense it is already possible, in what he claims not to have said, to detect sexual innuendo. The ladies are clearly satisfied with their guest as they take him in, place him by the fire and ply him with food, drink and spices. This *mise en scène* also remains traditional in texts referring to sexual gratification.[7] A doubt over the 'hero's' ability to keep silence persists however, and so an extra test is devised in which the women's 'ginger pussy' is dragged down the pilgrim's back. The pilgrim-knight passes this test (it is, after all something of an heroic initiation to manhood) with results at once epically improbable and comic:

Tant las fotei com auziretz:
Cent et quatre-vinz et ueit vetz,
Qu'a pauc no.i rompei mos corretz
E mos arnes;
E no.us puesc dir lo malavegz,
Tan gran m'en pres.

(I fucked them as often as you shall hear:
One hundred and eighty-eight times,
So that I nearly broke my belts
And my harness;
And I cannot say how ill it left me
So hard did I take it.)

The warrior has indeed emerged from beneath the garb of the pilgrim; he has passed all tests, has proved himself more cunning that the women, and has regained his voice to sing of the exploit. Yet his success is presented as incomplete, for this heroic effort has left him near prostrate with exhaustion. Moreover, it is not on the macho boast that the poem ends, but with a repetition of the last two lines, thus emphasizing the comic rather than the heroic aspect of the text. The vehicle for the text also underscores this lighter side of the poem, since the metre and rhyme-scheme recall popular dance-forms, and assimilate the text to ribald, or parodic, folk-song.

A relationship to 'popular' forms is also claimed by the *pastourelle*, a narrative form, sometimes presented in the guise of a *chanson*, in which an I-persona leaves the court to find solace in the simple charms of a shepherdess. In this aim he is quite likely to be thwarted by the woman's quick wits or by the intervention of a group of shepherds. The underlying ideology of the *pastourelle* remains courtly, and part of its humour derives from the way the knight-poet-protagonist, escaping from the stifling sophistication of the court and its conventions, woos a non-courtly female in courtly terms, often bribing her with aristocratic rewards, while expecting a more immediate conquest than would be acceptable in a scenario of *fin'amor*. A variant on the shepherdess, used in the following example by Colin Muset, is that of the young girl in a garden. Whatever may be the relationship of such figures to amorous fairies or goddesses, the type as exploited in the Middle Ages derives doubly from the classical tradition of the nymph in the grove and from the Song of Songs tradition, presenting the garden, and its female occupant, as a place of delights whose beauty and freedom lie in its twin affiliations with 'wild nature' and elegant artifice. The poem begins:

> Volez oïr la muse Muset?
> En mai fu fete, un matinet,
> En un vergier flori, verdet,
>   Au point du jour
> Ou chantoient cil oiselet
>   Par grant baudor,
> Et j'alai fere un chapelet
>   En la verdor.
> Je le fis bel et cointe et net
>   Et plain de flor.
>   Une dancele
> Avenant et mult bele,
>   Gente pucele,
>   Bouchete riant,
>   Qui me rapele:
> 'Vien ça, si viele
> ....
> Ta muse en chantant
> Tant mignotement!'[8]

> (Will you hear Muset's musing?
> It was composed one morning in May,
> In a garden, full of flowers and green,
>   At dawn

> When the little birds were singing
>   For sheer pleasure,
> And I went to make a chaplet
>   In the greenery.
> I made it beautiful and elegant and clean
>   And full of flowers.
>   A young lady,
> Attractive and very beautiful,
>   A noble girl,
> With smiling mouth,
>   Who called out to me:
> 'Come, play your fiddle
>   ....
> Singing your muse
> so prettily!')

The narrator approaches the girl, who is dressed in expensive Spanish silk, and sings a song, a couple of lines of which are quoted. After this she grants him *merci* (specified as a kiss and 'something else I much desire'). Following their love-making they share food and wine. The poem ends:

> Or a Colin Muset musé
> Et s'a a devise chanté
> Pour la bele au vis coloré [. . .]
>   Mult se cointoie,
>   Qu'Amors veut servir,
>   Si a grant joie
>   El vergier ou dognoie,
>   Bien se conroie,
>   Bon vin fet venir
>   Trestout a loisir.

> (Now Colin Muset has mused
> And sung to his heart's content
> For the beauty with the fine complexion [. . .]
>   He is greatly amusing himself,
> For he wants to serve Love,
>   So he has great joy
> In the garden where he makes love,
>   He is well supplied,
> He has good wine brought
> Quite at his leisure.)

As its editor, Joseph Bédier, points out, this poem is much more complex than it seems at first sight. The setting, the emphasis on physical attraction and well-being, on the discreetly referred to but none the less obvious satisfaction of desire, the poetic form and the repeated use of affective diminutives in the first two stanzas all relate this text to the *pastourelle* tradition. Yet the vocabulary and many of the underlying ideas are those of *fin'amor*; the poet constantly refers to his joy, to the young woman's *merci* (the granting of her favours), to his service of Love, which is also making love (in all senses from the most Victorian to the most modern). What really complicates the poem though is that it is put clearly in the poet's own name in the first line. The uttering voice is now 'I', now an impersonal narrator referring to a 'poet', Colin Muset, in the third person. To what extent should we equate 'I' with the third-person hero Colin Muset? At one level totally, in the anecdotal text; but 'I' is also the traditional 'hero' both of the courtly *chanson* and of the *pastourelle* and as such has no extra-textual existence, despite a constant temptation to equate 'I' with the poet. For the medieval audience this question of identity is made even more complex by its being used to confronting a singing or reciting 'I' which was not identical to the composing 'I'. Unlike modern texts which 'read themselves' in the reader's head, the medieval text was embodied in a physical presence saying 'I' on behalf of an absent sensibility. The contemporary audience accustomed to such conventions would change its perceptions between the two parts of the poem, only asking itself afterwards about the role of Muset in the central adventure. Certainly, the poet has carefully associated himself with both personae, there is a gentle sliding from 'he' to 'I' via the song as autonomous creation in the first stanza, while in the last there is an explicit reference to the first line, so closing the circle of the text, and to the content of the intervening lines. The very idea of a *muse(t)* being some feature of the poem, or the poem itself, is a hard one. It is, as Bédier pointed out, otherwise unknown as a designation for a poem. It usually refers either to a bagpipe or to a day-dream. One interpretation would add to the comic effect of the piece (the peasant instrument in a courtly setting), the other would relate it to the tradition of Guillaume IX composing enigmatic erotic fantasies in his sleep. It is also, of course, and most blatantly, a pun on the poet's name. What it tells us most clearly is that 'Colin Muset' and his text exist only as functions of each other.

Part of the complexity arising from the interpretation of Colin's poem is caused by its inseparability from lyric genres. When Colin's near contemporary Rutebeuf (active *c.* 1248–77) writes about himself, he no longer does so in lyric form. His so-called 'personal poems' are mostly written in unbroken flows of verse, like the romance, but differentiated from that kind by the use of a rhyme scheme *aabbbcccd* . . ., and by grouping lines in threes by length, $8 + 8 + 4$ syllables. In the definitive edition of his complete works these texts are referred to as 'Poems of Misfortune', and the poet's hard luck is indeed a central theme. He presents himself as addicted to dice, married to an ugly shrew of a wife, sick and reduced to penury. However, the character he creates in these poems is totally literary, and the *Griesche* (Dicing) poems are such virtuoso pieces of rhetorical writing that the text and its verbal exuberance take over completely from any 'realistic' portrait. This is particularly noticeable in the opening of 'La Griesche d'esté' (Summer's Dice):

> En recordant ma grant folie
> Qui n'est ne gente ne jolie
>   Ainz est vilaine
> Et vilains cil qui la demaine,
> Me plaing set jors en la semaine
>   Et par reson.
> Si esbahiz ne fu mes hom,
> Qu'en yver toute la seson
>   Ai si ouvré
> Et en ouvrant m'ai aouvré
> Qu'en ouvrant n'ai rien recouvré
>   Dont je me cuevre.
> Ci a fol ouvrier et fole oevre
> Qui par ouvrer riens ne recuevre:
>   Tout tourne a perte;
> Et la griesche est si aperte
> Qu'*eschec*' dit 'a la descouverte'
>   A son ouvrier,
> Dont puis n'i a nul recouvrier.
> Juignet li fet sambler fevrier;
>   La dent dit 'Cac',
> Et la griesche li dit 'Eschac'.
> Qui plus en set s'afuble sac
>   De la griesche.[9]

> (Remembering my great folly
> Which is neither noble nor jolly,
>   But vile
> And vile the man who commits it,
> I lament seven days a week
>   And rightly.
> No man was ever so distracted,
> For all winter long
>   I've done this job
> And working has been the sort of work
> Where working has earned me nothing
>   To cover myself.
> It's a mad workman at a mad job
> Who works for nothing:
>   All is loss;

And the Greek game is so expert
It forces 'Fool's Mate'
    On its player
From which there's no escape.
It makes July seem like February:
    Your teeth chatter
And the game says 'Check'.
The most expert player wears a sack
    After the game.)

This poem like others by Rutebeuf on this theme combines apparent personal confessions with social generalizations. It opens with a reference to the earlier Winter's Dice and assures a continuity of presentation. This appears as autobiography, yet the heavy use of *annominatio* (a type of punning involving roots, suffixation and prefixation), the equivocal rhymes and the insistent *anaphora* (repetitions of identical elements) at varying positions in the line and the metrical and rhyme schemes themselves, reinforced by Rutebeuf's love of leonine rhyme (involving the penult as well as the final stressed syllable) provide a surface for the text which distracts from the personal element. This all contributes to a universalized 'abstract' portrait in which Rutebeuf presents himself as Everyman.

The image of extreme poverty Rutebeuf gives of himself in these poems (and the image of a man so addicted to gambling that he has no time for anything else) is actually contradicted by his vast and varied output, ranging from *fabliaux* to religious drama to poems in support of the Crusades to polemics in support of the University of Paris in the face of what was seen as a take-over by the Mendicant Orders.

In the midst of this vast output of polemics and apparent self-pity Rutebeuf also found time to offer some reflexions on the plight of the poor which show a remarkable poetic insight. Here we note an absence of the intrusive rhetoric which marks his 'personal' poetry:

Ribaut, or estes vos a point:
Li aubre despoillent lor branches
Et vos n'aveiz de robe point,
Si en avreiz froit a vos hanches.
Queil vos fussent or li pourpoint
Et li seurquot forrei a manches!
Vos aleiz en estei si joint
Et en yver aleiz si cranche!
Vostre soleir n'ont mestier d'oint:
Vos faites de vos talons planches.
Les noires mouches vos ont point,
Or vos repoinderont les blanches.[10]

> (Porters, now you're well set up:
> The trees are baring their branches
> And you haven't got any clothes,
> So you'll get cold in your haunches.
> How you'd love doublets now
> And fur-lined long-sleeved surcoats!
> You go so sprightly in summer
> And in winter simply creak along!
> Your shoes don't need any wax;
> Your heels are your pattens.
> The black flies have stung you,
> Now its the turn of the white ones.)

This simple poem of only one stanza offers just two rhymes, and one of them constantly reuses the same word (*point*) in a variety of meanings. This is an extreme case of *annominatio* but the effect is surprisingly spare, probably because it is a simple masculine rhyme alternating with a single feminine rhyme without any hint of equivocation. Certainly parts of the poem can be read ironically (like La Fontaine's fable of the Grasshopper and the Ant): the porters have enjoyed summer, if they had thought winter would come they could have made some provision. Yet the present tenses of ll. 3, 9 and 10 indicate an eternal state of affairs from which there is no escape. Moreover, any temptation to read this as a satirical jibe at the expense of the poor is suppressed by the vivid images of what constitutes wealth (warm clothes and leather shoes), of the unchanging hardships of the poor (flies in summer and snow in winter) and by the fact that Rutebeuf has elicited our pity for himself with just this image in another poem. We are thus left contemplating one of the first, and most enduring, non-formulaic portraits of the unemployed in French literature.

It is just this visual quality which marks the work of the two later medieval poets whose manner is closest to that of Rutebeuf. Not that it is likely that either was a conscious successor to the thirteenth-century poet. Despite his works being preserved in a dozen manuscripts he seems very quickly to have sunk into oblivion. It is really from the tradition of Jean de Meun and the second *Roman de la Rose*,[11] combined with the lyric innovations of Machaut mentioned in the last chapter, that Eustache Deschamps and François Villon take their inspiration. Deschamps was a prolific love-poet and also wrote a long satirical poem on marriage, a neo-dramatic piece on the catering at court, a number of treatises, in verse and prose, and verse epistles. It was, however, when his work as a diplomat and civil servant took him to 'barbaric' countries like Bohemia and Flanders that his poetic verve found its true strain. Suddenly he uses the *ballade* and even more pithy *rondeau* to their best advantage, capturing an atmosphere in a few sounds and images that stick, like the mud of the Flanders fields:

Car g'i ay eu toute chetiveté;
En cheminant la boe m'afubla
D'un ort mantel; je fu dedanz bouté,
Et mon sommier jusqu'au coul se plunga;
Bahu et tout long temps y demoura.
Quant g'issi hors et lui, nous semblions cendres;
Complaigne soy des Flamens qui voudra,
Mais ne me plaing fors du païs de Flandres.[12]

(For there I have known all wretchedness;
Travelling I put on mud
Like a filthy cloak; I was shoved down in it,
And my packhorse sank to its neck;
Coffers and all stayed there a long time.
When I got out, and he, we looked like ashes;
Let any who will complain about Flemings,
I'll only complain about the land of Flanders.)

However, whereas Rutebeuf's poems were inspired by pity or partisanship for a specific (and doubtless worthy) cause, Deschamps was inspired by pure xenophobia, especially in his treatment of Bohemia:

Poux, puces, puor et pourceaux
est de Behaigne la nature,
Pain, poisson salé et froidure,
Poivre noir, choux pourris, poreaux,
Char enfumee, noire et dure;
Poux, puces, puor et pourceaux.
Vint gens mangier en deux plateaux,
Boire cervoise amere et sure,
Mal couchier, noir, paille, ordure,
Poux, puces, puor et pourceaux
est de Behaigne la nature,
Pain, poisson salé et froidure.[13]

(Lice, fleas, stink and pigs
Are natural to Bohemia,
Bread, salt fish and cold,
Black pepper, rotten cabbage, leeks,
Smoked meat, black and hard;
Lice, fleas, stink and pigs.
Twenty people eating off two plates,
Beer to drink, bitter and sour,
Bad beds, blackness, straw, filth,
Lice, fleas, stink and pigs
Are natural to Bohemia,
Bread, salt fish and cold.)

The *rondeau*, bringing back its refrain in ll. 1–3, 6 and 10–12, makes a particularly enclosed and obsessive world out of a very small number of images. The incessant hammerblows of the repeated sounds and the all but absent syntax make the whole poem little more than an example of *iteratio* or listing. Although, as we saw when considering Deschamps's occasional poetry, he can be longwinded and mesmerized by rhetoric, here, and in his much lighter farewell to Paris with its refrain,

> Adieu Paris, adieu petiz pastez
> (Adieu Paris, adieu little tarts)

he is prepared to let a kaleidoscope of images speak for him. This lapidary aspect of his work is that which re-emerges most sharply in the poetry of Villon, who undoubtedly was aware of Deschamps's work through his contacts in the poetic milieux of Paris and at the courts of Orléans and Bourbon.

Villon, as we saw at the beginning of this chapter, thrust himself in the guise of a poor man into the midst of a conventional list of great men of the past. Much of his *Testament* is indeed concerned with presenting the picture of someone both broken in health (the results of injustice and torture) and poverty-stricken. The *Epitaph*, which comes appropriately towards the end of his Will, provides a summation of these features while also reducing him to the level of object:

> Cy gist et dort en ce sollier
> Qu'Amours occist de son raillon,
> Ung povre petit escollier,
> Qui fut nommé Françoys Villon.
> Onques de terre n'eust sillon.
> Il donna tout, chascun le set;
> Tables, tresteaulx, pain, corbeillon.
> Gallans, dictes en ce verset:
>
> Repos eternel donne a cil,
> Sire, et clarté perpetuelle,
> Qui vaillant plat ni escuelle
> N'eut onques, n'ung brin de persil.
> Il fut rez, chief, barbe et sorcil,
> Comme un navet qu'on ret ou pelle.
> Repos eternel donne a cil.
> Rigueur le transmit en exil
> Et luy frappa au cul la pelle,
> Non obstant qu'il dit: 'J'en appelle!'
> Qui n'est pas terme trop subtil.
> Repos eternel donne a cil.[14]

(Here lies and sleeps in this upper room
Whom Love killed with his dart,
A poor little student,
Who was named François Villon.
He never had a furrow of land.
He gave away all, everyone knows:
Tables, trestles, bread and basket.
Revellers, recite this verse for him:

Grant him eternal rest,
Lord, and perpetual light,
Who never had dish or platter
Of any worth, or a sprig of parsley.
He was shaven, head, beard, eyebrows,
Like a scrubbed, pealed turnip.
Grant him eternal rest.
Rigour consigned him to exile,
And the spade smacked his bum,
Despite his saying 'I appeal!'
Which isn't terribly subtle.
Grant him eternal rest.)

Although many critics have taken these and other references in the *Testament* literally as proof of Villon's ill-health, premature ageing and so on, we must actually note that what he gives us here is an epitome of all the masks he has adopted throughout not only the *Testament* but also the earlier *Lais* (Legacies) of 1456. He is turn and turn about martyr to love, in the tradition of Alain Chartier, student, fool or jester (the shaven head), criminal and so on. Some of these things François de Montcorbier, alias Des Loges, alias Villon, was in real life, but what we have here is a purely literary re-creation. The whole portrait is framed by a quotation from the *Requiescat*, the opening of the Requiem Mass. The suggestion appears to be that Villon is putting all these personalities behind him.

We lose track of Villon very soon after the appearance of the *Testament*. Conventional scholarly views hold that he must have died about this time, but a tradition already rife in the sixteenth century and reported as an anecdote by Rabelais, has him living on producing passion-plays in Poitou. It may be that having given up the world of poetry voluntarily, he retired, as did Rimbaud, to lead the life of a clerk, for which his education had prepared him. Yet whatever the biographical facts of Villon's existence, or indeed those of the other poets considered in this chapter, the important phenomenon is the persistent tradition of (pseudo-)autobiographical writing in which the poet presents himself as an outsider – a version of the court-jester with licence to satirize.

4

Love-Poetry in the Age of Humanism

PETER SHARRATT

Most poets in the Renaissance at some time or other wrote about love, and, whatever their own personal experience, they wrote within a fairly rigid formal tradition. This poetry may be seen as a pointer to the new sensibility which was nourished by the humanist movement. Our understanding and enjoyment of it today can be enriched by a knowledge of the literary and cultural forces which helped to shape it, and an awareness of the expectations of a Renaissance reader. This indeed is the only way we can appreciate the interplay between the lived emotion and its formal expression.

In order to give some idea of the flavour of Renaissance love-poetry, it is better not to start with a passionate poem but rather with a more detached and distant one which is much more typical:

> Je ne suis point, Muses, acoustumé
> De voir la nuict vostre dance sacrée:
> Je n'ay point beu dedans l'onde d'Ascrée,
> Fille du pied du cheval emplumé.
> De tes beaulx raiz chastement allumé
> Je fu poëte: et si ma voix recrée,
> Et si ma lyre, ou si ma rime agrée,
> Ton oeil en soit, non Parnasse, estimé.
> Certes le ciel te debvoit à la France,
> Quand le Thuscan, et Sorgue, et sa Florence,
> Et son laurier engrava dans les cieux:
> Ore trop tard beaulté plus que divine,
> Tu vois nostre âge, helas, qui n'est pas digne
> Tant seulement de parler de tes yeulx.[1]

(Muses, I am not accustomed
To watch your sacred night-time dance;
I have not drunk from the Ascrean waters,
Sprung from the step of the winged horse.
Chastely set alight by your lovely eyes
I became a poet, and if my voice is pleasing,
And if my lyre or my rhyme finds favour,
Your look, and not Parnassus, should be praised.
Heaven should in fact have given you to France
At the time the Tuscan poet wrote on high
The river Sorgue, his laurel-tree and Florence.
Now (too late) o more than godly beauty,
You see our age, alas, which is unworthy
Even to speak about your eyes.)

In this poem, taken from his first collection of love-poetry, Ronsard seems to be as interested in himself as a love-poet as he is in the woman he claims as his only inspiration, and he has much to say about his poetic aims. The very form he has chosen, the sonnet, recently imported from Italy where it had flourished for over two centuries, indicates a conscious acceptance of the Italian literary tradition and a wish to naturalize it in France. The language is elevated, quite different from everyday speech, and this is enhanced by the combination of formal rhythmic patterning with a clear grammatical or logical structure and a rhetorical colouring (periphrasis, hyperbole, and negation which amounts to affirmation). The poem gains in resonance by its rich allusiveness. Firstly, in spite of his protestations, the poet has drunk deeply from the springs of Latin and Greek literature. He takes it for granted that the reader can follow him, or that he is prepared to take the trouble to find out. This is clearly elitist, and we know that many of his contemporary readers found him obscure. Secondly, when he praises Petrarch's life-long love for Laura ('le Thuscan ... et son laurier'), and his poetic celebration of her, Ronsard expects the reader's recognition and assent. This homage to the master was a commonplace among the earlier Italian followers of Petrarch, and Petrarch himself acknowledged his debt to Virgil and Homer. In this way Ronsard is able to reach out to other poetic worlds and bring them into his own.

This poem is a carefully structured and crafted piece of writing, self-contained and yet part of a larger whole in which the poet has set himself the programme of creating a new poetic idiom. There can be little doubt about the artistry involved. Yet this is supposed to be love-poetry, and many people today who come across this sort of writing for the first time are disconcerted because they were looking for something else. Whatever has happened, they may ask, to Cassandra, the girl to whom the collection is addressed? She scarcely seems present in the poem, at least as a person of flesh and blood.

Now the reality and identity of the poetic mistress is an important subject to which I shall return at the end, when I come to discuss how Renaissance love-poetry may be read today. For the moment, as I talk about individual poets and their poems, I should like the reader to bear in mind the following questions: who is the 'je' who is speaking in the poem, to whom is the poem addressed, and what is the true subject of the poem? I believe that a consideration of these questions will lead to a better understanding of what this kind of poetry is about.

Before returning to Ronsard and his fellow-poets I would like to say something about the cultural context in which they wrote and of some of the forces which helped to determine their writing, in order to bring out the difference between this period and our own. The history of poetry is one of continuous evolution rather than of sudden radical change, and the Renaissance is no exception. Yet it did create what Du Bellay called 'une nouvelle, ou plustot ancienne renouvelée poësie' (a new, or rather renewed old poetry) and the practice of it was vibrant, urgent and widespread, in this age of intellectual and artistic renewal.

The rediscovery of Greek and Latin literature had brought with it an awareness of the history and myths of the pagan, pre-Christian world, made people aware of the relativity of thought and behaviour, proposed a different idea of virtue as personal energy and perfection no longer dependent entirely on God, and provided a new aesthetic and imaginative stimulus. 'Humanism' meant both the accurate scholarly study of the classics ('humane letters') and the adoption of new social and personal attitudes derived in part from them. Humanists at first attempted to carry on the tradition by writing their own poems, plays and essays in the purest possible classical Latin (in contrast to the debased, living, Latin of medieval discourse). Some poets were equally at home in Latin and French; their Latin poetry was often, curiously, less inhibited, and was enriched by intertextual references to the ancient models. Although it was written for a small band of scholar poets, it was more than an intellectual game: apart altogether from its poetic qualities it improved the poets' linguistic facility, helped them to master complex metrical skills and taught them to handle new poetic genres and verse-forms, all of which was to be put to good use in the writing of French poetry.

The study of the classics and the practice of Latin soon made poets wish to return to French. The Italians had long ago extended the scope of Italian to include subjects previously written about in Latin and had developed an extensive literature of the imagination. French writers were torn between seeing Italian as a third classical language to be admired and imitated, and wanting to go beyond all three and create a new and distinctive literature in French. But first they steeped themselves in classical literature, either in the original or in translation. In so far as love-poetry is concerned, the favourite Greek authors were Homer, with his vast mythological resources (of which we have seen something in Ronsard's poem), Plato, the Anthology and anacreontic writings, and in Latin, the elegiacs, Catullus, Tibullus and Propertius, and especially Ovid. Italian was even more influential.

It is not possible to appreciate Renaissance love-poetry without understanding how and why Petrarch and his followers captured the imagination of European writers for two hundred years and more and dominated writing in the vernacular and the new literary consciousness, first in Italy in the Quattrocento and Cinquecento, then in France, England, Scotland, Spain, the Low Countries and elsewhere too.[2] Petrarch, the first great humanist, wrote mainly in Latin, but it was his Italian poetry which held the widest appeal. His *Canzoniere*, a collection of love-poems, addressed to one woman, Laura, became the model for countless collections. It begins with the description of the first moment of love, the *innamoramento*, a love at first sight which leads to the adoration of a woman, who is usually married, ideally beautiful and goddess-like and who does not return the poet's love. The poet, condemned to serve this cruel lady (Petrarch's debt to the troubadours is clear), is frustrated sexually and psychologically, and describes his anguish and tormented suffering, to the point, even, where he experiences a *dolendi voluptas* or pleasure in his pain. In Petrarch the final outcome is that Laura dies, and then leads him to a spiritual perfection which makes him turn to God and see his earlier love for her as adulterous and therefore as an obstacle to perfection. (On this last point it should be said that Petrarch's imitators often part company with him.) These strong emotional tensions are conveyed by characteristic poetic techniques. The sonnet, exploited by Petrarch, though not invented by him, is the main verse-form used and in its small space, the tightly-knit balance of octave and sestet, with almost infinite possibilities of harmonic variation, admirably captures both the sameness and distinctiveness of love; and the juxtaposition of sonnets within the sequence, by means of textual cross-reference, reproduces individual moments and moods within the whole experience and shows the links between them. The familiar rhetorical technique of antithesis conveys the tensions and the ambiguities of love; and the repetitions, exclamations, questions and exaggerations all help to convey the perception of this experience as at once ecstatic and down-to-earth. There is also a literary code of conceits (or physical images which give life to abstract ideas), and a stress on the parallels between the poet's mood and the world of nature.

It was also from Italy that Platonism came into France, through Marsilio Ficino's Latin translation and his commentary on *The Symposium*, Ebreo's *Dialoghi d'Amore*, and other treatises on love. Plato's idealizing view of love had a great attraction for writers of the Renaissance, partly because it seemed possible to reconcile it with Christian spirituality. Sometimes Petrarch's view seems close to Plato's, at least in the sonnets written after Laura's death, in which the woman leads the man from a contemplation of her beauty to spiritual perfection. Yet the two attitudes are very different because the woman's rejection of the man conflicts with the Platonic notion of a common pursuit of virtue, and in any case Plato's main concern is with male homosexual love rather than love between men and women.

In spite of the dominant idealizing theory of the Petrarchan and Platonist tradition, Renaissance love-poetry is obviously also very sensual. Yet even here it is often easy to detect reference to a literary tradition, such as that of the Latin elegiacs and their Neo-Latin imitators, especially in genre poems about kissing. Moreover there is present sometimes a popular current of writing, close to song and the oral tradition, and to the *tradition gauloise* of bawdy which overlaps with it. We shall see that Petrarchism quickly leads to anti-Petrarchism, a rejection of artificiality and a celebration of enjoyment.

This then is the context in which the poets we shall be considering wrote, and it has been necessary to set it out in some detail precisely because they themselves were aware that they were writing to a programme.

Maurice Scève, bourgeois, humanist and man of learning, published several books including pastoral, and scientific or cosmic poetry about the creation, but today he is best remembered for his *Délie, Object de plus haulte vertu* (1544). This is the first French *Canzoniere* or collection of love-poems written in honour of one woman. It is not in the form of sonnets but written in *dizains* or ten-line poems, a medieval form, interspersed with a series of woodcut emblems. (Scève was not the first French Petrarchan, since Clément Marot had already translated some of his sonnets and adapted some of his techniques and themes, but Marot emerges rather as playful, cynical, Ovidian, and was sensual in a way that Petrarch was not.)

The *Délie* does not narrate in detail the story of a love-affair. There is a broad sweep of incidents, from the *innamoramento* of the first poem to the author's gradual decision to abandon his pursuit of an unresponsive woman, and the firm lucid statement of the concluding poem, yet there is no linear, temporal development. The opening *dizain* of the *Délie* will give an idea of the kind of writing it is:

> L'Œil trop ardent en mes ieunes erreurs
> Girouettoit, mal cault, à l'impourueue:
> Voicy (ô paour d'agreables terreurs)
> Mon Basilisque auec sa poingnant' veue

Perçant Corps, Cœur, et Raison despourueue,
Vint penetrer en l'Ame de mon Ame.
   Grand fut le coup, qui sans tranchante lame
Fait, que vivant le Corps, l'Esprit desuie,
Piteuse hostie au conspect de toy, Dame,
Constituée Idole de ma vie.[3]

(My eyes, too ardent in my youthful roving,
Spun round like a weather-cock, imprudently, idly,
When suddenly (o fear of terror and pleasure)
My Basilisk with her sharp look
Piercing body, heart and reason all at sea,
Came deep into the recess of my soul.
The blow was great, without a cutting blade,
Which, while the body lives, made spirit die,
Pitiable host in sight of you, my Lady,
The constituted idol of my life.)

After a deliberate echo of Petrarch's first sonnet ('giovenile errore') Scève compares Délie's look with that of a basilisk, a mythical animal whose glance could kill. The theological image in the last two lines (provocative in 1544 because of the debates about the Catholic mass, and about the veneration of images) makes him into a sacred host, a sacrificial victim offered up to her, his idol. The natural compactness of the decasyllabic *dizain* and Scève's taut use of juxtaposition and inversion, together with the neologism 'girouettoit' and the unusual Latinate syntax of 'au conspect de toy' have a forceful intellectual impact.

In another poem, 'Plus tost seront Rhosne, et Saone desioinctz', Scève uses the rivers and hills of Lyon in a heightened form of the Petrarchan topos of nature supporting and amplifying emotion: the powerful sexual imagery in the confluence of the virile fast-flowing Rhône and the slower, calmer Saône shows the unthinkableness of separation, and this is further stressed by the figure *adynaton*, or impossibility (the rivers flowing backwards and the hills becoming fused together). Another *dizain* has an even greater violence of tone:

Seul auec moy, elle auec sa partie:
Moy en ma peine, elle en sa molle couche.
Couuert d'ennuy ie me voultre en l'Ortie,
Et elle nue entre ses bras se couche.
   Hà (luy indigne) il la tient, il la touche:
Elle le souffre: &, comme moins robuste,
Viole amour par ce lyen iniuste,
Que droict humain, & non diuin, à faict.
   O saincte loy a tous, fors a moy, iuste,
Tu me punys pour elle auoir meffaict.   (*Délie*, 161)

(Alone by myself, she with her partner,
Me in my pain, she in her soft bed.
Gripped with anguish I wallow in nettles,
And she lies naked in his arms.
Ah! (unworthy man) he holds her, touches her.
She lets him, and, as the weaker one,
Violates love by this unjust bond,
Which human law, and not divine, has made.
O holy law, just to all but me,
You punish me for her misdeeds.)

In this poem about physical jealousy and frustration it is her marriage which is seen as the obstacle to true love. The short contrasting half-lines, the dramatic exclamations, the odd syntax of the personal construction in the last line and the ironic generalization (her sin is to sleep with her husband) all combine to convey his dejection and despair.

In the last *dizain* 'Flamme si saincte en son cler durera' the poet returns to Petrarch with an allusion to the *Trionfo del tempo*, asserting that although their relationship is over it will continue to live in their memories and ours like the evergreen juniper bush. Unlike Petrarch he does not reject their passionate desire and their experience of love. Délie has not led him to spiritual perfection but to self-awareness and pagan virtue.

This sequence is shot through with vivid original imagery and conceits, the language is elevated and yet expressive and innovatory, and the syntax is sometimes loose and sometimes curiously strained. The form of the *dizain* (only ten lines and shortish ones too) lends itself to concentration of meaning and compact brilliance. Scève draws on great resources of learning and cultural reference: courtly love and allegory, Marot and the *rhétoriqueurs*,[4] scientific and hermetic thought, the classical elegiac poets, Petrarchism for images and techniques, Platonism for purifying love (especially the Italian theorists, Ebreo and Speroni) and for the presentation of Délie as the ideal of beauty and virtue. Perhaps the greatest single inspiration is classical mythology: Venus/Diana/Artemis, the moon-goddess and chaste huntress, but also nature-goddess, and Hecate as goddess of the underworld. The deep psychological resonances of this mythology echo through the whole poem, and help us to appreciate Scève's exploration of emotion, and the conflict between physical and spiritual aspiration and its ultimate resolution.

Five years after the publication of *Délie* Du Bellay[5] published his *Deffense et illustration de la langue françoise*, and at the same time a collection of fifty sonnets called *L'Olive* (increased in 1550 to 115). This volume is the first collection of love-sonnets in French, and is addressed to a woman of uncertain identity and even reality, seen as the goddess of wisdom. The general colouring is Petrarchan (because, as he says, he could find no better model) and the collection ends with a group of Platonist-Christian poems expressing a deepened religious awareness in terms of repentant humility and of a love purified of sensual attraction.

Some of the earlier poems give a sense of romantic melancholy if not despair and two bitter poems on jealousy stand out. Du Bellay also published *XIII Sonnets de l'Honneste Amour*, in a cerebral Platonist manner, an approach favoured also by Peletier and Pontus de Tyard. Quite different from this are his robust Latin *Amores*, addressed to Faustina, who appears, at least, to be more real. The theme of these poems is that he has lost Faustina and wants her back. His *De poetarum amoribus* invokes at length the poetic mistresses of the Latin elegiacs, Petrarch, the Neo-Latins and contemporary French writers, and is a good example of the poet's need to relate to other poets. Du Bellay is better known for his satirical and apparently personal account of his unhappy years in exile in Rome, but his love-poetry, while low-key and not totally compelling, is an integral part of a communal interactive poetic movement.

If Du Bellay appears as a diffident love-poet, cold and rather distant, striving rather than achieving, then Louise Labé is exactly the opposite. She was one of the few women poets of the Renaissance[6] and virtually her total poetic output is contained in one small volume: twenty-four sonnets, one of which is in Italian, three Ovidian elegies and a prose *Débat de Folie et d'Amour*. The dedicatory epistle sets out a deliberate programme of writing on behalf of women and she encourages other women to take advantage of the new possibilities in education previously denied to them, and by their writing to cover themselves with literary glory rather than with jewellery and beautiful clothes, so that men will take them seriously. Labé firmly places her collection in the Petrarchan tradition and sets herself more or less the same formal constraints as her contemporaries and yet shows that she has a total mastery of the medium and is able to project her own poetic voice. Her sonnets alternate between the joys of love (remembered, dreamed of, longed for) and the aching sadness of an absence which is becoming permanent. The following poem embodies these tensions when the blackness is at its deepest:

> Tant que mes yeus pourront larmes espandre,
> A l'heur passé avec toy regretter:
> Et qu'aus sanglots et soupirs resister
> Pourra ma voix, et un peu faire entendre:
> Tant que ma main pourra les cordes tendre
> Du mignart Lut, pour tes graces chanter:
> Tant que l'esprit se voudra contenter
> De ne vouloir rien fors que toy comprendre:
> Je ne souhaitte encore point mourir.
> Mais quand mes yeus je sentiray tarir,

Ma voix casses, et ma main impuissante,
Et mon esprit en ce mortel sejour
Ne pouvant plus montrer signe d'amante:
Prirey la Mort noircir mon plus cler jour.[7]

(As long as my eyes can cry for you;
Trying to recall our happy days together,
As long as my voice can rise above sobs and sighs
And make its message heard;
As long as my hand can pluck the gentle strings of my lute
To celebrate your charms;
As long as my spirit is willing and content
To give itself to your embrace alone,
Then I have no desire at all to die.
But when I feel my eyes begin to dry,
My voice to break and my hand to fail,
My spirit flag upon this earth of ours,
And fail to show the slightest sign of love,
I'll call on death to darken my bright day.)

Other poems convey sensual and psychological harmony (though it may be muted by the illusory quality of dream or day-dream), and in this case too it is the intensity of the emotion expressed which strikes the reader. Labé is spontaneous, sincere, passionate, or at least gives the impression of being so. She does use the Petrarchan language of love and recall poetic texts currently in vogue, but her borrowings are discreet. The technical skill is evident: she varies the division of the sonnet and has a developed sense of harmonics in the way words and images correspond from sonnet to sonnet. It is necessary to stress this artistic skill since there is a danger in her case of playing it down in favour of the expression of spontaneous passion.

Labé's achievement is to establish a balance between the ordinariness and universality of love (by the conscious deployment of the commonplaces) and the quality and variety of personal experience (by her psychological subtlety and individual expression). The view of love which emerges is pagan, sensual, self-aware.

Labé (like Scève, whom some think she was addressing) lived and wrote in Lyon, the second commercial and cultural centre in France. The most prolific poetic activity, however, was centred on Paris, with a secondary focal point in the Loire valley because of the presence of the court, and the most productive of all French Renaissance love-poets was Pierre de Ronsard with whom I began. Like Du Bellay, a friend of his, he was a minor aristocrat; familiar with the court, a humanist and highly proficient scholar in Greek and Latin, he became the acknowledged leader of a small but variable group of poets known as the Pléiade. He is still best known for his love-poetry, though this is only about a sixth of his poetic work, which embraces court-poetry, philosophy, poems of religious polemic, epic and pastoral and much else besides. His love-poetry extends from the first poem he published almost to the very last and includes three major collections and several smaller ones, for the most part in sonnet form but including elegies and *chansons*.

In 1547 Ronsard published his first poem 'Des Beautez qu'il voudroit en s'Amie' in the *Œuvres poétiques* of his friend Jacques Peletier du Mans. This is a poem of delicate erotic imagination picturing his ideal mistress in physical terms. He says also that he expects her to know by heart the work of two of the traditional writers about love who will inspire his own poetry: Jean de Meun's *Roman de la Rose*[8] and 'tout cela qu'a chanté / Petrarcque en Amours tant vanté' (everything sung by Petrarch celebrated for his love-poetry). Although not addressed to a particular woman, this is a poem about love, and shows the possibility of writing unfocussed love-poetry.

At the start of his poetic career Ronsard was more concerned with his *Odes* (1550 and 1552) either in the difficult Pindaric vein or in the more approachable Horatian mode of urbanity and moderation, including however four love-odes to Cassandre inspired by Catullus and the Renaissance Dutchman Joannes Secundus and other Neo-Latin poets on the theme of kissing and evanescent beauty. His first collection of love-poems, *Les Amours* of 1552 and 1553, was addressed to Cassandre de Salviati, a young girl he had met at the Château de Blois, but who remained inaccessible to him. The first edition contained an appendix of polyphonic music in four parts by leading musicians, thus underlining the connection between poetry and song.

This love-sequence, like so many others, describes the sufferings as well as the joys of love. From the first meeting the poet is madly and inevitably in love with this goddess newly come down from heaven. Her divinity and inaccessibility are described in 'Quand au matin ma deesse s'abille' (p. 28) in which she is compared to Venus rising from the waves. Ronsard is not suggesting that this is a scene with which he is familiar and it is scarcely even a vivid erotic fantasy. Although he describes Cassandre's combing, waving and curling her 'beaulx cheveux blondz' in sensuous terms, it is rather Venus he is talking about, or love, or womanly beauty.

Yet beauty can be cruel and love is not all ecstatic delight. Love is a 'fureur', a frenzy or madness, a physical or perhaps a psychological disorder. When he writes 'Franc de raison, esclave de fureur, / Je voys chassant une Fére sauvage' ('Deprived of reason, a slave of frenzy, I am hunting a wild beast', p. 71) the violent image contrasts with reason and order. The poem which begins 'Qui vouldra voyr dedans une jeunesse, / La

beaulté jointe avec la chasteté' (He who would like to see in a young
person beauty joined with chastity, p. 41) ends on a note of happiness, yet
his praise of her virtue is reluctant, anguished, and some of the sensual
sonnets are totally opposed to anything Petrarch wrote about Laura, as
can be seen from the following poem:

> Je vouldroy bien richement jaunissant
>   En pluye d'or goute à goute descendre
>   Dans le beau sein de ma belle Cassandre,
>   Lors qu'en ses yeulx le somme va glissant.
> Je vouldroy bien en toreau blandissant
>   Me transformer pour finement la prendre,
>   Quand elle va par l'herbe la plus tendre
>   Seule à l'escart mille fleurs ravissant.
> Je vouldroy bien afin d'aiser ma peine
>   Estre un Narcisse, et elle une fontaine
>   Pour m'y plonger une nuict à sejour:
> Et vouldroy bien que ceste nuict encore
>   Durast tousjours sans que jamais l'Aurore
> D'un front nouveau nous r'allumast le jour.   (p. 15)

> (I so much want, turning richly yellow
> To fall in golden rain, drop by drop,
> Into the lovely breast of beautiful Cassandre,
> When slumber slips into her eyes.
> I so much want, into a seductive bull
> To change, and take her by surprise,
> Walking alone on the young grass
> Far from her friends, and plucking flowers.
> I so much want, in order to ease my pain,
> To be Narcissus and for her to be a pool,
> In which to plunge myself the whole night long:
> And I would like that night to have no end
> And never see the breaking of the dawn,
> Bringing light upon the face of a new day.)

Ronsard's application of classical mythology (the story of Narcissus
and of Jupiter's seduction of Danae and Europa) taken largely from Ovid's
Metamorphoses with which he clearly felt a great affinity, is highly original
and has a powerful psychological impact: and even though Petrarch both
uses the Danae myth and has a similar reference to an endless night,
Ronsard's poem has a force all of its own. He assumes the reader is aware
of Ovid's stories and goes beyond them. He is often, of course, more
recondite and erudite than he is here.

Petrarch and the Petrarchans (above all Bembo and Ariosto) are very
much present too. Yet Ronsard goes far beyond Petrarch in his personal

pursuit of an ideal of beauty. His detached attitude to Petrarchism may be seen from the fact that in 1553 he published anonymously his *Folastries* containing some bawdy poems in the *tradition gauloise*, in which caricatural sexuality contrasts with apparent pastoral innocence. In a similar vein in 1555 he published his *Meslanges* which contains a poem 'Quand au temple nous serons' contrasting prayerfulness in church with playfulness in bed. There are two different attitudes in Ronsard's writing at this time, an evocation of ideal, ethereal beauty and chaste perfection, but also explicit sexual description.

Ronsard's second collection of love-poems, the *Continuation des Amours*, appeared in 1555 and was augmented in the following year in the *Nouvelle Continuation des Amours*, both addressed, for the most part, to a girl called Marie, though Ronsard insists on the multiplicity of loves. There is a new tone here, with many references to nature, country life and fertility. Marie appears as an intimate, an equal, a willing partner in love (though some poems talk bitterly of her cruelty). The use of the alexandrine, rather than the decasyllable, allows more space for narrative, and the intermingling of sonnets, *chansons* and elegies creates variety, and makes the poems lighter and more popular. Yet whatever may have been the real character and personality of 'la pucelle angevine', the simplicity and lack of mythology correspond to another literary tradition, that of the pastoral, and bookish echoes abound.

This new direction in Ronsard's writing corresponded to the contemporary vogue of anti-Petrarchism. The work of humanist poets writing in Latin, such as the *Poemata* of Théodore de Bèze and *Juvenilia* of Ronsard's teacher Muret, both indebted to the *Basia* of Secundus, helped to start off this movement, and in 1553 Du Bellay published a poem 'A une dame', later called 'Contre les Pétrarquistes', in which he rejects Petrarchan conceits and other techniques in favour of 'jouyssance'. Moreover in 1554 the humanist publisher Henri Estienne published in Paris poems attributed to Anacreon, and other lyrical poems whose light-hearted sensuality greatly influenced subsequent French poetry. Ronsard, for his part, made a formal break with Petrarch two years later in his *Elégie à son livre*, which he added to the poems to Marie. His praise of the 'beau style bas, populaire et plaisant' however still has an explicit reference to Catullus, Tibullus and Ovid.

After these two early collections of love-poetry Ronsard devoted most of his energies over many years to his philosophical *Hymnes*, to his Catholic polemical *Discours* at the start of the wars of religion, and to the exercise of his official functions as court-poet. For twenty years he published no full-scale collection of love-poetry. He did, however, produce several smaller collections. The first of these, containing sixteen sonnets, to a noblewoman 'Sinope', in the Secundan vein, appeared in 1559 in the *Second Livre des Meslanges*. They present an analysis and expression of desire, a discussion about love and marriage, as well as a commentary on his own professional status as a tonsured cleric.

Another group of poems, three *Discours en forme d'Elégie*, addressed to a young bourgeoise called Genièvre, recount an affair which lasted for a year, from the summer of 1561 onwards. Ronsard relates how he was swimming naked in the Seine one July evening and left the water to join Genièvre who was dancing with friends on the bank, and promptly fell in love with her. He sees her again by chance standing at her own door and declares his love to her but she rejects him, Later she tells him that she is in mourning for her lover who has just died, and as he consoles her, Ronsard persuasively asks for a place in her love. With much incidental anecdote the poet describes the ecstasy of their relationship, then their mutual gradual cooling off and the transference of their affection to others.

If the Genièvre poems have a ring of veracity about them (whatever relation this may have to biographical reality), there are some other love-poems which are much more ambiguous. On occasion Ronsard wrote on behalf of noble or royal patrons (which does suggest that love-poems were in fact intended to be sent). He addressed Isabeau de Limeuil on behalf of Louis Prince de Condé (probably in order to regain his favour – see *Les Amours*, pp. 297 ff. and 306 ff.). In the *Sonnets et madrigals pour Astrée* he addressed Petrarchan and mythological poems to Françoise d'Estrée on behalf of her lover (it has been suggested that Ronsard ended up loving her himself); and in *Les Amours d'Eurymedon et de Callirée* he tells of the platonic relationship between Charles IX and Anne d'Acquaviva.

In the *Sonnets pour Hélène* (1578), Ronsard's last collection of love-poems, written against the background of the civil wars, he writes about his love for a *demoiselle d'honneur* at the court of Charles IX. These poems owe something to a new vogue of Petrarchism in the literary salons; unlike Petrarch, however, he asserts that his love for Hélène was not destined but the result of choice, and she may have been pointed out to him by Catherine de Medicis as a suitable poetic subject. Ronsard exploits the association with Helen of Troy, 'la belle grégeoise', and the effects of her beauty, though he tempers this with unflattering comments about his own Hélène. She is an intellectual interested in the spiritual philosophy of Plato, wanting to maintain a virtuous chastity, to which Ronsard opposes hedonistic enjoyment. The main theme of the poems is the resistance she offers to Ronsard's urgent attempts at seduction, a contrast heightened by an age difference of twenty-five years and the poet's melancholic disenchantment, and pessimistic reflections on the approach of death. He is jealous of younger men ('l'Olympique jeunesse, / Pleine d'un sang bouillant' – (Olympian hot-blooded youth), p. 430) and he feels that because of his age he is being ridiculous and unreasonable. Love, he admits, is an escape from oneself and love-poetry is an escape from the horrors of the religious wars: 'Au milieu de la guerre, en un siecle sans foy, / Entre mille procez, est-ce pas grand folie / D'escrire de l'Amour?' (In the midst of war, in a faithless age, / Surrounded by lawsuits, is it not great madness to write about love?, p. 468)

Yet he does write about love, and in spite of his earlier protestations he has returned to the Petrarchan manner. But these later poems are different. When we come across the topos of Hélène's icy chastity, Ronsard is not simply showing the alternating moods of the lover and the intransigence of the mistress. He is rather describing Hélène's withdrawn temperament, her introverted make-up, in terms which owe nothing to Petrarch in the end and little enough to any literary convention. In the poem 'Te regardant assise aupres de ta cousine' (Looking at you sitting next to your cousin, p. 394) the reference to Petrarch is clear, yet in addition we see Hélène in contrast to her cousin 'comme paresseuse, et pleine de sommeil' (looking lazy and sleepy) and hear her described as 'Pensive toute à toy, n'aymant rien que toymesme' (Pensively wrapped up in yourself, loving nothing but yourself). Two other poems, intended for the *Sonnets pour Hélène* but not included until later, go even further and present a picture of her frigid rejection of love-making which is not unsympathetic: 'Je trespassois d'amour assis aupres de toy' and 'Le mois d'Augst bouillonnoit d'une chaleur esprise' (*Les Amours*, pp. 498 and 463). It seems that here Ronsard is talking about a real growth in understanding and perhaps affection on his part as the collection progresses.

Renaissance poetry is grounded in the logical and rhetorical structures which contemporary education instilled in the writer, and is overlaid with the new sensibility derived from classical and Italian literature. It is, moreover, highly formalized in its rhythms, metres, language and imagery, and this attention to craftsmanship is part of a deliberate programme. It is necessary to bear firmly in mind these characteristics of Renaissance poetry when we try to find an answer to the questions I posed earlier.

Firstly, who is the 'je' in the poem? The problem is not specific to love-poetry: whenever a poet talks in the first person (and sometimes even when he does not) we may wonder about the truthfulness, and the sincerity, of what he says about himself, and whether the lyrical 'je' is the same as the real-life poet (see also above, Chapter 3). A good example is the impression of sincerity which Du Bellay gives us in his satirical *Regrets* when he describes his unhappy exile in Rome, because in spite of the ring of authenticity not everything he says is true. The problem is especially acute at a time when all poetry was seen as a form of feigning or lying,[9] when imitation was the main road to poetry, and when formal patterns, codes and conventions were preferred to creative originality or the representation of real feelings and emotions. If we wish to know who is talking, it is as important to know that it is a Renaissance poet as to know that it is Scève, Labé or Ronsard, perhaps even more important.

In Renaissance love-poetry (and to some extent in all love-poetry) the 'je' is a poet/lover writing in a poetic fashion about love, writing in the character of a love-poet. I have suggested that we do hear the poets' individual voices, not the personal living voice of the poet (though some would say that we do), but his or her poetic voice. Criticism today has gone beyond this idea of voice and there is indeed much to be gained also from considering love-poetry as texts to be unravelled, or structures to be dismantled. Mariann Sanders Regan, for example, talks of 'the voice of a poem, not the voice in a poem' and sees the text as an equivalent to self with a life of its own. She also says that we cannot separate *Poet* and *Lover*: 'they are both everywhere and nowhere in a given love-lyric – they are not things or even personae but desires, motivations "behind" processes, *Triebe* (drives) of poetics.'[10] Doranne Fenoaltea has studied this in Scève, pointing out that lyrical poems proceed by association, not sequence, so that true anecdote is out of place; what we find is a 'narrative pre-text', a story explicitly or implicitly supplied by the reader.[11] In a sense, the answer to the question, 'who is talking?' is 'the text'. If we accept this critical approach and consider that the 'je' is a poet/lover who is almost synonymous with his own text (and it is an idea which Renaissance writers would, I believe, have readily understood), then the identity of the real-life poet loses its importance and the poetry gains in stature.

This also has a direct bearing on the second question we should ask: to whom is love-poetry addressed? In the poem with which I began, when Ronsard ('Ronsard'?) says 'tu', is he directly addressing Cassandre who really existed or 'Cassandre' whom he has invented? Is there a poetic mistress in the same way as there is a poet/lover who exists only in the poems?

I have not said much about the real people whom the poets addressed in their love-poetry. Earlier critics, literary historians and biographers were very interested in this question and have discovered much information, some of it archival and some anecdotal. The poems themselves were often used, illogically and unhelpfully, as a source of information, as were poems by fellow-poets, which is not much better. More recent critical writing, with its emphasis on the text and its structure, has not, however, made the loved one irrelevant. It is not without interest that successive generations of young readers, coming to Renaissance poetry for the first time, do look for a real-life love-story behind the poetry, start by assuming that the poet is 'really in love with' the person he is addressing, and are disturbed when they discover he may not be. This critical innocence is refreshing and has much to recommend it; it reflects the perceptions of earlier critics which

were themselves based on the post-Romantic search for subjective experi-
ence, and it is in accord both with later love-poetry and the contemporary
interest in autobiography and frank confession.

Whether we look at these poems from the point of view of intertextu-
ality, voice, structure, or with any other critical *parti pris*, it is not idle to
ask what is the relation between the poet's experience and the poetry,
provided this enriches our understanding of it. For in spite of the
importance they accorded to craftsmanship and the literary tradition,
Renaissance poets did write from experience and did think it was necessary
for poetry (see for example, Du Bellay's *Deffense*, Peletier's *Art Poetique*,
and Ronsard's posthumous preface to the *Franciade*). There are many
different ways in which love-poetry is related to experience. Sometimes
poets admit that they have invented the loved one (as Baïf did afterwards
about Méline); sometimes, as we saw in the case of Ronsard, a poet may
write on someone else's behalf, or choose a real person as a *passion-prétexte*.
In none of these kinds of poetry is it possible to talk of sincerity, though in
the last two there may in the end be a real emotional experience. Love-
poetry may be generalized or unfocussed, without reference to a particular
person; it may, on the other hand, call for a multiplicity of loves, addressing
more than one woman in the same collection as Marot and Ronsard some-
times did. Finally, it may be the account of a real lived experience.

The question remains: how are we to decide? At first glance it seems
that poems which give the impression of passion and spontaneity are
bound to be more sincere than others, but this will clearly not do. The
anti-Petrarchan profession of simplicity and call for 'jouissance' soon turn
into a literary convention; in any case, some Renaissance love-poetry is
frankly and explicitly spiritual, not sensual, and other poetry is at least
reticent and discreet. The direct erotic approach of Baïf, for example, is not
more sincere than the chaster idealizing approach of Peletier in the *Amour
des amours* or of Pontus de Tyard in the *Erreurs amoureuses*. It is possible
that Du Bellay shows greater sincerity in his Latin poems to Faustina than
his French poems to Olive, but not because they are more passionate.

All in all sincerity does not seem to be a useful term of literary criticism.
We are left in the end with the notion that to be good, love-poetry must
be convincing. Louise Labé has this quality, not because her poetry is
passionate (though this is part of the reason) but because, whatever the
biographical or historical facts, she has created 'the expression of *significant*
emotion' to use T.S. Eliot's phrase.[12] Ronsard usually has it too, though
not always to the same degree in each collection of poems. Sinope,
Genièvre and Hélène are all more convincing than Cassandre and Marie,
or than Du Bellay's Olive, because in spite of some literary allusiveness,
they come across as consciousnesses, as psychologically coherent women.
In each case there is a strong narrative element (Sinope instigates the

meditation on his professional celibacy, Genièvre is unpredictable, yet the mutual relationship is compelling, and Hélène incites Ronsard to respond with some subtlety). I do not wish to suggest that it is the narrative which on its own makes for convincingness, and the narrative or implied narrative may indeed be part of a literary strategy, yet I find it hard to believe that *this* narrative and the resulting emotion are not directly nourished by experience, and this is why they are capable of persuading the reader.

Once again it is the reader who matters. The very fact of publication changes the poet's attitude to the loved one and her attitude to him within the poem; it shows that this is not just a private communication, but a work of art. Even if the poem is addressed primarily to the loved one, it is also addressed to others. Sometimes within a love-sequence we find poems addressed to fellow-poets, a small circle of like-minded friends. Moreover, all the poets we have been looking at make it plain that they have one eye on the small body of readers capable of appreciating them. This is elitist poetry. And yet we can see that they wished to reach a much wider readership and were trying to educate people's poetic sensibilities and extend their taste.

My third question was, what is the poet writing about? The answer may seem obvious; he or she is writing about love, but is that sufficient? Renaissance love-poetry seems to be about much else besides. Grahame Castor has shown that Petrarchism is as much about the quest for beauty as about love,[13] and Donald Stone has argued that the celebrated ode of Ronsard, 'Mignonne, allons voir si la rose', is not just erotic but also philosophical (it concerns the idea of love, the passage of time and the evanescence of beauty).[14] And as Fenoaltea says, 'For the learned and humanist sixteenth century, the significant formal pattern was an essential part of man's concept of the world of art ... a means of access to relationships in creation and therefore to knowledge and truth'.[15]

One last word – implicit in all I have been saying is the importance of the role of the reader. (It is often stated that Renaissance poetry was meant to be sung, or read aloud rather than privately; in so far as this is true, the hearer takes the place of the reader.) The reader participates in the creation of the work, according to some recent critical theories. Some Renaissance theories of rhetoric and poetics emphasize the audience in a similar way, and we can suppose that they would not have found this modern view totally alien. In love-poetry, then, the readers would help to create the experience. In the first place they would discover the 'narrative pre-text' as Fenoaltea has shown, the story behind what is narrated on the page, and in the second they would bring to their reading their own experience (or lack of it), their wishes, aspirations, desires, and so create a new experience.

5

Poetry and Imagination in the Renaissance

BRIAN BARRON

In a well-known passage in the final act of Shakespeare's *Midsummer Night's Dream*, Theseus relegates the experiences recounted by the four lovers to the realms of fantasy, the common territory of the lunatic, the lover and the poet, who are 'of imagination all compact'. Shortly afterwards, he is required to comment on the mechanicals' description of their play:

> 'A tedious brief scene of young Pyramus
> And his love Thisbe; very tragical mirth.'
> Merry and tragical! Tedious and brief!
> That is, hot ice and wondrous strange snow.
> How shall we find the concord of this discord?

Yet the play is all it claims to be, as Philostratus confirms with a reference to the tears of mirth he shed at the rehearsal. In this scene, Shakespeare thus sums up some of the central preoccupations of Renaissance poetry, and indeed of all Renaissance writing. On the one hand there is the uncertain value attaching to the imagination, which, while it may well permit the poet's eye 'in a fine frenzy rolling' to move from earth to heaven and back again, remains a faculty more readily associated with disorders of the mind and not therefore to be taken too seriously by grave Dukes of Athens and their sixteenth-century counterparts; on the other hand there is, splendidly displayed in the parodic tragedy we are about to witness, the reconciliation of opposites which is the ultimate aim of the Renaissance writer of poetry. This chapter will explore this reconciliation of opposites, the ways in which the poet seeks to find 'the concord of this discord' in fulfilling his stated aim, which is to 'imitate nature'. I shall be

examining the constant sense of paradox which informs all the best
Renaissance writing and provides both the creative force and formal
underpinning of some of the most remarkable (and sometimes neglected)
sixteenth-century French poems.

Paradox is apparent in contemporary understanding and discussion of
the concept 'imagination' itself. Imagination is at best an ambiguous
concept for sixteenth-century writers.[1] While it is recognized as an
essential 'faculty' in the process of cognition – one which is necessary for a
proper ordering of perceptions and understanding of the world – it is at
the same time a dangerous and unstable force. In so far as the poet's art
involves deliberate stimulation of this faculty, he is putting himself at risk.
'Stimulation' should not of course here be taken to equate to the raptures
of the Romantics, far less the 'dérèglement de tous les sens' of Rimbaud
(see below, Chapter 10, p. 162), and the risk involved is not the extreme
neurosis or even madness that afflicts some Romantic or post-Romantic
poets. The Renaissance poet stimulates his imagination by his reading,
by an attempt to absorb the great works of the past and to achieve
encyclopedic knowledge so that he can express the world or 'imitate
nature' in his own writing. The ambition is huge, and the principal danger
lies in the frequency (indeed inevitability) of failure. The surge of con-
fidence that comes with inspiration most often gives way to disillusion-
ment and sometimes depression when the power of the imagination is
revealed to be illusory. The poet is favoured by Apollo, but is also a child
of Saturn. Exhilaration inevitably gives way to melancholy. This alter-
nation is one of the most constant and appealing features of Renaissance
poetry, and is linked to the antithetical nature of much Renaissance
thought, anticipating the method of Montaigne. Every experience implies
its opposite. The alternation is often found in a single image; the
Renaissance poet's love of Petrarchan oxymoron is well known, and
celebration of the 'bitter-sweet' quality of love is universal. Lyric poetry
involves vituperation as well as praise, and the vogue for 'blasons'
celebrating the female anatomy is matched by the popularity of 'contre-
blasons' which are the opposite of idealization.

The ambiguous quality of the imagination, and the alternation of its
positive and negative qualities, may be found in a single love-sonnet: the
attempt to make concrete the presence of the absent beloved, followed by
the fading of the vision, is a frequent theme in Ronsard's love-poetry and
is much imitated by Baïf and other of his followers. It is worth pausing to
consider one sonnet in more detail:[2]

> Si mille œilletz, si mille liz j'embrasse,
> Entortillant mes bras tout alentour,
> Plus fort qu'un cep, qui d'un amoureux tour
> La branche aymee impatient enlasse:

Si le souci ne jaunist plus ma face,
Si le plaisir fonde en moy son sejour,
Si j'ayme mieulx les ombres que le jour,
Songe divin, cela vient de ta grace.

Avecque toy je volleroys aux cieulx,
Mais ce portraict qui nage dans mes yeulx,
Fraude tousjours ma joye entrerompue.

Et tu me fuis au meillieu de mon bien,
Comme l'esclair qui se finist en rien,
Ou comme au vent s'esvanouist la nue.

(If I embrace a thousand carnations, a thousand lilies,
Entwining my arms all around
More firmly than a vine, which lovingly
And impatiently clings to the beloved branch:

If care no longer makes yellow my face,
If pleasure takes up residence within me,
If I prefer darkness to day,
Divine dream, that comes from your favour.

With you I would fly to the heavens,
But the portrait which swims in my eyes,
Always betrays my interrupted joy.

And you flee from me in the midst of my enjoyment,
As the flash of lightning finishes in nothing,
Or as the cloud vanishes in the wind.)

The poem uses largely conventional imagery (flowers, the vine embracing the branch, the flight to the heavens). It expresses both the intensity and urgency of desire through its control of rhythm and assonance, and through the repetition of 'mille' in the first line (a favourite device of Ronsard's). Exactly half-way through the sonnet, the reader receives his first hint of the disillusionment to come ('ombres') and this is confirmed when the image of the beloved begins to fade ('ce portraict qui nage dans mes yeulx') even before it has been fully realized. The use of the conditional ('volleroys') in l. 9 subtly introduces the move from intensifying to declining desire, and prepares the reader for the nostalgia which is all that remains at the end of the poem. Renaissance love-poetry is rarely concerned only with love. Here, the lover's attempt to create the presence of his beloved by (literally) compressing powerful but insubstantial sense-impressions (colour, scent, texture) into a concrete reality reflects the creative effort of the poet himself, and his disappointment that he is unable to give permanent and tangible form to the world his imagination encourages him to penetrate. In the words of Shakespeare's Theseus, he seeks '[to give] to airy nothing/A local habitation and a name', but the poem is never quite worthy of its subject. For the French Renaissance poet, 'songe' cannot help calling up the spectre of 'mensonge'. Dream and falsehood are inextricably bound up with one another, and both partici-pate in the ambiguous nature of the imagination. This sonnet stands as an icon of poetic creativity. The poet is constantly straining to achieve a permanent, sustainable image of the ideal, and is at the same time aware of the impossibility of the task.

The alternation may be the leitmotif of a whole collection: the 'Première Journée' of Remy Belleau's *Bergerie* is a single sustained vision, culminat-ing in the poet's experience of the dance of the Muses (an image of inspiration) which then fades with the coming of dawn, leaving the poet with nothing but regret for the perfect world he has lost. Belleau further develops the theme when he comes to write the second 'day' of his *Bergerie*, and contrasts the ideal world of Joinville in 1565 with the civil strife which divides France in 1572.[3]

It may also appear in the form of contrasting moods at different phases of the poet's career, connected with his own psychological development and with the pressures of external reality. Du Bellay's *Regrets* are the best known example of this, contrasting as they do the confidence and ebullience of the early years, and the hopes of the humanist setting out for Rome, with the mundane reality he has to deal with there, and the sense of his own fading powers. A complex tissue of themes comes together in this sonnet sequence, many of which are illuminated by the notion of the paradoxical imagination. The overall subject of the sequence is the poet's suffering, which comes about because of what might be called his dislocation in place and time. In France, his imagination made him impatient to get to Rome (the Rome of the humanist, which no longer exists); in Rome he yearns for Anjou, for the France of the past and for the France of his return. The *Regrets* establish clearly that both of these are illusory. Du Bellay is quick to realize the danger that the imagination represents, inviting him as it does to waste his life in an idealized elsewhere. He rejects nostalgia, and uses his gifts as a poet to master the situation which threatened to master him. I shall illustrate this with just one poem from the 'elegaic' section of the collection. (The elegaic and satirical sections are themselves an illustration of the ambivalence of the imagination. The scorn Du Bellay directs at Rome with his 'rire sardonien' is his way of dealing with his neurosis; the satirical imagination, stimulated by his reading of Horace and Juvenal, and of contemporary Italian poets, takes over from, and cures, the home-sick imagination, modulated by Du

Bellay's knowledge of Ovid). Sonnet 36 recounts how time seems endlessly prolonged by the poet's homesickness in Rome:

> Depuis que j'ay laissé mon naturel sejour,
> Pour venir ou le Tybre aux flotz tortuz ondoye,
> Le ciel a veu trois fois par son oblique voye
> Recommencer son cours la grand' lampe du jour.
>
> Mais j'ay si grand desir de me voir de retour,
> Que ces trois ans me sont plus qu'un siege de Troye,
> Tant me tarde (Morel) que Paris je revoye,
> Et tant le ciel pour moy fait lentement son tour:
>
> Il fait son tour si lent, et me semble si morne,
> Si morne, et si pesant que le froid Capricorne
> Ne m'accourcist les jours, ny le Cancre les nuits.
>
> Voila (mon cher Morel) combien le temps me dure
> Loing de France et de toy, et comment la nature
> Fait toute chose longue avecques mes ennuis.[4]
>
> (Since I left my natural abode
> To come where the Tiber flows with twisting waves,
> The sky has three times seen the great lamp of the sun
> Start three times over its oblique course.
>
> Yet I have such a strong desire to see myself back,
> That these three years are to me more than a siege of Troy,
> So much I long, Morel, to see Paris again,
> And so slowly does the sky turn for me:
>
> It turns so slowly, and seems so dreary to me,
> So dreary and so heavy that cold Capricorn
> Does not shorten my days, nor Cancer my nights.
>
> That, my dear Morel, is how time drags for me,
> Far from France and from you, and how nature
> Makes all things long with my woes.)

This sonnet is remarkable primarily for its gravity, for the ennobling of the poet's suffering by the representation of time dragging in the extended periphrasis of the first quatrain, by the elevated language and imagery, and by the control of rhythm, reinforced by repetitions and assonances. The background of the flowing Tiber generalizes the theme and at the same time personalizes it by inviting the reader to identify with the exile watching the river – and time – flow away from him. The three years of the periphrasis become a heroic Trojan ten, before resolving themselves into the endless succession of the seasons. The poem does not express a neurotic obsession with time, nor is it a lament. It is a limpid account of the poet's awareness of his vulnerability, explicitly recognized ('tant le ciel *pour moy* fait lentement son tour'; *'m'*accourcist'), and an illustration of how linguistic and cultural resources have been brought to bear on the problem in order to overcome it. The imagination is both the source and the cure of the sickness.

It is therefore a mistake to see Du Bellay as the poet of lamentation and self-pity. It is true that failure is a constant motif in his writing. Poetic creativity is seen in terms of the commonplace of flight followed by fall, and Icarus becomes a symbol of the poet's doomed aspirations. Comparison with the achievements of Ronsard, and the constant attempt to free himself from the dominance of his friend, also mark the development of his work. Complaint and comparison are not however ends in themselves, and Du Bellay uses the admission of his own lesser imaginative powers as a springboard for the assertion of his originality. This is clear in the *Regrets*, where he associates himself with the art of the portrait-painter, while comparing Ronsard with Michelangelo (Sonnet 21).

Du Bellay is not the only poet to worry about failure, and in particular the failure of the imagination. Ronsard too recounts his illness and the sense of listlessness which afflicts him in the 1560s after the death of Du Bellay and during the period of political instability following the death of Henri II. As part of this new mood he sets out to contrast the inconsequential nature of poetry as he apparently now conceives of it with the elevated social function he had attributed to it in the 1550s and early 1560s. The poems of the later 1560s show us Ronsard again and again in this kind of mood, itself a combination of cynicism and playfulness which is not far from the 'rire sardonien' deployed in Du Bellay's *Regrets*. Sometimes the tone is negative and depressed, sometimes (and far more frequently) playfulness dominates. The 1569 'Ombre du Cheval' is a good illustration of this aspect of Ronsard's work. The poet has been sent a poem about a horse:

> Amy Belot, que l'honneur accompagne,
> Tu m'as donné non un cheval d'Espagne,
> Mais l'ombre vain d'un cheval par escrit,
> Que je comprens seulement en esprit.

> (My friend Belot, may honour be your guide,
> You have given me, not a Spanish steed,
> But the empty shadow of a horse in writing,
> Which I comprehend only in my mind.)   (Pl. II, 373)

This horse is a 'fantôme' which only becomes real in the poet's dream, and when it becomes too pressingly real, the dream ends:

> Plus en songeant ton cheval je me donne,
> Plus il me trompe, et fuit sur la Garonne,
> Aux crins espars, au jarret souple et pront,
> A l'estomac refait, au large front,
> A la grand' queue, à la drillante oreille,
> Et hanissant bien souvent il m'esveille,
> Ou bien je l'oy, ou je le pense ouir,
> Puis comme idole en l'air s'esvanouir.

> (The more I give myself your horse in my dream,
> The more it eludes me, fleeing to the Garonne,
> Its mane flying, its hock supple and quick,
> Its chest deep, its forehead broad,
> Its great tail, its gleaming ear,
> And often it wakes me with its neighing,
> Either I hear it, or I think I do,
> And then I seem to see it vanish into the air like a spectre.)

The precipitous list of the horse's physical qualities leads the reader into the poet's imaginative world – his dream – where the animal is real, and lets the reader down with a bump when the poet starts awake, not quite sure whether what he can hear is real or not. Note also the recurrence here of the image of something insubstantial vanishing into thin air. Similar images recur throughout Ronsard's poems, and in those of the many writers who imitate his themes and style. To return to Belot's horse; its lack of substance has its advantages, since it costs nothing to feed and groom; it is a non-horse, which cannot be compared to the great horses of history, like Bucephalus, but which can be related to the animals of myth and legend:

> Il vole en l'air, boit en l'air, d'air se paist;
> C'est un corps d'air, l'air seulement luy plaist
> Et la fumee et le vent et le songe,
> Et dedans l'air seulement il s'allonge.

> (It flies in the air, drinks in the air, feeds on air,
> It is an airy body liking nothing but air
> And smoke and wind and dream,
> And only in air does it stretch out.)

Its cousins are to be found in the *Thousand and one Nights* and in the service of the gods of the Greek pantheon, including among others 'le dos-ailé Pegase/Et le cheval de l'Aurore' (Wing-backed Pegasus/And the steed of Dawn). Its lack of substance is thus a necessary concomitant of its nobility, and it has the rare gift of making the poet dream, not only in the vivid way related above, but also by setting in motion within his

imagination the thrilling list of mythical and poetic creatures he has
encountered in his reading. This list leads ultimately to Homer. Ronsard
relates his own illness to the prophecy of Achilles's death in the *Iliad*, and
concludes, not gloomily, but with a celebration of the escapist value of
poetry:

> Aurois-tu leu, o teste rare et chere,
> Dedans les vers du fantastique Homere,
> Qu'un des chevaux d'Achille s'avança,
> Et le trespas a son maistre annonça?
> Tu crains, voyant ma longue maladie,
> Que ton cheval en parlant ne me die
> Prophetisant quelque funebre mot:
> Garde-le bien, je n'en veux point Belot.
> Mon cher ami, j'ai bien voulu t'escrire
> Ces vers raillards pour mieux te faire rire
> Apres ta charge, et le souci commun
> De conceder audience à chacun,
> Haut-elevé au throne de Justice,
> Aimant vertu et chastiant le vice.
> Dieu, qui sous l'homme a le monde soumis,
> A l'homme seul le rire a permis
> Pour s'esgayer, et non pas à la beste,
> Qui n'a raison ny esprit en la teste [...]
>   ainsi tu pourras rire
> De ma folie, et de t'oser escrire
> Je ne scay quoy qui est encor plus vain
> Que ton cheval qui n'a selle ny frain.

> (Could you have read, dear friend,
> In the poems of fanciful Homer
> That one of Achilles's horses came forward
> And announced to his master his death?
> You fear, seeing my long illness,
> That your horse might speak out and say to me
> Prophetically some funereal word.
> You can keep it, I don't want it Belot.
> My dear friend, I wanted to write you
> These mocking verses the better to make you laugh
> After your work, and the daily care
> Of giving audience to one and all,
> Seated high on the throne of Justice,
> Loving virtue, and punishing vice.
> God, who has placed the world under man,
> Has given laughter to man alone
> To raise his spirits, and not to the beast

Who has neither reason nor sense in his head [...]
    and so you can laugh
At my folly, and at my daring to write
I know not what that is even emptier
Than your horse which has neither saddle nor bit.)

While the theme and tone of this poem are a long way from the solemn claims and elevated style of many earlier poems, 'L'Ombre du Cheval' is arguably more representative of Renaissance poetry at its best, and is certainly to be seen as a necessary counterweight to the earlier seriousness. The playful tone, reinforced by the decasyllabic metre, underlines the profundity of the message rather than detracting from it; literature, and the imagination which it feeds and which feeds it in turn, is both escapist and, like laughter, of deep moral and social significance. The poet is at one and the same time a prophet or magus, and the whimsical practitioner of a 'frolicsome trade' ('folâtre métier').

While I have chosen to illustrate this paradox with a poem written in 1569, and therefore one of the mature works of the greatest French poet of the sixteenth century, it should not be thought that the antithesis of seriousness and frivolity is restricted to this period of Ronsard's development, or to his works alone. Indeed it runs through the whole of his work, and is present in that of his contemporaries. Imagination is the source of an art which is at the same time profoundly serious and entirely frivolous, whose constructions may be seen as approximating to the Platonic 'ideas', or as no more than insubstantial shadows. It is thus part of the network of paradoxes which provides the creative framework of sixteenth-century poetry; ultimately the poet's awareness of the illusory nature of his endeavours serves to confirm his belief in the value of his art. While the temporary and transient nature of inspiration can produce depression, poetry also provides the means of recovery. In this way, the pressures the poet is subjected to, and the insecurity which relates to the ambiguous nature of the imagination, become themselves the subject of poetry, as part of the wider paradox illustrated in the love-sonnet with which I began.

This wider paradox concerns at base the contradiction between a transcendental reality which the poet postulates as his subject, and to which he claims to have privileged access through his imagination, and the means he has at his disposal to express this reality. Language, like the carnations and lilies of the love-sonnet, is too insubstantial to make real the ideal. The poet thus finds himself required to deploy his virtuosity and to extend the range of his medium, accumulating images in an attempt to transform the real into an ideal embodiment of itself. Lyrical technique explicitly involves the celebration of a subject by the accumulation of appropriate images and epithets. This is what the sixteenth century means by 'describing' or 'imitating nature'.[5] The deliberate cultivation of excess is the hallmark of the *Odes* (1550) with which Ronsard first thrust himself on the attention of established literary circles:

> it is the true aim of the lyric poet to celebrate to the extreme the subject whose praise he undertakes ...   (Pl. II, 973–4)

This view is confirmed in the posthumous preface to the *Franciade*, where the poet is distinguished from the historiographer by his function, which is to embellish reality as a way of acceding to truth:

> [Les] Poëtes [...] ne cherchent que le possible, puis d'une petite scintille font naistre un grand brazier, et d'une petite cassine font un magnifique palais, qu'ils enrichissent, dorent, et embellissent par le dehors de marbre, jaspe, et porphire, de guillochis, ovalles, frontispices et pieds-destals, frises et chapiteaux, et le dedans de tableaux, tapisseries eslevées et boffées d'or et d'argent, et le dedans des tableaux cizelez et burinez, raboteux et difficiles a tenir és mains, a cause de la rude engraveure des personnages qui semblent vivre dedans.   (Pl. II, 1021)

> (Poets [...] seek only the possible, then from a little spark they create a great fire, and from a little hut they make a magnificent palace, which they decorate, gild and beautify outside with marble, jasper and porphyry, with guilloches, ovals, frontispieces and pedestals, friezes and capitals, and inside with reliefs, tapestries raised and inlaid with gold and silver, and the interior of the reliefs chiselled and engraved, coarse and difficult to hold in the hands, because of the rough engraving of the characters that seem to live within it.)

I have given the French text of this curious passage because the quality of the prose is itself an illustration of the feature of poetry it seeks to illustrate. The image of architectural decoration, and the sustained quality of the language which develops it, echo Belleau's descriptions of art objects in the *Bergerie*, and here, as there, serve to obscure the line between reality and the imagined ideal. I shall return later to this important definition of the poet's activity. For the moment, it is enough to stress the decorative build-up which seems to be required to bring the ideal to life. An interesting example of this technique in action can be found in the 1553 'Harangue de tres-illustre François, Duc de Guise aux Soldats de Metz'. (Pl. II, 304–11) In this poem, Ronsard, taking his cue from Homer, describes the arming of the Duke in decorated armour depicting the glorious past of the House of Guise. Thus 'clothed' in his own glory, he is transformed into a hero of mythological proportions, who can legitimately address his troops in 'vers Tyrteans'.

The relationship between language (the vernacular which must be 'defended' and 'illustrated' to make it a suitable vehicle for poetry) and its aim to express the inexpressible ideal is an important part of the debate in the sixteenth century about the relative importance of 'art' and 'nature' in poetry.[6] On one level, 'art' is everything that is learned, primarily by study and imitation of ancient sources, while 'nature' is the poet's innate genius. But the fruitful tension between 'art' and 'nature' is reinforced by the multiple values which attach to the idea of nature itself. In their mythology of poetry, the poets look back to a golden age, when poetry, the language of the gods, was a universal form of discourse, and communication between human and divine levels of existence was constant rather than intermittent, direct rather than indirect.[7] Nature, in this pre-fall state, is nature as God (or the gods) created it, and it exists out of time. It has the perfection of the static, and is depicted as permanent springtime, but a springtime which, as in Botticelli's 'Primavera', is complemented by the automatic provision of the fruits of the earth to indolent and perfectly happy mankind. 'Natura naturata' is doubled however in the poet's experience by 'natura naturans', the sublunar universe which is characterized by the excitement of movement and change – 'inconstant and variable in its perfections', to use Ronsard's phrase.[8] The poet, in seeking to 'imitate nature', looks to a transcendental reality – permanent and static – which it is his particular gift to perceive and record, and at the same time prescribes a method for acceding to that reality which is firmly anchored in the imperfect world governed by time and characterized by movement and change.

By 'imitation of nature' the Renaissance poet does not therefore mean any simple description of phenomena, but rather an investigation and elaboration of their significance. The paradox lies in the attempt to reach some essential truth by means of this process of elaboration and the search for 'copia' and completeness. Poetry seeks to communicate truth by accumulation of images, and the poet's 'inventions' are the results of his researches in the image-thesaurus constituted by the works of the ancient (and Italian) poets, or in the compendia derived from them, like Boccaccio's *De genealogia deorum*. Imagery is above all mythological, and myth, with its emblematic qualities and its ability to communicate layers of meaning, is the poet's primary means of acceding to truth through language. Ultimately, however, since truth is perceived as simple and uniform, it involves a synthesis which is beyond the capacities of the human imagination. Poetry is therefore the record of human effort to encapsulate a truth, into which, at its best, it provides momentary insight. In the process leading to the moment when truth clarifies, the poet piles up his fragmented and partial perceptions as the Titans piled mountain upon mountain in their defiance of the gods, and like the Titans, he risks the punishment reserved for human presumption. In this context, Du Bellay's *Antiquitez de Rome*, which stress the vanity of human endeavour and make recurrent reference to the Titans and their punishment, may be

seen as yet another reflection of the poet's sense of the inevitability of
failure.[9] The 'vanitas vanitatum', here as throughout Renaissance thought
and art, is a counterpoint to the 'dignitas hominis'.

This ambiguity, fundamental to Renaissance poetics, is found in
Ronsard's presentation of the idea of poetry as 'allegorical theology' in his
Abbregé de l'Art poëtique (1565). What is interesting here is less the idea,
which is found in the many volumes of poetic theory which were being
produced in sixteenth-century Italy, as the poet's attitude to it:

> for in the first age Poetry was nothing other than an allegorical Theology,
> to instil in the brains of coarse men, by pleasant and colourful fables, the
> secrets they could not understand, if truth were too openly uncovered to
> them.   (Pl. II, 996)

Here the phrase 'nothing other' translates 'n'estoit au premier age que . . .'
which contrives in the context to communicate both a sense of the
superiority of this primitive art, and at the same time to underline its
primitiveness (= 'nothing more than'). Ronsard goes on to develop the
idea of a chain of knowledge, initiated by 'the Oracles, Prophets, Seers,
Sybils, Interpreters of dreams' who pass on divine knowledge to the first
generation of 'divine poets', who in their turn expand this material to
make is accessible to men:

> for what the Oracles stated in few words, these noble persons amplified,
> coloured and increased, being towards the people what the Sybils and
> Seers were for them . . .   (ibid.)

Thus far, amplification is necessary and good. But there follows a
gradual dilution or degeneration; as successive generations of poets
imitate their predecessors, poetry becomes wordier, and ever further
distanced from its pure origins. The Roman poets are called 'human'
rather than 'divine' because they are 'more swollen with artifice and labour,
than with divinity', and only five or six are spared the general condemna-
tion of having 'brought more weight than honour to the libraries'. What is
required is 'learning, accompanied by perfect artifice', and Ronsard goes
on to advise his reader to avoid redundancy in his writing, using the image
of the gardener who is careful to prune useless branches. With the idea of
'perfect artifice' we find again the tension on which poetry thrives,
between the need to 'amplify' the subject on the one hand, and the
knowledge that amplification implies destruction on the other.

The art–nature tension, and the ambiguity attaching to the idea of
nature itself, provides the basis for some fine poems. Thematically,
Ronsard develops the contrast between the ideal past and the defective
present. The fragmentation of human experience of the divine is paralleled
in the loss of wild nature. This is a constant theme in his work, from early

odes like the 1550 poem in praise of the 'Forêt de Gâtine' (Pl. I, 452), seen as the home of the Muses on earth, to the late elegy 'Contre les Bûcherons de la Forêt de Gâtine', where the violation of this last refuge of the Muses is deplored because it will replace the life of which sound (poetry) is the guarantee with the silence of death, and (paradoxically) the silence which allows imagination to flourish with the clamour of modern civilization:

> Tout deviendra muet, Echo sera sans voix,
> Tu deviendras campagne, et en lieu de tes bois,
> Dont l'ombrage incertain lentement se remue,
> Tu sentiras le soc, le coutre et la charrue,
> Tu perdras ton silence, et, haletans d'effroy,
> Ny Satyres, ny Pans ne viendront plus chez toy.   (Pl. II, 117)

> (All will be silent, Echo will have no voice,
> You will become farmland, and in place of your woods,
> Whose uncertain shade slowly waves,
> You will feel the plough, the ploughshare and the coulter,
> You will lose your silence, and neither Satyrs nor Pans,
> Panting in fright, will come to you again.)

At the same time, there is a recognition that this age of gold is no more than an image of human aspiration. In 'Les Isles Fortunées', dedicated to his erudite friend Marc-Antoine de Muret (who had provided the learned glossary for the second edition of his *Amours*), Ronsard develops the theme of an ideal world where, free from all constraints, and from the contemporary horrors of war, the 'bons esprits' can commune with one another and with the gods. As the poem develops, this world is however revealed to be that of literature, of escape into the imagination through reading. Muret will read to his companions the works of the great poets of antiquity, and the natural world of this pre-fall paradise will respond:

> A ces chansons les chesnes oreillez
> Abaisseront leurs chefs esmerveillez,
> Et Philomele, en quelque arbre esgarée,
> N'aura souci du peché de Terée,
> Et par les prez les estonnez ruisseaux
> Pour t'imiter accoiseront leurs eaux.   (Pl. II, 413)

> (Hearing these songs, the ear-decked oaks
> Will lower their wondering heads,
> And Philomela, lost in some tree,
> Will lament no more Tereus's sin,
> And, in the meadows, the startled brooks
> Will quieten their waters to imitate you.)

The union between nature and poetry is re-established and fulfilled, with the natural world *imitating* the poet in a reversal of the normal image. We should note that this world is characterized by the absence of pain and sorrow (the nightingale ceases her lament) but concomitantly by silence, which, as we have just seen, indicates the absence of life. Only poetry can resolve this contradiction; thus, if the streams fall silent, it is to imitate the voice of the erudite humanist reading the great works of the past. A vision in which nature imitates art rather than the contrary is however bound to be illusory, and so the end of the poem returns to the image of war with which it began, reminding the reader that escape to these happy isles is only temporary, and that poetry is not the reflection, but rather the only remaining manifestation of the age of gold:

> Telles, Muret, telles terres divines,
> Loin des combats, loin des guerres mutines,
> Loin des soucis, de soins et de remors,
> Toy, toy, Muret appellent à leurs bors,
> Aux bords heureux des isles plantureuses,
> Aux bords divins des isles bien-heureuses,
> Que Jupiter reserva pour les siens,
> Lors qu'il changea des siecles anciens
> L'or en argent, et l'argent en la rouille
> D'un fer meurtrier qui de son meurtre souille
> La pauvre Europe! Europe que les Dieux
> Ne daignent plus regarder de leurs yeux,
> Et que je fuy de bon coeur sous ta guide,
> Laschant premier aux navires la bride,
> Et de bon coeur à qui je dis adieu
> Pour vivre heureux en l'heur d'un si beau lieu.

> (Such, Muret, such blessed lands,
> Far from battle, far from unruly war,
> Far from worries, cares, and remorse,
> Call you, you Muret, to their shores,
> To the happy shores of the fertile isles,
> To the divine shores of the happy isles,
> Which Jupiter set aside for his own,
> When he changed the gold of the ancient times
> Into silver, and silver into the rust
> Of murdering iron whose killing soils
> Poor Europe! Europe which the Gods
> Deign no more to look on with their eyes,
> And which I willingly flee with you as my guide,
> The first to give the ships their head,
> And to which I willingly say farewell,
> To live happily in the bliss of such a beautiful place.)

The contradiction is thus both endemic to the undertaking, and one which has a historical development and becomes gradually more acute in the poet's consciousness. To recreate in the context of Valois France, if not the primitive age of gold at least its human reflection in the social and political stability of Augustan Rome, characterized by the happy conjunction of an enlightened patron and poets of genius: such was the declared aim of Ronsard and his friends. If the context had seemed promising in the immediate aftermath of the reign of François Ier, it soon came to seem hopeless. The ambition remains, however, tempered by a powerful sense of the potential of poetry and also of its limitations.

If we consider now the effects of the art–nature paradox on technique, it will become clear that, in setting himself the task of bridging through language the gap between fallen man, with his partial and fragmented vision, and the transcendental unity of truth and beauty, the poet is again obliged to acknowledge the illusory nature of his undertaking. The technique of mythological embellishment is summed up in the idea of the 'fabulous mantle', which has been analysed by Terence Cave. Ronsard documents this crucial aspect of his poetics in the remarkable sequence of hymns, the 'Quatre Saisons de l'An'.[10] These poems illustrate the poet's elevated conception of himself as interpreter and imitator of nature, and, like Orpheus and Amphion, as a catalyst of civilization – of social and political harmony. They also contain a demonstration of the progressive maturing of Ronsard's views on how poetry functions. Two of the Hymns (Autumn and Winter) contain major statements on how poetry is written. The long preamble (86 lines) to the 'Hymne de l'Automne' contains the much-anthologized section where Ronsard describes the sense of awe he experienced as a boy in wild nature and his subsequent consecration by the Muse. The youth of the poet here merges with the youth of the world to allow direct imaginative experience of the divine. In this context, the next phase of the poet's development, undertaken with the end of the Muse's peroration still ringing in his ears, cannot but be anti-climactic and unsatisfactory:

> 'tout paisible et coy
> Tu vivras dans les bois pour la Muse et pour toy.'
> Ainsi disoit la Nymphe, et de là je vins estre
> Disciple de Dorat, qui long temps fut mon maistre,
> M'apprist la Poësie, et me monstra comment
> On doit feindre et cacher les fables proprement,
> Et à bien desguiser la verité des choses
> D'un fabuleux manteau, dont elles sont encloses.   (Pl. II, 241)

> ('peaceful and quiet
> You shall live in the woods for the Muse and yourself.'

Thus spoke the Nymph, and from there I came to be
A pupil of Dorat, who was a long time my master.
He taught me poetry, and showed me how
One should cleverly feign and hide fables,
And how to disguise well the truth of things
With a fabulous mantle in which they are enclosed.)

The change of tone, and the banality of the description of the apprentice-
ship with Dorat, underlines the tension between nature and art, an
unbridgeable gap, here emphasised in the sudden move from the woods
to the schoolroom. The creation of the 'fabulous mantle' is the core of
Ronsard's technique, a technique imitated by his contemporaries, and
where the build-up of images (usually mythological) ennobles and trans-
forms the subject. But here he finds it wanting, although he will use
it for his Hymn to Autumn. This dissatisfaction with an art that seeks
to 'hide' and 'enclose' is the context of the desire for something new
expressed at the beginning of the Hymn to Winter, and culminates in a
new image of the activity of the poet, here conceived as an earthly
philosopher – that is, not one who thinks in terms of the unattainable ideal
contained in the story of the 'divine poets' who are capable of conquering
Fortune and Destiny ('Et en pillant le Ciel, comme un riche butin,/Mirent
dessous leurs pieds Fortune et le Destin.' – And pillaging Heaven, like a
rich booty, They placed Fortune and Destiny beneath their feet), but
a human poet, conscious of his limitations and yet anxious to stretch his
human potential to the maximum. The human 'philosophie' with which
this poet has to work is described:

Elle a pour son sujet les negoces civiles,
L'equité, la justice et le repos des villes,
Et, au chant de sa lyre, a fait sortir des bois
Les hommes forestiers et leur bailla des lois.
Elle sçait la vertu des herbes et des plantes,
Elle va dessous terre, aux crevaces béantes,
Tirer l'argent et l'or, et chercher de sa main
Le fer qui doit rougir en notre sang humain.
Puis à fin que le peuple ignorant ne mesprise
La verité cognue, apres l'avoir apprise,
D'un voile bien subtile, comme les peintres font
Aux tableaux bien portraits, luy couvre tout le front,
Et laisse seulement, tout au travers du voile,
Paroistre ses rayons comme une belle estoile,
A fin que le vulgaire ait desir de chercher
La couverte beauté, dont il n'ose approcher.
Tel j'ay tracé cet Hynne, imitant l'exemplaire
Des fables d'Hesiode et celles d'Homere.   (Pl. II, 252)

> (Its subject is civil affairs,
> Equity, justice, and the peace of cities,
> And, to the song of its lyre, it led out of the woods,
> Forest-dwelling men to whom it gave laws.
> It knows the power of herbs and plants,
> It goes beneath the earth, into the gaping chasms,
> To bring out silver and gold, and to search out with its hands
> The iron which will grow red in our human blood.
> Then, so that ignorant people will not scorn
> Known truth, once they have learned it,
> It covers truth's face with a subtle veil,
> As painters do, with a well-made picture,
> Allowing to appear through the veil
> Only its rays, like a lovely star,
> So that the common throng will desire to seek
> The hidden beauty which it dare not come near.
> So have I drawn this Hymn, imitating the example
> Of Hesiod's fables, and those of Homer.)

Characteristically, the stated desire to break new ground is resolved into the assertion that here only the most prestigious of models have been used. This, we are being told, is true poetry, as practised by the greatest of the ancient poets. The shift from the 'fabuleux manteau' to the 'voile bien subtile' is to my mind instructive, and marks the culmination of a long period of reflection on poetry by the greatest French poet of the sixteenth century, bringing together many of the conflicting attitudes we have been considering. The technique of elaboration is ultimately only a means to an end, seeking to create the right mental conditions for an imaginative breakthrough by the poet and the reader working in co-operation, and from both of whom sustained effort is required. This breakthrough occurs when the necessary opacity of language dissipates – momentarily – to allow the light of truth to shine clearly. The full force of the extract from the preface to the *Franciade* quoted earlier now becomes clear; as the viewer of the 'magnificent palace' is expected to examine the decorative detail ever more closely until the figures come to life, in spite of the 'rough engraving' and the fact that they are 'difficult to hold in the hands', so also is the reader challenged by the opacity of language and expression in the poem. What is more, the poet, putting behind him the contradictions involved in maintaining the divine origins of poetry, accepts the ambiguities which are attendant on any human activity. The impetus toward socialization and civilization is seen as both bad and good; if philosophy has led men 'out of the woods' it has been to send them into the depths of the earth to extract silver and gold (ambivalent commodities) and also 'the iron which will grow red in our human blood'. (For Ronsard, mining always represents human discontent, greed and discord.) In this flawed world, shot through with such contradictions, the poet's vocation is so to stimulate and instruct his reader that the delicate social balance, itself an image of the tensions which hold the cosmos together, can be maintained.

Within this context, the image of the poet as painter is an essential feature of Ronsard's mature definition of the poet's activity. The conjunction of poet and painter is of course a commonplace of poetic theory in a century dominated by Horace's *Ars Poetica*, and is a leitmotif not only in Ronsard but in many of his friends and imitators. The word 'imagination' can itself mean the creation of visual images, and *Imagination poëtique* is the title of a collection of emblems by Barthelemy Aneau.[11] Emblem books, containing symbolic engravings with a corresponding versified text, were extremely popular. The conjunction of all the arts – literary, visual and musical – is itself a Renaissance ideal, and one which yet again quite obviously concerns the resolution of opposites. It is usual for poets to argue for the superiority of their art, seen as combining the melodic qualities of music and the visual qualities of painting, sculpture or engraving, and also (following Horace) as offering a permanence which is not possible for material monuments. Poetry is often also described as 'peinture vive', where life is seen as rhythm – as movement and respiration, opposed to 'la morte peinture'. The tension is once more between the static qualities of the allegorical or emblematic image, reflection of the transcendental world to which poetry aspires, and the qualities of movement, implying existence in time, which are an essential feature of poetry. The contradiction is never resolved, and it becomes a fertile source of poetic reflection and imagery. The painter strives to transcend the limits of his art and make his static image come to life (as happens in the baroque palace of the preface to the *Franciade* and – over and over again – in Belleau's *Bergerie*). The poet, for his part, has to seek through language to crystallize his message in a single pregnant image, culmination of his narrative. While in Scève's *Delie*, where the poems (concentrated *dizains*) are explicitly attached to a sequence of emblems, there is a sustained effort towards abstraction and compression which can be seen to justify the analogy of visual and literary, the expansive, accretive technique of the Pléiäde poets would seem to be wildly at odds with the visual medium.[12] Many poems do however take as their subject – or pretext – the description of a painting or art object. The supreme example is Ronsard's 'La Lyre'.[13] In this poem, Ronsard, suffering from depression, describes a decorated lyre which has been given him by a friend. The decoration depicts the mythological history of poetry, and in describing the 'fabulous mantle' which envelops the musical instrument, he is reinvigorated, and his flagging inspiration and his faith in his art are revived. The technique develops the same idea as the 'Harangue' of 1553.

Usually, descriptions of art objects underline their static quality, which is both a defect since it implies lifelessness, and an advantage, since it places them out of time. In Ronsard's 'La Défloration de Lède', the handle of the basket Leda carries is an allegorical representation of time, which thus literally stands still while the narration moves towards its climax, with Jupiter's seduction of Leda and her rapid production of the two eggs from which emerge Castor and Pollux and Helen of Troy. Acceleration and even instantaneity are features of the sexual activities of gods and semi-gods in Ronsard, and the phrase 'tout soudain' is nearly always there to underline it. The effect is at one and the same time serious – these beings are not subject to the laws of time, fortune and destiny as we are – and quite profoundly comic. In the case of Leda, the deflowering produces instant deification – 'Tu seras incontinant/La belle soeur de Neptune' (You will be at once/The lovely sister of Neptune) – and an accelerated pregnancy (the poem leaves us with the image of her rapidly swelling waistline). The timeless (and therefore eternally renewed) moment of the deflowering marks the impregnation of the mortal by the divine; from Leda's womb will emerge the essence of Greek (and therefore all) poetry.[14]

Many poems conclude with a single striking image summing up and crystallizing the message which may have been developed over several hundred lines of narrative. Thus the elegy entitled 'L'Orfée' consists of a multiple narrative, but leaves the reader with the image of the metamorphosis of Orpheus's lyre into a constellation in the heavens. The essential Orpheus is thereby ennobled and immortalized – fixed for eternity.[15] Similarly, the 'Hymne de l'Hiver' is epic in tone and dimension, and narrates the struggle against Winter as a cosmic battle which is assimilated to the battle of the gods and the giants (a leitmotif of French Renaissance poetry, as will by now be clear). At the end of the narrative, peace is restored and the combatants sit down to a banquet. The dinner service is decorated with mythological scenes depicting events which have just been narrated:

> Des Dieux et des Titans les victoires passées,
> Et comme Jupiter aux enfers foudroya
> Le Gean, qui le Ciel de cent bras guerroya.   (Pl. II, 258)

> (The past victories of the Gods and the Titans,
> And how Jupiter's thunderbolt cast into hell
> The Giant, who fought heaven with a hundred arms.)

The participants, and Ronsard's readers, thus have constantly before their eyes a powerful reminder of the effects and punishment of discord and disorder.

One final example will underline the poetic value of these tensions between the visual and the literary (and particularly the narrative). In Ronsard's 'Hymne de l'Eternité', faced with the difficulty of celebrating 'celle qui jamais par les ans ne se change' (the one who through all the years does not change) the poet chooses the device of the allegorical image or emblem. The present tense is used, and the visual qualities of the image are stressed by careful indication of relative positions and by frequent reference to colour. Eternity is a symbolic figure sustained by counterbalanced forces, and the rhythm of the alexandrines reinforces the tensions that bind the allegorical group together:

> A ton dextre costé la Jeunesse se tient,
> Jeunesse au front crespu, de qui la tresse vient
> Par flots jusqu'aux talons d'une enlasseure entorse,
> Enflant son estomac de vigueur et de force.
> Ceste belle Jeunesse, au teint vermeil et franc,
> D'une boucle d'azur ceinte desur le flanc,
> Dans un vase doré te donne de la destre
> A boire du Nectar, afin de te faire estre,
> Toujours saine et disposte, et afin que ton front
> Ne soit jamais ridé comme les nostres sont.
> Elle, de l'autre main, vigoreuse Déesse,
> Repousse l'estomac de la triste Vieillesse ...   (Pl. II, 123)

> (On your right stands Youth,
> Youth with the curly forehead, whose locks fall
> In waves to her heels in a twisting tangle,
> Her breast swelling with vigour and strength.
> This lovely Youth, with her ruddy open complexion,
> And an azure buckle fastened at her side,
> With her right hand has you drink from a golden vessel
> Nectar, so that you may be
> Always healthy and hearty, and so that your brow
> Will never be wrinkled as ours are.
> With the other hand this vigorous Goddess
> Pushes back the breast of sad Age ...)

At some points, narrative progression risks destroying the suspension of time created by the emblematic force of the description, but the poet deploys his device of instantaneity to sustain, and even reinforce the narrative-descriptive tensions of the poem, making them a perfect reflection of their subject. Discord is the enemy of eternity, constantly threatening to destroy, but held in check by the delicate balance of forces on which the continuity of the universe depends:

> Discord ton ennemy, qui ses forces assemble
> Pour faire mutiner les Elemens ensemble

A la perte du monde et de ton doux repos,
Et voudroit, s'il pouvoit, r'engendrer le Chaos.
Mais tout incontinent que cest ennemy brasse
Trahison contre toy, la Vertu le menasse,
L'eternelle Vertu, et le chasse en Enfer,
Garroté, pieds et mains, de cent chaisnes de fer.   (ibid.)

(Your enemy Discord, who gathers his forces
To cause the Elements to rebel together
For the loss of the world and your sweet repose,
And he would, if he could, being Chaos back into being.
But just as soon as that enemy conspires
Treason against you, Virtue threatens him,
Eternal Virtue, and banishes him to Hell,
Bound hand and foot in a hundred iron chains.)

The cluster of contradictions surrounding the imagination and its projection in poetry thus produces a complex and invigorating vision of the world, a world which is itself characterized by ambiguity and ambivalence, and one which, both in terms of contemporary cosmology and historical reality, is poised on a knife-edge, ready to return to disruption and chaos. The poet, marked out to feel both the exhilaration of the imagination and its counterpart in depression, is himself a model of the world, a microcosm of the macrocosm. And in this context poetry, the product of an imagination both stimulated and controlled, of insight, learning and wisdom, of nature and art, is in the fullest sense an imitation of the world, and at the same time, through its dynamic and subtly didactic relationship with its reader, an exhortation to virtue. Poetry reflects, channels, and directs the forces that ensure the continuity of the universe.

All this is very serious. Did the sixteenth-century poet really believe in his God-given role as interpreter of the divine purpose, instructor of the people, and indeed guide of kings? In a chapter devoted to contradiction and paradox, the answer can only be yes – and no. I began with Shakespeare and the complementarity of tears and laughter. I want to end with an early poem in which the young poets-to-be of the Collège de Coqueret and their tutor Jean Dorat take a break from the obscurer early Greek poets, and the austere allegorical interpretations which were Dorat's speciality, and set off for a picnic by the Seine. The poet's imagination is inflamed by the gifts of Bacchus:

Je voy cent bestes nouvelles,
        Pleines d'ailes,
Sur nos testes revoler,
Et la main espouvantée
        De Penthée
Qui les poursuit parmy l'air,

Evan! que ta teste folle
    Me rafolle
De vineux estourbillons;
Je ne voy point d'autres bestes
    Sur nos testes
Qu'un scadron de papillons.   (Pl. II, 457)

(I see a hundred new beasts
    Full of wings,
Flying around our heads,
And the horror-struck hand
    Of Pentheus
Pursuing them through the air.

Evan! how my mad head
    Drives me mad
With vineous spinnings;
I see no other beasts
    On our heads
Than a flight of butterflies.)

And so Ronsard, unquestioned leader of the group, encourages his companions in a butterfly-chase, using vocabulary reminiscent of his claim to have brought first to France the glory and dignity of true poetry. Monsters or butterflies? The Renaissance poet answers: both.

6

The Poet as Self: Thought and Feeling in the Poetry of the 'Premier Dix-Septième Siècle'

IAN REVIE

The reputation of the poets of the first half of the seventeenth century has been sufficiently rescued from the authoritarian strictures of Boileau and sufficiently discussed with regard to such notions as the baroque, the metaphysical, the *précieux*, the mannerist and so on, for critical discussion now to have alighted on the term the 'premier dix-septième siècle[1] to refer to a period sufficiently distinguished to be acknowledged in its own right. And while it is undoubtedly true that the influence of Ronsard remained an extremely important factor during this period, it is equally true that the work of the poets I shall discuss in this essay deserves to be seen in terms other than the 'post-Renaissance' or the 'pre-classical'. In looking at the poetry of Théophile de Viau, Saint-Amant, Tristan L'Hermite and (briefly) Etienne Durand I shall be exploring those aspects of their work which make of their poetic production something more personal and more original than their immediate posterity valued. It should, however, be said that the perspective which Boileau led many to take, seeing Malherbe as almost the sole predecessor of Classicism, surrounded and succeeded by a chorus of worthless voices, also ignores the fact that the poetry of Théophile was republished many more times than that of Malherbe in the course of the century, showing its continuing popularity with the readers of the age, if not with the self-appointed arbiters of taste.

Without wishing to make Malherbe too much of a touchstone in the discussion, it is none the less highly instructive to compare his 'Consolation à M. Du Périer' with Théophile's 'A M. de L.. sur la mort de son père'. The comparison has frequently been made, and the contrast frequently pointed in the Christian resignation of Malherbe with the pagan epicureanism of Théophile:

> Vouloir ce que Dieu veut, est la seule science
> Qui nous met en repos.

> (To want what God wants is the only science
> Which brings us peace.)

This is Malherbe's conclusion and there can be no greater contrast than with Théophile's astonishing vision of a universe in which all things are subject to the final disintegration, in which death, at first seen as an outrage to Nature, is subsequently seen to be Nature itself, a fact accepted in the poem's vigorous conclusion (while Malherbe's conclusion is lameness itself, following, as it does, his far superior penultimate stanza):

> Celuy qui formant le Soleil,
> Arracha d'un profond sommeil
> L'air et le feu, la terre et l'onde,
> Renversa d'un coup de main
> La demeure du genre humain
> Et la base où le Ciel se fonde:
> Et ce grand desordre du Monde
> Peut-estre arrivera demain.   (III, 303)[2]

> (He who in forming the Sun,
> Awoke from their deep sleep
> Air, Fire, Earth and Water,
> Overturned with one sweep
> The mansion of mankind
> And the base whereon Heaven sits:
> And this great disorder of the World
> Perhaps will happen tomorrow.)

What is, however, more interesting in the comparison of the two poems is the fact that while Malherbe's consolation to his friend is spoken from a real personal awareness of the suffering caused by the death of a child and refers directly to his own experience of it, it is Théophile's poem which is vibrant with a personal voice, whereas Malherbe's sense of self is eclipsed in his Christian stoicism. It is this notion of the presence of self in his poetry which sets Théophile apart, not just from Malherbe but from many of his contemporaries,[3] and which I wish to use to shape this discussion of his poetry; but it is with a glance at the poetry of Durand that it is appropriate to begin.

The early and violent death of Etienne Durand is generally held to have deprived French literature of possibly one of its finest lyric poets, and this on the evidence of only a handful of poems. His much anthologized 'Stances à l'Inconstance' allow us to see his great gifts as a composer of harmonious lines, and serve as a fine introduction to the baroque theme par excellence of inconstancy:

> Je peindrais volontiers mes légères pensées,
> Mais déjà, le pensant, mon penser est changé,
> Ce que je tiens m'échappe, et les choses passées
> Toujours par le présent se tiennent effacées,
> Tant à ce changement mon esprit est rangé.
>
> (Willingly I'd paint my fleeting thoughts,
> But already, in the thinking, my thought is changed,
> What I grasp escapes me, and all things past
> By the present are always held in eclipse,
> So is my mind to changing attuned.)

This poem, which appeared in his *Méditations* of 1611, his only published book of poems, can stand as a marker for the beginning of a period during which several notable poetic talents continued to produce a lyrical and satirical poetry which refused to be bound over by the prescriptions of Malherbe, yet which also sought to break free from the more automatic forms and conventions to which the legacies of the Pléiade had dwindled. Like Théophile de Viau, as we shall later see, we find Durand both playing and mocking the game of amorous servitude, yet while there is originality and considerable skill in those verses Durand has left us, there is at the same time at least as much of the elegant player of the amorous game:

> La constance en amour fait d'étranges miracles.
> Quoi donc, faut-il aimer? Faut espérer aussi,
> Car les refus de femme ont l'effet des oracles
> Qui, jurés, bien souvent n'arrivent pas ainsi.
>
> (Constancy in love works strange miracles.
> Why then, should one love? And hope also,
> For women's refusals like the oracle's words
> Though sworn true come often not to pass.)

Had he survived to meet Alceste, no doubt he would have met with the same arguments as Oronte (see below, p. 110) and, perhaps, there would have been some right on Alceste's side.

In the love-poetry of Théophile we find his almost constant insistence upon the element of personal experience that is necessary to him as a poet. Not that he never exercises himself in the all but automatic play of Petrarchan and Ronsardian themes; but he does make his poetry the locus of a tension between the expected conventional discourse of the poet-lover and the thinking author who chafes at the constraints imposed by both the role of lover and the conventions of a poetic form that insist upon the lover's need to continue in his suffering. For Théophile, it is only worth loving if one is loved in return, and his poems frequently break off from their ostensible, initial subject to become a comment upon the rhetoric.

Thus the poem 'Cloris pour ce petit moment …', which Streicher sees as expressing a 'violent accès de dépit',[4] may well be just that, but it is even more interesting as an expression of Théophile's refusal to allow his reason to be overwhelmed by a passion that is merely poetic:

> Lors que mes ardeurs sont passees
> La raison change mes pensees   (II, 156)

> (When my ardour has gone
> Reason alters my thoughts)

He gives full voice to his rejection of the Petrarchan tradition which spiritualizes love through the suffering of the rejected lover:

> Toutes les complaisances feintes
> Où tes affections mal peintes
> Ont trompé mes sens hebetez,
> Je les tiens pour foibles feintises,
> Et n'appelle plus que sottises
> Ce que je nommois cruautez.   (II, 157)

> (All those favours feigned
> Wherein thy ill-painted affections
> Deceived my bewildered senses
> I hold them for weak deceptions
> And call now only foolishness
> What once I called cruelty.)

And there is the familiar sense of his own worth which prevents him both from regretting the verses already written in the lady's honour and also from continuing in the role of ardent but rejected suitor:

> Je ne veux point mal à propos
> Mes vers ni ton honneur détruire   (II, 157)

> (For no good reason I will not
> My verses or your honour destroy)

Amorous servitude, however, cannot withstand the twin forces of reason and the beloved's refusal to love in return, and typically for Théophile the poem charts a movement in his mind and feelings to end with his freeing himself from the image and state of the suffering, rejected suitor:

> C'en est fait, je sens que mon ame
> Souspire sa dernier flame,
> Tous ces regards sont superflus,
> Je ne vois rien, rien ne me touche,
> Je suis sans oreille et sans bouche,
> Laisse moy, ne me parle plus.   (II, 160)

> (It is over, I feel that my soul
> Breathes its last flame,
> All thy glances are in vain,
> I see nought, nought touches me,
> I have nor ear nor mouth,
> Leave me and speak no more.)

Yet Théophile is a highly complex personality and for a poet so sensual, so insistent upon the essentially personal nature of experience, if it is to nourish poetry, can the sensory deprivation he imposes on himself here be seen as a triumph? Might it not be better considered as an even more effective and personal image of pain than the fires and chains of other poets? Elsewhere, as in 'Je n'ay repos ny nuict ny jour' (I, 445), he can be found fitting more easily into an existing mould. It would clearly be wrong to overstress the personal independence of Théophile's experience or to insist that his poetry only ever seeks to reflect the realities of his existence; but it is equally clear that there is a veritable drama that is played out around the persona that inhabits his poems and that it is driven by the energy which it derives from the tensions in the making of the poem, which for Théophile (whatever he may say about the ease with which he writes – 'Un bon esprit ne faict rien qu'aisement') is a quest for originality.

This clearly explains why he was able to acknowledge the influence of Malherbe while finding no difficulty in setting much of Malherbe's conception of poetry aside. It is in his 'Elégie à une dame' (I, 342), which he places at the very heart of the 1621 edition of his works, that we find the clearest assertion of the independence of Théophile, for while the poem begins by seemingly according to love the power of inspiration, it progresses through the well-worn topos of the triumph of ignorance to proclaim that what pleases him in the lady is the sharpness and subtlety of her intelligence, which makes her a suitable reader of the verses that Théophile writes:

> Mais vous à qui le Ciel de son plus doux flambeau,
> Inspira dans le sein tout ce qu'il a de beau,
> Vous n'avés point l'erreur qui trouble ces infames,
> Ny l'obscure fureur de ces brutalles ames,
> Car l'esprit plus subtil en ses plus rares vers,
> N'a point de mouvemens qui ne vous soient ouvers: (I, 347)

> (But you to whom Heaven with its gentlest flame
> Inspired in your breast all that is most beauteous,
> You harbour not the fault which governs the infamous
> Nor the obscure fury of those coarse souls,
> For the subtlest mind in its finest verses
> Moves not in ways you cannot discover.)

But while he is content to acknowledge his previous efforts in more traditional and conventional modes, what Théophile now proclaims to be the measure of his poetry is reason, yet it is reason not so much in the sense of the avoidance of extravagance as in the sense of a proper independence. What pronouncements Malherbe may have made are good, but they apply to his poetry and not to all; there is no merit in trying to emulate him:

> Imite qui voudra les merveilles d'autruy,
> Malherbe a tres bien fait, mais il a fait pour luy,
> Mille petits voleurs l'escorchent tout en vie:
> Quant à moy ces larcins ne me font point d'envie:
> J'approuve que chacun escrive à sa façon   (I, 349)

> (Let who will follow the marvels of another,
> Malherbe spoke well, but for himself alone,
> A thousand petty thieves strip the very flesh from his bones:
> But for myself I hold this theft as nought
> And declare each poet must to his own hold true)

He further goes on to chastise and parody the imitators of Malherbe, laughing at their struggle to emulate some of Malherbe's rhymes (while, as many have noted, not having been averse to imitating these same rhymes himself). The necessary freedom of mind which Théophile requires for himself as poet will not allow him to be held by preconceived notions of the form a poem should take nor by dictates concerned with the mellifluousness of verse.

> D'une insensible ardeur peu à peu je m'esleve,
> Commençant un discours que jamais je n'acheve.
> Je ne veux point unir le fil de mon subjet,
> Diversement je laisse et reprens mon object [...]
> La reigle me desplaist, j'escris confusément,
> Un bon esprit ne faict rien qu'aisement.   (I, 352–3)

> (With a flame scarce felt little by little I grow hot,
> Beginning my discourse but never ending it.
> I do not wish to have a subject that is unified,
> In divers ways I leave and return to it [...]
> Rules I dislike, I write without them,
> A fine mind does all with ease.)

There follows a complaint about the difficulties of writing for the stage, of earning a living as writer to a company, and features such as these make it relatively easy to see in Théophile's work the traces of an autobiography which perhaps serves only to obscure the more interesting perception of a poetry dependent on a dramatic persona. It has been noted that Théophile says 'I' more often than any other contemporary and while it is necessary to be aware of the fierce Gascon spirit, of the Protestant then *libertin* and, finally, Catholic mind that displays a roughness so opposed to the virtues of Classicism, it is more interesting to see this 'I' as a poetic persona moving in a landscape imbued with the ambiguities of a post-Renaissance *décor*. Several of the poems which were once considered to display pre-Romantic or even surreal characteristics as aspects of the more personally original side of Théophile's verse have now been more accurately placed in the context of one or other fairly ancient topos. One such clear example would be the nightmare vision of 'Un corbeau devant moi croasse' (S.i, xlix) now generally considered to belong to the ancient tradition of 'the world turned upside down'. But when we take Théophile's poetic production as a whole, albeit without too great an insistence on unity of purpose or inspiration, we find its essential characteristic to be the dramatic qualities inherent in the evolution of a persona constantly tempted by roles both poetic and amorous; roles to be played out in a theatre of metamorphosis, where landscape represents a natural refuge from the merely decorative and mythological qualities (both early exploited then later satirized by Théophile), within which reason can free itself from false logic and image. The world of Théophile's poetry is a constantly changing world, since such, for him, is Nature, and also because it has become a landscape of the mind in which the presence of a certain classical literature is almost tangible.

Most criticism rightly insists upon the superiority of the Théophile of the elegies. Certainly he is no great lover or exploiter of the sonnet. Yet in two or three of his sonnets the compression of the form is well suited to the daring compression which Théophile brings to bear on the conventional imagery of spiritual experience arising from amorous suffering. In the sonnet 'Chere Isis tes beautez ont troublé la nature' he pushes the notion that the lady's beauty is a temptation even to the gods themselves far enough into the realm of the explicitly sexual for it to have been one of the many subjects of accusation brought against him at his trial in 1624:

> Et tandis que le ciel endure que tu m'aimes,
>
> Tu peux bien dans mon lict impunement coucher;
> Isis que craindrois-tu, puis que les Dieux eux mesmes
> S'estimeroient heureux de te faire pecher.
>
> (And while Heaven allows that thou lovest me,
>
> Thou may'st in my bed fearless lie;
> Isis, what need'st thou fear, for the gods themselves
> Would think them happy didst thou but lie with them.)

It has been suggested that the frequent practice of using churches as places of assignation may have contributed to the creation of poems which instead of using the profane as a way to the sacred, drew on sacrilege and near blasphemy to give force to their metaphors of profane love. This may well be, but in the sonnet 'A quoy bon me presser tant d'aller à confesse' the urgency of the lover's voice carries a sexual charge which marks most of Théophile's poems as suitor:

> L'amour pour le salut n'a rien qui soit fatal,
> Et le dire tout bas, marqueroit ma foiblesse [...]
> Mon crime est que j'enrage, et peste en tout lieu,
> Malgré tous mes respects, et ma perseverance,
> Que vous ne vouliez pas me faire offenser Dieu.   (III, 311)

> (Love for salvation holds nought that is fatal,
> To say this but softly, would be a mark of my weakness [...]
> My crime is to rage and to curse in any place,
> For in spite of my respect and my persistence
> You would not lead me to offend God.)

Théophile could and did go even further than that, even if, under threat, he was to deny authorship of several such poems. There is surely no more vigorous rebuttal of the entire Petrarchan and Platonic traditions in love-poetry than his 'Je songeois que Phyllis des enfers revenue' in which his vigorous obscenity once again stems from the compression of a certain language of convention:

> Son ombre dans mon lict se glissa toute nue
> Et me dit: cher Thyrsis, me voicy de retour,
> Je n'ay fait qu'embellir en ce triste sejour
> Où depuis ton despart le sort m'a retenue.
>
> Je viens pour rebaiser le plus beau des Amans,
> Je viens pour remourir dans tes embrassements.
> Alors quand cette idole eut abusé ma flamme,
>
> Elle me dit: Adieu, je m'en vay chez les morts,
> Comme tu t'es vanté d'avoir f...tu mon corps,
> Tu te pourras vanter d'avoir f...tu mon ame.   (III, 256–7)

> (Her shade into my bed quite naked slipped
> Saying: Dear Thyrsis, here I am come back,
> I have but grown more lovely in that sad place
> Where, since thy departure, fate has held me.
>
> I come to kiss again the handsomest of lovers,
> I come to die again in thy embraces.
> And when this idol had abused my flame,

> She said: Farewell, I return to the dead,
> As thou hast boasted of having f.....d my body,
> Now thou mayst boast of having f.....d my soul.)

Théophile, of course, was not alone in his satirical rejection of certain conventions. Indeed the above poem comes from a collection of many such by numerous authors. But it is a consistent feature of his poetry that it should display the restlessness that both challenges and returns to these conventions. As Chauveau has remarked, amorous inspiration remained for the seventeenth century what it had been for the sixteenth, namely the dominant source of poetic creation; and before the later years made of it a merely futile game of the *salons*, it retained a vitality that bears comparison with the preceding century.

It is in the elegist, however, that we find the best of Théophile. Here he is capable, in this relatively free form, in the rhyming couplets which Malherbe disdained, of allowing himself to discourse on love, giving emphasis to the experience as the encounter between two free and necessarily imperfect human beings. In poems such as 'Souverain qui regis l'influence des vers' we find the very best of a personal lyrical talent that offers a note of truthful description of human relationships rather than the stereotypes of a certain type of poetry.

Many have consequently concluded that the best of Théophile coincides with the loosest of poetic forms; but this is to ignore 'La Maison de Sylvie', the sequence of ten odes probably begun while Théophile was in Chantilly, but subsequently elaborated during his imprisonment.[5] It is clear that the ambiguous circumstances of the author contribute to the fascination of this sequence: a landscape of tranquillity remembered in the degradation of prison, yes; but a landscape already created and transfigured by myth, so that this is no merely decorative treatment of landscape; the classical garden becomes a place in which the poet exists in the same way that the statuary and the cultivated plants exist. These are some of the most complex and subtle of all of Théophile's poems. They mix some of the descriptive elements of the landscape poem, with mythological elements (largely derived from Ovid's *Metamorphoses*), with the main features of encomiastic poetry, with the bitterness and horror of the poet's predicament, imprisoned, abandoned by many of his friends and already burned in effigy. Even without Théophile's earlier rejection of 'la sotte Antiquité', there would necessarily be a more than merely decorative use of the descriptive and mythological elements in such poems. What seems to me to give this sequence its unique force is the figure of the poet who is, in turn, the observer of the *décor*, the singer of the praises due to Sylvie (Marie-Félice Orsini, wife of his powerful protector Henri II de Montmorency), and, as both such, the possessor of the sensibility which operates the metamorphoses, but who is also the persecuted and

imprisoned figure, his life at stake, whose ultimate recourse against his
enemies lies in the power of his language, in the beauty of his song.

   In the first of the odes, Théophile establishes the basis for the complex
interweaving of strands that is to follow: the magical properties of a nature
that is inhabited by the gods and demi-gods of antiquity is evoked but
distanced:

> Si quelques arbes renommez
> D'une adoration profane,
> Ont esté *jadis* animez
> Des sombres regards de Diane;   (III, 133)

> (If some famous trees
> With a profane adoration
> Were *long ago* animated
> By the sombre glances of Diana;)

for the presence of the mythological elements in the poem will depend
upon the human participants in the drama and will never be assumed
(however tongue in cheek) to be real. It is Théophile the reader of Ovid,
together with his friends and protectors, who creates this dimension.
What follows therefore becomes not the familiar exaggeration of encomi-
astic verse, in the identification of the Duchess with mythological figures,
but a recognition of Sylvie as the creator of this place, as the poet is the
creator of these verses.

> Je sçay que ces miroirs flotants
> Où l'objet change de place,
> Pour elle devenus constans
> Auront une fidele glace,
> Et sous un ornement si beau
> La surface mesme de l'eau
> Nonobstant sa delicatesse,
> Gardera seurement encrez
> Et mes characteres sacrez,
> Et les attraits de la Princesse.   (III, 135)

> (I know that these floating mirrors
> In which reflections move,
> For her become constant
> Will be faithful mirrors,
> And beneath so beautiful an ornament
> The very surface of the water
> Despite its delicacy,
> Will surely keep fixed
> Both my sacred script,
> And the attractions of the Princess.)

It is through these identifications that it becomes possible for the second ode to recount the metamorphosis of the tritons into white stags and the story of Acteon, while the third portrays the death of Phaeton and the mourning of Cygnos. These three odes serve as preparation for the entry of the poet into this landscape as a participant. In the fourth ode Théophile speaks as himself, the references to his personal, and highly dangerous, situation are precise. Herein lies the fascination of this sequence of poems; the third ode could well have served with very little addition as a discreet enough allusion to Théophile's situation and to the faithful friendship of Thyrsis (probably Jacques Vallée des Barreaux) but discretion was never Théophile's chosen style. The fourth ode is a hymn to friendship in which he vigorously attacks his accusers:

> Les sottes limites,
> Que prescrivent les imposteurs,
> Qui sous les robbes de Docteurs,
> Ont des ames de Sodomites.   (III, 150)

> (The foolish limits
> Laid down by impostors,
> Who beneath their doctoral robes
> Have the souls of Sodomites.)

The opening apostrophe to the swan and the integration into the poem of the poet's own assessment of the interest and justification of his subject fuse the landscape of myth with his personal situation. And, when in the fifth ode Thyrsis recounts his dream in which the death of Damon (Théophile) is announced to him by a messenger from the underworld, the oneiric and imaginary worlds become even less distinguishable from the real, since Théophile reveals that he has indeed already been executed in effigy and that the refuge of Chantilly (site of the gardens celebrated in the poems) is where he has fled. The links across the three poems are further strengthened by the use of the stark imagery of black and white coupled with the general theme of metamorphosis as reversal.

Despite the fact that if the odes are read as a chronicle of the events of Théophile's flight, imprisonment and trial, then the sixth ode must be close to the nadir of his personal suffering, since it equates with the long imprisonment in the vilest of conditions, much of the anger which characterizes the two preceding odes is absent from this poem. Indeed what happens is that the prison simply becomes the garden; as Thyrsis's dream of Damon's fate runs in exact parallel to the decree of the Parlement which led to Théophile's misfortunes, the poet dreams the landscape of his security and eventual vindication:

Nous estions lors tous deux couverts
De ces arbres pour qui mes vers
Ouvrent si justement ma vene [...]
Nous estions dans un cabinet
Enceint de fontaines et d'arbres,   (III, 161–2)

(Then were we both roofed o'er
By those trees for whom my verses
Unlock so well my inspiration [...]
Then were we in a bower
Surrounded by trees and fountains.)

The three remaining odes develop the story of Philomèle, who was transformed into a nightingale, from *Metamorphoses*, but again, as with the story of Cygnos and Phaeton, they place *in parallel* the poet and the nightingale, rather than simply accepting one as the symbol of the other. Due praise is, of course, offered to his protectors Henri and Marie, but what Théophile primarily achieves in this sequence of poems is the most complex expression of a poetic persona which is called into being on the various complex levels of meaning which the poems touch, revealing the poet as being created by the poem rather than the reverse, but all still finally subject to that consistent note of Théophile's poetry – the restlessness of a mind which can find infinity in any subject but which knows there are an infinity of subjects also. 'La Maison de Sylvie' represents the peak of Théophile's poetic achievement, perhaps because it presents the greatest complexities and subtleties in the use of the poetic 'I'. The poet who speaks here is aware that he inhabits the countries of the mind; he is equally aware that that is where his existence is at stake.

The differences between the poetry of Théophile and that of Saint-Amant are at least as great as the similarities, and their frequent association in anthologies or essays such as this is a product of the history of literary criticism more than anything else. Certainly they both shared a whole-hearted appetite for the coarse and the grotesque which does much to explain Boileau's harshness towards them, but Théophile could never have penned *Moïse sauvé*. Anthologies frequently represent Saint-Amant by extracts from his longer poems, and it is certainly true to say that many of these are apparently fuelled by the desire simply to continue the creation of verses. But if his Biblical epic does in some ways merit the contemporary jibe of *Moïse noyé* (Moses drowned), it also contains passages of high quality and originality. Considerable verve, great variety of inspiration, and a taste for fantastical and humorous decoration are the hallmarks of Saint-Amant's poetry.

In the early 'La Solitude' we find both a theme and aspects of imagery

which invite close comparison with Théophile's poem and also with
Tristan's 'Le Promenoir des deux amants', which probably surpasses both:

> O que j'ayme la solitude!
> Que ces lieux sacrez à la nuit,
> Esloignez du monde et du bruit,
> Plaisent à mon inquietude! [. . .]
>
> [. . .] Là se nichent en mille troux
> Les couleuvres et les hiboux.
>
> L'orfraye, avec ses cris funebres,
> Mortels augures des destins,
> Fait rire et dancer les lutins
> Dans ces lieux remplis de tenebres.
>
> (Solitude it is that I love,
> How these places sacred to the night,
> Far from the world and all noise,
> Please my unquiet mind! [. . .]
>
> [. . .] There in a thousand hollows nest
> Vipers and owls.
>
> The screech owl[6] with its mournful cries,
> Mortal auguries of destiny,
> Make the gnomes laugh and dance
> In these places full of darkness.)

But there is in Saint-Amant's dark places rather less that is genuinely
disturbing than there is in Théophile's 'Un corbeau devant moi croasse',
even if they both have literary origins rather than real nightmare roots.

While Saint-Amant's poetic output is very varied in form, it is most
interesting to consider the persona of *le bon gros Saint-Amant* who inhabits
many of his poems, especially the sonnets of his *Raillerie à part*. For
whereas the former contain much exuberant verse (e.g. 'Le Melon'), which
is in its exaggeration and extravagance a challenge to the easy acceptance of
moribund forms and dead metaphors in poetry, it is the self-mocking
figure of the lazy, gluttonous drunkard, author of the highly skilful verses,
which again shows something of the concept of a personal presence in
poetry as one of the more interesting characteristics of the individual and
the age. Not that pure inspiration drew from an unlettered poet the verses
that we read, as Saint-Amant would often have us believe. But what
Boileau was to turn against him is, in fact, the best of his talent:

> Ainsi tel autrefois qu'on vit avec Faret
> Charbonner de ses vers les murs d'un cabaret.
>
> (*Art poétique* I, 21–2)

>(Such one saw then in company with Faret
>Blacken with his scribbles the walls of a tavern.)

While many of the longer poems are sustained by an imagination which is allowed to flit from topic to topic but little constrained by structure or at times even subject-matter, the sonnets turn on the gusto with which the voice which speaks them matches for compression and wit the requirements of the higher modes of expression, as it dwells contrapuntally on the sordid and the grotesque of the subject-matter. Here is a quatrain from one of his most famous:

>Là, faisant quelquefois le saut du sansonnet,
>Et dandinant du cul comme un sonneur de cloche,
>Je m'esgueule de rire, escrivant d'une broche
>En mots de Pathelin ce grotesque sonnet.

>(There, hopping around like a starling,
>Arse bobbing up and down like a bell-ringer,
>I laugh my head off, writing with a skewer
>In words like Pathelin's this grotesque sonnet.)

But the final tercet leads the reader into as neat a trap as was ever devised for any amorous play (there is no rhyme for *ongles*):

>Nargue: c'est trop resver, c'est trop ronger ses ongles;
>Si quelqu'un sçait la ryme, il peut bien l'achever.
>...

>(I give in: it's too much thought, too much biting my nails;
>If anyone knows the rhyme, he can finish it)

The presence of the poetic persona here is crucial to the success of the joke; the sense of the poem being written almost as it is read is vital.

The success of poems such as 'Les Goinfres' and 'Le Paresseux' undoubtedly owes as much to their author's experience as to any literary tradition, but when they are juxtaposed (as they were in the original volumes of Saint-Amant's verse) with such others as 'L'Hyver des Alpes' and the sonnet 'Sur la moisson d'un lieu proche de Paris' they do not merely reveal a complex personality capable of both the most bizarre humour and the most highly developed aesthetic sensitivity. Both types of poem show themselves to depend on a nature that is subject to change and instability, but which knows itself to be capable of giving voice to both in well wrought verse. A nature, then, which constructs itself into a persona to affirm its existence in poetry, built as it is upon paradox and antithesis, mutation and instability.

L'or tombe sous le fer; desjà les moissonneurs,
Despouillant les sillons de leurs jaunes honneurs,
La desolation rendent et gaye et belle.

L'utile cruauté travaille au bien de tous,
Et nostre œil satisfait semble dire à Cybelle:
Plus le ravage est grand, plus je le trouve dous.

(Gold falls before iron; already the mowers
Stripping the furrows of their golden honours,
Make the desolation both gay and beautiful.

This useful cruelty works for the good of all,
And our eye, with satisfaction, seems to say to Cybele:
The greater the ravage is, the sweeter I find it.)

The burlesque poetry which Saint-Amant developed (with others) looks not only to Italy and to Spain, but back to the satirical traditions of the late sixteenth and early seventeenth centuries of French poetry. Wherever we turn in his poems, we meet in Saint-Amant a well-read writer who is aware of the uses he can make of what he finds and who allows himself to be seen on stage as he does so. If we take one possible example among many from the anonymous anthologies of the grotesque development of the baroque sonnet, and contrast it with Saint-Amant's poems, one difference which immediately appears is the way in which Saint-Amant is himself a presence in his own poems, whereas the other poem lacks any such dimension, while still displaying the same objectives in terms of antithetical effects, the juxtaposition of high verbal and prosodic skills with low and comic subject-matter:

Don Diègue est de retour avec sa barbe blanche,
Son teint de ramoneur, sa mine de Chinois,
Sa démarche d'oison et sa jambe de bois,
Qui représente aux yeux la forme d'une éclanche [...]

Enfin le verre en main, sans chapeau, sans rabat,
O dieux, s'écria-t-il, si jamais rien m'abat,
Permettez que ce soit ce flambant cimeterre.

Son souhait arriva, le goinfre fut devin;
Car Bacchus à l'instant le culbuta par terre
Où je lui vis verser moins de sang que de vin.
(*Recueil Sercy*, Ière partie, 1653)

(Don Diego has returned with his beard so white,
His sweep's complexion and Chinaman's look,
His gosling's waddle and his wooden leg,
Which looks like a shoulder of mutton [...]

At last, glass in hand, hatless and shirt open,
O gods, cries he, should ever I be laid low,
Let it be by this glowing scimitar.

His wish came true, the glutton became an prophet;
For Bacchus instantly cast him backwards to ground
Where I saw him spill less blood than wine.)

I do not wish to claim that Saint-Amant writes a poetry of self-exploration, but it does seem to me that what really distinguishes his poems, when they are after all simply on set-piece themes of the period, is that they draw the force of their paradoxes and antitheses from the identity of the speaking voice with the subject of the poem. The anonymous piece quoted above quite simply takes burlesque to be an end in itself and that is precisely what the mode for the burlesque became, a cul-de-sac of ever more grotesque invention until invention failed.

In Saint-Amant's 'Le Paresseux' it may indeed be the poet who wears the comic mask, but the poem is the stronger for it:

Accablé de paresse et de melancholie,
Je resve dans un lict où je suis fagoté
Comme un lievre sans os qui dort dans un pasté,
Ou comme un Dom-Quichot en sa morne folie.

(Overwhelmed with laziness and with melancholy,
I dream in a bed where I lie bundled
Like a hare boned and sleeping in a pie,
Or like some Quixote in his sad folly.)

This is not of course simply a matter of the use of the first person, as the last lines show:

Et hay tant le travail, que, les yeux entr'ouvers,
Une main hors des draps, cher BAUDOIN, a peine
Ay-je pu me resoudre à t'escrire ces vers.

(And so hate work, that, eyes half open,
One hand out of the sheets, dear BAUDOIN, scarce
Was I able to resolve to write you these verses.)

It is also clearly a question of the poet inhabiting his own composition, being both satirist and satirized.

The ability to write fluent verses on themes and images of the day was one of the greatest of the abilities of Tristan L'Hermite; in a variety of modes, as imitations of foreign models (chiefly Marino), or as a response to poems written by friends, Tristan possessed the talent to create some of the most musical verse of the period. His works taken as a whole are the most substantial of any of the poets of the first half of the century. Between 1633 and 1648 he published five separate volumes of poetry in a wide range of subjects and styles, throughout which it is possible to see that personal voice which transforms many a poem.

In an early poem 'Les Cheveux blonds',[7] Tristan shows many of the traits which were to remain typical of his verse whatever the subject-matter: the love of antithesis and paradox, the cultivation of detail in description, the passionate tone, the sureness of rhythm:

> Fin or de qui le prix est sans comparaison,
> Clairs rayons d'un soleil, douce et subtile trame
> Dont la molle étendue a des ondes de flamme
> Où l'amour mille fois a noyé ma raison.
>
> Beau poil, votre franchise est une trahison.
> Faut-il qu'en vous montrant vous me cachiez madame?
> N'était-ce pas assez de captiver mon âme
> Sans retenir aussi ce beau corps en prison?
>
> Mais, ô doux flots dorés, votre orgueil se rabaisse;
> Sous la sévérité d'une main qui vous presse
> Vous allez, comme moi, perdre la liberté.
>
> Et j'ai le bien de voir une fois dans ma vie,
> Qu'en liant le beau poil qui me tient arrêté,
> On ôte la franchise à qui me l'a ravie.   (p. 33)
>
> (Fine gold whose price is beyond comparison,
> Bright rays of sunlight, sweet and subtle web
> In whose soft spread lie waves of flame
> Wherein love a thousand times has drowned my reason.
>
> Beautiful hair, your freedom is a betrayal.
> Must your display hide from me my lady?
> Was it not enough to hold captive my soul
> That you hold also that fair body in prison?
>
> But, oh sweet tide of gold, your pride is brought low;
> By the severity of a hand which presses on you
> You will, as did I, lose your liberty.

> And I rejoice to see, for once in my life,
> That that fair hair is bound which does arrest me,
> And liberty lost by what deprived me of mine.)

There is none of the occasional roughness of Théophile here, but the drowning of reason mentioned in the fourth line has often been turned into an accusation against Tristan by those who found his poetry too precious, too decorative. Such has often been the judgement brought on Marino and on baroque poetry as a whole; and it was certainly in the poems of Marino that Tristan found much inspiration. A poem such as 'La Belle en deuil', however, is developed by Tristan from one line of the Italian's 'La Bella Vedova' and shows us an aspect of Tristan's work which is not merely justified by the value accorded to imitation at that time, but which also illustrates the way his personal treatment of a set-piece theme makes of him one of the great lyrical poets of the age:

> Que vous avez d'appas, belle nuit animée!
> Que vous nous apportez de merveille et d'amour!
> Il faut bien confesser que vous êtes formée
> Pour donner de l'envie et de la honte au jour.
>
> La flamme éclate moins à travers la fumée
> Que ne font vos beaux yeux sous ce funeste atour,
> Et de tous les mortels, en ce sacré séjour,
> Comme un céleste objet vous êtes réclamée.
>
> Mais ce n'est point ainsi que ces divinités
> Qui n'ont plus ni de voix ni de solennités,
> Et dont l'autel glacé ne reçoit point de presse.
>
> Car, vous voyant si belle, on pense à votre abord
> Que par quelque gageure où Vénus s'intéresse
> L'amour s'est déguisé sous l'habit de la Mort.   (p. 31)

(Many are your attractions, beautiful, animate Night!
Much do you bring of marvels and of love!
It must be confessed that you are so made
That you inspire envy and shame in the day.

Flame shines out less through surrounding smoke
Than do your fine eyes beneath their mournful surround,
And above all mortals, in this holy place,
As a heavenly being you are sought out.

But it is not as are sought those other divinities
Who receive no more vows nor ceremonies,
And before whose cold altars nobody stands.

For, seeing you so beautiful, and standing by your side
It is as if for some wager that Venus had engaged
Love had disguised itself in the weeds of Death.)

The entire sonnet is built on the extension of the identity of love and death, which is of course no new theme; but Tristan's development of it depends on the tension that is found in the paradoxes, on the (Malherbian) balance of lines such as 'La *flamme* éclate moins à travers la *fumée*/ Que ne font vos *beaux* yeux sous ce *funeste* atour'. The rhythm gives new life to metaphors and antitheses that were the commonplaces of the period. Later poems such as 'La Belle Gueuse' and 'La Belle Esclave maure' exploit similar themes and are certainly worthy of the admiration Baudelaire felt for them. And while the latter is a fairly close imitation of a sonnet by Marino, yet clearly having its origins in the Song of Solomon, Tristan's version stands out among the many to be found in the period. This aspect of Tristan's work is perhaps a measure of the poet; he is able to choose from a gamut of possible means of expression, a range of the elegant subjects of the day, yet he seldom falls into the mere five-finger exercise which often typifies the lesser poetry of the numerous anthologies published both at the time or more recently. While his treatment of themes may be at times precious, it never remains simply that; 'La Belle Esclave maure' may, for example, lack the resonance that the treatment of such a theme would have found in Italy, or even more so, in a Spain in which the literary topos is to be set against the brutal realities of the treatment of a remaining Moorish population, yet the skill with which Tristan constructs his verses never lapses into the merely mechanical. It is a skill which we find at its most interesting when we consider the achievements of those poems which bridge the conventional situation and the personal level of expression. It is not true of Tristan, as it is of Théophile, that we find his impatience with the conventional forms taking him away from the apparent direction of a poem in midstream, nor do we find him restricting the play of verse forms to allow the greater play to thought; but we do find the expression of a real impatience with the role of supplicant as both lover and courtier which is forced upon him by his status in life.

Les Vers héroïques[8] are more than adequate testimony to Tristan's ability to provide the occasional verse demanded by the need for patronage, and the lines written to be spoken in masques or sent in the name of another are not necessarily less eloquent than those he wrote only on his own behalf. Yet Tristan has left us a corpus within which his own voice can be heard clearly expressing the frustrations of his condition. His life is, itself, a worthy subject of study, some of it more or less fictionalized in *Le Page disgracié*, but in his poetry, where the question of registers and forms was much less open to experimentation, he has provided some very interesting

examples of the fusion of a personal voice with forms which might
otherwise have been only the vehicle for low comedy. 'La Belle Banquière'
(pp. 59–62) immediately strikes an interesting note in that its combination
of love and money is much more a subject for the stage than for poetry,
especially since the poem is not merely a satire. The verses which set out
the things which the poet is able to appreciate in life without benefit of
riches are developed as much as though they were part of any of his poems
describing Nature. The biting tenor of the final verse may be no more than
is to be found in many of the epigrams of the period, including Tristan's
own, the disdain for money in the name of love possibly hypocritical in the
mouth of one who spent so much time in pursuit of patronage. Even so,
simply to couple the words 'belle' and 'banquière' in his title and not give
way to the merely, and impersonally, satirical is Tristan's achievement.
Indeed the poem is an intriguing mix of forms, for the conventional
opening complaint:

> Philis, vous avez eu tort
> D'avoir rebuté si fort
> Mes vœux et mes sacrifices.
>
> (Philis, you were wrong
> To reject so strongly
> My avowals and my offerings.)

gives way to a brief narrative of first meeting, the awakening of affection,
and then the inadvertent betrayal by a friend, asked presumably by the
poet to speak on his behalf. The verses which follow constitute a
denunciation of the mercenary attitude displayed by the *banquière*, even
though her father should expect her to marry for wealth, but instead of
leaning towards the satirical they become an apology for Tristan and his
way of life:

> Mes désirs sont limités;
> Je n'ai point les vanités
> D'aller ni suivi, ni brave;
> Nul soin ne me va chargeant,
> Et je ne me rends esclave
> Des hommes, ni de l'argent [...]
> Le doux concert des oiseaux,
> Le mouvant cristal des eaux,
> Un bois, des prés agréables,
> Echo qui se plaint d'Amour,
> Sont des matières capables
> De m'arrêter tout un jour.

> (My wants are limited;
> I have not the vanity
> To have followers or great display;
> I am burdened by no cares,
> And make not myself a slave
> Either to men or money [. . .]
> The sweet concert of the birds,
> The moving crystal of the waters,
> A wood, some gentle meadows,
> Echo who complains of Love,
> These things are able
> To hold my attention all day.)

The personal tone combined with imagery of the kind which he frequently exploited in his poems ('Le doux concert des oiseaux,/ Le mouvant cristal des eaux') as well as the particular circumstance of paying suit to a banker's daughter make this one of Tristan's most interesting, personal and original poems. It also shows us the rather dreamy side to his character, which he presented as being a necessary prerequisite for the creation of poetry. In a celebrated letter, published in his *Lettres meslées*,[9] he gives his definition of poetry: 'Poetry is a gift from Heaven; but we may say that it is never properly nurtured but by idleness, and that it is a quick and sudden fire drawn from still waters.' Such a life (of contemplative idleness) was not of course one which was open to Tristan with his lack of wealth, and it is therefore no surprise to find that many of his poems – some among his best – express the impatience he felt with the condition of the poet as courtier. For all his quarrelsome nature and his passionate independence, Tristan's main complaint is that his chosen patrons were not sufficiently appreciative of his services, and his verse, just as much as Malherbe's, might have served the dignity of King and State, had circumstances been different. Even so, the poet who could, early in his career, both imitate and surpass Théophile's 'Solitude' in his 'Le Promenoir des deux amants', clearly was confident of speaking with his own voice and we can continue to hear that voice throughout his career; in the cruelty of 'La Gouvernante importune' or in the wittier 'Le Portier inexorable', the poems of *Les Amours* renew the conventions of the poetry of the obstacles to love:

> Si l'amour du bon vin, qui ton visage enflamme,
> Adoucit quelquefois ton courage irrité,
> Suisse, rabats un peu de ta sévérité,
> Et permets ce matin que j'aille voir Madame [. . .]
>
> Dieux! pour éterniser la rigueur de mes fers,
> Mettrez-vous point Cerbère à garder cette belle?
> Il suffit de ce Suisse à garder les enfers!   (p. 63)

(If the love of good wine which enflames thy face
Sometime abate the fierceness of thy courage,
Swiss gateman, leave off a little thy severity
And allow me in to see Madame [...]

Gods! To prolong forever the rigours of my chains,
Could ye not set Cerberus to guard this lady?
For this Swiss will serve at the gates of hell!)

And 'Le Miroir enchanté' surely represents the very best of the poetry to be found on the confines of the baroque and the precious. Undoubtedly Malherbe would have been horrified by such a poem, yet Tristan learned much of his music from his straight-laced predecessor and acknowledged it in 'Les Miséres humaines' (from *La Lyre*):

Malherbe qui fut sans pareil
A trouvé le dernier sommeil
A la fin de ses doctes veilles,
Lui dont les écrits, en nos jours,
Sont des plus savantes oreilles
Les délices et les amours.   (p. 88)

(Malherbe the peerless
Found that last sleep
After all his learned hours,
He whose words, today,
Are to the knowing ear
The substance of delight and love.)

There should be space also to acknowledge Tristan's achievement as a religious poet, if only to underline the fact that the libertinism of Théophile and Saint-Amant was not the only factor leading to the production of a poetry in which thought and feeling combine to outwit the dangers of order. But the last word is best left to a remarkable sonnet from *Les Vers héroïques*:

C'est fait de mes destins; je commence à sentir
Les incommodités que la vieillesse apporte.
Déjà, la pâle Mort, pour me faire partir,
D'un pied sec et tremblant vient frapper à ma porte.

Ainsi que le soleil, sur la fin de son cours,
Paraît plutôt tomber que descendre dans l'onde,
Lorsque l'homme a passé les plus beaux de ses jours,
D'une course rapide il passe en l'autre monde.

Il faut éteindre en nous tous frivoles désirs,
Il faut nous détacher des terrestres plaisirs
Où sans discretion notre appétit nous plonge.

Sortons de ces erreurs par un sage conseil,
Et cessant d'embrasser les images d'un songe,
Pensons à nous coucher pour le dernier sommeil.   (p. 134)

(My fate has run its course, I begin to feel
The discomforts old age brings with it.
Already pallid Death, to urge my departure,
With his dry, trembling step, comes knocking on my door.

Just as the sun, at the end of its course,
Appears more to fall than sink into the sea,
When man has spent the best of his days,
Rapidly he passes into the world beyond.

We must snuff out in us all frivolous desires,
We must detach ourselves from earthly pleasures
Wherein, without discretion, our appetite has plunged us.

Let us leave off such errors through wise counsel,
And no more embracing the images of dreams,
Think us to lie down for that last sleep.)

As 'I' becomes 'We' in the last sleep, so a personal lyricism was eclipsed in the stability of a classicism which sought to order space as a proof that it could order time. The slow metamorphosis of the last three centuries has found the turbulent voices of instability to be the lasting poetry of the century.

The Language of the Gods: Uses of Verse 1650–1800

PETER FRANCE

Les Amours de Psyché, which Jean de la Fontaine published in 1669, is a reworking of the famous story from Apuleius, framed in a polite conversation among four friends in the gardens at Versailles. In it the author tries to blend two different modes of writing, the noble (*héroïque*) and the entertaining (*galant*) in what he calls a 'juste tempérament'. The work is written in a mixture of prose and verse; La Fontaine presents this in his preface as a way of combining the 'agréable' and the 'solide'. Here is one of his transitions from prose to verse (the narrator is telling how Venus makes a triumphal departure for Cythera):

> La cour de Neptune l'accompagna. Ceci est proprement matière de poésie: il ne siérait guère bien à la prose de décrire une cavalcade de dieux marins: d'ailleurs je ne pense pas qu'on pût exprimer avec le langage ordinaire ce que la déesse parut alors.

> > C'est pourquoi nous dirons en langage rimé
> > Que l'empire flottant en demeura charmé;
> > Cent Tritons, la suivant jusqu'au port de Cythère,
> > Par leurs divers emplois s'efforcent de lui plaire.   (p. 136)[1]

(The court of Neptune accompanied her. This really calls for poetry: prose is hardly suited to describing a cavalcade of marine deities; indeed I do not think one could express in ordinary language how the goddess appeared on this occasion.

> That is why we say in rhyming language
> That the floating empire was enchanted by her;
> A hundred Tritons, following her to the port of Cythera,
> Attempt by their various actions to please her.)

The mix of prose and verse was not an invention of La Fontaine's; in France it goes back to the Middle Ages. But the author of the *Fables* was fond of it, using it particularly in semi-private letters such as those he wrote to his wife on his journey to Limoges. Such 'mixed' works appeal by reason of their variety and apparent freedom. It often appears as if the choice between verse and prose is random, and La Fontaine declares in the preface to *Les Amours de Psyché* that he finds prose, often considered 'the natural language of all men' (p. 123) as hard to write as verse. In the passage just quoted, however, the shift is in fact motivated. Certain subjects such as highly wrought descriptions, key points in the narrative, invocations or hymns call out to be treated in what contemporaries liked to call 'le langage des dieux'. It is clear, though, that the idea of a 'language of the gods', with its allusion to a tradition of high and inspired poetry, is not to be taken quite seriously here. As in his *Fables*, La Fontaine is playing on different registers, one supposedly down-to-earth, the other elevated. In the same way, the young Racine in a letter from Uzès dated 17 January 1662, pretends that the verse section of his letter (a pleasant little poem describing the beauties of a southern winter) is the product of a moment of inspiration or poetic fury: 'the fire of poetry carried me away to such an extent that I did not notice that time was passing and that I was too late to catch the post'.[2]

Verse and prose may be mingled in a natural way, but this sort of play is only possible because they are perceived as belonging to different linguistic systems. What then constitutes the 'language of the gods'? If one compares juxtaposed passages in texts such as the ones I have mentioned, it emerges that the primary features of verse language are those produced by the demands of rhyme and metre – inversion, epithets, the replacement of simple terms by longer, often figurative equivalents (e.g. 'votre cœur' for 'vous') – and by the various types of patterning – antithesis, symmetry, repetition – which verse encourages.[3] Then there are other figures which are by no means peculiar to verse, but which are particularly at home there. Thus Bernard Lamy in his *Art de parler* (1675) writes of the poets: 'Since all they say is extraordinary, their expressions, to match the dignity of the subject-matter, must be extraordinary and remote from ordinary speech. Hyperbole and metaphor are absolutely necessary in poetry . . .'[4] To these one would need to add the allusions to classical mythology which may well figure in prose, but flourish in verse. Taken together, all of this produces a type of language which is clearly distinguishable from prose of all kinds.

Lamy's view did not go unchallenged in classical France. There were those who believed that the greatest virtue of French poetic language was precisely its unobtrusive quality. 'Verse only pleases us in so far as it is natural. We have very few poetic words, and the language of French poets is not, like that of other poets, very different from everyday language', wrote the Jesuit critic Dominique Bouhours in his dialogue 'De la langue française', which expresses the up-to-date position of the 1670s.[5] Even so, it would have been difficult for Molière's contemporaries to disagree with Monsieur Jourdain's philosophy teacher as he divides the whole world of language into two hemispheres – 'all that is not prose is verse, and all that is not verse is prose'.[6] The two could be juxtaposed, they remained separate.

Note that Jourdain's teacher talks about verse, not about poetry. In his 1928 introduction to Ezra Pound's *Selected Poems*, T.S. Eliot wrote, against the grain of our century, that 'no-one is competent to judge poetry until he recognizes that poetry is nearer to "verse" than it is to prose poetry'.[7] For most readers in seventeenth- and eighteenth-century France – as indeed for many people ever since – the equation of verse with poetry seemed evident enough. The language of the gods demanded rhyme and metre. And it seemed to some critics of the classical period that French prosody, like the French language, had finally attained a correct and dignified form after its earlier stumblings; as Boileau famously put it,

> Enfin Malherbe vint, et le premier en France
> Fit sentir dans les vers une juste cadence.
>
> (*Art poétique*, I, 131–2)

> (Finally Malherbe came, and for the first time in France
> Introduced a proper cadence into verse.)

But during the same period, 'poetry' was slowly beginning to dissociate itself from verse, and to be understood more as a particular *quality* which may be present in either prose or verse. The 1718 edition of the *Dictionnaire de l'Academie* added to its earlier, more formal definition of 'poésie' the words: 'an extraordinary activity of the spirit, caused by an inspiration which is, or seems to be, divine'.[8] There was room therefore for the idea to germinate that poetry can do very well without verse. What matters, on this view, is the genius of the writer, his or her capacity to stir the passions of the reader. Seen in this light, poetry may well draw closer to the eloquence of the inspiring orator.

A key figure in this development was Fénelon, both in his theoretical writings and in his *Télémaque*. His *Dialogues sur l'éloquence*, written about 1685, contain the declaration: 'People take themselves for poets when they have spoken or written in metre. On the contrary, however, many people write verse which is devoid of poetry, and many others are full of poetry without writing verse; let us therefore ignore versification'.[9] In his *Lettre à l'Académie* (1714) he speaks enthusiastically of the poetry of the Bible, even where the language shows no sign of versification. *Télémaque* (1699) is an edifying moral fable, but it should also be seen as an epic poem for its time, a Virgil-inspired continuation of the *Odyssey*. As such, it puts into practice Fénelon's ideas of a poetry of powerful, harmonious eloquence that dispenses with rhyme and metre. Given its immense popularity throughout the eighteenth century, one may fairly see it as a prime source for modern French poetic prose, which received a new boost some sixty years later with the publication and speedy translation into French of the biblical-seeming prose of Macpherson's Ossian. It is thanks to such examples, for instance, that in 1787 Parny was able to publish his 'Chansons madécasses' (Malagasy Songs). These are presented (like Ossian) as adaptations of a primitive type of song. Their poetry (now very dated) lies mainly in the deployment of figures of repetition and symmetry and in the 'sublime' simplicity of diction which can be glimpsed in these lines:

> Nahandove, ô belle Nahandove! l'oiseau nocturne a commencé ses cris, la pleine lune brille sur ma tête, et la rosée naissante humecte mes cheveux. Voici l'heure: qui peut t'arrêter. Nahandove, ô belle Nahandove?[10]

> (Nahandove, oh beautiful Nahandove! the night bird has begun to sing, the full moon shines on my head, and the dew begins to dampen my hair. This is the hour: who can stop you, Nahandove, oh beautiful Nahandove?)

The idea was gradually gaining acceptance, therefore, that prosody, and above all rhyme, was an obstacle to true poetry, an obstacle to the faithful depiction of reality, and even more so an obstacle to the expression of genuine feeling. Fénelon says as much in his *Letter à l'Académie*, though he stops short of condemning versification outright and merely defends greater freedom and greater stress on the emotional and truth content of poetry as opposed to its form. His contemporary, Houdar de la Motte, a champion of modernity, wrote against rhyme, though paradoxically he attempted to translate Homer into fashionable rhyming verse, as opposed to the dull prose of the classical purist Madame Dacier. And later in the eighteenth century, we can find much more forthright condemnations of verse, for instance in the devastating pages on versification in Du Cerceau's *Réflexions sur la poésie française* (1742).[11] What presents itself as a defence of a truer poetry may of course be an attack, direct or indirect, on poetry itself. If, as Rivarol, puts it, 'nothing is said in verse that cannot be equally well said in prose',[12] this can be read as a condemnation of the whole poetic enterprise. For many writers of the age of reason (and indeed their successors), the very notion of poetry implies childish frivolity. Descartes, one of the founders of rationalism, jokes about the poets ('these speakers of nothing') with his colleague Huyghens. Their work may be amusing, but it should not get in the way of the main business, the search for truth. It is for such reasons that the encyclopaedist d'Alembert speaks with a kind of regret of the inevitable decline of poetry in a philosophical age.[13]

The problem is that whereas the Renaissance poets had kept alive the ideal of a philosophical poetry capable of expressing the truths and mysteries of the universe (see above, Chapter 5), the post-Cartesian world sees a separation between truth and imagination which almost necessarily marginalizes poetry or condemns it to triviality. It has often been noted that in the course of the seventeenth century poetry became more and more influenced by *salon* sociability. It is for the amusement of polite society that a Benserade will put Ovid's *Metamorphoses* into *rondeaux* – a game that could not appeal to the serious-minded reader, or even to the sensible Molière, who mocks it in *Les Précieuses ridicules*. Poetry became associated with polite frivolity, then, but it was also connected with childhood, the childhood of the individual and the childhood of society. And by an equation which was something of a commonplace in classical France, childhood was associated not only with primitive peoples, who spoke in poetry being incapable of reason, but also with the common people. Peasants are like children, taking pleasure in rhymed verse of all kinds. It should not be forgotten that throughout the period considered here, popular song pursues a very fruitful career. Indeed, many of the most popular French songs (now children's songs in some cases) find their more or less definitive form at this time. Moreover, the seventeenth and eighteenth centuries saw a considerable flourishing of popular political songs, notably the *mazarinades*, directed against Cardinal Mazarin during the Fronde.

It would be wrong (as the example of the *mazarinades* makes clear) to see popular song as belonging to a quite separate world from that of the *salon* poets. Both, moreover, were vulnerable to the scorn of sensible good taste. It is instructive in this respect to look at the famous scene in Act I of Molière's *Le Misanthrope* (Act I, Scene 3) where two poems, one from the *salons*, the other from the people, are set face to face – or back to back. There is little doubt that we are meant to laugh at the sweet nothings of Oronte's sonnet with its *chute*:

> Belle Phyllis, on désespère,
> Alors qu'on espère toujours.
>
> (Fair Phyllis, one despairs,
> When one is condemned to hope.)

Against this, Alceste sets the 'pure passion' of his sweetly jingling folk-song ('J'aime mieux ma mie, au gué'), but it is not obvious that this is really supposed to be any more worthy of a rational adult, however much it might appeal to a certain post-Romantic taste. And it is all the more piquant that all of this is framed in the proper, relatively unobtrusive alexandrines that are the mark of 'serious' comedy. For of course verse did have its place and its uses.

Among the contemporaries and successors of Fénelon there are many defenders of the 'language of the gods'. Voltaire, for all his rationalism, is one of the most prominent, writing of the way in which the constraints of prosody actually lead to new insights and discoveries and valuing the superior energy that verse can impart to language. Diderot too, though himself no poet in the normal sense of the word, was very sensitive to the power of the imitative harmony in a classic line of verse in Boileau's *Lutrin*:

> Soupire, étend les bras, ferme l'oeil et s'endort.
>
> (Sighs, stretches out his arms, shuts his eyes and goes to sleep.)

This, he says, creates a 'hieroglyph' or 'emblem', an indissoluble fusion of matter and form, which makes of poetry something very different from prose (though here, it seems, there is no need for versification).[14] The basic point, however, is that verse, whether original, hieroglyphic or entirely derivative, continued to be seen by most people as the obligatory formal mark of the higher forms of poetry, tragedy, epic, ode and even serious comedy. Verse on its own did not guarantee quality, but it served to indicate clearly what in our century Russian formalism called the 'literariness' of certain types of text.

This decorum may be seen as a survival of the high seriousness of Renaissance poetry, but can also be regarded as a sort of distinguished costume which fitted certain types of writing for polite upper-class society. It is interesting to see how this worked in the theatre. By the time Molière and Racine were writing, there was a fairly clear division: tragedy, opera and high comedy (i.e. ambitious plays in five acts) are written in verse, whereas shorter, less obviously literary comedies may be in prose. Occasionally such intermediate genres as the *comédie-ballet* allow for a mixture of the two. Molière's experience is instructive. Most of his great five-act comedies (*Tartuffe*, *Le Misanthrope*, etc) are in alexandrines, but *Dom Juan* and *L'Avare* are in prose. This seemed improper to many spectators of the time, and Thomas Corneille's flabby verse adaptation of *Dom Juan* (*Le Festin de Pierre*) was preferred to the original at the Comédie-Française for the following century or more. It would appear, incidentally, that Molière was in the habit of writing his scripts in prose first, even when they were later versified. In Act II of *La Princesse d'Elide*, a court entertainment, the verse text suddenly breaks off and we find a touching note: 'The author's intention was to treat the whole of his play in this style. But an urgent order from the King forced him to hurry and to finish the rest in prose, passing quickly over certain scenes which he would have made longer had he had more time.'[15] Verse is here an optional ornament or amplification. Even Racine, strange as this seems, may have written at least a first draft of his dialogue in prose. We still have the

outline, with some prose dialogue, of an unwritten *Iphigénie en Aulide* –
a tantalizing half-open door on the unexplained genesis of Racinian
poetry.[16]

The eighteenth century saw much discussion about the possibility of
prose tragedy. This novel idea was championed – naturally – by Houdar
de la Motte, who supported his thesis with feeble prose versions of
Sophocles and Racine. Voltaire, as one might expect, resisted the idea. But
some years later Diderot emerged as the great theorist of the serious drama
in prose; thereafter, although verse tragedy continued to be written
throughout the nineteenth century (taking on a new lease of life with
Hugo's Romantic drama) there was no longer to be the same necessary
connection between serious drama and verse. A similar debate – to our
eyes perhaps equally foreign – concerned the translation of poetry.
Assuming that it was written in verse, was it necessary or desirable to
translate it into verse? British writers such as Dryden generally answered
yes, but the French were more divided. If one believed that the true value
of poetry lay in translatable thought (and not, as is now something of an
unexamined commonplace, that poetry is what gets lost in translation),
then it was only natural that the majority of translations of Virgil, for
instance, were in prose. Abbé Desfontaines, among others, defended this
practice, claiming in a preface to his new translation of Virgil that poetry
resides essentially in 'boldly drawn images, vivid colours, vigorous expres-
sions, concise and expressive turns of phrase, and a pleasing language,
flowing and melodious, with nothing feeble, languid or prolix about it.'[17]
He and those who thought like him saw the dangers of the kind of padded
poetic versions that the Earl of Roscommon stigmatized in his versified
Essay on Translated Verse (1684):

> The weighty bullion of one sterling line
> Drawn to French wire would through whole pages shine.

This long-running debate is interestingly exemplified in the translations of
Alexander Pope into French in the eighteenth century.[18] The major works
were repeatedly translated; for the *Essay on Man*, for instance, Silhouette's
prose vied with Du Resnel's verse (among others) and both were printed
together in the *Œuvres complètes* of 1776. Readers took sides on this tricky
issue. Voltaire, of course, emerged as one of the leading champions of
verse translation, and his own version of a few lines from the *Rape of the
Lock* (printed in Chapter 22 of his *Lettres philosophiques*) is in fact the nearest
the French ever came to a good translation of Pope. Shakespeare was to
provide far knottier problems.

These then are some of the areas of choice (La Fontaine's fables offer
another example, to be discussed in the next chapter). What they suggest
is that poetry was not seen by the contemporaries of Racine or Voltaire

as some essential quiddity – it was rather one of the forms of verbal communication and shaded off easily into prose eloquence. In particular they were far removed from the belief that took hold in the nineteenth century that the ideal poem is the brief lyric utterance which communicates an imaginative view of the world for which prose would be inadequate. Rather, poetry was understood as the more agreeable, moving or eloquent expression of ideas and states of mind which might well have been expressed more prosaically.

One should not exaggerate this point of course. Robert Finch among others has argued for the survival throughout the eighteenth century (seen by Margaret Gilman from a more or less Romantic perspective as the 'nadir of poetry') of a strain of individual poetry that depends more on imagination, inspiration and personal feeling than on a formal conception of the art.[19] His division of the realm of eighteenth-century poetry into three different provinces, the individualist, the didactic and the dogmatic, is a dubious one, as is the attempt to 'rescue' this poetry by showing that it is really lyrical after all, but it would certainly be wrong to overlook the quiet poetic achievements of such writers as Segrais, Gresset or Bernis, to name just three of his 'individualist' poets. Or take this 'Chanson triste' by Antoinette Deshoulières, a poet of the late seventeenth century who was greatly admired in her own time and the following generations, though now she is often – and wrongly – thought of as simply the author of trivial society verse and insipid pastoral lyrics:

> Ah! que je sens d'inquiétude!
> Que j'ai de mouvements qui m'étaient inconnus!
> Mes tranquilles plaisirs, qu'êtes-vous devenus?
>   Je cherche en vain la solitude.
> D'où viennent ces chagrins, ces mortelles langueurs?
>   Qu'est-ce qui fait couler mes pleurs
> Avec tant d'amertume et tant de violence?
> De tout ce que je fais mon cœur n'est point content.
> Hélas! cruel Amour, que je méprisais tant,
> Ces maux ne sont-il point l'effet de ta vengeance?[20]

> (Ah, what disquiet I feel!
> What emotions I never knew before!
> My tranquil pleasures, what has become of you?
>   I seek in vain to be alone.
> Whence come these griefs, this mortal langour?
>   What makes my tears flow
> With so much bitterness, so much violence?
> My heart is not content with anything I do.
> Alas, cruel Love, whom I so much despised,
> Are these pains not the effect of your vengeance?)

It is not exactly easy, in the post-Romantic period, to approach poetry such as this. It is not poetry which, as one twentieth-century writer puts it, makes you feel as if the top of your head had been blown off. Although there is no overt reference to shepherds and the proper names of pastoral (Tircis, Alcandre and the rest of them), it clearly belongs to this tradition. The initial capital of 'Amour' suggests as much – and yet the invocation of this deity also links this short poem with the classic of unrequited woman's love, *Phèdre*. Like her enemy Racine, Deshoulières moulds verse, in this case free stanzaic verse, to convey an emotion which finds expression in the mix of short lines of simple statement ('Je cherche en vain la solitude') and longer lines which are balanced and combined with a subtle musicality. The vocabulary of love, as in so much classical writing, is made up of abstractions ('mouvements', 'amertume', 'violence'), all of them hovering on the edge of the metaphorical and allowing the reader to invest her or his own feelings in their capacious semantic space.

There is a good deal of this kind of quiet, unpretentious recreation of private, yet easily shareable feeling in the poetry of Madame Deshoulières and her contemporaries. Arguably, it has been underrated by those who too quickly wrote off this age as an age without poetry. But for all that, the great poetic achievements in the classical period are to be found rather on the borders of eloquence. I shall discuss some aspects of the poetry of persuasion in the next chapter; here I should like to dwell on two other cases, the tragedy of Pierre Corneille and Racine, and the evocation of the Revolutionary Terror in André Chénier's *Iambes*.

As we have seen, verse was the obligatory form for tragedy at least until the end of the seventeenth century – and verse almost always meant alexandrines. Dramatic theorists, obsessed as they were with verisimilitude, tended to present the alexandrine as the equivalent of prose. The play might be known as a 'dramatic poem', but it was not thought unduly 'poetic' for one character to address another in a long sequence of verse lines, each twelve syllables long, with a caesura after the sixth, and alternating masculine and feminine rhymes. 'Poetry' only emerged consciously in the theatre in those infrequent moments – usually soliloquies, dreams, oracles and the like – when the alexandrine was replaced by a noticeable stanza form with a changed rhyming pattern and usually an alternation of shorter and longer lines. Such were the opera libretti that Quinault wrote for Lully. And at the end of his career, in his biblical tragedies *Esther* and *Athalie*, Racine introduced operatic choruses where music invades the eloquent world of the alexandrine.

The great advantage of this *passe-partout* verse form – comparable in this to Shakespearian blank verse – is its flexibility as a dramatic medium. It adapts itself equally well to business-like talk, to violent and rapid dispute, to high formal speech, and to the vehement eloquence of passionate persuasion. All of these are present in Corneille's great tragedies. Let us look at part of a famous speech from *Sertorius* (1662) where the hero, a self-exiled Roman general, replies to Pompée, who is trying on behalf of the tyrant Sylla to tempt him back to Rome:

> Je n'appelle plus Rome un enclos de murailles
> Que ses proscriptions comblent de funérailles:
> Ces murs, dont le destin fut autrefois si beau,
> N'en sont que le prison, ou plutôt le tombeau;
> Mais pour revivre ailleurs dans sa première force,
> Avec les faux Romains elle a fait plein divorce;
> Et comme autour de moi j'ai tous ses vrais appuis,
> Rome n'est plus dans Rome, elle est toute où je suis.
> Parlons pourtant d'accord. Je ne sais qu'une voie
> Qui puisse avec honneur nous donner cette joie.   (Act III, Scene 1)

> (I no longer give the name of Rome to a ring of walls
> Which his [Sylla's] proscriptions fill with funerals:
> Those walls, whose destiny was once so great,
> Are now only her prison, or rather her grave;
> But to live elsewhere in her original strength,
> She has utterly separated herself from the false Romans,
> And since around me I have all her true supports,
> Rome is no longer in Rome, she is entirely with me.
> But let us try to agree. I know only one way
> Which could honourably give us this joy.)

This is not apparently the poetry of personal feeling – though there is nothing to prevent an actor from endowing these ringing lines with the self-confidence, or perhaps rather the desperation, that he wants to convey in Sertorius. But what one hears here above all, against the prosaic ground bass of reasonable conversation ('Mais parlons plutôt d'accord') is the swelling of the voice in two opposing tableaux, powerful by reason of that opposition. First we see a desolate city. The rhyming of 'murailles' with 'funérailles' and of 'beau' with 'tombeau' and the accumulation of nouns (which form such strong symmetrical groupings within the frame of the alexandrine) intensify the contrast of old splendour and recent decay. The first sequence of four alexandrines is made up of two balanced, mutually reinforcing couplets which execute variations on the same fundamental idea. Then, announced by the rhetorical 'mais', comes a second such sequence, again a symmetrical grouping of two statements, linked as so often by an oratorically effective 'et' at the beginning of the third line. This time though, the second couplet carries the movement on to a culminating formulation, memorably antithetical and hammered home in a series of monosyllables with the repeated mention of the name of Rome (which had begun the movement). The whole series of eight lines, with its effects of symmetry and patterning, achieves the monumental force of a Roman inscription or civic building. It is in no sense lyrical, but rather the poetry of persuasive affirmation, and it is not for nothing that it imprinted itself so strongly on the minds of generations. Memorability is one of the great qualities of poetry at this time.

Such eloquent effects are typical of Corneille, but are by no means his prerogative. In Racine's tragedies there are many scenes of grand affirmation. But in his work, as indeed in many of his rival's plays, this eloquence is often undermined from within; those who speak so nobly are seen as actors defending themselves, seeking their advantage, or even self-indulgently revelling in their own speech. Take for instance another evocation of a ruined city, Troy, as painted in *Andromaque* (1667) by Pyrrhus in his attempt to persuade the Greek ambassador Oreste that there is no chance of Hector's infant son reviving the fortunes of the defeated enemy:

> Je songe quelle était autrefois cette ville,
> Si superbe en remparts, en héros si fertile,
> Maîtresse de l'Asie; et je regarde enfin
> Quel fut le sort de Troie, et quel est son destin.
> Je ne vois que des tours que la cendre a couvertes,
> Un fleuve teint de sang, des campagnes désertes,
> Un enfant dans les fers; et je ne puis songer
> Que Troie en cet état aspire à se venger.   (Act I, Scene 4)

> (I think what this city once was
> In ramparts so magnificent, so fertile in heroes,
> Mistress of Asia, and then I consider
> What was Troy's fate, and what her destiny is now.
> I see only towers covered with ashes,
> A river dyed with blood, a deserted country,
> A child in chains, and I cannot think
> That Troy in this state can aspire to revenge.)

In its piercingly elegaic quality this is arguably a more powerful piece of poetic writing than the lines from *Sertorius*. The rhythm is far less four-square than Corneille's. Here again are the two blocks of four, balanced against one another, but in each block the movement of accumulation reaches forward into the middle of the third line – the 'et' which divides each block is asymmetrically placed. And the physicality of the images (ashes, towers, blood, rivers, a child) is more immediate than in *Sertorius*. What is most interesting, though, is that this haunting passage is not spoken from fullness of heart – or at least not apparently so. There are other evocations of fallen Troy in the play, put in the mouth of Andromaque the victim; Pyrrhus, however, is not the victim (not literally at any rate), but the cause of this desolation. When he speaks these wonderful words, therefore, the spectator is simultaneously carried forward by their poetic force and intrigued by the relation between their beauty and the unexpressed feelings of the speaker.

There are of course many other scenes in Racine where the dramatic poetry seems to express in a more directly lyrical way the love, hate, grief or joy of the speaker. At such times, Racine's theatre attains a moving intensity which one rarely finds in that of his contemporaries. So Bérénice, as she pleads with Titus not to dismiss her from Rome, utters the words which have since become a classic (by now somewhat shop-soiled) evocation of the pain of separation.

> Dans un mois, dans un an, comment souffrirons-nous,
> Seigneur, que tant de mers me séparent de vous,
> Que le jour recommence et que le jour finisse,
> Sans que jamais Titus puisse voir Berénice,
> Sans que de tout le jour je puisse voir Titus?
> 				(*Bérénice*, Act IV, Scene 5)

> (In a month, in a year, how shall we endure,
> My lord, that so many seas separate me from you,
> That the day begins and the day ends
> Without Titus ever being able to see Bérénice,
> Without my being able all the day to see Titus?)

One hesitates to say anything about such lines. It is obvious enough how the repetitions, the sound patterns, produce a hallucinating kind of music that sinks deep into the mind of the hearer – and the hearer is not only Titus on the stage, but the spectator in the auditorium or the reader of the text. Again, however, it would be wrong to overlook the dramatic dimension of this poetry, to forget what is going on between the figures on stage. Bérénice's outpouring appears as an unexpected tangential movement in a speech of passionate persuasion, of which it nevertheless remains a part. It may be played in a tone of self-absorbed meditation, a personal song of grief with no care for the hearer. But the line immediately following suggests something different:

> Mais quelle est mon erreur, et que de soins perdus!

> (But what a mistake this is, and what wasted effort!)

Having transfixed his audience with Bérénice's lament, Racine then ironically undermines it – it is only words, self-indulgent words even, and the cruel situation remains what it was.

In the early part of the twentieth century, there was much talk of 'pure poetry', and Racine was quarried for these quotable moments of lyrical intensity which seem to float free of the dramatic context. The corollary was sometimes to downgrade the more obviously dramatic verse, in which Racine uses the resources of poetry to portray action, passion and conflict. This is to impose on seventeenth-century theatre concepts which belong in a post-Romantic world. It is to take too much to heart Verlaine's praise of music in poetry and his injunction: 'Take eloquence and wring its neck'. No doubt the seventeenth-century audience were susceptible to the purely poetic qualities of plays which were after all called 'dramatic poems', but the poetry they valued is more akin to prose eloquence than to the lyric of personal feeling. Much of its force lies in its construction, and in what the rhetoricians called the figures of speech – to which one must add (*pace* La Motte and the advocates of prose tragedy) the resources of the alexandrine, which permitted, as we have seen, a versatile eloquence of which prose was hardly capable.

The greatest master of French verse in the century following Racine's death was André Chénier, even if he left only a small body of finished work.[21] In Chénier's verse, as in Racine's, music and eloquence alternate or coexist. Before Hugo, he shows the heights to which eloquence could reach when allied to the musical possibilities of traditional prosody. His theory of poetry, expressed in the remarkable *Ars Poetica* entitled *L'Invention*, stresses once again the need for the genius and enthusiasm which enable the poet to overcome the much lamented inadequacy of the French language for high poetry (something of a cliché in the late eighteenth century). This poetic fire, however, finds its form not in a wild freedom, but in the ability to forge texts which will imprint themselves, like bronze inscriptions, in the minds of readers. This is how he describes the result:

> Leur sublime torrent roule, saisit, entraîne
> Les tours impétueux, inattendus, nouveaux,
> L'expression de flamme aux magiques tableaux
> Qu'a trempés la nature en ses couleurs fertiles,
> Les nombres tour à tour turbulents ou faciles:
> Tout porte au fond du cœur le tumulte et la paix,
> Dans la mémoire au loin tout s'imprime à jamais.   (p. 131)

> (Their sublime torrent rolls, seizes, bears onward
> The impetuous, unexpected, original turns of phrase,
> The fiery expression with its magic pictures
> Which nature has dipped in its fertile colours,
> The harmony alternately turbulent and gentle:
> All carries tumult and peace deep into the heart,
> All imprints itself for ever on the distant memory.)

The old adage said that orators are made, poets are born. Chénier would not have disagreed, I think, but the qualities he admires are not so dissimilar from those which his contemporaries prized in Demosthenes – or indeed in the orators of the French Revolution. He shared the didactic ambitions for poetry which are discussed in the next chapter. What he was looking for was the expression, transposed into the 'language of the gods', of the great truths that the modern age had unveiled, the truths of Newton, Kepler, Galileo. It is not surprising, then, to be able to trace in his works the process whereby prose becomes poetry. Not only do most of his planned philosophical poems exist only as prose outlines, but for one poem at least, the 'Hymne à la justice', we have a prose draft (p. 881) where we can see, as Chénier himself put it in *L'Invention*, the potential statue emerging from the marble. The result is what the rhetoricians called an eloquent 'amplification'.

Chénier has many strings to his bow. In the beautifully orchestrated *Bucoliques*, taking his cue from certain exotic lines in Racine, he blends the sonorities of classical names with the suave music of modern French:

> Là s'arrêtent en foule auprès d'une fontaine
> Anticlès et Procris, Aréthuse et Cyrène.   (p. 5)

> (There close by a fountain gather in a crowd
> Anticles and Procris, Arethusa and Cyrene.)

In the *Elegies*, he moves between relatively simple self-expression and the rolling deployment of rank upon rank of alexandrines that we find for instance in Elegy XX, yet another variation on the theme of ruined cities which appealed perhaps even more strongly to his contemporaries than to those of Racine. He was writing at the time when Hubert Robert was painting his 'sublime' visions of imaginary ruins, whose equivalent in alexandrines is to be found in such lines as these:

> Où sont ces grands tombeaux qui devaient à jamais
> D'une épouse fidèle attester les regrets?
> L'herbe couvre Corinthe, Argos, Sparte, Mycènes;
> La faux coupe le chaume aux champs où fut Athènes.   (p. 72)

> (Where are those great tombs which were meant
> To bear eternal witness to a faithful wife's grief?
> Grass covers Corinth, Argos, Sparta, Mycenae;
> The scythe cuts the stubble on the fields where Athens stood.)

Notice again the way in which the capacious alexandrine accommodates the list of proper names. Magnificent, if a bit easy.

To modern readers it is probably the *Iambes* which show to best advantage Chénier's poetic eloquence. These are unfinished poems, written in 1794 in the prisons of the Revolution where the author was waiting to be executed. They have the vivid appeal of the sketch, yet they too rely above all on the skill with which Chénier manipulates the verse forms that came down to him from his predecessors. He departs from the successions of alexandrines that were the norm in most of his previous poetry; the *Iambes*, modelled on the Greek, are written throughout in alternating lines of twelve and eight syllables, with rhymes alternating *abab*. But this fixed form is twisted, as Chénier imposes on it the jagged rhythms of his indignation. There is nothing mysterious here, nothing of the ambiguity and irony which modern readers like to find in lyric poetry. Everything is out in the open. The vehement vocabulary, the violent metaphors, the abrupt syntax, the obsessively recurring short lines, all fix the poet and his enemies in a tableau comparable to some of David's paintings that Chénier so admired in the early years of the Revolution:

> On vit; on vit infâme. Eh bien? il fallut l'être;
>   L'infâme après tout mange et dort.
> Ici même, en ses parcs, où la mort nous fait paître,
>   Où la hache nous tire au sort,
> Beaux poulets sont écrits; maris, amants sont dupes;
>   Caquetage, intrigues de sots.
> Et sur les gonds de fer soudain les portes crient.
>   Des juges tigres nos seigneurs
> Le pourvoyeur paraît. Quelle sera la proie
>   Que la hache appelle aujourd'hui?
> Chacun frissonne, écoute; et chacun avec joie
>   Voit que ce n'est pas encore lui:
> Ce sera toi demain, insensible imbécile.   (pp. 192–3)

> (We live, we live ignoble. What then? It was bound to be so.
>   The ignoble eat and sleep after all.
> Even here, in his sheepfolds, where death makes us graze,
>   Where the axe draws lots for us,
> Pretty love-letters are written; husbands, lovers are duped;
>   Tittle-tattle, fools' intrigues.
> And on the iron hinges suddenly the gates groan.
>   Of our lords the tiger judges
> The supplier appears. What will be the prey
>   Called by the axe today?
> All shudder, listen, and all see with joy
>   That their turn has not yet come.
> It will be you tomorrow, insensible imbecile.)

There is no reason why poetry should not exist as sociable and entertaining verse that makes no great demands on its leisured audience – in this respect much eighteenth-century French verse could be compared to the innumerable musical creations of the contemporaries of Rameau all over Europe. But verse in the classical period could also rise to the heights of a special kind of eloquence. As such, it seemed to many critics not essentially different from prose, which increasingly invaded its terrain, and was preferred to it by those who had grown impatient with an aesthetic of 'la difficulté vaincue'. Nevertheless, it could, in certain gifted hands, achieve its own special memorability, thanks to its colour, its harmonies, its patterns and its rhythms. It would be a pity, in our post-Romantic age, to lose sight of this important conception of poetry.

8

The Poet as Teacher

PETER FRANCE

Une morale nue apporte de l'ennui:
Le conte fait passer le précepte avec lui.
En ces sortes de feintes il faut instruire et plaire,
Et conter pour conter me semble peu d'affaire.   (p. 153)[1]

(Moral teaching by itself is boring:
The story wins a hearing for the lesson.
In this kind of fiction one must both teach and please,
And story-telling for its own sake seems trivial to me.)

This passage, from the beginning of Jean de La Fontaine's sixth book of fables, has become all too familiar. It is no doubt one of the most often repeated pronouncements of classical poetics, and, while being specifically concerned with the fable ('ces sortes de feintes'), it sums up a central precept of what has been called 'la doctrine classique'. The apparent simplicity of these sentences conceals the complexity of the issues at stake; the practice of poets in the seventeenth and eighteenth centuries often corresponds to quite different impulses. Nevertheless, it is worth reminding oneself, if an age when poetry seems far removed from teaching, that the poets of classical France (for La Fontaine was not alone) felt the need to stake their claim to be taken seriously as useful writers.

This is of course an ancient tradition. Not only had the moral value of tragedy been amply debated by Plato, Aristotle and hosts of commentators, but the poetry of Greece and Rome offered notable examples of overtly philosophical, didactic poetry. The *De rerum natura* of Lucretius and Virgil's *Georgics*, to name only two of the most important, were present in the minds of those who attended the colleges of the *ancien régime*. Throughout the Middle Ages, poetry (or verse) had been used as a medium for instruction, and the Renaissance period had given the poet an exalted place as a teacher of mankind. At its simplest, verse was an aid to impressing truths on the memory (the grammatical instructions in the schoolroom Latin grammars were encapsulated in pieces of Latin doggerel). At its most elevated, the 'language of the gods' endowed important subjects with an appropriate grandeur.

At the beginning of the French Wars of Religion, for instance, Ronsard addressed a series of verse discourses on topics of great current concern to the King, the Queen, the people of France and his Protestant adversaries; the first of these are like lay sermons, the later ones move increasingly to satire and personal invective. Agrippa d'Aubigné's *Les Tragiques*, mostly written in the middle of the same wars, though published only in 1616, reads like a counterblast from the Protestant side, and it remains unique in French poetry. Writing with the passion and hyperbole of religious commitment, d'Aubigné piles alexandrine on alexandrine, moving between satire and denunciation, and creating in his seven cantos a sequence of massive visions of violence, corruption, suffering, judgement and resurrection. As he says in his presentation of the poem, it is not meant so much to instruct as to move the reader – and it is at the same time an outpouring of its author's passions – but like Ronsard's discourses, it is a poetry whose prime aim is persuasion.

As we saw in the previous chapter, the position of verse, and indeed of poetry, did not go unchallenged during the reigns of Louis XIV and Louis XV any more than it had in the thirteenth century.[2] Reason was often opposed to rhyme, serious philosophy to childish art. Nevertheless, the proceedings of academies, the contents of journals, and the curricula of schools make it clear that poetry retained its traditional central position within the literary culture of the time. This being so, it was essential that it should be seen as more than merely a pleasurable pastime. 'Conter pour conter' was not only trivial, in the puritanical perspective of much contemporary devotion it might come to seem positively sinful, wasting time and distracting people from their proper duties. To combat such a perception, it is no wonder that critics and writers alike proclaimed the usefulness of poetry, a usefulness which depended above all on the capacity of poetry to teach.

The theorists of the time weave a variety of schemes which bring together the twin imperatives, pleasure and instruction. Rapin is fairly characteristic in saying that 'the principal aim of poetry is to be useful', but that 'poetry is only useful in so far as it pleases'.[3] To put it crudely, pleasure sugars the pill of instruction. Most discussions of the problem concern not so much the overtly didactic or discursive poetic genres as those which are in some way narrative, the most important of these being epic, tragedy and comedy (the novel not yet having conquered a significant place). The dramatic genres pose special problems which go beyond the limits of this chapter, but it is worth saying something here about the epic.

The 'heroic genre' (as it was also called) has largely dropped out of the modern poetic consciousness. In the period that concerns us, France did not produce any epic masterpieces to set alongside *Paradise Lost*, but the genre continued to occupy a position at the summit of the poetic hierarchy. The dominant theoretical work on the subject was Le Bossu's *Traité du poème épique* (1675), and this explicitly presents the epic as an instructive genre. In Le Bossu's view (which is of course a different thing from actual poetic practice), the lessons of epic are above all moral ones; he imagines his authors starting from a 'moral truth' and then seeking a 'fable' which will embody it. Homer and Aesop (or La Fontaine) are thus engaged on similar business, the difference between the Trojan war and a fight between two dogs being one of scale and of suitability to a given audience. The *Iliad* is therefore allegorized to produce a universally valid lesson about human conduct, which may then be reinforced by various means, including the *sententiae* or maxims uttered by the narrator or given to the characters.

Nearly 100 years after Ronsard's *Franciade* (1572), and a little before Le Bossu wrote, there was a remarkable flowering of epic poems in France, almost all of them being concerned with national or biblical (rather than classical) subjects, the most famous being Saint-Amant's *Moïse sauvé* (see above, p. 94). As an example of these now forgotten heavyweights, we may take *Clovis*, published by Jean Desmarets de Saint-Sorlin in 1657, though begun some twenty years earlier.[4]

The 1657 version of Desmarets's poem (it was reissued in a revised form in 1673) consists of twenty-six 'books', written throughout in alexandrines. It has one central subject, the conversion of the first Christian king of France. His baptism is delayed until Book 24, the action of the poem coming from a series of adventures – enchantments, abductions, mistaken identities – which are more akin to the romance tradition than to ancient epic. There are, of course, fights and battles from which Clovis emerges victorious, but these are overshadowed by the love interest, for the baptism of Clovis involves also his marriage to the Christian princess Clotilde, from whom he has been repeatedly separated throughout the poem.

Clovis would thus appeal to the taste of those who devoured the long pseudo-historical novels of the mid-seventeenth century. But Desmarets had higher ambitions. His poem was conceived originally during the lifetime of his great patron Richelieu (whose memory is amply praised in it), and it corresponds to Richelieu's cultural aims, celebrating the greatness of the French monarchy and the power of the *monarque très chrétien* over his subjects and his neighbours. In Desmarets's epic, as in the many other historical epics produced in the sixteenth and seventeenth centuries, modern France and its rulers are given legitimacy, as Augustus had been in Virgil's *Aeneid*, by a narrative of origins. As Desmarets puts it, comparing France favourably with Rome, 'only the empire of France has a clearly great foundation, having been conquered by Clovis alone, and a clearly divine one, thanks to the miracles which brough this great king to Christianity' (p. 711). The mythological panoply of ancient epic is replaced by what was called the *merveilleux chrétien*, the better to enhance the grandeur of France's rulers.

Clovis is therefore an example of what the twentieth century was to call committed literature. The commitment here may strike modern readers as little more than flattery at times, particularly when Desmarets rewrites his epic in the 1673 version to incorporate more extended praise of Louis XIV. But as in much writing of this kind, praise, whether sincere or not, goes along with the desire to influence those in power. As David Maskell puts it, 'epic did not only have a moral purpose – this was the purpose of most literature – but was also directed towards the most illustrious audience, the ruler'.[5] This comes across most clearly in Desmarets's original epistle to the King, who in 1657 was still not twenty. In traditional manner he lists the duties of a Christian king, in particular his duties towards the Catholic church at a time when the protestant 'heresy' was being more and more successfully suppressed, and concludes: 'Sire, it is by following these great examples of heroic virtue [Clovis's execution of sacrilegious soldiers] that you will overcome the vices of your kingdom' (p. 31).

As this suggests, the inculcation of moral values is done very largely through example, through the depiction of admirable heroes and heroines, and of wicked, treacherous villains. From time to time, however, Desmarets includes a moralizing speech, as for instance in Book 23, where the ambassador of Theodoric exhorts the victorious Clovis to clemency and where subsequently Clovis, over-excited by the sweet sounds of the lute, speaks of the dangers of music for the heroic warrior. It is interesting to note that in the second case Desmarets draws a parallel with the classic episode of Odysseus and the sirens:

> Comme le sage Ulysse, en son vaisseau léger,
> Redoutant des beaux chants l'appât et le danger,
> Ouït les doux accents des charmantes sirènes,
> Puis s'enfuit de leurs bords sur les humides plaines,
> Clovis ainsi se dompte [...]   (p. 584)

> (As the wise Ulysses, in his light vessel,
> Fearing the attraction and the danger of beautiful songs,

> Heard the sweet strains of the enchanting sirens,
> Then fled from their shores across the humid plains,
> So Clovis masters himself [...]

Now the episode of the sirens, together with all the other tall stories of the *Odyssey*, was a favourite example for all the rationalist allegorizers of ancient epic, who felt obliged to find useful moral lessons in these childishly improbable (yet highly respected) texts. Critics such as Le Bossu subordinate all poetic pleasure to the idea, the lesson. In the case of Desmarets, one may wonder how firmly the moral impulse controls his poetic undertaking. It was against him in particular (though for reasons that have not a great deal to do with the nature of his writings) that the Jansenist Pierre Nicole wrote in the eleventh of his *Lettres sur l'hérésie imaginaire* that dramatic poets and novelists were public poisoners. Gaston Hall writes perceptively of the 'numerous unresolved tensions' in Desmarets's writing.[6] As he mused about music, Ulysses and the sirens, was he perhaps aware that there were elements in his long and convoluted narrative – violence, metamorphosis, sorcery, eroticism – which were incompatible with moral and political usefulness? There are, too, in among the long expanses of undistinguished narrative, not a few moments when poetic perceptions give a pleasure that has nothing to do with instruction. Here, for instance, is the description of grandees at Clovis's baptism (Book 24):

> Tous en longs manteaux blancs, et d'argent recouverts,
> Comme au lever du jour, dans les rudes hivers,
> Lorsque le sombre ciel fait tomber dans les plaines
> L'éclatante blancheur de ses volantes laines;
> On voit par les chemins tout passant, tout berger,
> Couvert également de cet argent léger.   (p. 599)

> (All covered in long white cloaks and in silver,
> As at daybreak, in the harsh winter,
> When the dark sky lets fall on to the plains
> The gleaming whiteness of its flying wool;
> On the roads one sees every passer-by, every shepherd
> Equally covered with this light silver.)

This lacks the thrilling energy of Desmarets's contemporary, Milton, but it is more interesting than what we generally find in the epic of his more famous successor, Voltaire.

Like *Clovis*, Voltaire's *La Henriade*[7] is a national epic, though set in the much more recent past – its hero is Henri IV, its subject the defeat of the ultra-Catholic Ligue at the end of the Wars of Religion. Having grown up in a culture which placed the epic at the top of the poetic hierarchy, Voltaire no doubt wanted to stake a claim to fame by succeeding where so many of his French predecessors appeared to have failed. To many readers he seemed to have done just this, and his poem was favourably compared with the great epics of Greece and Rome. Posterity has been less indulgent. *La Henriade* seems very much written to a formula, with the idealized hero, the language heavily dependent on the classics of the previous reign, the set-piece scenes of battle or deliberation and the prophecies which allow the writer to look forward from the time of the action to the time of writing. Like *Clovis*, it comes accompanied with an exhortatory and flattering 'Discourse to the King', though Voltaire eventually decided not to publish this. Naturally, though, the message is very different from that of Desmarets. Voltaire's king is not just magnanimous; he has the virtues of a philosopher, a tolerant man of reason. Where *Clovis* was dedicated to a strong Catholic monarchy, *La Henriade* (while apparently approving Henri's conversion to catholicism), has as its high point a graphic description of the St Bartholemew Massacre, in which the horrific forces of fanaticism are led on by the figure of Discord (one of the many allegorical characters who replace both the pagan Gods of ancient epic and the *merveilleux chrétien* of Voltaire's more recent predecessors). This too is committed writing; epic composition is a sign of high poetic ambition for Voltaire, but it also gives him the chance to offer a counterblast to his greatest predecessor Racine, whose biblical drama *Athalie* (1699) was in his eyes a masterpiece, but a deplorable incitement to religious intolerance.

In *La Henriade*, Voltaire used a weighty narrative form to communicate moral and political beliefs; subsequently, in *Zadig*, *Candide* and the other *contes philosophiques*, he was to use a lighter and more effective form of story-telling for instructive – or at least philosophical – purposes. Elsewhere, however, he is more direct. The *Discours en vers sur l'homme*, for instance, published in 1738–9, correspond fairly exactly to Pope's 'essays' and to the familiar norms of the verse epistle. Voltaire uses the attractive qualities of verse to interest readers, to carry them along with him, and to leave them with the memorable expression of some important ideas. To use Pope's phrase, it is 'what oft was thought, but ne'er so well expressed'. It could be argued, however, that it is not so much the ideas that count as the tone of voice of the poet as he pursues elusive questions of ethics and metaphysics.

In these discourses Voltaire is less witty than Pope; his language is less dense and spiky, his couplets have less bite. But as with Pope, the image given is of a person of good company whose thought flows naturally into verse. In the sixth discourse, entitled 'De la nature de l'homme' (no less!), he builds his poem round a dialogue. A reader, tired of the frivolities of fashionable society, asks the poet, whose 'great study is man', to describe

the great chain of beings which Pope and Plato had seen in the world. The
poet demurs (such talk is dangerous in France), and approaches his subject
in a roundabout way, with a tale that purports to come from a Chinese
original. Eventually, however, he begins to speak, indeed to preach, in his
own name, and is well-launched in a disquisition on the way to make a
short life seem long, when suddenly the flow is interrupted:

> On peut vivre beaucoup sans végéter longtemps:
> Et je vais te prouver par mes raisonnements . . .
> Mais malheur à l'auteur qui veut toujours instruire!
> Le secret d'ennuyer est celui de tout dire.[8]

> (One can live a great deal without vegetating a long time:
> And I am going to prove to you by reason . . .
> But ill betide the author who wants always to be teaching!
> The secret of being boring is to leave nothing unsaid.)

It is a well-tried tactic, of which several examples are to be found in
Boileau's satires and epistles. A tone of modesty and naturalness is created,
the solemnity of didactic poetry is (it is hoped) avoided, and Voltaire can
go on:

> C'est ainsi que ma muse, avec simplicité,
> Sur des tons différents chantait la vérité.

> (That is the simple way in which my muse
> Sang the truth in varied tones.)

And indeed his tone is varied, rising at times to high eloquence as he
evokes the cosmic order, but then moving from the cosmic to the comic.
There is room in this agreeable, easy-going poetry for jokes, irony and
throw-away remarks. To Romantic ears, it may seem like versified prose,
but this epistolary verse is a significant achievement of the classical period.

Such a wordly style was acceptable for the lay discussion of moral topics,
but less appropriate for the religious poetry which makes up such a large
part of the poetic output of the seventeenth and eighteenth centuries in
France. Innumerable are the odes, *stances*, sonnets, meditations and so
forth on Christian themes. And whereas the general consensus of critical
opinion in the classical period was hostile to extravagant language, even
in poetry, religious feeling authorized at least a relative boldness. As
the English poet Traherne put it, writing of divine love, 'excess is its true
moderation'.[9] What is more, the model for much religious writing was the
Hebrew poetry of the Bible (in particular, the Psalms), filtered of course
through Latin translation, but still challengingly different from the norms
of salon poetry.

Those who wrote on religious topics were probably sincere in their effusions; it is also likely that they found here an opportunity to write a kind of poetry which was otherwise inadmissible. The verbal extravagance of the religious poets of the baroque era (Du Bois Hus, for instance) was certainly pruned by their successors, but such a classic poet as Jean-Baptiste Rousseau ('le grand Rousseau'), was enabled by his model, Psalm 48, to begin his ode 'Sur l'aveuglement des hommes du siècle' with this stanza:

> Qu'aux accents de ma voix la terre se réveille!
> Rois, soyez attentifs; peuples, ouvrez l'oreille!
> Que l'univers se taise et m'écoute parler!
> Mes chants vont seconder les accords de ma lyre:
> L'esprit saint me pénètre, il m'échauffe et m'inspire
> Les grandes vérités que je vais révéler.[10]

> (Let the earth awaken to the sound of my voice!
> Kings, be attentive; peoples, open your ears!
> Let the universe be silent and listen to my speech!
> My songs will echo the sounds of my lyre:
> The holy spirit fills me, he animates me and inspires in me
> The great truths that I am about to reveal.)

The style here is like that of the high priest Joad in Racine's *Athalie*. Rousseau's prophetic manner accords well with the rather conventional enthusiasm of the ode – an exalted genre that shared with the epic the prestige of antiquity. The poet is seized by what in Platonic terms was known as a state of 'divine fury'. The fiction of inspiration, and the prestige of the Christian religion and its sacred texts, allow him to get away with a grandiose tone (exclamations, imperatives, superlatives) which might otherwise verge on the ridiculous.

An ode is not formally a didactic poem, but a lyric. It purports to be a song in which the poet pours out his feelings. Nevertheless, the last lines of the stanza just quoted make it clear that what we are reading is in fact a poetic sermon. Religion offered the most incontrovertible way of harnessing the potentially dangerous pleasures of poetry to edifying purposes. Thus the sonnet, associated above all with love poetry, offered possibilities – as it had in the late sixteenth-century writing of Chassignet, Sponde, La Ceppède and others – for a memorable form of religious instruction. Take Rousseau's 'Sur la grâce':

> D'un père infortuné portant le châtiment,
> Tout homme est aux enfers soumis dès sa naissance,
> Si la grâce ne vient terrasser leur puissance
> Unie aux saintes eaux du premier sacrement.

L'arbitre franc et libre à pécher seulement
Devient libre par elle à suivre l'innocence,
Et méritant pour nous, elle nous récompense
Du bien dont nos efforts ne sont que l'instrument.

Mais si l'âme, sans elle à périr condamnée,
Ne saurait mériter qu'elle lui soit donnée,
Dois-je donc m'endormir, ou me désespérer?

Non: sans la mériter tous ont droit d'y prétendre,
Elle est le prix du sang qu'un Dieu voulut répandre,
Et c'est déjà l'avoir que de la désirer.[11]

(Bearing the punishment of an unfortunate father,
All men are condemned to hell from birth,
If grace does not come to destroy its power,
United with the holy waters of the first sacrament.

The human will, free only to sin,
Becomes through grace free to live in innocence,
And grace, giving us its merits, rewards us
For the good for which our efforts are only the instrument.

But if the soul, condemned without grace to perish,
Cannot deserve to receive it,
Must I then abandon the struggle, or despair?

No: without deserving it, all may lay claim to it,
It is the price of the blood which God deigned to shed,
And to desire it is already to possess it.)

One sees here how well the sonnet form lends itself to didactic writing on a subject of great contemporary concern. The four-square solemnity of the two quatrains – each of them made of a single complex but well-balanced sentence – is contrasted with the urgent question of the first tercet, answered by the emphatic 'No' of the final section. In time-honoured manner, the sonnet is crowned by a memorable formulation, for which Rousseau was perhaps indebted to the equally striking sentence in Pascal's *Pensées*: 'Tu ne me chercherais pas, si tu ne m'avais trouvé.'

The Christian religion continued to offer a career to the didactic poet in the eighteenth century, but the age of the Enlightenment had other subjects to offer. If the mid-seventeenth century was the period of epic ambitions, these were replaced in the second half of the eighteenth century by the attempts to write great philosophical or scientific poems. Such an ambition had of course been familiar to the Renaissance poets. In France the *Semaines* of Du Bartas, encyclopedic epics of the Creation, could offer models alongside the *De rerum natura*, but the scientific discoveries of the eighteenth century proposed new and stirring challenges to the poets of the time. Ponce-Denis Ecouchard-Lebrun (Lebrun-Pindare to his contemporaries), writes in the third canto of his unfinished *La Nature* (begun about 1760) about the role of genius in recovering the 'divine characters' of the lost 'book of gold' of the Universe. The genius in question is not only Newton or Buffon; the poet too has his role to play. The section devoted to the new astronomy concludes with the lines:

> Telle on voit la physique embrasser l'univers,
> Et sa hauteur n'a rien d'inaccessible aux vers.[12]
>
> (So we see physics embracing the universe,
> And its loftiness is not inaccessible to poetry.)

To 'embrace the universe' implies a new mastery. Celebrating the order of the world, poetry will enable a non-specialist public to possess in imagination the riches which science has been revealing. It will do this in language which steers a middle course between technical terminology – where this is not too obscure and repelling – and the conventional grandiloquence of the 'language of the gods' (a phrase used yet again by Lebrun in the canto just quoted). Many are the descriptive, scientific or philosophical poems which set out to do this. André Chénier, whose gifts might have allowed him some degree of success, left only small fragments and prose sketches of his *Hermès* (on the natural order) and *L'Amérique* (on human history), both of which reveal a grandiose design. In the early nineteenth century Népomucène Lemercier (1771–1840) left over a dozen complete epics, including *L'Atlantiade, ou la théogonie newtonienne* (1812), a poem in six cantos which is itself part of a vaster whole embracing almost every subject imaginable. Lemercier transforms the new physics into a strange epic in which Bione (life), Electrone (electricity) and similar figures replace the deities of classical epic. The result is bizarre, clumsy, virtually unreadable, but remarkable all the same.

More successful, indeed very successful with his contemporaries (though not with a mocking posterity), was Jacques Delille (1738–1813).[13] In 1770, following Saint-Lambert's *Les Saisons* (1769), itself an imitation of the fashionable *Seasons* of the Scottish poet James Thomson, Delille began by returning to the source of such poetry, publishing a translation of Virgil's *Georgics*. Such edifying poems on country life chimed in well with the ideas propagated by the enlightened Encyclopaedists, encouraging landowners and city dwellers to take a more positive attitude to the work of the land, preaching a degree of social reform and popularizing new developments in agricultural technique. Delille went on to pursue these and wider themes in his own long poems, *Les Jardins* (1782), *L'Homme des champs* (1800), *L'Imagination* (1806) and *Les Trois Règnes de la nature* (1808).

His stance is summed up in these lines from Canto 6 of *Les Trois Règnes* (devoted to the vegetable kingdom):

> Tout est désenchanté; mais, sans tous ces prestiges,
> Les arbres ont leur vie, et les bois leurs prodiges,
> Je veux les célébrer [...]   (vol. IX, p. 150)

> (The magic spell has gone from everything; but, without these enchantments,
> The trees have their life and the woods their marvels,
> I want to celebrate them [...])

His poetry is to be a poetry of fact, and will gain its appeal from the extraordinary variety of the natural world. He does not so much explain this world as describe it and arrange it according to the taxonomies of the time, marvelling as he does so. It is not for nothing that he sang the praises of gardens, and in particular of the less formal English garden; like a gardener, he takes on nature and reduces it to a manageable and (to his contemporaries) attractive state.

Delille's involvement with the garden was less personal and less subtly imaginative than that of Théophile in 'La Maison de Sylvie' (see above, pp. 91–4). He was very conscious of writing didactic poetry, and comes back in several of his prefaces to the problems this involves. To those who reproach him with writing on uninteresting subjects (in *Les Jardins*), he admits that he cannot offer the strong sensations provided by the poetry of the passions, but claims that poetry can have other, quieter charms. In this context, questions of style are crucial. What is needed – in order to sugar the pill of instruction – are 'accurate ideas, vivid colouring, abundant images, charming variety, unexpected contrasts, enchanting harmony, sustained elegance' (vol. VII, p. 6). It is a tall order, and Delille hardly matched his own requirements. One of the crucial questions was that of poetic diction. In his early writing he championed an enlarging of the classical poetic vocabulary to cope with new material, and he does indeed use a lot of technical terms, but he is also a devotee of the elegant periphrasis, which sometimes verges on the riddle ('Ce reptile gluant qui traîne sa maison' – This slimy reptile who drags along his house). This style was the source of much of the contempt heaped on him by the later Romantic generations.

His contemporary reputation was no doubt exaggerated, as was the reaction to it. His poetry does not offer 'those violent shocks and deep impressions which belong to other types of poetry' (vol. VII, p. 5), but it has the leisurely (not to say long-winded) charm of an untroubled walk through the endless variety of the world. So, in the third canto of

L'Homme des champs (subsequently to be expanded in *Les Trois Règnes*), the man of leisure is encouraged to discover the worlds revealed by geology, the fossils for instance:

> Souvent deux minces lits, léger travail des eaux,
> L'un sur l'autre sculptés par les mêmes rameaux   (vol. VII, p. 240)
>
> (Often [there are] two thin strata, the insubstantial work of the waters,
> One sculpted on the other by the same branches)

The effect is gently enigmatic, but all is explained at the end of the poem in one of the numerous prose notes, in this case referring to a memoir read by Jussieu to the Academy of Sciences.

Delille and Jean-Baptiste Rousseau are little read nowadays, however well their works met the demands of the contemporary public. Even Voltaire's didactic verse has fallen by the wayside. Indeed, if we are looking for an eighteenth-century poet whose persuasive powers have lasted, we will need to turn to Rouget de l'Isle, author of the 'Marseillaise', though the French anthem can hardly be classed as *instructive* poetry. In the didactic genres, the two success stories of the classical period both belong to the reign of Louis XIV – Boileau and (above all) La Fontaine. And in both cases what most modern readers of poetry value in them is precisely the interplay between instruction and poetic pleasure.

Boileau's *Art poétique* (1674) is cited by Delille as one of the few successful modern didactic poems. But although its author is sometimes called the 'schoolmaster of Parnassus' ('régent du Parnasse'), misusing a phrase that he used ironically of himself, he is better described by another *sobriquet*, 'le satirique'. For the genre of Juvenal and Horace was where he was most at home; although he tried to draw a line between satire and the more respectable epistle, his satiric verve continues to show through. What is more, some of his most interesting works show him reflecting on the value and purpose of the genre and his practice of it.

There was of course a classic moral case to be made for satire, one which was often made by the Latin satirists and by Boileau's French predecessors (such as Mathurin Régnier). Satire is defended here as comedy was often defended by Molière. This is how Boileau puts it in Satire IX:[14]

> La satire en leçons, en nouveautés fertile,
> Sait seule assaisonner le plaisant et l'utile,
> Et d'un vers qu'elle épure aux rayons du bon sens,
> Détrompe les esprits des erreurs de leur temps.
> Elle seule, bravant l'orgueil et l'injustice,
> Va jusque sous le dais faire pâlir le vice;
> Et souvent sans rien craindre, à l'aide d'un bon mot,
> Va venger la raison des attentats d'un sot.   (p. 74)

(Only satire, fertile in lessons and novelties,
Is capable of blending the pleasing and the useful,
And with a line purified in the rays of good sense
Disabuses minds of the errors of the age.
Only satire, braving pride and injustice,
Ventures beneath a dais to make vice grow pale;
And often, fearlessly, with the help of clever word,
She avenges reason for the attacks of a fool.)

This is Boileau on his high horse, keeping up an elevated moral line, and giving the satiric muse a part to play in a brief but edifying allegorical drama. The 'fearless' denunciation of the vices of the age is indeed to be found in some of his satires, which may attack easy targets, such as avarice, or more dangerous ones, such as religious hypocrisy. In some ways this is timeless moral satire, railing at the corruptions of Paris, the arrogance of power and wealth, and all the follies of humanity, just as Juvenal had in Rome. But the reference to 'nouveautés' reminds us that satire can also have a more topical function. And it is here that its instructive purpose tends to merge into something rather different.

Satire IX, like several of Boileau's writings, shows that satire was an ambiguous genre, enjoyed and feared by readers. Boileau was fiercely criticized, the main thrust of the attack being that he was using his poetic gift to satisfy petty spite and conduct personal vendettas. One of the perennial debates surrounding the genre concerned the propriety of naming names, since it was here that the supposedly didactic function of satire seemed less evident. Boileau named his victims copiously in his first nine satires; only after 1669, in order to achieve the respectability required by royal favour, did he become more discreet, and marked this by entitling his poems 'epistles' (only returning to satire many years later).

The majority of the figures named in the early satires are writers and poets, though there are a number of lawyers, tax-farmers, ecclesiastics and others. It may be that Boileau was right to pillory the writings of Chapelain and Cotin, to name only his two most constant victims – certainly posterity has accepted his verdict, often without looking any further. As he presents it, he is exercising a useful social function in defending reason and good taste against the pernicious work of what Pope would call the 'dunces'. It does seem, though, that critical judgement here is less important than personal hostility – or indeed, at times, a joyful irresponsibility, for it often seems that bad poets are there above all to make good lines. So, in Satire VII, Boileau writes:

Faut-il d'un froid rimeur dépeindre la manie?
Mes vers, comme un torrent, coulent sur le papier.
Je rencontre à la fois Perrin et Pelletier,
Bonnecorse, Pradon, Colletet, Titreville.   (p. 53)

(Have I to paint the mania of a dull rhymer?
My lines pour like a torrent on to the paper.
I find at once Perrin and Pelletier,
Bonnecorse, Pradon, Colletet, Titreville.)

This is the final version, but in earlier editions the list of names is quite different.

The point in noting this is not so much to condemn Boileau for irresponsibility as to stress the spontaneous pleasure he takes in writing satirical alexandrines full of proper names – the comic equivalent of the type of accumulation we saw in Chénier's verse (see above, p. 120). This pleasure can infect the reader too, even if he or she does not know anything about the writers being mocked. The lines just quoted are followed by the cry 'Aussitôt je triomphe' (Forthwith I triumph). As he puts it, it is at such moments that he knows he is a poet. At one time, Boileau tended to be seen as a dogmatic and rather prosaic critic, but recent work has underlined how the undoubted urge to lay down the law mingles in his writing with irony, self-deprecation and fun. Frequently in his satires and epistles there is a sudden turn (which we noted also in Voltaire's *Discours*) from apparently serious preaching to apologetic amusement at his own pretensions. Often he speaks with two voices; Satire IX, for instance, is a dialogue between himself and his wit ('esprit'), in which he urges himself to give up satire. His wit seems to agree, and announces:

'Puisque vous le voulez, je vais changer de style.
Je le déclare donc: Quinault est un Virgile.
Pradon comme un soleil en nos ans a paru.
Pelletier écrit mieux qu'Ablancourt ni Patru.
Cotin à ses sermons traînant toute la terre,
Fend les flots d'auditeurs pour aller à sa chaire.
Saufal est le Phénix des esprits relevés.
Perrin . . .' – Bon, mon esprit, courage, poursuivez.
Mais ne voyez-vous pas que leur troupe en furie
Va prendre encor ces vers pour une raillerie?   (p. 75)

('Since that is your wish, I shall change my style.
I declare then: Quinault is a Virgil.
Pradon has appeared like a sun in our age.
Pelletier writes better than Ablancourt or Patru.
Cotin, pulling the whole world in to his sermons,
Forces his way to the pulpit through floods of listeners.
Saufal is the phoenix of elevated minds.
Perrin . . .' – Splendid, my wit, take courage, continue.
But don't you see that the infuriated legion of them
Will take these lines too as mockery?)

One notes here the skilful modulation of tone, rising from the 'plain man' simplicity of the opening to the burlesque grandeur in the ironic image of a successful Cotin. In Satire VII, written when he was still a mad young dog, Boileau said self-deprecatingly:

> Je sais coudre une rime au bout de quelques mots.
> Souvent j'habille en vers une maligne prose;
> C'est par là que je vaux, si je vaux quelque chose.   (p. 54)

> (I know how to sew a rhyme on to the end of a few words.
> Often I dress some malicious prose in verse.
> This is my merit, if I possess any merit.)

There is more to it than this, of course, but the emphasis on verse-making is undoubtedly the right one.

In his fables, La Fontaine was engaging with a more clearly didactic genre. Fables, as they were written by the Greek Aesop and the Roman Phaedrus, were meant to instruct children; a simple and memorable story, sometimes accompanied by a picture, would impress on the young mind a useful lesson for the conduct of life. However, these fables were also studied in the colleges of the *ancien régime* by boys learning Latin, and they provided the basis for early exercises in rhetoric (what we might now call creative writing). In his teens, La Fontaine may well have had to 'amplify' the bare story of, say, the wolf and the lamb, adding such ornaments as dialogue or description and bringing into play all the various figures of speech.[15]

Such fables were generally in prose. La Fontaine tells us in his preface how he had gone against the advice of an expert (the lawyer and writer Patru) by giving them what he describes in his dedication as 'the ornaments of poetry'. He remarks that since the fables were familiar to everyone (and he is clearly thinking of adult readers as he writes this), he would be wasting his time if he did not 'make them new by adding some touches which would make them less insipid'. The reference to novelty and seasoning reminds one of the passage quoted above from Boileau's Satire IX. Nevertheless, as we saw at the beginning of this chapter, La Fontaine also made claims for the instructive value of his little narrative poems: affirming that 'this work should be judged not so much by the form I have given it as by its usefulness and its content', he goes on to liken his fables to Christ's parables.

Now some of the parables of the New Testament are notoriously difficult to interpret, and the same may be said of La Fontaine's fables. They are lively, witty, beautiful, but what lesson are we meant to take from them? Sometimes, to be sure, the lesson is clear enough. The last fable of all, 'Le Juge arbitre, l'hospitalier et le solitaire', written shortly before its author died in 1694, is based on an edifying story from Arnauld d'Andilly's *Les Vies des Saints Pères du désert*, and like his model, La Fontaine expounds the religious message (the value of the solitary life) in a quite unambiguous way. Nearly thirty years earlier, in the first book of fables, the moral of such fables as 'La Grenouille qui veut se faire aussi grosse que le bœuf' appears similarly unequivocal. The frog puffs itself up until it bursts, and the fabulist draws the moral:

> Le monde est plein de gens qui ne sont pas plus sages:
> Tout bourgeois veut bâtir comme les grands seigneurs,
> > Tout petit prince a des ambassadeurs,
> > > Tout marquis veut avoir des pages.   (p. 37)

> (The world is full of people who are no more sensible:
> Every bourgeois wants to build like the great lords,
> > Every princeling has ambassadors,
> > > Every marquis wants to have pages.)

Even so, this is not simply a piece of general moralizing; the way in which La Fontaine spells it out in social terms means that for the contemporary reader it is transformed into a topical satire on individuals who could be named (and are named in the notes to scholarly editions).

Sometimes even the basic moral of the tale is a good deal more obscure. In *Emile*, his book on education, Jean-Jacques Rousseau amuses himself by imagining a child getting hold of the wrong end of the stick on hearing various well-known fables. One example is the 'Le Loup et le chien', in which a lean and hungry wolf is tempted by the fat life of a guard dog, but changes his mind and runs off on seeing the mark left on the dog's neck by its collar. Rousseau tells how he once saw a little girl crying at this fable, because she was tired of being kept in order: 'she felt her neck rubbed bare; she cried because she wasn't a wolf'. He assumes that the fable was meant as a 'lesson in moderation', but was read as a 'lesson in independence'.[16] Against this, one of La Fontaine's sources, Phaedrus, begins this fable with the words: 'I am going to show in a few words how sweet liberty is'. La Fontaine himself gives no overt moral; he transforms the fable into a comic and rather touching dialogue, in which the two animal characters are strongly individualized as human beings (and yet still animals), and leaves us with the tantalizing ending:

> Cela dit, maître loup s'enfuit, et court encor.   (p. 39)

> (Saying this, Master Wolf ran off, and is still running.)

The disabused lesson that an adult reader draws from the fable is something like: how nice it would be if we could be both independent and comfortable, but alas, we cannot – a lesson well known to Jean-Jacques incidentally.

Many of La Fontaine's best fables are like this. As he put it in the
dedication to Book 12, 'these fictions are in fact a kind of history in which
no-one is flattered' (p. 316). Whatever their overt moral, the 'lesson' these
marvellous little tragi-comedies communicate is more like that of the
novelist than that of the preacher or teacher. It seems appropriate to
conclude this chapter on the didactic function of classical poetry by citing
a fable of La Fontaine's which is mentioned by Voltaire in his *Discours en
vers*, the comic tale of 'The Acorn and the Pumpkin' ('Le Gland et la
citrouille') in which the fabulist seems (but with him, can one be sure?) to
be making fun of the whole business of moralizing by example, and
perhaps also the actual moral with which he begins:

> Dieu fait bien ce qu'il fait. Sans en chercher la preuve
> En tout cet univers, et l'aller parcourant.
>   Dans les citrouilles je la treuve.   (p. 249)

> (God does well what he does. Without scouring
> The whole universe in search of a proof of this,
>   I find it in pumpkins.)

A mocking tone is established from the start in the grotesque contrast of
the second and third lines. The fable itself concerns a villager, who thinks
himself cleverer than the local priest, and indeed than the God who created
the world so incompetently. Why should little fruits like acorns grow on
great oaks, and big pumpkins on little plants? Tired by his mental
exertions, he goes to sleep under an oak, and an acorn drops on his nose.
He sees the light:

> 'Oh! oh! dit-il, je saigne! et que serait-ce donc
> S'il fût tombé de l'arbre une masse plus lourde,
>   Et que ce gland eût été gourde?
> Dieu ne l'a pas voulu; sans doute il eut raison,
>   J'en vois bien à présent la cause.'
>   En louant Dieu de toute chose,
>   Garo retourne à la maison.

> ('Oh! oh! he says, I am bleeding! what would it be like
> If a heavier weight had fallen from the tree,
>   And the acorn had been a gourd?
> God did not wish it so; no doubt he was right,
>   I see the cause clearly now,'
>   Praising God in all things,
>   Garo returns to his house.)

One wonders what the children of *Emile* would have made of this
conclusion.

9

The Romantic Renaissance

PETER DAYAN

Serait-ce déjà lui? C'est bien à l'escalier
Dérobé.[1]

(Is he already here? That certainly came from the hidden
Staircase.)

No translation can convey the reason for which the last of these eleven words, which begin Hugo's play *Hernani*, was immediately recognized as the symbol of a revolution in French verse, and set off a tumult in the theatre. The reason is this: 'Dérobé' (hidden) is a past participle used adjectivally; and it is separated from the noun which it qualifies ('escalier') by a line-break. There is thus no natural pause in the rhythm of the sentence at the end of the first line. The pause comes after 'Dérobé', and this is emphasized by the full stop, by the stage directions (there is a portentous knock on the door at this point), and by the fact that 'Dérobé' almost rhymes with 'escalier'.

To ears used to the harmonies of the type of alexandrine which had dominated serious French theatre for a century and a half, this displacement of the pause seemed shockingly and wilfully discordant. The audience at the first night of *Hernani* was composed partly of people with such ears, who had come to have them shocked – they were known as the 'Classiques'; and partly of friends and partisans of Hugo, known as 'Romantiques', who were determined to defend the new poetic style. There was a famous and picturesque battle between the two sides. The 'Classiques', of course, lost the battle – and the war.

According to the English poet Swinburne, the year of that battle, 1830, will remain 'famous for ever beyond all others in the history of French literature'.[2] And the reason for this is not the quality of the play (neither Swinburne nor the poets who supported Hugo at the time maintained that *Hernani* was his masterpiece), but the new freedom in poetic style that the play made France accept. It may seem strange that this new freedom should be symbolized by the mere separation of a noun from a participle. But the issue of variety in rhythm was central to the Romantic revolution, as the poet Théodore de Banville makes plain in his splendid manual of Romantic versification, the *Petit Traité de poésie française*. This is how he describes the establishment of the convention that *Hernani* rejected:

> It was decreed that the meaning of the sentence, divided at the caesura, would stop at the end of the line, and that every line would resemble every other line, just as one twopenny biscuit resembles another twopenny biscuit.[3]

In thus condemning every line of poetry to repeat the rhythm of every other line, this decree, to Banville, had killed poetry. For repetition, to the Romantics, was death:

> The rule demanding the regular suspension of sense at the caesura and the rule dictating that the sense come to a halt at the end of the line had, between the two of them, quite simply condemned poetry to death. (p. 79)

This assassination of poetry, to Banville (and here as always, Banville's perspective on history is very much the accepted view of the Romantic poets), is no mere metaphor, but a historic event, an arbitrary exercise of usurped power by one uniquely untalented petty tyrant. French verse, he writes,

> remained free until the seventeenth century, or to be precise, until Boileau appeared, and said: 'I'm changing all that; from now on, the heart will be on the right.' – But why? – And Boileau answered: 'It will be on the right, because I wish it to be on the right.' (p. 83)

After Boileau murdered it, French poetry remained dead for over a century. But this period of death was both preceded and followed by life:

> With the exception of the great men of the seventeenth century, Régnier, Corneille, Racine, Molière, La Fontaine, the history of French poetry jumps from the sixteenth century to the nineteenth. Everything contained in the interval MUST NOT BE READ. (p. 61)

Poetry, then, according to Romantic history, flowered in the sixteenth century, died in the seventeenth despite the efforts of a few, and was resuscitated in the nineteenth – or, to be more precise, in the half-century after the French Revolution. This resuscitation was accomplished by two men: André Chénier and Victor Hugo. They delivered French verse from its ignoble bands. Chénier was the first to revive the rich variety of French verse rhythms – and according to Banville, was guillotined for this crime. (Chénier was indeed guillotined, in 1794; it was really for writing articles and having friends disapproved of by Robespierre, rather than for the rhythms of his verse, but Banville was plainly unable to resist equating poetic with political revolution, and the political intolerance of Robespierre with the literary intolerance of the post-Boileau 'Classiques'.) For thirty years after Chénier's death, his poetry, though largely unpublished, served as a reference point: praised by the poets who were gradually acquiring the label 'Romantiques', derided by their opponents. Apart from the vivacity of his images, the quality which made his verse so controversial was the sure-footed freedom, the measured flexibility of his rhythms, which, while they do not openly flout Boileau's rules, bend them to strikingly original effect. Examples of lines which are not really end-stopped are easy enough to find in his work. But perhaps more subtle – and more influential – is his attitude to the traditional virtue of balance in verse. For example, at the end of his last 'Iambe', written under threat of execution, Chénier thrice shifts the main pause towards the beginning of the line, throwing single-word invocations into sharp relief. This does not actually break an established rule. (There is a comma in the middle of his alexandrine, where the caesura should be, after 'haine'; the other two lines are octosyllables, and there was no firm convention concerning the place of the caesura in such shorter lines.) None the less, a sense of balance would have been expected, especially at the end of such a serious work. Chénier gives instead a remarkably disturbed and disturbing rhythm which, in each line, accelerates from the main pause towards the end. The result is an unmistakably Romantic effect of uncontainable emotional charge.

> Allons, étouffe tes clameurs;
> Souffre, ô coeur gros de haine, affamé de justice.
> Toi, Vertu, pleure si je meurs.[4]

> (Come, stifle your clamour;
> Suffer, o heart heavy with hate, hungry for justice.
> Thou, Virtue, weep if I die.)

Hugo carried further the movement begun by Chénier; after Hugo, says Banville, the rhythm of French verse was no longer fixed by tradition, but depended on the poet's 'inspiration' and 'génie'. This was universally felt to be a revolutionary conquest. Hugo puts it thus, in lines of which the second is splendidly and defiantly lop-sided:

> sur les bataillons d'alexandrins carrés
> Je fis souffler un vent révolutionnaire.[5]

(on the four-square ranks of alexandrines
I let loose a revolutionary wind.)

In a way, Hugo's revolution was incomplete; it left intact the traditional rules governing rhyme, and those determining the ways in which the number of syllables per line were calculated. Those rules remained in force for another sixty years, and they make Romantic verse seem, to the modern reader, still quite rigorously conventional and regular. None the less, the deep-seated need to push at boundaries which led to the questioning of all such rules towards the end of the century was clearly already at work in the verse of 1830. And so, albeit in a relatively naïve form, was the dramatic theme that always accompanied that need to push at boundaries: mystery. The knock at the door at the beginning of *Hernani* comes from a secret, hidden staircase; it disturbs the woman who hears it, as well as the rhythm of the alexandrine; and the man behind the door turns out to be, not the expected one, but a masked stranger. Cloak-and-dagger stuff, perhaps; but after all, melodrama was merely the more comfortable version of the great Romantic obsession with a threatening, disturbing, and always hidden truth. Visible truth had gone out of fashion, along with Boileau's clear rules governing poetic form.

Banville is certainly right to describe the Romantic 'révolution' as 'immense, incalculable, vertigineuse'. One might say that its consequences have been giving poets vertigo ever since. The disturbance, the irregularity at the heart of that revolution did not kill the urge towards rhythm – on the contrary: all the best-known poets of the century were, in Mallarmé's phrase, 'hantés du Rythme' (haunted by Rhythm). But it did make the situation of that rhythm infinitely problematic. One could no longer write poetry by following precept or example – not even Hugo's example; for he said that he 'would condemn no less imitators who attach themselves to so-called romantic writers, than those who pursue so-called classic authors'.[6] Hungry for an absolute rhythm, but forbidden to seek for a definition of it: Romantic poets often seemed to feel that their art condemned them to the pursuit of a ghost.

But before we return to follow the spectre of Rhythm, it is worth examining further the Romantic notion of the history of French verse, for the sense it gives of the basic values espoused by the Romantics themselves. Those values, which are at work in the poetry of Mallarmé as much as in that of Baudelaire, Nerval, Gautier and Banville, are perfectly expressed in the metaphors used by Banville when describing the evolution of French verse.

They are metaphors built around the notions of death and rebirth, of sterility and fertility. Death and sterility are associated with tradition, convention, repetition; life and fertility are the products of individual freedom and effort, unpredictable, always original, impossible to regulate. The poetry of the eighteenth century was flat, mechanical and lifeless because it was rule-bound and bowed to authority; the poetry of the sixteenth and nineteenth centuries was alive because it was the constantly renewed result of the poet's struggle. One word, used by Banville, Nerval, Gautier, Hugo and many others, sums up both the sense that the nineteenth century represented a rebirth of poetry, and the proud claim that the poetic quality of the sixteenth century had been rediscovered: renaissance.

> It must be difficult for the present generation to imagine the spiritual effervescence of that age; a movement like that of the Renaissance was taking place ... It was as if we had rediscovered the great forgotten secret, and indeed we had, we had rediscovered poetry.[7]

But what was the secret of poetry, that had thus been forgotten and rediscovered? The French Romantic definition of poetry varies, of course, from poet to poet, but there is one essential feature from which it can always be recognized. It is closely connected with the metaphors of rebirth and of originality mentioned above. It is this: the force of Romantic poetry wells up from an always obscure depth, and inscribes itself in poetic discourse both in a formal beauty which has always characterized its manifestations, and as a disruption of the known and the accepted. Its expression (but expression is hardly the right word, since, despite all, its source remains mysterious, remains half-hidden) must always be new, because it cannot be held still by rule, explanation or example, but must be caught on the up-swing.

Caught on the up-swing: there is, of course, a paradox in that notion, since if it were caught, it would cease to swing up, cease to be force. The poetry of the period exists, indeed, in a state of paradox. On the one hand, it must hold and represent its secret; on the other, it must be dominated by that secret, unable to fix it, wind-blown by its force.

This definition of poetry corresponds to a peculiar moment in the history of human ideals. It has often been said that the literature of the time was marked by an inability to accept that God had died. This contention, however, is at best a half-truth. God, for most of the poets of Hugo's and of Banville's generations, was not dead; he was merely hiding. It was not divinity, but the face of the Divinity that had vanished. Poetry was, as much as ever, seen as a sacred activity; the difference was that instead of being about a God whose life-story could be found in the Bible, it was concerned with a more absolute, less definable principle, which, unlike the God of the Catholic tradition, gave no clear orders, and seemed to refuse reduction to human time or reason. Just as they rejected Boileau's rules for regulating rhythm, but in the name of a freer, purer, more vertiginously absolute Rhythm, so the Romantic poets rejected the God of the Bible and his rules, but in the name of a purer, more distant, more absolute ideal.

Of course, the rejection of Boileau's rules and the rejection of the rules of God created a poetic principle with a less stable basis. The Romantic definition of poetry which I have given above could be called formal, in that it defines the way in which poetic discourse relates to its central subject, but does not define the subject itself – except negatively, by refusing it the right to inhabit the world of things that can be satisfactorily fixed, once and for all, in language. Such a mobile and invisible subject, though it could be conceived of as a divinity, did not need to be so; and it seems that, in the course of the century, while poets continued to refer themselves to an ideal, they gradually ceased to feel the need to equate that ideal with a divinity that existed before and outside the mind of man. Did Baudelaire, Rimbaud, Lautréamont, Mallarmé believe in God? The question is, in the end, irrelevant; because whatever they believed in, it does not speak with the authority of the Christian God. Whatever speaks, in their work, has no absolute authority; and wherever the ideal is, it does not speak. This slow fading of the absolute God is paralleled, though with a time-lag of three or four decades, by a slow fading of the absolute Rhythm. But that is another story, to which we will return in Chapter 11.

I should like, at this point, to illustrate my Romantic definition of poetry with a few examples, taken from poets with very different ideas of what the subject of poetry might be, in order to bring out the similarity in its operation, wherever it is situated.

Marceline Desbordes-Valmore was born in 1786 – twenty-four years after Chénier, and sixteen before Hugo. The 'génération de 1830' saw her, as it saw Chateaubriand, Lamartine and Vigny, as one of the precursors of its movement, a herald of the new Renaissance. Though relatively little read today, she was widely admired by other poets in her lifetime. Even Baudelaire, who normally maintained that women were unable to appreciate, let alone to create art, had more praise for her than for any other French poet born before 1810 except Hugo. In his essay on her, Baudelaire is, of course, concerned to prevent his admiration for a poetess from invalidating his standard misogyny; so he characterizes the talents which she indubitably possesses as 'feminine', while suggesting that there are other, 'male' talents which she lacks. However, 'feminine' or not, the talents which he attributes to her are certainly peculiarly Romantic:

> Hers are great and vigorous qualities which make an indelible mark on memory, profound breaches made suddenly, unexpectedly, in the heart, magic explosions of passion.[8]

What appears through the breaches she creates in the heart? What is the magic force of her explosions? In one sense, the answer is clear enough. Desbordes-Valmore is primarily a poet of love; of love for lovers, for children, and in her political poems for the suffering people. It is that love which creates the explosions, and it is the frustration of love which creates the breaches in the heart. Indeed, most of her poems are about love frustrated – usually by death, infidelity or absence. Many commentators on her work have portrayed her as a sort of *mater dolorosa*. This is easy enough to do; all her children except one died before her, and she had more than one unhappy love-affair. But this biographical explanation does not account for the fact that the very poetic quality of her writing seems inseparable from her experience of loss. A historian of the poetic idea must be concerned to ask why it is that poetry, for her, should have had such a privileged relationship with the frustration of love. And the answer to that question is perhaps clearest in those poems where the obstacle to love does not take the form of an irreversible separation, such as death; in other words, where the removal of the obstacle could be envisaged. For in such poems, we can see how the removal of the obstacle would threaten the poetic effect.

La Jalousie

Qu'as-tu fait d'un aveu doux à ton espérance?
Mes pleurs, qu'en as-tu fait? ton bonheur d'un moment.
Les secrets de mon âme ont aigri ta souffrance,
Et pour y croire enfin, tu voulus un serment.

Le serment est livré: tu ne crois pas encore.
Tu doutes des parfums en respirant les fleurs;
Tu voudrais ajouter des rayons à l'aurore,
Au soleil des flambeaux, à l'iris des couleurs.

Incrédule, inquiète, ingrate jalousie!
Amour, aveugle amour qui méconnaît l'amour,
Qui regarde un ciel pur, et demande le jour!
Oh! que je ... que je t'aime, aimable frénésie![9]

(Jealousy

(What did you make of a confession that flattered your hopes?
What did you make of my tears? but a moment's happiness.
The secrets of my soul sharpened your suffering,
And you demanded an oath, so that you might at last believe.

The oath has been sworn; still you do not believe.
While breathing flowers you doubt their perfume;
You would have rays added to the dawn,
Torches to the sun, colours to the spectrum.

Incredulous, insecure, ungrateful jealousy!
Love, blind love that cannot recognize love!
Which sees a pure blue sky, and calls out for daylight!
Oh! how I ... how I love you, lovable frenzy!)

One gust of the 'vent révolutionnaire' which was blowing on the alexandrine can be felt in this poem: it is in the peculiar hesitation and repetition in the last line, which, like many of Hugo's most daring rhythmic innovations, seems to reproduce an impassioned speech rhythm – and a sort of foreseeable surprise.

Up to that line, the poem scarcely seems to be in praise of jealousy. Jealousy is presented as an irrational impulse which, as soon as it receives what it asks for, demands more – even when that 'more' is impossible. It is a desire apparently for something concrete – a promise, a tear, light, colour, perfume –, but in fact for a certainty which it cannot name, and which is beyond the concrete. It seems an attempt to pierce its apparent object, to find beyond it a form of that object which would be more real – or perhaps less real, in that it would be less contingent, more absolute. Plainly, to the object which it seeks thus to pierce, it is destructive in its refusal to satisfy its hunger with earthly food. So one might suppose that the poet, frustrated by this unreasonable passion, would react against it. And that is indeed the implication of the first 'que je ...' One expects some violent reaction against the perverse demands of jealousy.

But no. After a pause, the lover states that she loves this jealousy. Or rather, she states that she loves an 'aimable frénésie', addressed in the second person – as her lover, and not his jealousy, had been in the rest of the poem. Is it really jealousy that is this 'frénésie'? or the lover? or his love? or the whole emotional nexus evoked in the poem? If it is the latter, then one could contend that it is the poetic frenzy itself. For the force of Romantic poetry is, in a sense, nothing other than this: a passion that appears to attach itself to a real object, but is in fact directed by an image beyond that object, beyond reality, impossible to grasp; a passion destructively impractical and an endless source of tears, but none the less, somehow, preferable to any other. It is an image that provokes the desire which makes, to use Baudelaire's word, a 'trouée', a breach in the heart; it is an image which appears beyond that 'trouée'. Nothing real can have the desired effect. And had the last line of this poem not been in praise of an unreasonable frenzy, had it merely castigated jealousy, as if to abolish jealousy would simply bring peace, it would not have been a Romantic poem. There is no Romantic love without frustration.

Hernani, written at about the same time as this poem, also concerns itself with love; and it is clear in the play, too, that there can be no Romantic love without frustration. Death, indeed, is as present in the play, and as closely associated with passion, as it is in Desbordes-Valmore's poems. It may seem paradoxical that a movement which thought of itself as a renaissance, a rebirth, fighting sterility and promoting a resurgence in poetic energy, should be so fixated on frustration. But the paradox is only apparent. For to the Romantic mind, a desire satisfied is a dead desire. A passion which can be contented by real objects is condemned to be as simple, as obvious, as shallow and as repetitive as the alexandrine according to Boileau. The force of the poetic rebirth is that of an aspiration, an aspiration to and of something always beyond reach, an image beyond an image. One could say, indeed, that the Romantic rebirth was a perpetual travail; its Messiah, its truth incarnate, was always on the way, but must never arrive. The Catholic Church was surely right to mistrust the spirit of the new literature.

It was Gérard de Nerval who provided the subtlest poetic description of the situation of the Romantic Messiah. 'Le Christ aux Oliviers' is a series of five sonnets, first published in 1844, which portrays a Christ who has sounded the heavens – and failed to find a positive God. This failure, however, does not lead to simple materialism. The universe that Christ discovers has no visible guiding spirit; but it does have an extraordinary profundity. The shadow of its mystery lies across our world; and it is into that mystery that life leads us.

> En cherchant l'œil de Dieu, je n'ai vu qu'une orbite
> Vaste, noire et sans fond, d'où la nuit qui l'habite
> Rayonne sur le monde et s'épaissit toujours;
>
> Un arc-en-ciel étrange entoure ce puits sombre,
> Seuil de l'ancien chaos dont le néant est l'ombre,
> Spirale engloutissant les Mondes et les Jours![10]
>
> (Seeking the eye of God, I saw only an orbit,[11]
> Vast, black, and bottomless, inhabited by a night
> Constantly thickening, which radiates onto the world;
>
> Surrounding this dark well, a strange rainbow,
> Threshold of the ancient chaos whose shadow is the abyss;
> Spiral swallowing up Worlds and Days!)

There is a 'rayonnement', a source of illumination in this universe; but it is a negative illumination, a black light, from which comes, not knowledge, but ignorance. The more we look, the less we are certain – except of the necessary, life-preserving distance that separates us from the source and end of all.

This truth, of course, is distressing. It was distressing to Nerval, who more than once said that it would, perhaps, have been more comfortable to be able to believe, naïvely, in a simple religion. But for him as for his Christ, it was too late.

Given that fact, there was a practical question to be answered. God was the source of authority; even after stating that he does not exist, Christ continues, in Nerval's poem, to address him as 'Father', and his life's work, the establishment of his religion, would collapse without at least the shadow of that authority. It is clear that even after the death of the Father, something like his authority is wanted.

The doom-laden but, in the end, symbiotic relationship between the desire for and the denial of authority is one of the central sources of Romantic poetic tension. In this work, that relationship is balanced in a typically tortuous way. On the one hand, Christ, on an immediate, emotional level, is unable to live without a master, without someone whose exercise of force will create a continuing drama, and thus give him a role to play. As is usually the case in Romantic poetry (especially in Baudelaire's work), the character who exercises that force, acting to allow this life to continue, is evil.

> Mais prêt à défaillir et sans force penché,
> Il appela le *seul* – éveillé dans Solyme:
>
> 'Judas! lui cria-t-il, tu sais ce qu'on m'estime,
> Hâte-toi de me vendre, et finis ce marché:
> Je suis souffrant, ami! sur la terre couché . . .
> Viens! ô toi qui, du moins, as la force du crime!'
>
> (But near faltering, bent, without strength,
> He called on the *only one* – awake in Salem:
>
> 'Judas! he cried, you know how I am valued;
> Sell me without delay, conclude the bargain;
> I suffer, friend! as I lie on the earth . . .
> Come! you who have, at least, the strength of crime!')

Crime has strength; the ideal, in the end, has none. The true Romantic always places in positions of power those who will act to cause disaster. In *Hernani*, to take another, less subtle example, the stranger who knocks on the door at the beginning is responsible for the failure of the hero Hernani's initial plans to elope with his beloved; he turns out to be none other than the Emperor Charles V. In the final act of the play, Hernani has overcome the Emperor's resistance to his marriage – only to be stopped by another authority-figure, his beloved's uncle, who, reminding Hernani of an oath he had sworn on the head of his father, demands that he kill himself. Those who aspire to an absolute, whether in love or in religion, needs to be frustrated by worldly authority. In 'Le Christ aux Oliviers', Caesar symbolizes that authority; Judas and Pilate are its agents.

Frustration alone is not enough, though. The Romantic poem also requires the constant rebirth of idealizing aspiration. The question is: how could such aspiration find the force to refuel itself? Since God cannot be found, one might think that in 'Le Christ aux Oliviers', the authority of Caesar would be impossible to challenge, and any opposition to it would soon appear futile. The only effective force appears to be of this world.

Fortunately, there is another source of power at work in the poem. The defeated Christ, despite his terror and submission, causes the universe to tilt on its axis, and shifts Caesar's world towards the abyss. Why? Where does his power come from? Precisely from that insane courage which led to his downfall. He had gone as far as one can towards the eye of darkness. And that journey leads back to the mystery of creation.

> L'augure interrogeait le flanc de la victime,
> La terre s'enivrait de ce sang précieux ...
> L'univers étourdi penchait sur ses essieux,
> Et l'Olympe un instant chancela vers l'abîme.
>
> 'Réponds! criait César à Jupiter Ammon,
> Quel est ce nouveau dieu qu'on impose à la terre?
> Et si ce n'est un dieu, c'est au moins un démon ...'
>
> Mais l'oracle invoqué pour jamais dut se taire;
> Un seul pouvait au monde expliquer ce mystère:
> – Celui qui donna l'âme aux enfants du limon.
>
> (The augurer interrogated the victim's entrails,
> The precious blood made the earth drunk ...
> The dazed universe tilted on its axles,
> And for an instant Olympus stumbled towards the abyss.
>
> 'Answer! cried Caesar to Jupiter Ammon,
> Who is this new god being imposed on the earth?
> And if he is no god, he is at least a devil ...'
>
> But the invoked oracle was silenced for ever;
> Only one could explain this mystery to the world:
> – He who gave a soul to the children of clay.)

Who is this mysterious and unique provider of soul? Obviously not Caesar, nor anyone on this earth. It cannot be Christ's God, since he is apparently dead. Nor can it be some older god, since the 'mystère' which he alone could explain involves the demise of previous religions. The answer is at once infinitely simple, and infinitely complex. He is someone about whom we can know almost nothing except the form of his mystery. To investigate that form is to court death, and to renew life.

The peculiar twist in the tail at the end of 'Le Christ aux Oliviers' (the lines quoted above are the last of the poem) is similar, in one important way, to that at the end of 'La Jalousie': Nerval, like Desbordes-Valmore, appears to give a positive value to a kind of force which had previously been presented as treacherous. In the work of Baudelaire, positive values are harder to find. None the less, twists in the tail are quite common. And Baudelaire's twists, like Nerval's, refuse to let us think we know where truth comes from.

His sonnet 'Remords posthume' (Posthumous Remorse) has, like 'La Jalousie' and 'Le Christ aux Oliviers', a theme which initially appears conventional. The poet, addressing his 'belle ténébreuse' (dark beauty), predicts what she will hear when she has exchanged her life of non-chalance, pleasure and luxury for the immobility of a damp grave. The tomb, he says,

> Te dira: 'Que vous sert, courtisane imparfaite,
> De n'avoir pas connu ce que pleurent les morts?'
> – Et le ver rongera ta peau comme un remords.[12]

> (Will say to you: 'What good has it done you, imperfect courtesan,
> Not to have known what the dead weep?' –
> And the worm will gnaw your skin like a pang of remorse.)

At first sight, this might appear a standard reproach for a wasted life. But it is by no means clear in what sense, or from what moral point of view, the courtesan's life has been wasted; for there is no indication of what might have constituted a better life. In fact, the tomb's words are magnificently obscure. What is it that the dead weep, and that the courtesan has not known? Is it life, which they have lost, or a secret normally revealed only to the dead? Should the courtesan have tried to learn this secret, whatever it is? Would it have done her any good if she had? Does the poet know it, and if so, what good has it done him? Will he not feel the remorse which he ascribes to her?

As one meditates on the tomb's words, they at once become steadily more enigmatic, and turn into a peculiarly acute questioning of the poet's apparently superior stance. Like the certainty of being loved in 'La Jalousie', the secret which would allow us to understand how and why to judge the courtesan slips away. It is at once created and rendered quite invisible by the images, of death, of idle luxury, of the worm of remorse, of after-life, behind which it seems to lurk. The force of the poem derives again from an impossible, unsettling desire, that seems to feed on but never to be content with a real, living relationship; it is unbalanced by the search for an uncertifiable certitude.

There are relatively few examples in Baudelaire's verse of the kind of dramatic rhythmic irregularity which sets off *Hernani*. The three lines quoted above, all end-stopped and with reasonably secure caesuras, are quite typical. It is as if Baudelaire, aware of the need for both regularity and irregularity in poetry (he liked to say that the two fundamental requirements of the human spirit were monotony and surprise), had transferred the irregularity in his verse from the formal rhythm to the sense. Many readers find that the smooth rhythms of Baudelaire's poems lull them into a sense of security, of reliable formal beauty which serves as a kind of tether for aspirations so vertiginous that they threaten the hold of words. On close reading, one almost always finds that the subjects of Baudelaire's poems are either as provocatively elusive as 'what the dead weep', or aggressive, even sadistic in their refusal of the bourgeois search for stable, regulated satisfaction in this life. Certainly, even if Boileau had passed Baudelaire's verse for scansion, he would have balked at its content – as, indeed, did the public prosecutor in 1857, when Baudelaire first published his book of verse, *Les Fleurs du Mal*: he was fined for outraging public decency ('outrage à la morale publique et aux bonnes mœurs'), and ordered to remove six poems from his book. The essence of Romanticism is not in the external form of its revolution; it is in the way in which it needs to revolt.

The revolt of Stéphane Mallarmé seemed to many to be against sense itself – and in a way, it is. Born some twenty years after Baudelaire, and forty after Hugo, he was much influenced by both in his youth, but went further than either in his rejection of comfortable convention in verse. He liked to distinguish between two types of language; one, journalistic, was to be used in politics, economics, and other such contingent and narrowly contextualized spheres of human activity; the other, poetic, sought to evoke 'autre chose' (something else), a principle at once of beauty and of rhythm, and the original source of those aspirations which, in their debased form, attempted to satisfy themselves through journalistic language. Mallarmé's 'something else' was at least as inaccessible as Baudelaire's secret, or certitude for the jealous lover. But, unlike his predecessors, he was never content to portray the effect on a character of a Romantic aspiration. He compulsively questioned the fundamental, unchanging forms of that aspiration, and the ways in which it operated. The lessons which he learnt from that questioning were not and could not be presented as discursive philosophical argument; for they concerned a type of desire beyond the reach of the discursive. Rather, he integrated those lessons into his poetry, which he turned into the stage for the drama of poetic aspiration itself. In that drama, the role of Rhythm is multiple and central.

Une dentelle s'abolit
Dans le doute du Jeu suprême
A n'entr'ouvrir comme un blasphème
Qu'absence éternelle de lit.

Cet unanime blanc conflit
D'une guirlande avec la même,
Enfui contre la vitre blême
Flotte plus qu'il n'ensevelit.

Mais, chez qui du rêve se dore
Tristement dort une mandore
Au creux néant musicien

Telle que vers quelque fenêtre
Selon nul ventre que le sien,
Filial on aurait pu naître.[13]

(A piece of lace abolishes itself
In the doubt of the supreme Game
To half-open as if a blasphemy
Nothing but bed's eternal absence.

This unanimous white conflict
Of one garland with the same
Flown against the window-pane
Floats more than it buries.

But, in the home of the dream-gilded one,
A mandola sadly sleeps
In the hollow musical nothingness

Such that towards some window
According to no other belly
As a son one might have been born.)

Like every late Mallarmé poem, this sonnet gives the reader a lot of work
to do. The concrete objects mentioned – bed, lace, window, mandola (the
mandola was a lute-like instrument used in the Renaissance) – inspire the
urge to construct an image, a scene, a tableau in the mind's eye; and the
'Mais' (But) seems to indicate a shift in that tableau, an event. But what
scene? what shift? The clearest feature of the tableau seems to be blanks –
hollows, emptinesses, absences. And indeed, the commonest interpreta-
tion of the scene is as a bedroom with no bed in it, seen through lace
curtains that have nothing to hide.
But the space which those curtains vainly defend is the fertile one of

dreams. No birth will take place there; but in the multiple hollows evoked, by their presence or absence – bed, bedroom, the belly of the musical instrument, which sadly sleeps – one might have been able to be born. Who might? according, precisely, to whose belly (Mallarmé's possessive pronoun 'sien' could mean 'hers', 'its' or 'his', so to preserve the ambiguity I have not translated it)? As whose son? And under what circumstances? These questions only matter in that, like the curtains, they veil the fertile space. It is and remains unreal, denied; yet in the poem, and thanks to the rhythm of the poem, it acquires a strange kind of existence.

The lines of this sonnet, like those of Baudelaire's 'Remords posthume', are, on the whole, comfortably end-stopped. Like the music evoked by the mandola, like lace-work, this sonnet makes use of a traditional rhythmic scheme; and there is a dance, a play of appearance and disappearance, here as in most of Mallarmé's work, which makes the reader feel in the presence of an unmistakable and constant pulse. Yet these rhythms are always also disturbed, made uncomfortable; and that disturbance is also produced, in a sense, by rhythm – by the bizarre and complex sense-rhythms of Mallarmé's syntax, and by the rhythms of the poem's sounds: the dense repetition of sounds in 'Tristement dort une mandore' and 'Telle que vers quelque fenêtre', for example, seem to expand and perturb the metre as much as Hugo's 'Dérobé'. One might say that the characteristic texture of Mallarmé's poetry is that of recognizable patterns disrupted by other recognizable patterns just enough to suggest the space where another kind of pattern, less concrete, less analysable, more ideal, might have existed.

Mallarmé's ideals are far from the world of positive facts, and that which is born in his poems has but a tenuous life, and dies often. Indeed, it dies every time there is a positive attempt to regulate it. But its death, like the death of poetry at the hands of Boileau, is not definitive. From the Romantic genius, in the end, the secret is always reborn; the secret, at least, of pretending that a secret exists, and of longing for it.

Visions and Voices: the Nature of Inspiration from Romanticism to the Birth of Surrealism

KEITH ASPLEY

The famous letters addressed by Rimbaud in May 1871 to Georges Izambard and Paul Demeny respectively (the so-called 'Lettres du voyant') clearly reveal that he believed that a poet's visionary power is a crucial criterion for judging him: both generations of Romantics are assessed in relation to their prowess in this domain: 'The first Romantics were *seers* without really realizing it. ... Lamertine is sometimes a seer, but he is stifled by his archaic poetic form. In the last poems of the too mulish Hugo there is a lot of the seer. ... The second Romantics are very *visionary*: Th. Gautier, Lec. de Lisle, Th. de Banville. But since exploration of the invisible and hearing of the unheard is not the same as recapturing the spirit of things dead, Baudelaire is the first seer, the king of poets, *a veritable god*' (*PSI*, 204–05).[1] Yet despite this praise, Baudelaire was not perfect, in Rimbaud's eyes at least: 'He lived in too artistic a milieu; and the form of his poems, that has been so highly vaunted, is petty: discoveries of the unknown demand new forms' (*PSI*, 205).

As the strictures on Lamartine and Baudelaire show, there was a fundamental problem of finding an adequate means of translating the vision into words, a problem recognized by Wordsworth in *The Prelude*:

> but I should need
> Colours and words that are unknown to man,
> To paint the visionary dreariness.

In the 1820s Alphonse de Lamartine planned, and even began to write, a vast epic to be entitled *Les Visions*. The different sections of *La Chute d'un ange* (1838) were designated 'Visions'. In the evocation of its heroine, Daïdha, he writes of 'a vision of Eve', but here the term seems to be employed rather loosely: many a beautiful woman on earth could inspire such a thought.

A few days after the idea of *Les Visions* first came to him, Lamartine presented the experience as a veritable moment of inspiration: 'As I left Naples on Saturday 20 January I was illuminated by a ray from on high: I have conceived. I feel myself to be a great poet.'[2] The sceptic might wonder whether he was merely seeking to forge or foster his own particular poetic persona. Nevertheless, influenced by thinkers such as Louis-Claude de Saint-Martin, Lamartine often portrayed himself as one of the 'men of desire', or to use the Hugolian term, one of the 'magi', a poet-prophet with a mission to pass on to ordinary mortals his own insights. In the 'Fragment du Livre Primitif', the eighth 'vision' of *La Chute d'un ange*, for example, he proclaims (ll. 283–90):

> Il est parmi les fils les plus doux de la femme
> Des hommes dont les sens obscurcissent moins l'âme,
> Dont le cœur est mobile et profond comme l'eau,
> Dont le moindre contact fait frissonner la peau,
> Dont la pensée en proie à de sacrés délires
> S'ébranle au doigt divin, chante comme des lyres,
> Mélodieux échos semés dans l'univers
> Pour comprendre sa langue et noter ses concerts.   (*LP*, 274)

> (There are amongst the gentler sons of woman
> Some men whose souls the senses conceal less,
> Whose hearts are deep and mobile as the waves,
> Whose skin can tremble at the slightest touch,
> Whose thought, a prey to sacred frenzies,
> Moves with God's finger, sings like lyres,
> Melodious echoes scattered through the universe
> To comprehend its tongue and note its harmonies.)

Yet near the beginning of the same poem (ll. 53–6, 81–4) he seems suspicious of those who claimed to have *seen* the Divine:

> Si quelqu'un parmi vous, soleils, ma créature,
> Hommes, anges, esprits, dit: J'ai vu sa figure,
> L'invisible à nos yeux visible est apparu;
> Pitié, dérision sur ceux qui l'auront cru. [...]

> Le seul œil qui me voit c'est votre intelligence:
> Force qui ne connaît ni masse ni distance,
> Substance transparente où mon ombre se peint,
> Nuit qui de ma clarté s'illumine et se teint!   (*LP*, 268–9)

(If anyone among you, suns, my creature,
Men, angels, spirits, proclaims: 'I have seen his face,
The invisible has appeared before my eyes';
Pity, derision on those who give it credence. [. . .]

The only eye that sees me is your intelligence:
A force that knows nor mass nor distance,
A transparent stuff on which my shade is painted,
The night which by my brightness is illumined and tinted.)

Indeed, with Lamartine, who certainly did not reject the role of reason, it seems to be more frequently a case of reflection, or meditation, than veritable vision; the title of the collection that first made his name was *Méditations*. Although this contains poems with such titles as 'Dieu', 'La Prière', 'La Foi', 'Génie', probably the most famous of all is 'Le Lac' (or 'Le Lac de B.'), which is reflective, nostalgic, and simply lyrical, rather than visionary.

It has been claimed that the 'Fragment du Livre Primitif' was possibly in the memory of Victor Hugo when he composed 'Ce que dit la bouche d'ombre'.[3] It has also been claimed that *La Chute d'un ange* is, with 'Ce que dit la bouche d'ombre', the great philosophical poem of the nineteenth century.[4] Commentators on Hugo's poem, the penultimate and arguably the most powerful one in *Les Contemplations* (1856), initially tended to concentrate more on the message – such themes as the Great Chain of Being, metempsychosis, animism, free will, love, suffering, redemption – than the medium, but more recently some critics have begun to turn the spotlight on the writing and the rhetoric.[5] The rhetoric involves the creation of a persona, a speaking voice. Hugo makes it evident that here he is playing the role of an intermediary between his fellow-men and the divine, or the Muse, or whatever else the 'mouth of shadow' might purport to be. His situation is comparable with that of St John on Patmos, but at the start of the poem itself Hugo tells how he was wandering near the dolmen above Rozel when he was borne away to the top of the rock by a spectre who proceeded to dictate the remainder of the text.

In the opening lines of this 'oration' (ll. 7–10 of the poem) visions and voices, sight and hearing are brought together in a curious image:

Sache que tout connaît sa loi, son but, sa route;
Que, de l'astre au ciron, l'immensité s'écoute;
Que tout a conscience en la création;
Et l'oreille pourrait avoir sa vision.   (*LC*, 462)

(Understand that everything knows his law, his goal, his path;
That from the star to the mite the boundless cosmos listens to itself;
That everything in creation has a conscience;
And that the ear might have its vision.)

One notes the Pascalian ring of the second line of this sequence, the Swedenborgian note in the suggestion of 'correspondences', the indication of a universal animism. More than once in this poem Hugo skilfully, or so it seems, plays on an opposition between dialogue and monologue; in l. 11 he writes 'Car les choses et l'être ont un grand dialogue' (For there is a great dialogue between things and being); in l. 51 the mysterious speaker utters the first-person plural imperative, 'Causons' (Let us chat), pauses, but then, in fact, resumes his monologue to the no doubt awe-struck poet; but seen or heard from another angle, Hugo the poet continues his lesson to his reader. As Lamartine had already suggested, Hugo is told, or tells, that real revelation must wait until death:

> Un jour, dans le tombeau, sinistre vestiaire,
> Tu le sauras; la tombe est faite pour savoir;
> Tu verras; aujourd'hui tu ne peux qu'entrevoir,
> Mais, puisque Dieu permet que ma voix t'avertisse,
> Je te parle.   (*LC*, 468)

> (One day, within the tomb, the sinister antechamber,
> You shall know; the grave is made for knowing;
> You shall see; today you can but glimpse;
> But since God lets me warn you with my voice,
> I address you,)

For Hugo (or the spectre) it is not merely a question of the sounds of nature but a *message* the natural world transmits to all who can listen with an attentive and responsive ear, as l. 41 indicates: 'Tout dit dans l'infini quelque chose à quelqu'un' (Everything in the infinite says something to somebody). The poet, or the reader, or mankind, is invited to draw closer and *look* (ll. 228–31):

> Viens, si tu l'oses;
> Regarde dans ce puits morne et vertigineux,
> De la création compte les sombres nœuds,
> Viens, vois, sonde.   (*LC*, 470)

> (Come, if you dare!
> Look into this dismal, giddying pit
> And count creation's sombre knots,
> Come, look, investigate.)

On the face of it, the speaker and his kind are the 'voyants du ciel supérieur' (seers of the upper reaches of heaven) in l. 361, and his listener is the 'songeur' (dreamer) two lines later, but since we know that, at one level, Hugo himself is the author of these words, he himself would be ranked among the visionaries.

After 680 alexandrines in *rimes plates*, the poem ends with 16 sextains, rhyming *aabccb*, in which the third and sixth lines are hexasyllabic. This formal change reflects a movement from a review of the present to a more than utopian vision of the future in which, for example, God Himself will no longer be able to distinguish Belial (or Satan) from Jesus; and by the end the listener's visionary qualities seem to be on a par with those of his interlocutor (ll. 776–7):

> Et, quand ils seront près des degrés de lumière
> Par nous seuls aperçus   (*LC*, 487)

> (And when they are near the grades of light
> Perceived by us alone)

It is difficult in Hugo's case to evaluate fully the importance of spiritualism for this conception of the sacred mission of the poet. Among his fellow-exiles on Jersey in 1853 was Mme de Girardin, the wife of the editor of *La Presse* and a poet in her own right. She believed in spirits and organized seances involving table-turning. Hugo was convinced when he heard the voice of his daughter Léopoldine who had been drowned ten years previously and was not sceptical even when the spirits of Aeschylus, Dante and Shakespeare addressed him in French, in alexandrines. Hugo is certainly on record as stating that the 'experience of the tables' confirmed beliefs he already held: 'The truths that man discovers need to be confirmed by God. Fifteen years ago I found the ones that emerged from the phenomenon of the tables. I have written a book about these very truths.'[6]

In 'Les Mages', another poem from the final book of *Les Contemplations*, Hugo argues forcefully that poets are the real priests, the inspired ones. In ll. 269–70 they are 'ces contemplateurs pâles/Penchés dans l'éternel effroi' (those pallid contemplators/Bowed in endless awe). In one stanza (the thirtieth) they are successively 'messiahs', 'poets', 'apostles', 'prophets'. In two of its melodramatic exclamations the emphasis is placed on the act of *looking*: 'Comme ils regardent!' (How they look!) and 'Quels spectateurs démesurés!' (What inordinate spectators!); and in stanza 36 they are depicted fully engaged in their questing:

> Eux, ils parlent à ce mystère,
> Ils interrogent l'éternel,
> Ils appellent le solitaire,
> Ils montent, ils frappent au ciel.
> Disent; es-tu là?   (*LC*, 446)

(*They* speak to that mystery,
They examine the eternal,
They call out to the solitary,
They ascend and knock at heaven's door
And say: Are you there?)

This lengthy poem of 710 lines not only lists the men Hugo regards as magi, from Isaiah and Virgil to Piranesi and Beethoven, but also evokes some of their attributes: the bright ray that links their soul to the eye of Jehovah, their souls bared before God but seeing the Unknown, and above all their capacity to see and hear.

As a metaphor of the visionary, the choice of the astronomer Herschel in stanza 49 is possibly the most interesting, since for a man of Hugo's generation he would represent the scientist whose exploration of the physical universe took him, through the agency of his eyes and his telescope at least, to its furthest confines; and in the penultimate *dizain* Hugo attempts once more to put into words the experience of *voyance*:

N'est-ce pas que c'est ineffable
De se sentir immensité,
D'éclairer ce qu'on croyait fable
A ce qu'on trouve vérité,
De voir le fond du grand cratère,
De sentir en soi du mystère
Entrer tout le frisson obscur,
D'aller aux astres, étincelle
Et de se dire: Je suis l'aile!
Et de se dire: J'ai l'azur! (*LC*, 457)

(Is it not ineffable
To feel immense,
To shed light on what one thought was fable
From what one finds is truth,
To see the bottom of the vast crater,
To feel the obscure shudder
Of mystery enter within one,
To fly to the stars like a spark
And to say to oneself: I am the wing!
And to say to oneself: I hold the blue of heaven!)

When Hugo appears to go over the top like this, it may be his attempt to convey something of the awe he feels in the face of the marvellous potential of language or the sublime mystery of poetry and creation. The Senegalese statesman-poet, L.S. Senghor, has related Hugo's mode of expression not only to the biblical prophets but also to the Bantu of his own continent: 'His vision is in depth. The Initiate is endowed with those

inner eyes that pierce the wall of appearances. It is thus that the image of
the visionary poet is *symbol*, or more exactly, contingent expression of the
moral world, the sole true one: *sense* by *sign*.'[7]

Alfred de Musset, on occasions, did raise his eyes to the skies and
meditate. In the second verse of 'Ballade à la Lune', he wonders:

> Lune, quel esprit sombre
> Promène au bout d'un fil,
>   Dans l'ombre,
> Ta face et ton profil?   (*MP*, 58)

> (Moon, what sombre spirit
> Dangles on the end of a thread
>   In the shadows
> Your face and your profile?)

but most of the time Musset portrays inspiration in its conventional
personified guise. One might well regard Hugo's 'bouche d'ombre' as a
dark avatar of the Muse; with Musset's series of 'Nights' we are left in
no doubt. 'La Nuit de mai', 'La Nuit d'août', 'La Nuit d'octobre' are
structured in the form of a dialogue between the poet and a female figure
who often sounds as much like a lover as Erato or Polymnia. In the first
poem in the series the opening words are given to 'La Muse': 'Poète,
prends ton luth et me donne un baiser' (Poet, take your lute and give me a
kiss), and her third 'speech' begins in a truly Dionysiac tone:

> Poète, prends ton luth; le vin de la jeunesse
> Fermente cette nuit dans les veines de Dieu.
> Mon sein est inquiet; la volupté l'oppresse,
> Et les vents altérés m'ont mis la lèvre en feu.
> O paresseux enfant! regarde, je suis belle.
> Notre premier baiser, ne t'en souviens-tu pas,
> Quand je te vis si pâle au toucher de mon aile,
> Et que, les yeux en pleurs, tu tombas dans mes bras?   (*MP*, 192)

> (Poet, take your lute; the wine of youth
> Ferments tonight within the veins of God.
> Uneasy is my breast, oppressed by pleasure,
> And thirsty winds have set my lips ablaze.
> O slothful child, look, I am beautiful.
> Do you not remember our first kiss,
> When I saw you so pale at the touch of my wing,
> And, with tearful eyes, you fell into my arms?)

Were it not for the reference to the wing at the end of the penultimate line
in this sequence, the reader could easily substitute for the Muse some very
real woman. In the exchange the figure of the Muse oscillates between her

immortal nature – at one point an insatiable spectre – and an all too human one, in which she is addressed successively as 'ma blonde', 'ma maîtresse et ma sœur'. Yet she plays her conventional role to the full, stimulating the poet to create and providing him with ideas:

> Inventons quelque part des lieux où l'on oublie;
> Partons, nous sommes seuls, l'univers est à nous.
> Voici la verte Ecosse et la brune Italie,
> Et la Grèce, ma mère, où le miel est si doux.   (*MP*, 193)

> (Let us invent somewhere places where one may forget;
> Let us depart, we are alone, the universe is ours.
> Behold the verdant Scotland and Italy the brown,
> And Greece, my mother, where honey is so sweet.)

These particular lines are trite. The two epithets of colour are almost redundant; the metaphor of 'ma mère' and the reference to 'le miel' are redeemed only by their alliteration. Yet Musset (or his Muse) on occasions does produce apparently very simple lines that have a strangely haunting quality: 'Les plus désespérés sont les chants les plus beaux' (The most despairing of songs are the finest of all). The paradoxical note is a hallmark of the famous Romantic irony.[8]

The special relationship between the poet and the Muse here has been explained in terms of two conflicting tendencies within the former, who becomes simultaneously an actor and a spectator.[9] One could see the Muse in Jungian terms as the Anima, the female element in the male, but at times in this poem this figure disguises a literary source, for example the list of Greek place-names that Musset took from Book II of the *Iliad* (Argos, Ptéléon, Messa, Pélion, Titarèse, Oloossone and Camyre, ll. 74–9), as if the Muse who spoke to Musset was indeed one of Homer's Muses of Olympus. This makes the verse sound somewhat secondhand. The legend of the pelican offering its own heart to feed its young – with its associations with Christ – seems melodramatic when applied to the poet, despite Musset's claim, a few lines from the end, that he has known martyrdom.

In 'La Nuit de décembre' the characteristic pattern of a dialogue between the poet and his Muse is replaced by a lengthy monologue from the former, followed right at the end by a so-called 'vision'. The monologue is initially a narrative, a series of anecdotes about meetings with his double. The verse-form then changes from sextains of octosyllabic lines to more complicated nine-line stanzas in which decasyllables and octosyllables alternate in a particular manner. Here the poet addresses a 'tu', who may be a previous lover.[10] In the penultimate stanza of this section of the poem she comes and sits on the poet's bed, but then he, in confusion or a state of delirium, wonders whether or not he is in fact contemplating his own image in a mirror or even the phantom of his youth. For the final three stanzas, Musset reverts to the pattern of octo-syllabic sextains in which the enigma is resolved, albeit in a paradoxical fashion: 'Ami, je suis la Solitude' (Friend, I am loneliness).

In his letter to Demeny Rimbaud poured scorn on the 'fourteen times execrable' Musset and his failure to *see*: 'Musset did not know how to do anything: there were visions behind the gauzy curtains, but he closed his eyes' (*PSI*, 205). The image of the 'gauzy curtains' may suggest that Rimbaud felt that Musset was too salon-bound, even too sheltered, despite his Don Juan side and despite his alcohol problems. The figure of the Muse implies that Musset examined the process of inspiration, but her frequent recourse to rhetorical questions in the three poems of the series in which she appears reveals that she often had no answers.

So how much of a *voyant* was Rimbaud himself? In both of the 'Lettres du voyant' he claimed that he was working at making himself into such a being, but it is in the one to Izambard that he explains what form this 'work' took: 'I am now going in for as much debauchery as possible. . . . It's a matter of arriving at the unknown by the disturbance (or the dissoluteness)[11] of *all the senses*. The suffering is enormous, but one must be strong, one must be born a poet, and I have recognized that I am a poet' (*PSI*, 200). This letter is not specific about the forms of debauchery that Rimbaud had in mind. It has been claimed that 'Matinée d'ivresse' may be the result of a hashish-induced hallucination. Apart from a reference in paragraph 1 to a 'poison' that will stay within the veins, the text's final word 'Assassins' has been used as justification for this theory, since etymologically this word comes from the Arabic for 'hashish-eater'.

Despite the apparent contradiction between the ideas of being 'born a poet' and of having 'to work to make oneself a poet', Rimbaud obviously believed that he had a poetic vocation. Certainly in a poem such as 'Le Bateau ivre' there are many images which demonstrate to the reader the power of the vision, the revelatory quality of the experience. A number of the quatrains begin with the key words 'J'ai vu' (I have seen). Others commence with variants, 'J'aurais voulu montrer', 'J'ai rêvé', 'J'ai suivi' (I would like to have shown, I have dreamed, I have followed) or with expressions that call into play other senses: 'J'ai heurté' (I have collided with). It is a well-known fact that when Rimbaud wrote 'Le Bateau ivre', he had not seen the sea. This prompts the query: what was the nature of the 'vision'? Was it entirely and pristinely personal? Was the poem the fruit of his reading? There are undoubtedly echoes of Hugo in places.[12] Jean Richer has offered a rather different kind of exegesis, suggesting, for example, the role played by the Tarot cards in the poem's composition.[13] We shall never know the full story. Certain of the expressions do seem to point to a visionary experience, e.g. 1. 40: 'Et j'ai vu quelquefois ce que l'homme a cru voir' (And I have sometimes seen what man has thought he saw). In an attempt to put into words the extraordinary or even the preternatural nature of the experience, Rimbaud has recourse to diverse devices: neologisms ('nacreux'), the use of the plural of words normally employed only in the singular ('bleuités', 'rousseurs', 'Florides'), but above all curious images (like the surreal apparent contradiction of 'les azurs verts').

The texts of *Une Saison en Enfer* and *Illuminations* are dotted with suggestions of strange poetic gifts. One paragraph in 'Adieu' is especially interesting and important from this point of view:

> Quelquefois je vois au ciel des plages sans fin couvertes de blanches nations en joie. Un grand vaisseau d'or, au-dessus de moi, agite ses pavillons multicolores sous les brises du matin. J'ai créé toutes les fêtes, tous les triomphes, tous les drames. J'ai essayé d'inventer de nouvelles fleurs, de nouveaux astres, de nouvelles chairs, de nouvelles langues. J'ai cru acquérir des pouvoirs surnaturels. Eh bien! je dois enterrer mon imagination et mes souvenirs! Une belle gloire d'artiste et de conteur emportée! (*PSI*, 151)

> (Sometimes I see in the sky endless beaches covered with joyous white nations. Above me a great golden vessel flaps its multi-coloured flags in the morning breeze. I have created every feast, every triumph, every drama. I have tried to invent new flowers, new stars, new flesh, new tongues. I believed I had acquired supernatural powers. Ah well! I must bury my imagination and my memories! That's the end of a glorious reputation as an artist and a storyteller!)

The image of the golden vessel in the skies is almost prophetic, like the 'navire en marche' in Hugo's 'Plein ciel'. It may also be hallucinatory like the Spanish galleon in Tournier's *Vendredi ou les limbes du Pacifique*, whose quick-work is golden too.[14] The 'vaisseau d'or' has also been explained in relation to Rimbaud's concept of the Alchemy of the Word,[15] which presumably evokes the transmutation of the base metal of ordinary discourse into verbal gold. The realization of the ambition to create new flowers and new stars would seemingly have placed the poet on a par with God, but the last two sentences of the paragraph contain a characteristic Rimbaldian admission of failure. Yet at the level of language he did invent not just a few new words but a host of novel images, many of which continue to baffle the would-be interpreter. It is significant that Rimbaud himself employs the verbs 'créer' and 'inventer' in the above paragraph, showing that he believed he was a veritable innovator and that he fully appreciated the etymological connection between 'poetry' and 'creation'. He terminates 'Parade' with the teasing declaration: 'J'ai seul la clef de cette parade sauvage' (I alone have the key to this wild parade – or perhaps the word 'parade' should be understood in terms of the 'curtain raiser', the show that took place outside the tent); and in 'Mauvais Sang' (Bad blood) he claimed, perhaps ironically, that what he said was oracular ('C'est oracle, ce que je dis'), but he instantly added another perplexing explanation: 'Je comprends, et ne sachant m'expliquer sans paroles païennes, je voudrais me taire' (I understand, but not knowing how to explain myself without using heathen words, I would prefer to remain silent). Rimbaud himself was thus aware that he was having to operate on the far frontier of communication.

In this respect he was unquestionably one of the main precursors of the Surrealists. Surrealism was at first defined in terms of automatic writing and began with an investigation of the subconscious as a possible source of poetry. That movement's chief theoretician, André Breton, believed that an important initiator was Tristan Corbière:

> It was undoubtedly with *Les Amours jaunes* that verbal automatism was installed in French poetry. Corbière must have been the first in date to be borne along by the wave of words which, beyond conscious control, expires every second on our ears and to which the common run of men opposes the barrier of immediate sense.[16]

Breton cited as supporting evidence Corbière's phrase 'Je parle sous moi' (I speak beneath me). It would be fascinating to know the precise nature of this special kind of *sotto voce* mode. If Breton's account of Corbière's method of composition is correct, the subconscious voice would appear to manifest itself in curious images or juxtapositions of words, like the line 'Dans un clair rayon de boue' (In a bright ray of mud) from the poem 'Après la pluie' (After the rain).[17] The use of rhyme, often very clever rhyme, which would suggest a fair degree of conscious control on Corbière's part, would camouflage what automatism there may have been. More recently P.-O. Walzer has argued that the reader's initial impression of an unrefined poetry is pure *trompe-l'oeil* and that in fact the manuscript evidence indicates careful re-working of the material. Walzer prefers to think in terms of an avalanche of words constantly generating other words rather than of dictation by the unconscious mind.[18]

Corbière without doubt exerted some influence on Jules Laforgue. Laforgue criticism has also highlighted the influence of the nineteenth-century German philosopher Eduard von Hartmann and his very personal conception of the unconscious, which is related to instinct. Laforgue may well have read the works of Hartmann, but the refinement of his own poems seems cerebrally controlled, as does the series of outlandish but intriguing neologisms such as 'sexciproques' and 'éternullité'. If he had lived long enough to be able to digest the very different presentation of the unconscious (or the subconscious) by Freud and Jung, his way of writing might not have been the same.

Breton certainly paid tribute to Freud in the first *Manifeste du surréalisme* (1924). Although a later chapter is devoted to that movement, it seems appropriate here to stress that the twin phenomena of visions and voices have continued to feature in French poetry in the twentieth century. The Surrealists were proud to bring back to prominence the role of inspiration in the creative process: in the *Second Manifeste du surréalisme* (1930) André Breton argues that it is inspiration that has 'catered for the supreme needs of expression at all times and in all places'.[19] Automatic writing, the discovery of which was really the starting-point of Surrealism, depended on the ability to make oneself receptive to the dictation of the subconscious voice. In the context of that movement, however, the strangest case is that of Robert Desnos. In the domain of voices, he claimed that all the 150 'aphorisms' of his 1923 collection entitled *Rrose Sélavy* were produced during hypnotic trances by telepathic communication across the Atlantic with the artist Marcel Duchamp. Duchamp himself had already published in the review *Littérature* a set of similar pronouncements using the oddly spelt pseudonym that Desnos borrowed for his title. Doubts have been cast on the authenticity of Desnos's claims, but the fact remains that we have the actual text, the end-product, regardless of the manner in which it was produced. Perhaps the individual examples read more like linguistic games or experiments relying on devices such as puns and spoonerisms than poetry proper, but that is largely a matter for the reader's judgment. The sentence that constitutes number 143 is 'Dites les transes de la confusion et non pas les contusions de la France' (Speak of the trances of confusion and not the contusions of France) (*CB*, 46).

The first crucial text for an appreciation of the 'vision' side of the Desnos diptych is his 'Journal d'une apparition',[20] in which he writes of a mysterious nocturnal visitor. In the introductory section he affirms:

> Mais je me refuserai toujours à classer parmi des hallucinations les visites nocturnes de ★★★ ou plutot je me refuserai, le mot hallucination étant admis, à le considérer comme une explication de ce qui pour le vulgaire est peut-être un phénomène mais qui ne saurait l'être pour moi.
>
> ★★★ est réellement venue chez moi. Je l'ai vue, je l'ai entendue, j'ai senti son parfum et parfois même elle m'a touché.[21]

> (But I shall always refuse to classify as hallucinations the nocturnal visits of ★★★ or rather I shall refuse, if the word hallucination is accepted, to consider it as an explanation of what is, for the common herd, perhaps a phenomenon but which could not be so for me. ★★★ really came to my apartment. I have seen her, heard her, smelt her perfume, and sometimes she even touched me.)

In one of the subsequent entries he adds:

> Et, doucement, sans bruit, ★★★ entre dans mon atelier. C'est elle, à n'en pas douter. Je reconnais son visage, sa démarche, l'expression de son sourire. Je reconnais encore sa robe: une robe très reconnaissable qu'elle ne porte que dans certaines circonstances.
>
> Elle s'approche de moi et s'assoit à quelque distance de mon lit, sur un fauteuil où j'ai posé mes vêtements avant de me coucher. Elle se pose commodément et me regarde fixement.[22]

> (And softly, without a sound, ★★★ enters my studio. It is her beyond doubt. I recognize her face, her walk, her smile. I also recognize her dress: a very distinctive dress that she wears only in certain circumstances.
>
> She comes up to me and sits down some distance from my bed, on an armchair where I put my clothes before getting into bed. She makes herself comfortable and stares at me.)

The figure seemed to Desnos to be surrounded by a bluish phosphorescent halo. The reader is obliged to speculate whether the night visitor actually was the singer Yvonne George, for whom the poet's love was unrequited, or rather some kind of 'apparition', as the title suggests, or simply a dream or a special manifestation of the Muse. We could also ask ourselves whether there is a distinction between a figment of the imagination and a creation of the imagination. The reader of the collection *A la Mystérieuse* (1926) is certainly tempted to wonder to what extent this curious experience was the source of some of its poems. In 'O douleurs de l'amour' (*CB*, 89), there are appeals to the 'muses of the desert' and the 'demanding muses' but also sentences that do resemble aspects of the descriptions in the diary entries:

> Mon rire et ma joie se cristallisent autour de vous. C'est votre fard, c'est votre poudre, c'est votre rouge, c'est votre sac de peau de serpent, c'est vos bas de soie … et c'est aussi ce petit pli entre l'oreille et la nuque, à la naissance du cou, c'est votre pantalon de soie et votre fine chemise et votre manteau de fourrure.

> (My joy and laughter crystallize around you. It's your make-up, your powder, your rouge, your snakeskin bag, your silk stockings … and it's also that little fold in the skin between your ear and the nape of your neck, it's your silk trousers and your fine blouse and your fur coat.)

And in the poem 'Vieille Clameur' (*CB*, 123) from the 1927 collection, *Les Ténèbres*, a shadowy figure slips into the poet's room in a way that recalls the stealthy entrance of the 'heroine' of the 'Journal d'une apparition':

> La serrure se ferme sur l'ombre et l'ombre met son oeil à la serrure
> Et voilà que l'ombre se glisse dans la chambre

La belle amante que voilà l'ombre plus charnelle que ne l'imagine perdu dans son
 blasphème le grand oiseau de fourrure blanche perché sur l'epaule de la belle
 de l'incomparable putain qui veille sur le sommeil

(The lock is fastened on the shadow and the shadow puts its eye to the lock
And behold the shadow slips into the bedroom
That beautiful lover there the shadow more carnal than is imagined lost in its
 blasphemy by the great bird of white fur perched on the shoulder of the
 beautiful the incomparable whore who watches over sleep)

The metamorphosis of the guardian angel into a prostitute is interesting
psychologically and may be seen as an expression of the poet's frustration
or jealousy or anger; and the extraordinary length of some of Desnos's
lines – the last one in this sequence is a good example – not only mirrors
the remarkable nature of the experience but also points to an uncontrolled
quality in the writing, no doubt this poet's individual brand of auto-
matism.

The varied nature of these visions and voices raises all kinds of questions,
fundamental and otherwise. To what extent was Desnos's night visitor
similar to the 'tu' at the end of Musset's 'Nuit de décembre', ultimately
revealed to be Solitude, who ostensibly came to sit on the poet's bed?
Are hallucinations, certain preternatural or even 'out of body' experiences
extreme forms of the phenomenon of inspiration? Or should they, in the
context of poetic creation, be viewed in another light? Michel Riffaterre
has claimed that in 'Ce que dit la bouche d'ombre', for instance, the spectre
of the dolmen of Rozel 'is psychologically a hallucination. But on the
literary plane, it is a myth; stylistically, ... the episode is not a description,
serving to suggest a reality, but simply a preface. The reader sees in that
supernatural being a supernumerary of the legendary repertory, a close
relation of the bit parts of melodrama or the epic; he recognizes in it a
process, the traditional introduction of scenes of revelation ... Hugo's
myths are not tacked on to his philosophical poems, for they correspond
quite often to the archetypes of the collective unconscious and thus impose
themselves on the imagination of the modern reader'.[23]
 A number of the poems we have examined also invite speculation about
the exteriority or the interiority of inspiration, the extent to which the
material of (visionary) poetry is taken from the outside world or from
within the poet himself. For example, is the figure of the Muse usually
based on a real woman, or is it a metaphor of the creative process? We
also have to ask whether certain poets, especially those associated with
Romanticism, are guilty of deceiving the reader, or of distorting the
situation, in preferring to place the emphasis on inspiration and genius
rather than on perspiration and application. All the time we have to bear in

mind the words of Baudelaire: 'Inspiration is undoubtedly the sister of daily work'.[24] Even within the few texts by Rimbaud I have cited there is an interesting ambiguity or dialectic, with references to work and suffering on the one hand and to the idea of being born a poet on the other. Ultimately one is obliged to accept that this balance between inspiration and perspiration is, with tilts either way, a constant in poetry, or at least in the image that poets offer of the making of poetry. A certain school of critics would argue that what matters most of all is the text of the poem, its unique and sometimes magical marriage of words, regardless of everything else. It is an attitude that has some appeal, but the processes whereby the words appear on the page remain a source of fascination to anyone who sits down to write.

Poetry Dies Again

PETER DAYAN

In 1842, a little book called *Gaspard de la Nuit* was published in Angers. *Gaspard de la Nuit* is now generally considered as the first French collection of prose poems, though its author, Louis (or Aloysius) Bertrand, would not have called it that; the term was first used in its modern sense by Baudelaire, twenty years later. Bertrand had been trying to publish his book since 1833, but did not live to see it appear. He died in 1841.

What is a prose poem? For Théodore de Banville, the answer is simple: it is a contradiction in terms.

> Can a prose poem exist? No, despite Fénelon's *Télémaque*, despite Charles Baudelaire's admirable *Prose Poems* and Louis Bertrand's *Gaspard de la Nuit*; for it is impossible to imagine a piece of prose, however perfect, in which one could not, with a superhuman effort, add something or remove something; prose is therefore never done, once and for all.[1]

Banville's argument only works if one accepts that a poem can and must be perfect. This notion was certainly current in Bertrand's day. It was soon to become one of the received ideas of a school of poets known as the Parnassians, with which Gautier, Banville, Leconte de Lisle, even Verlaine and Mallarmé were linked at various times; the Parnassians, rejecting what they saw as the formless spewing forth of emotions that characterized many early Romantics, sought to make of the poem something permanently fixed by its own internal dynamic, the concretization of an immutable ideal. But equally characteristic of the period was the despairing admission that the immutable ideal either did not exist, or was inaccessible to the poet; and that to reflect this admission, a poem should be, not petrified in a false perfection, but unsettled, open on to the unknown.

Baudelaire certainly accepted that his *Petits Poèmes en prose* corresponded to no pre-formed ideal. Indeed, as he says in his preface to the collection, they do not even work as imitations of the model that inspired him to write them – *Gaspard de la Nuit*.

> Sitôt que j'eus commencé le travail, je m'aperçus que non-seulement je restais bien loin de mon mystérieux et brillant modèle, mais encore que je faisais quelque chose (si cela peut s'appeler *quelque chose*) de singulière- ment différent, accident dont tout autre que moi s'enorgueillirait sans doute, mais qui ne peut qu'humilier profondément un esprit qui regarde comme le plus grand honneur du poète d'accomplir *juste* ce qu'il a projeté de faire.[2]

> (As soon as I set to writing it, I realized not only that my work remained far removed from my mysterious and brilliant model, but also that I was doing something (if one can call it *something*) singularly different, an accident which would doubtless have been a source of pride for anyone other than myself, but which can only be felt as profoundly humiliating by a spirit which considers that the poet's greatest honour consists in doing *exactly* what he intended to do.)

So the poet's honour consists in carrying out a plan absolutely; but art has gone its own way, and dishonoured him. The poet, one might say, has lost the ability to circumscribe his own poem. Gautier and Banville liked to compare poems to jewels, or sculptures in marble: hard, perfectly delin- eated, given fixed contours by the artist's hand. But Baudelaire's prose poems have a less clear-cut status. They are fragmentary, full of 'soubre- sauts', of fits and starts, undulating; within them, says Baudelaire, beginnings and ends are everywhere and nowhere. In this disconcerting world, what becomes of Beauty? Nothing that would allow us to determine the form of a poem; indeed, nothing clear at all, perhaps, except that it defeats the artist, who, in the third poem of Baudelaire's collection, cries for mercy:

> Cesse de tenter mes désirs et mon orgueil! L'étude du beau est un duel où l'artiste crie de frayeur avant d'être vaincu. ('Le Confiteor de l'artiste', p. 26)

> (Cease to tempt my desires and my pride! The study of beauty is a duel in which the artist cries out in terror before being defeated.)

Why should beauty terrify Baudelaire, whereas it appeared more generous to Banville? The answer is that for Baudelaire, the channel of communication between the artist and the infinite has become blocked. The absolute no longer consents to incarnation in poetic forms, because poetic forms are necessarily finite. The prose poem is, in fact, the poetic form born of the loss of faith in poetic form.

Though Bertrand's poems are strikingly different from Baudelaire's, the implications of the use of the form of the prose poem are just as strikingly similar. For Bertrand as for Baudelaire, poems are no longer eternal diamonds; the poet strives to define and dominate his art, but fails. Bertrand's collection is preceded by a curious text which, while explaining the titles, reduces the artist to a hollow fiction, a mere shadow of a man. The narrator recounts how the manuscript of the poems came into his possession. He begins by describing himself, sitting on a bench. He compares himself to a minutely realistic statue in his town, Dijon. The implication of the comparison is that, like the statue, from a distance he might seem to be alive; but from close up, one can see that he is nothing but plaster, only an imitation of a man.

Then a bizarre and lunatic stranger appears, sits beside him, and tells of how he has spent his life searching for 'l'art absolu' – and failed to find it. The narrator confesses that he has similarly sought, and found nothing; he likens art to a needle in a haystack. The stranger, however, has at least managed to produce one manuscript, the sole result of thirty years of effort. It is signed 'Gaspard de la Nuit'. He leaves it with the narrator, and the narrator soon discovers that 'Gaspard de la Nuit' is just a local name for the devil – who, as Gaspard himself says, does not exist, except, of course, in books.

So the poems in the book are presented as having been written by a fictional character who has failed to find art, and published by an even more fictional character – a mere plaster statue – who has equally failed to find art, and has given up the search. And just in case the message that *Gaspard de la Nuit* is a collection of non-poems was not clear enough, there is a 'postface' whose only aims seem to be to declare the poet mad or a jester – 'un fou' – and to deny to the book the status to which 'l'art absolu' necessarily aspires: immortality.

Ce ne sont point ces pages souffreteuses, humble labeur ignoré des jours présents, qui ajouteront quelque lustre à la renommée poétique des jours passés.[3]

(These poor pale pages, a humble labour unsung in its own time, are not of a kind to add a new gloss to the poetic glory of past ages.)

Beauty as a permanently victorious enemy; Art as an ill-defined but plainly poisoned needle in a haystack; the artist as an unconvincing fiction, his creations destined to remain deservedly unknown ... in denying to

Gaspard de la Nuit all the positive virtues of Romantic poetry, Bertrand provokes the reader to ask: what, then, is the value of the book?

The answer is provided by the peculiar characteristics of the episodes, the prose poems, that constitute the collection. Let us take an example: 'La Tour de Nesle'.

> 'Valet de trèfle! – Dame de pique! je gagne!' Et le soudard qui perdait envoya d'un coup de poing sur la table son enjeu au plancher.

> Mais alors messire Hugues, le prévôt, cracha dans le brasier de fer avec la grimace d'un cagou qui a avalé une araignée en mangeant sa soupe.

> ★

> 'Pouah! les chaircuitiers échaudent-ils leurs cochons à minuit? Ventre-dieu! c'est un bateau de feurre qui brûle en Seine!'

> L'incendie, qui n'était d'abord qu'un innocent follet égaré dans les brouillards de la rivière, fut bientôt un diable à quatre tirant le canon et force arquebusades au fil de l'eau.

> Une foule innombrable de turlupins, de béquillards, de gueux de nuit, accourus sur la grève, dansaient des gigues devant la spirale de flamme et de fumée.

> Et rougeoyaient face à face la tour de Nesle, d'où le guet sortit, l'escopette sur l'épaule, et la tour du Louvre d'où, par une fenêtre, le roi et la reine voyaient tout sans être vus.

> (pp. 115–16)

> ('Knave of clubs! – Queen of spades! I win!' And the trooper who had lost sent with a bang of his fist on the table his stake flying to the floor.

> But then messire Hugues, the provost, spat into the iron brazier with the grimace of a hermit who has swallowed a spider while eating his soup.

> ★

> 'Pouah! Are the pork-butchers scalding their pigs at midnight? By God! it's a boat full of straw burning on the Seine!'

> The fire, at first merely an innocent will-o'-the-wisp lost in the river mists, soon became a devil let loose firing cannon and many a musket volley as he drifted downstream.

> A crowd of countless jesters, cripples, and bedless vagabonds came running to the river-bank, and danced jigs before the spiral of flame and smoke.

And facing each other two towers glowed red, the Tour de Nesle, from which the watch emerged, blunderbusses shouldered, and the Tour du Louvre from which, through a window, the king and queen saw all without being seen.)

I should like to list four characteristics of this poem which it has in common with almost all the others in *Gaspard de la Nuit* – and which, variously developed, became basic features of most of the best prose poetry of the next sixty years.

First, the physical setting. Though picturesque, it is simple, and quite conventional. The Tour de Nesle, the Louvre, and the Seine at night appear in countless productions of the Gothic branch of French romanticism. (The language of the soldiers is in a corresponding pseudo-mediaeval register.) The narrator is therefore able to assume his reader will know that the Tour de Nesle was a fortification on the left bank of the Seine, opposite the Louvre. But like the Paris of Baudelaire's *Petits Poèmes en prose* and of Lautréamont's *Chants de Maldoror*, like the parks, streets and theatres of Mallarmé's prose poems, this familiar and well-defined setting serves as a foil for characters whose half-revealed emotions remain both unfamiliar and ill-defined. What are the unseen king and queen thinking? In *Gaspard de la Nuit* as in Baudelaire's prose poems, an inordinate amount of time is spent looking out of or into windows, climbing in and out of them, even throwing things through them. The characters are constantly looking towards another world, outside their own, as if it could help to define emotions which neither they nor the poet can express. Romantic poetic prose does not encapsulate a poetic moment; it is the expression of a state of aspiration, of tension. The prosaic, the conventional, is one pole of that tension.

Second, violence. The violence here is contained, and the pleasure in it vicarious; but it is certainly present. The gesture of the soldier who loses at cards seems to promise a fight; the peculiar and awkward rhythm of the sentence (eighteen words without punctuation) adds to the sense of unease. The fight does not happen, doubtless because of the distraction of the burning boat. The burning boat itself, however, represents a real disaster, although we hear nothing of its consequences or victims – we see only the crowd gleefully dancing the jig by the light of the flames, and the king and queen, who, like the crowd, obviously enjoy the boat's spectacular destruction. Bertrand, unlike Baudelaire or Lautréamont, is careful not to shock the reader by openly provoking sadistic pleasure. None the less, throughout *Gaspard de la Nuit*, enmity, loss, death and destruction fire a liberation of feeling which gives the scenes their force. It is pleasure in violence that fuels the escape from the prosaic, and projects us towards what might have been the poetic, if only it had existed.

The last gesture, typically violent, of Maldoror in Lautréamont's *Chants de Maldoror* is to hurl his hapless victim Mervyn across Paris. Mervyn flies over the Louvre, the Seine, and the site of the Tour de Nesle, and finally lands – the impact is fatal – on the dome of the Pantheon. The Pantheon is the last resting-place of the great men of France, and the symbol of that single, institutionalized, immortal glory in which neither Bertrand nor Lautréamont believed. Victor Hugo lies buried there; but no prose poet does.

Third, illumination. Not all violence has the peculiar power that propels Mervyn across Paris and inspires the jig outside the Tour de Nesle. What is needed is a violence that illuminates, that is, changes perceptions, like the red glow from the burning boat. Those changed perceptions suggest a removal of the ordinary conditions of life, a strange realm where the laws of time and gravity do not apply. That strange realm constitutes a pole of tension opposite the prosaic. It is never reached, only glimpsed, in sudden flashes that leave the reader wondering in what sense it exists. It is Rimbaud's prose poems that generate the most powerful of these flashes. They are called, precisely (though possibly not by Rimbaud), *Les Illuminations*.

Finally, open ends. In this poem, four individual characters appear. Each is named only once. None appears elsewhere in the book. Two anonymous groups, the motley dancing crowd and the watch, also appear; each group similarly lasts for only one sentence, then disappears for ever. We never discover what became of the boat, or of the card-players' quarrel. Such open ends serve, in a way, the same purpose as violence: projection. They invite readers away from the text, into a space where only their imaginations and desires can guide them. In spite of what Banville says, to the prose poet, no poem is ever complete.

Mallarmé's favourite way of describing this incompleteness was to say that what mattered in a poem was to be sought, not in the poem's words, but between its lines, and in the blank paper around the text. Bertrand added to his manuscript a note to the page-setter, which begins thus: '*General Rule*. – Use blanks as if the text were poetry.' Bertrand particularly indicates that he wants '*large blank spaces*' between the paragraphs or couplets of each piece, 'as if they were verse stanzas'. Of course, publishers have frequently ignored his instructions. Mallarmé similarly wanted blank paper to feature prominently in his poetic prose – and had similar trouble with publishers. But although Mallarmé and Bertrand compare the blanks around their prose to blanks around traditional verse, their function is completely different. The blanks traditionally left around verse may be compared to a frame for a painting, or a setting for a jewel. They form an outline, a clean limit to the poem or stanza. For Mallarmé and Bertrand, on the contrary, the blanks are there, in Bertrand's words, to 'faire foisonner', to multiply the poem, to invite its continuation beyond its limits. They are not raised borders to contain the poem, but margins into which it leaks.

Arthur Rimbaud was less interested in physical gaps on paper than Mallarmé or Bertrand. But there are other kinds of gap in his life and work which have exercised a unique fascination on readers of French poetry over the last century. To begin with, there is the well-known fact that he completely abandoned literature before he was twenty-three years old. Like Baudelaire, he always saw poetry as the expression of a desire to go further than was reasonably possible. But Baudelaire, Mallarmé and Verlaine, in moving away from poetry within the tradition, never went too far beyond its boundaries. They thought of poetic production in the new intellectual atmosphere as an oscillation; writing poetry meant alternately refusing and accepting the constrictions of poetic language. But Rimbaud's urge to refuse was so much stronger than his urge to accept that in the end, he refused to follow the pendulum back. The result was silence.

There is plenty of silence in his prose poems. There is also a powerful expression of the Romantic urge to refuse this world. And there is, as in Mallarmé, the post-Romantic projection of 'something else', another world – not a spiritual realm of angels, souls, God or ghosts, but a glory always to be created, reached in poetry through unstable metaphors for its qualities. For Rimbaud, that other world represents above all liberation – just as normal life represents, above all, oppression.

Qu'on me loue enfin ce tombeau, blanchi à la chaux avec les lignes du ciment en relief – très loin sous terre.
Je m'accoude à la table, la lampe éclaire très vivement ces journaux que je suis idiot de relire, ces livres sans intérêt. –

A une distance énorme au-dessus de mon salon souterrain, les maisons s'implantent, les brumes s'assemblent. La boue est rouge ou noire. Ville monstrueuse, nuit sans fin!

Moins haut, sont des égouts. Aux côtés, rien que l'épaisseur du globe. Peut-être les gouffres d'azur, des puits de feu. C'est peut-être sur ces plans que se rencontrent lunes et comètes, mers et fables.

Aux heures d'amertume je m'imagine des boules de saphir, de métal. Je suis maître du silence. Pourquoi une apparence de soupirail blêmirait-elle au coin de la voûte?[4]

(Let me be allowed at last to rent[5] this tomb, whitewashed, with the lines of its mortar in relief – very far below the earth.

My elbows are on the table, the lamp lights very brightly these newspapers that I am a fool to re-read, these books of no interest. –

At an enormous distance above my subterranean living-room, houses take root, fogs assemble. The mud is red or black. Monstrous town, endless night!

Less high, are the sewers. To the sides, nothing but the thickness of the globe. Perhaps the sky's abyss, wells of fire. It is perhaps on this plane that moons and comets, seas and fables meet.

At moments of bitterness I imagine balls of sapphire, of metal. I am master of the silence. Why should the semblance of a small window turn pale the top corner of the vault?)

The setting of this poem, the fifth part of 'Enfance', could be said to belong to the same Romantic-Gothic register as the setting of 'La Tour de Nesle'. It has the colours (black and red), the thick-walled building (the tomb is a sister-cliché to the tower), the dark city, the window, the flames and the water. But Rimbaud's Gothic is less familiar and less comfortable than Bertrand's, because he goes much further in following the logic of illumination. No earlier poet would have dared, one feels, to imagine anything as impenetrable as Rimbaud's ball of sapphire. It has neither existence nor function in any sphere that one could call real or realistic. Because it is round, one cannot get a grip on it. Hard and inflexible, it will fit into no context. Only light can pass into it – and the light that emerges from it will bear no images. The ball of sapphire says nothing. Its master is the master of silence.

In this poem, fables meet seas; a recognized form encounters the form-less. When Rimbaud mentions forms of discourse in *Les Illuminations*, it is normally either to reject them, or to couple them with an image that refuses their practical, time-bound use. So it is here with the fable. One can hardly imagine Æsop or La Fontaine telling their tales to Rimbaud's comets. A language that communicates is doubtless a necessary starting-point for poetry. But Rimbaud uses it as a springboard, to leave behind the world where communication matters. When he speaks in these poems, when he says 'I', he speaks to no one. He is interested, not in the com-munication of messages, but in the freedom to create texts with their own substance.

This aim is dangerous. It is within language used communicatively that we normally constitute our sense of identity, by interchange with and delimitation from others. Rimbaud loses both the limits and the inter-change. He can only present the result as both splendid and deadly. It is alone in a tomb, far below the earth, unwilling to admit the attraction of the light of day, that he finds the voice which speaks in this poem. The previous poem, the fourth in the series 'Enfance', is even more explicit. Its voice is that of an anchorite, an isolated 'savant', a lone long-distance walker or a child abandoned 'sur la jetée partie à la haute mer' (on the pier set out for the open sea – as if the pier, infected in turn by the urge to move, had left its moorings). Where could their journey be leading?

> Que les oiseaux et les sources sont loins! Ce ne peut être que la fin du monde, en avançant.   (p. 124)

> (How far away are the birds and the springs! It can only be the end of the world, going on.)

According to Mallarmé, Victor Hugo, who never showed any interest in prose poems, was convinced as he died that he was taking French poetry into the grave with him. In other words, as far as Hugo was concerned, the younger generation's poetry was still-born. And so, in a sense, it was. It is certainly not a poetry that affirms life, as Hugo understood it. For immediate evidence, one need look no further than its apparent effects on those who wrote it. It is easy to laugh at the myth of the 'poète maudit', the accursed poet, rejected by society, slave to a parcimonious and ungrateful muse, unable to take life seriously enough to hang on to it for long. But for the prose poets (except, in some senses, for Mallarmé), the reality comes uncomfortably close to the myth. Bertrand, Baudelaire, Lautréamont, Rimbaud and Mallarmé each produced only one volume that might have been called a collection of prose poems; each died before or soon after its publication. And none produced more than one major volume of verse. Hugo's literary output was ten times that of all five prose poets put together. His works were read in his life-time by millions; those of Baudelaire and Mallarmé were read only by a few, those of Bertrand, Rimbaud and Lautréamont by almost no one. Hugo also lived much longer than any of the prose poets – more than twice as long as Rimbaud or Bertrand, more than three times as long as Lautréamont. It is difficult not to see in these simple facts a reflection of their attitudes to art. For Hugo, poetry meant life endlessly reborn, in hope and aspiration as well as in mystery and fear; a link between man and a glorious immortal sphere. But in prose poetry, from *Gaspard de la Nuit* on, a kind of terrifying honesty enters literature. The prose poets admit that it is more comfortable to believe, as Hugo did, in an ideal or divine guarantee for poetry. But, seeing the intellectual flaws in that belief, they refuse to entertain it, and brave the consequences.

No one has ever taken the refusal within poetry of Romantic poetic ideals further than Lautréamont. His *Poésies* are not poetry in any sense of the word that would have been recognized by his predecessors or contemporaries. They are a bewildering concentrate of irony, parody, plagiarism, inverted cliché, perverse paradox, invective, and provocative absurdity, which constantly undermines its only proclaimed purpose. That purpose is the denigration of all literature that expresses doubt, describes pain or evil, or questions the perfection of God or of contemporary society.

> Depuis Racine, la poésie n'a pas progressé d'un millimètre. Elle a reculé. Grâce à qui? aux Grandes-Têtes-Molles de notre époque.[6]

> Since Racine's day, poetry has not advanced by one millimetre. It has lost ground. Thanks to whom? to the Great-Soft-Heads of our time.

He lists no less than seventeen of these Great-Soft-Heads, including Gautier, 'l'Incomparable-Epicier' (the Incomparable-Grocer); Lamartine, 'la Cigogne-Larmoyante' (the Tearful-Stork); Hugo, 'le Funèbre-Echalas-Vert' (the Gloomy-Green-Spindleshanks); and Musset, 'le Gandin-Sans-Chemise-Intellectuelle' (the Intellectually-Shirtless-Beau). And he attacks the schoolteachers of his day for asking their pupils to translate poetry by Musset whose subject, according to Lautréamont, is evil.

> A quoi bon regarder le mal? N'est-il pas en minorité? Pourquoi pencher la tête d'un lycéen sur des questions qui, faute de n'avoir pas été comprises, ont fait perdre la leur à des hommes tels que Pascal et Byron?   (p. 373)

> (What is the point of contemplating evil? Is it not in the minority? Why fill schoolboys' heads with questions which, for want of not being understood, have caused such men as Pascal and Byron to lose theirs?)

At a superficial reading, this could be taken to mean that one loses one's head if one thinks about the questions posed by evil without understanding them. But if one looks more carefully, one finds a peculiar negative in the middle of the sentence ('faute de *n'*avoir *pas* été comprises') that suggests an opposite sense. Pascal and Byron (and doubtless Musset and all the other Great-Soft-Heads, poets of Evil and Doubt) lost their heads precisely because they *did* understand those questions.

What are the questions concerned? Lautréamont makes it clear enough, and they are not new ones. Given that we know pain and injustice, can we believe in an omnipotent, eternal principle of good? If there is no eternal principle of good, can we believe in ideal forms? And if there are no ideal forms, can aesthetic and moral convention be anything more than arbitrary laws designed to keep our rulers in power? Once one has understood the import of these questions, one loses one's head whether one decides to answer 'yes' or 'no' to them. One can only answer 'yes' by incorporating into one's thought a series of sophisms, of metaphysical subterfuges which, though they had been common currency for centuries, constitute a kind of accepted insanity. The poets of the nineteenth century, and Lautréamont more than anyone else, show that insanity for what it is. But if one answers 'no' to those questions, refusing the acceptable insanity, autism threatens; one loses one's tongue. For the old insanity is not simply a diseased organ that can be excised from the body of our thought; without it, language in the traditional sense ceases to function. As it does in *Poésies*.

Those metaphysical subterfuges on which our language depends have been investigated with incomparable thoroughness by Jacques Derrida. Chief among them, and inseparable from the poetic belief in ideal forms, is a belief in the value of imitation, of representation. To Lautréamont as to Rimbaud, Baudelaire and Mallarmé, traditional poetry presented itself as an expression of something outside it – whether it be of the poet's soul, nature, human nature, Beauty, the Ideal, or God's will. Indeed, it claimed to draw its value from its adequacy as an imitation or reflection. But, as Derrida has shown, such claims rest on a very peculiar logic, that refuses to reflect upon itself.

If poetry situates the source of its value outside the text (in the realm of that which it imitates), that is because we cannot conceive of a text as itself a source of value, an origin of the breath of life. But if one investigates the realms in which poets put their faith, the gods and ideals and natures to which they appeal, one discovers that they, too, function in the manner of texts – as if they were themselves imitating something beyond them. In order to believe in them as sources of value, one has to prevent oneself from making this discovery, from seeing them as textual in nature. That is why such poetry necessarily presents itself as an *imperfect* imitation. As well as being a reflection, it is a veil, concealing the nudity of the divinity.

The prose poets refused to leave that veil in place. With them, poetry becomes what, for many, it still is today: a dance of the veils, a game played with the conventions of imitation. In this game, no ideal permanently escapes reduction to the level of an imitation, a text; none, therefore, remains a sufficient source of value. Lautréamont is a compulsive, ferocious and brilliant player of this game. His writing, like all Romantic poetry, is saturated with an intense, unsatisfied desire. But Lautréamont's desire refuses to be channelled into Romantic aspirations towards a poetic absolute. On the contrary, it finds a cruel satisfaction in prising open the logical gaps inherent in all such aspirations. In *Poésies*, every variety of poetic goal and aspiration, including those of Lautréamont's own earlier work, is explored and exploded. There is no form and no idea which, by the end of the book, still seems to have a privileged status.

In order to expose the ideal of Romantic poetry, Lautréamont places

beside it the ideal most opposed to it, that of the crassest right-thinking
self-satisfaction, implying mindless faith in the goodness of God, man, and
the authoritarian social order.

> Les gémissements poétiques de ce siècle ne sont que des sophismes.
> Les premiers principes doivent être hors de discussion.   (p. 361)

> (This century's poetic moanings are nothing but sophisms.
> There must be no discussion of first principles.)

It is, of course, plain that the Romantic-poetic ideal and the right-
thinking ideal are incompatible. But it gradually becomes equally plain
to the intrepid reader of *Poésies* – and no reader who is not intrepid will
get past the first page – that both ideals function in the same way,
and therefore have equivalent claims to validity. Both require a certain
blindness or bad faith from their adepts which Lautréamont's irony turns
into ridiculous stupidity. *Poésies* demonstrates that it is as dishonest to be a
Romantic as to be a right-thinking bourgeois – and vice versa; placed thus
side by side, the two ideals destroy each other, and nothing rises in their
place. It is impossible to resist the feeling that the urge to wreak this
destruction and the pleasure taken in it are, obscurely but intensely, poetic
in nature. But it is equally impossible to define their results in terms of any
tradition that might be called poetry. Let us not forget that *Poésies* is in
prose.

The rejection of poetry is not as obvious or as unambiguous in Mal-
larmé's work as in Lautréamont's. To believe in poetry, in the traditional
or Romantic sense, one has to believe in an absolute, unchanging ideal.
Lautréamont did not believe in such an ideal; Mallarmé, in an unusual and
subtle way, did. He thought that the absolute, even though it had no
logical status, current objective existence or divine sanction, could genui-
nely and honestly be held to exist in a future society that will believe in it,
and know that its only source is in the common aspiration of all humanity.
(He liked to describe that future absolute as expressed in an ideal book,
sole end of the humanly perceived universe.) But in his own society, the
true absolute had no credibility, and therefore no home.

Mallarmé was not alone in believing that contemporary society was no
place for poetry. Almost all the Romantic poets of the generations of
Hugo, Nerval, Baudelaire and Banville (the main exception was Hugo
himself) abandoned their youthful political enthusiasm when the revolu-
tions of 1830 and 1848 ended in a reinforcing of bourgeois materialism.
Most of the poets of Mallarmé's generation, growing up after those
disillusionments, were from the outset political pessimists; they expected
French society to remain divided, and hostile to art, ideals, and all grand
ideas. But Mallarmé differed from most of the other poets of the time in

maintaining that the poet and the notion of poetry needed society, as much as society needed the poet.

> I believe that poetry is made for the pomp and the ceremonies of a constituted society where there would be a place for the glory of which people seem to have lost all notion.[7]

To Mallarmé, the absolute is the oxygen of the poet. But only society can bring the absolute to life; and his society failed to do so. Since the absolute was, albeit temporarily, dead, what could a poet do? The answer is simple: spend his life preparing to join the absolute where it now resides – in death.

> For me, the case of the poet, in this society which does not allow him to live, is that of a man who isolates himself to sculpt his own tomb. (p. 869)

For Mallarmé, the only good poet was a dead poet; dead, at least, to the world of his time. That is why so many of his poems are 'tombeaux', tombs, homages at once to dead artists, and to the idea that death, that 'peu profond ruisseau calomnié' (shallow slandered brook), leaves art where it belongs.

So what, in this desultory world of ours, is the status of the poem? That, perhaps, of a hors d'oeuvre, whetting the appetite for a feast that can only be imagined; or a carefully constructed ruin, a 'cloître brisé' (broken cloister), inviting us to dream of what an architectural ensemble might have been. Mallarmé liked to denigrate his poems, in prose and in verse, by calling them mere album pieces, fragments, anecdotes or occasional verse; as if the production of a satisfactory, complete work was now beyond him – or any poet. Poetry was a broken art.

But perhaps not quite. Once, just once in his life, one year before his death and three before the end of the nineteenth century, Mallarmé allowed himself to publish a work described, without qualification, as a 'poème': *Un Coup de Dés jamais n'abolira le hasard (A Throw of the Dice will never Abolish Chance)*.

Its form is unique. It is not in continuous prose. Nor is it in regular verse. Is it in free verse? Not really. In his preface to the work, Mallarmé indicates its affinities with both the prose poem and free verse, which had first appeared in France a decade earlier;[8] but he emphasizes, too, its originality. To Mallarmé, free verse and the prose poem were both invented in the wake of the realization that 'the old verse forms' were not 'absolute, unique and immutable' (p. 867); *Un Coup de Dés* inaugurated a third new genre consequent on that realization.

How is *Un Coup de Dés* original? Most obviously, in its physical appearance. The work is divided into eleven double pages (each double page is to be taken as a single unit). The first four words of the title sentence appear alone on the first page, in large capitals:

UN COUP DE DÉS

The fifth word, JAMAIS, appears in the bottom right-hand quarter of the second double page. Below it are a dozen words in smaller capitals; above and to the left of it, the page is blank. On the third page begins an increasingly elaborate interplay of motifs in various still smaller typefaces, some in italics, some not, some appearing to form syntactically complete units, some not; and in the middle of these the remaining words of the title sentence, still in large capitals, stand out like moons among stars. No double page contains much more than a hundred words. One frequently feels that blank paper predominates, just as, despite the stars, black predominates in the night sky.

Blank paper, of course, was also a feature of *Gaspard de la Nuit*, written sixty years earlier. The purpose it served there is also one of the purposes it serves in *Un Coup de Dés*: it gives readers room, to continue for themselves in the multiple directions suggested by a poet who works by evoking rather than by exhaustively describing. Nor do the similarities between the two works end there. The other characteristics of prose poetry that I pointed out in 'La Tour de Nesle' are also present in *Un Coup de Dés*. There is a simple and conventional setting – a storm and a shipwreck – and a character, called 'LE MAITRE' (THE MASTER), whose half-revealed thoughts point to a world beyond ours. There is violence; LE MAITRE is plainly facing death. And there are illuminations, provided by images that appear with obscure force and suddenly alter our perspective on the scene set by the poem: the storm-tossed ship, a defiant fist, a floating feather (below which first a hat, then a prince emerge, only to be swallowed again by the storm), a rock, and finally the stars in the sky. But Mallarmé carries all these techniques incomparably further than Bertrand. His blanks not only give space to dream; they actually organize the rhythm, the pulsation of the various motifs, in a manner that is impossible to imagine until one sees the work.[9] His illuminations do not merely suggest possible other worlds; they appear as pointers to a single and coherent (though vertiginously distant) realm, and demand of the reader an extreme intellectual and emotional effort towards an understanding of that realm. Each image, motif, sentence and idea is clearly connected to all the others; but the precise nature of that connection is not clear, and indeed never becomes completely clear no matter how often one reads the work, for the vulgar notion of clarity implies a kind of transitive understanding whose value the work denies. In the place of such understanding, it offers an inexhaustible field of speculation in which, at each careful reading, ever more irresistible profound ideas and undeniably magnificent aesthetic pleasures begin to emerge – only to be drowned by the evidence that we have not understood the whole. The elements of the poem both fertilize and contradict one another endlessly, communicating, within each page and across the poem, in so many dimensions – syntax, disposition on page, typeface, image, concept, mood, register, reference, inference – that after *Un Coup de Dés* every other poem seems flat. One could be excused for thinking that this extraordinary virtuoso display, to which no quotation or description can do justice, might have been enough to bring poetry back to life.

The traditional notion of poetry had died with the traditional notion of ideals. For centuries, poets had accepted that Beauty prescribed certain poetic forms; but few of the poets of Mallarmé's circle believed in the existence of a Beauty that prescribed anything concrete and positive at all. Beauty, for the post-Romantics, was more subtle and distant than that; it said nothing, its form was not of a nature that permitted imitation or reflection. *Un Coup de Dés*, however, seemed to provide an alternative relationship with the ideal. Like traditional poetry, *Un Coup de Dés* is plainly concerned with what Mallarmé liked to call 'autre chose', 'something else', a realm beyond that which is ordinarily perceived. But unlike traditional poetry, it does not attempt to reflect or reveal that realm. In fact, it does not suppose that the 'something else' had any real existence before the poem. On the contrary: it is the poem, and its reading, that creates the 'something else', at a sufficient distance for it to remain other. Mallarmé is an idealist who knowingly creates his own ideal, with its own supply of veils, allowing readers to play for themselves the game whose operation suggests its existence. Might not this new creative game be enough to found a new, post-Romantic poetic tradition?

The answer is given by the simple fact that *Un Coup de Dés* continues to appear unique. Indeed, it seems to demand to be considered unique. To its devotees, its form and its ambition could never be imitated; it is the first and last example of its genre. Seen thus, it represents, not a new tradition, but the end of tradition. For there can be no tradition without a belief in definable values that transcend the individual work. But in *Un Coup de Dés*, Mallarmé demonstrates that such values can no longer be presupposed. The poem does not express its ideal: it creates it. And in creating its ideal, the poem necessarily breaks with tradition.

This new poetic creationism brought with it a frightening freedom. Poetry could no longer de defined by its relationship to an absolute, since the only absolute that continued to function from one poem to another was death. Nor could it be defined by its form; for how can any form be held to be innately poetic, if there is no pre-existing poetic ideal to decide it? After *Un Coup de Dés*, it becomes impossible to say what French poetry is. As a coherent category, it is dead.

The Banality of Modernism: Order and Adventure in Twentieth-Century Poetry

IAN REVIE

Labels such as Modernism, and even more so Post-Modernism, are not always useful or enlightening; but in at least one respect the idea of the modern and therefore the new, as something which engages with its own time, has been a salient feature of the art and the poetry of the early twentieth century. A simple comparison between the poetry of Mallarmé, in many other senses of the term the most modern poet of his times, and the poetry of Apollinaire will serve to show the extent to which the former kept the contemporary world at bay, or at least disguised it so heavily as to render it unrecognizable, whereas the latter, even in the period in which his poetry is laden with the vestiges of Symbolism, strove to open his verse up to the modern world. Such a definition of Modernism may appear to some to be the most trivial available, and it would be true to say that much verse written in this spirit has very quickly proved dated and uninteresting. None the less, there are few artists of the century whose work continues to attract attention of whom it is not true to say that the artefacts and events of the century are a powerful presence in their work. In the century of the common man this has necessarily meant that one of the battlegrounds of art, one which justifies the use of such terms as avant-garde, has been the articulation of that which had hitherto lain outside the realm of high art.

The origins of this tendency, in French poetry at least, can be found in the late nineteenth century. The work of Laforgue, Corbière, Cros, and Jehan Rictus can be seen as the beginning of a process which is carried on by Apollinaire, Cendrars and, although with certain differences, Queneau. Where much French poetry has sought, and continues to seek, the high and often abstract tone, denying any place to the immediate presence of the obviously contemporary world (e.g. the work of Yves Bonnefoy; see below, Ch. 11, pp. 213–15), in the years immediately before and after the Great War it is this Modernist current which defines the new in poetry and which therefore can be seen to be the vital element that makes poetry possible after the impasses of Symbolism. In this respect French poetry differs remarkably from the poetry of most other nations, since this aspect of Modernism surfaces earlier and is lost much earlier. A poem by René Char which arises from his experiences of the Occupation could never be identified as such by the casual reader, but without being creators of *vers de circonstances*, the three poets who form the main substance of this chapter created a poetry of modern Paris, France and the world – note the presence of the Eiffel Tower in so much of their verse – while also writing from the need to create a poetry of the self. Apollinaire is certainly among the most personal of poets, but his poetry was also seen, from its first reception, as being concerned with the heteroclite and often random nature of the external world – witness the now famous accusation brought against *Alcools* by Duhamel[1] as 'une boutique de brocanteur' (junk-shop). What is to be found of the self is externalized not merely for purposes of distance, as is, for example, the case with the 'mauvais garçon' of the opening lines of 'La Chanson du mal-aimé', but also because his is a poetry which begins from the premise of the dismemberment of Orpheus, from the fact of the existence of the only possible poetic voice as one which is disseminated throughout an experience which defies unification.

When in his 'Poème lu au mariage d'André Salmon' (A, 83–4) Apollinaire spoke of a table which threw him 'the last look of Orpheus dying', he was speaking very consciously as the poet at grips with the major problem of the new century, namely the absence of any centralized notions upon which any form of art could construct an agreed consensus as its own basis. The dismemberment of Orpheus is posited as the inevitable condition of the artist, but the look Apollinaire observed emanated from an external object. In several other major poems, mostly written and published after 1909 (the date of Salmon's wedding), Apollinaire attempted to reconcile what he saw as the poles of conflict in the artist's condition: order and adventure; but he did so with the knowledge that any victory achieved in the artist's struggle was co-terminous with the work in which it was achieved and could never be considered as laying the systematic foundation of a new art. Despite the attention he paid in his last years to defining and championing *l'esprit nouveau*, it is sufficient to glance at his writing on this subject to see that such common ground as there is among his chosen representatives of this new spirit consists almost exclusively of the desire to innovate. Perhaps more important was the ability Apollinaire shared with Picasso, in particular, to return to classical forms, just as, in England and the USA, Pound and Eliot were to call for a return to the hymnary as a model for verse.

Whether one considers that there is more continuity or discontinuity in the aesthetics of Apollinaire's poetry, it can none the less be seen that the central concern of his art lies in the encounter with the world as latent phenomenon from which art is to be made in the absence of aesthetic laws. The major achievements of Apollinaire's work all operate on the basis of this tension, from 'Zone', the first poem of *Alcools*, to 'La Jolie Rousse', the last poem of *Calligrammes*, allowing us to consider his poetry as part of the culture of the ready-made which is central to Modernism. For many, the invention of modern poetry is as much to be accredited to Blaise Cendrars as to Apollinaire, and it is certainly true that his poetry from the period 1911 onwards (see his salute to Apollinaire at the end of 'Hamac' (C, 64)) also exists in a relationship with the world which treats the questions of form and identity as secondary to the encounter with the object as random manifestation rather than as signifier of immanent unity. Cendrars has been labelled a poet of the cosmos, but that cosmos is as much the outward projection of the self as the inward direction of the universe upon the individual consciousness.

As for the poetry of Raymond Queneau, it is easy to find points of difference between him and the two earlier poets; the devices Queneau uses to give order to his work would be one such obvious heading. Nevertheless, he deserves to be considered alongside the other two because so much of his verse is concerned with the language of the century, the demotic forms of French, as well as with the places where he lived and worked, but also because, in the multiplicity of forms of poetry which he wrote, he defines the modern as variation on the past, which is to mark both its continuity and its difference with that past even more clearly than do his predecessors. Such a quality is fundamental to any valid definition of the term Modernism. A poem such as 'Si tu t'imagines' (Q, 120) modernizes Ronsard's 'Mignonne allons voir si la rose' but it also found an audience which was much wider (perhaps thanks to the singing of Juliette Greco) than that usually available to modern poetry, and as such it is an example of that other strand inevitably intertwined with the revolt against high art, the revolt against the appropriation of art by bourgeois society. None of the three poets had anything remotely approaching a socialist or socialist-realist period, but all three found the material of their poetry in the streets, much as a slightly earlier period of French painting found its images in similar places.

From 'Zone' to *Courir les rues* by way of the *Dix-neuf poèmes élastiques* there is a poetry of the modern world which is unhampered by any worries about the denotative functions of language. Here is Apollinaire:

J'ai vu ce matin une jolie rue dont j'ai oublié le nom
Neuve et propre du soleil elle était le clairon
Les directeurs les ouvriers et les belles sténo-dactylographes

Du lundi matin au samedi soir quatre fois par jour y passent
Le matin par trois fois la sirène y gémit
Une cloche rageuse y aboie vers midi
Les inscriptions des enseignes et des murailles
Les plaques les avis à la façon des perroquets criaillent
J'aime la grâce de cette rue industrielle
Située entre la rue Aumont-Thiéville et l'avenue des Ternes   (A, 39–40)

(This morning I saw a pretty street whose name I've forgotten
New and clean it was the bugle of the sun
The managers the workers and the beautiful shorthand-typists
From Monday morning to Saturday afternoon pass through four times a day
In the mornings a siren shrills out thrice
An angry bell barks out about noon
The inscriptions on the signs and on the walls
The plaques the notices like parrots squawk
I love the grace of this industrial street
Situated between the rue Aumont-Thiéville and the avenue des Ternes)

The modern industrial world is no longer unfit as a subject for poetry, so much is obvious. As with the rest of 'Zone', this extract is written in a new form of *vers libre* (of which there were many in the preceding thirty years) in which the looseness of length of line is played off against the maintained presence of rhyme, itself subjected to the occasional irregularity or substitution of assonance (e.g. the last two lines of the extract). The broken symmetry of the verse embodies the dislocated unity of experience.

Here is Cendrars in 'La Prose du Transsibérien et de la petite Jeanne de France':

Et voici des affiches, du rouge au vert multicolores comme mon passé
                                          bref du jaune
Jaune la fière couleur des romans de la France à l'étranger
J'aime me frotter dans les grandes villes aux autobus en marche
Ceux de la ligne Saint-Germain-Montmartre m'emportent à l'assaut de la Butte
Les moteurs beuglent comme les taureaux d'or
Les vaches du crépuscule broutent le Sacré-Coeur
O Paris
Gare centrale débarcadère des volontés carrefour des inquiétudes
Seul les marchands de couleur ont encore un peu de lumière sur leur porte
La Compagnie Internationale des Wagons-Lits et des Grands Express
                                          Européens m'a envoyé son prospectus
C'est la plus belle église du monde   (C, 32)

(And here are posters, from red to green multicoloured like my past
                                          in short yellow
Yellow the proud colour of French novels abroad
I like in the big cities to rub up against the passing buses

The ones on the Saint-Germain-Montmartre route carry me on to the
assault on the Butte
Their engines bellow like golden bulls
The cattle of evening browse on the Sacré-Coeur
Oh Paris
Central Station quayside of wills crossroad of worries
Only the paint sellers still have a little daylight on their doors
The International Sleeping-car and Grand European Express Company
has sent me its prospectus
It's the most beautiful church in the world)

Again the desire to produce images from the aggressive modern world
which set themselves off against the stock of more traditionally poetic
subjects is evident. 'Les moteurs beuglent comme les taureaux d'or/Les
vaches du crépuscule broutent le Sacré-Coeur' – the presence of the new is
signalled as a violation of the old, the industrial as a disruption of the
rustic/idyllic. Probably the most celebrated and successful example of this
comes with the opening of 'Zone':

A la fin tu es las de ce monde ancien

Bergère ô tour Eiffel le troupeau de ponts bêle ce matin

Tu en as assez de vivre dans l'antiquité grecque et romaine   (A, 39)

(In the end you're weary of this ancient world

Shepherdess oh Eiffel Tower the flock of bridges is bleating this morning

You've had enough of living amid ancient Greece and Rome)

In the case of both poets, the force with which the world enters the poem
derives largely from their insistence upon the daily and the trivial as
opposed to the objects redolent of Symbolism. The experience which both
shared of the army in the years of the First World War further reinforced
this aspect of their poetry, since it brought them into contact with a world
on which the poetic language of the preceding century had laid no hold
and in which they were forced to confront the realities of the transforma-
tion of that world through the language of the soldiery and the working
classes. Apollinaire in particular renews his verse through this contact in
much the same way that the musicians of the preceding century had turned
to folk and traditional tunes as a source for their works (see in particular
Apollinaire's poems in the sections of *Calligrammes* entitled 'Etendards'
and 'Obus couleur de lune' and Cendrars's 'La Guerre au Luxembourg').
What emerged from this period of writing, notwithstanding the strictures
of the Surrealists and others concerning the lack of an 'appropriate' moral

reaction to the phenomenon of war, was an awareness of the possibilities of language that lay outside the literary and polite registers to which poetry had largely been confined.

Apart from these aspects, the cityscapes of Apollinaire and Cendrars have in common the extent to which they are identified with the poetic voices themselves. Whatever the truth of Cendrars's claims to have influenced Apollinaire during this period – even to the extent of having suggested the opening line of 'Zone' – it is clear from 'La Chanson du mal-aimé' that this aspect of the world-self is present in Apollinaire's poetry long before 1912. From the London of the beginning to the Paris of the end, the external universe is both a projection of the poet's inner world and an aggressive challenge to any concept of unity which might lie within it. This is not just a matter of a poem which records the disarray of a rejected lover and which therefore displays disorder as evidence of the subjective experience it records, however much this aspect may be the source of some of the finest and simplest lines in the poem.

The scale of the poem, both in geographical and in cultural terms, its heterogenous mixture of well-known and obscurely erudite references, its medieval, classical, biblical and stridently modern sources of imagery, all this is evidence of the attempt to construct a lyricism in which the modern is the diversity and not merely the contemporary field of reference, even though this last is essential to any such reading of the poem. It is also, however, written in near-classical form and is the equal of any octosyllabic verse ever written in the French language. Its musical and formal qualities are a record of the struggle for expression which is underlined by the presence of the intercalated episodes – 'Aubade', 'Réponse des Cosaques Zaporogues' and 'Les Sept Epées' – as well as by the tensions operating between the cyclical features of the imagery and structure (the twenty-four hour and year time cycles and the journey from city to city) and the ragbag of tone and image:

> Voie lactée ô soeur lumineuse
> Des blancs ruisseaux de Chanaan
> Et des corps blancs des amoureuses
> Nageurs morts suivrons-nous d'ahan
> Ton cours vers d'autres nébuleuses [...]

> Soirs de Paris ivres du gin
> Flambant de l'électricité
> Les tramways feux verts sur l'échine
> Musiquent au long des portées
> De rails leur folie de machines

> Les cafés gonflés de fumée
> Crient tout l'amour de leur tziganes

De tous leurs siphons enrhumés
De leurs garçons vêtus d'un pagne
Vers toi toi que j'ai tant aimée

Moi qui sais des lais pour les reines
Les complaintes de mes années
Des hymnes d'esclaves aux murènes
La romance du mal aimé
Et des chansons pour les sirènes   (A, 58–9)

(Milky way oh luminous sister
Of the white streams of Canaan
And the white bodies of women in love
Shall we dead swimmers follow out of breath
Your course towards other nebulae [. . .]

Paris evenings drunk on gin
Blazing with electricity
The tramcars green lights on their spine
Music their way as far as the rails go
In their madness of machines

The cafés swollen with smoke
Call out all their gypsy love
From their nasal-dripping syphons
From their long-aproned waiters
To you you that I loved so much

I who know lays fit for queens
The complaints of all my years
The hymns slaves sang to Moray eels
The romance of the ill-beloved
And the songs the sirens sing)

The rag and bone shop of this heart is never foul; not the least of this poem's qualities is that it has entered the popular consciousness, perhaps the first and last poem, certainly long poem, of the century which is known to millions of French people.

This is not an irrelevant consideration, since the strand of Modernism which I am attempting to isolate has everything to do with the language and experience of the people and the way in which various writers and artists from the middle of the preceding century had turned to popular forms and images to find means of expression which might allow them to break out of a moribund tradition. The extent to which the poem, in the hands of Apollinaire and Cendrars, became the manifestation of the existence of a world that was new and changing is, of itself, obvious and was certainly insisted upon by the former in 'La Victoire' when he wrote:

> O mon amie hâte-toi
> Crains qu'un jour un train ne t'émeuve
> Plus   (A, 310)

> (Oh my love hurry
> Fear one day a train may move you
> No longer)

This particular aspect of their poetry represents one of the most character-istic strands and one which finds a continuation in the work of Raymond Queneau, whatever differences he would certainly have had with his two predecessors in the matter of form. To link his name to theirs in this context demands that due attention be paid to those aspects of Queneau's work which give it structure, all the more so when that structure is to some extent hidden. Nevertheless, on a level much more complex than merely that of the poetry of the city these three authors can be read as revealing the essential role played by banality in the reconquest of a voice for poetry in France.

The streets and buildings of Paris play as major a role in this poetry as they did in the previous half-century of French painting, and from 'Un fantôme de nuées' to 'Saint-Ouen's Blues' there is a revealing continuity. Both these poems can be said to partake in a tradition best demarcated by a title given to some of Apollinaire's occasional writings *Le Flâneur des deux rives* or perhaps by some such label as the existential promenade, for the combination of whimsy and *angst* in such a description is a fair assessment of the essential characteristics of this poetry. However, the scale of things needs to be expanded well beyond Paris for both Apollinaire and Queneau and certainly also for Cendrars, who, from his first poems 'Les Pâques à New York' and the 'Prose du Transsibérien' combines the world as phenomenon with the world as scale. What this does for us is to crystallize the notion that at the core of this attempt to re-invent poetry – indeed all art – is the figure of the artist as wanderer, not only in spatial dimensions but also in the labyrinth of culture which has ceased to be coherent for reasons which have to do with the fragmentation of the bourgeois world but also with the loss of underpinning to the language the artist must use.

It is evident that such a condition of art on the eve of the Great War will lead to even greater destructive tendencies. We find not only Dada and other anti-art movements as evidence of this but also the now fairly well-documented links between certain artistic avant-garde movements and extreme right-wing political movements, for example the relations between Italian Futurism and Fascism. Neither Apollinaire nor Cendrars partici-pated in the radically destructive aspects of the different contemporary movements, yet each felt it was essential for their works to be remade and fundamentally separated from any tradition other than the tradition of the new. The last stanzas of Apollinaire's 'Les Collines' show this particular clearly:

> Un chapeau haut de forme est sur
> Une table chargée de fruits
> Les gants sont morts près d'une pomme
> Une dame se tord le cou
> Auprès d'un monsieur qui s'avale
>
> Le bal tournoie au fond du temps
> J'ai tué le beau chef d'orchestre
> Et je pèle pour mes amis
> L'orange dont la saveur est
> Un merveilleux feu d'artifice
>
> Tous sont morts le maître d'hôtel
> Leur verse un champagne irréel
> Qui mousse comme un escargot
> Ou comme un cerveau de poète
> Tandis que chantait une rose
>
> L'esclave tient une épée nue
> Semblable aux sources et aux fleuves
> Et chaque fois qu'elle s'abaisse
> Un univers est éventré
> Dont il sort des mondes nouveaux
>
> Le chauffeur se tient au volant
> Et chaque fois que sur la route
> Il corne en passant le tournant
> Il paraît à perte de vue
> Un univers encore vierge   (A, 176–7)
>
> (A top hat is sitting on
> A table laden with fruit
> The gloves are dead beside an apple
> A woman wrings her neck
> Beside a gentleman who's swallowing himself
>
> Behind time the ball dances on
> I have killed the handsome conductor
> And I peel for my friends
> The orange whose savour is
> A marvel of fireworks

All are dead the headwaiter
Pours them an unreal champagne
Which froths like a snail
Or like the brain of a poet
While a rose was singing

The slave holds a drawn sword
Resembling springs and rivers
And each time it comes down
A universe is eviscerated
And new worlds emerge

The chauffeur sits at the wheel
And each time on the road
He klaxons on taking a bend
There appears as far as the eye can see
A still virgin universe)

The level of invention which Apollinaire is striving for, however strange, proto-Surrealist, it may seem, remains firmly rooted in the possibilities of language and never posits the prior destruction of language itself as a precondition of the new art. But time and again the poet emphasizes the creation of new universes, worlds of the imagination, which are born through a certain violence (e.g. 'Un univers est éventré' and 'Il corne en passant le tournant'). Each new birth/creation is deemed to be merely one of a continuing series ('Et *chaque fois* qu'elle s'abaisse' and 'Dont il sort *des mondes nouveaux*') which clearly reveals the creative process as one of continuous invention and re-invention, not an entry into a new stability. There is to be no reassembling of the scattered limbs of Orpheus but rather continuous and fragmented rebirth.

In Cendrars's *Dix-neuf poèmes élastiques*, the presence of the city also gives rise to images which are intended to convey energy and invention arising from the most banal aspects of daily life, as he says in 'Contrastes':

Les fenêtres de ma poésie sont grand'ouvertes sur les boulevards
                                        et dans ses vitrines
Brillent
Les pierreries de la lumière
Ecoute les violons des limousines et les xylophones des linotypes
Le pocheur se lave dans l'essuie-main du ciel
Tout est taches de couleur
Et les chapeaux des femmes qui passent sont des comètes dans
                                        l'incendie du soir   (C, 56–7)

(The windows of my poetry are wide open to the Boulevards
                                        and in their shop windows

Shine
The precious stones of light
Listen to the violins of the limousines and the xylophones of the linotypes
The street-corner boy washes himself on the hand-towel of the sky
Everything is splashes of colour
And the passing women's hats are comets in the fire of the sky)

Comparisons are easy to draw with many of Apollinaire's poems as with the introduction of fragmented headlines and *papiers collés* into their paintings by the Cubists:

Il pleut les globes électriques
Montrouge Gare de l'Est Métro Nord-Sud bateaux-mouches monde
Tout est halo
Profondeur
Rue de Buci on cri *L'intransigeant* et *Paris-Sports*
L'aérodrome du ciel est maintenant, embrasé, un tableau de Cimabue

(Its raining electric globes
Montrouge Gare de l'Est Métro Nord-Sud passenger boats world
Everything is halo
Depth
In the Rue de Buci the seller calls *L'Intransigeant* and *Paris-Sports*
The aerodrome of the sky is now, afire, a painting by Cimabue)

Cendrars, unlike Apollinaire, never presented himself as the enchanter, able to create a new external world, but, like Apollinaire, he did rejoice in the new poetry which could arise from the artefacts of modernity:

La lettre-océan n'a pas été inventée pour faire de la poésie
Mais quand on voyage quand on commerce quand on est à bord quand
on envoie des lettres-océan
On fait de la poésie   ('Lettre-océan', C, 143)

(The ship-to-shore telegram was not invented for writing poetry
But when you're travelling when you're dealing when you're
on board when you send ship-to-shore telegrams
You're writing poetry)

For all this, Cendrars saw the external world essentially as a projection of himself. He lived within a subjectivity which was acted upon by a cosmos, but a cosmos as he perceived it, as is clear from the following extract from 'Paris' (despite the title a globetrotting poem from *Feuilles de route*):

Je suis resté toute la nuit sur le pont écoutant les messages
qui arrivaient par T.S.F. en déchiffrant quelques bribes
Et les traduisant en clignant des yeux pour les étoiles
Un astre nouveau brillait à la hauteur de mon nez
La braise de mon cigare   (C, 157)

(I stayed up all night on deck listening to the messages
                    coming in on the wireless deciphering a few scraps
And translating them blinking my eyes for the stars
A new star shone on the level of my nose
The tip of my cigar)

Poems such as this, even when there is a sadness in them, are mainly a record of the poet's *joie de vivre*, of his restlessness, but above all of the insistent notion: 'le monde est ma représentation', and that representation is of a fragmented self.

Other poets of the period such as Valéry Larbaud and Paul Morand also display certain of these aspects of the poetry of the modern world, but they both retain a distance between self and the world which makes their poetry much less interesting. While it is true that in Larbaud's case there is the adoption of an ironic persona filtering his observations in tones reminiscent of Prufrock, his view of the world retains an elegiac note that makes of it a mere valediction rather than a salute to the new; and Morand's often more apparently aggressive modernity is too inclined to end in a vaguely sociological generalization as in 'Southern Pacific':

Les machines sont les seules femmes
que les Américains savent rendre heureuses.[2]

(Machines are the only women
that Americans can make happy.)

But in Raymond Queneau we find another poet of the daily and sordid realities of the city, who is capable of a more interesting conjunction of self and the world:

Adieu ce grand pont ces horizontales
ses arches ses murs et ses escaliers
ses fers peints en rouge et ses balustrades
adieu ce grand pont qui baigne ses pieds

adieu la maison et ses verticales
sa toiture mauve et ses volets gris
sa radio béante et dominicale
adieu la maison d'où je suis parti   ('Adieu', Q, 77)

(Farewell the big bridge those horizontals
its arches its walls and its stairways
its red-painted ironwork and its balustrades
farewell big bridge with its feet in the water

farewell the house and its verticals
its mauve roof and its grey shutters
its radio blaring on Sunday
farewell the house I set out from)

With Queneau, as with Apollinaire, there is the frequent juxtaposition of verse forms with a subject which is beneath them socially, as it were, and there is also the delight in mixing the learned with the popular on the level of syntax and vocabulary (one of the titles he considered for *Courir les rues* was *Farraparigo*). Moreover Queneau's cityscapes are the sad suburbs and working-class districts; they are by virtue of their language or their characters the *Parigot*'s perception of the city:

Les petits pigeons pleins de fientaisie
allaient et venaient survolant Paris
donnant à ses murs la couleur exquise
du caca aviair couleur un peu grise
ne se doutant pas pauvres innocents
qu'un piège sournois en bas les attend

les voilà capturés!
ils ne sont pas contents

'Adieu Paris! adieu ma belle ville'   ('Propreté', Q, 389)

(The little pigeons full of witty shit
were coming and going over Paris
giving its walls the exquisite colour
of avial caca a greyish colour
not suspecting the little innocents
that a wily trap awaits them below

they're in the bag!
they're none too pleased

'Farewell Paris! farewell my fair city')

The last line highlights the extent to which the poem is to be read both humorously and as a modern version of a long line of songs of loss and separation since it alludes to the well-known traditional song 'La Marquise empoisonnée': 'Adieu ma mie! adieu mon coeur' (Farewell my love! farewell my heart). Such a combination of humour and sentiment is typical of Queneau. More than either Apollinaire or Cendrars, he is prepared to allow humour to invade his depiction of the life of the city and he has recorded in *Bâtons chiffres et lettres*[3] how his first attempts at writing French as it was spoken and not as it was more or less fixed by the grammarians of the seventeenth century rapidly led him to perceive the comic possibilities of such transcription.

Queneau shares with his predecessors the notion that there is a relationship between himself and the external world which is, in fact, where the self actually exists. But where Apollinaire and Cendrars struggled with dispersal as the perception of both outer and inner worlds, Queneau reveals a fascination with secret form. His conception of the poem, which he was to extend to the novel, is of something which *has* form, which *is* form; but the form of the poem, like the form of a life, arises from perceivable, almost mathematical, laws which none the less remain aleatory. His fascination with numbers is well attested throughout his writings; that both his first and last names consist of seven letters was to provide a basis for the structure of many of his works and his fondness for the sonnet, while not merely reducible to this, obviously derives from the fact that 14 lines $= 2 \times 7$. Thus when one of Queneau's sonnets deals with the apparently least personal of subjects, there is none the less for its author a particular relationship between his own existence and the existence of the poem. But Queneau has extended this idea to limits which surpass the ability of any individual to encompass, for in his *Cent mille milliards de poèmes* (Q, 333–45) he created a machine for the generation of sonnets, all necessarily composed from his words and according to the basic patterns established by him – rhymes, Petrarchan form – but in number more than many human lifetimes could ever contain. The ten original poems of this collection are written so that any first line can be substituted for any other first line, any second line for any other second line and so on; the result being a possible 10^{14} sonnets which, as the preface informs us, it would take more than a million centuries to read.

Through such numbers it would be true to say that Queneau has made himself a poet of truly cosmic scale, yet at the same time he has confined himself to one of the more intimate forms of poetry, subject to some of the most restrictive rules. The following sonnet is not one of the original ten in Queneau's volume but is randomly made up from lines drawn from them:

Il se penche il voudrait attraper sa valise	(6)
d'aucuns par dessus tout prisent les escargots	(9)
le chauffeur indigène attendait dans la brise	(4)
on espère toujours être de vrais normaux	(7)
Le cheval Parthénon frissonnait sous la bise	(2)
que n'a pas dévoré la horde des mulots?	(9)
nous avions aussi froids que nus sur la banquise	(1)
à tous n'est pas donné d'aimer les chocs verbaux	(8)

Du Gange au Malabar le lord anglais zozotte   (4)
on sale le requin on fume à l'échalotte   (3)
le chemin vicinal se nourrit de crottin   (9)

L'Amérique du sud séduit les équivoques   (1)
on mettait sans façon ses plus infectes loques   (6)
le Beaune et le Chianti sont-ils le même vin   (5)

(He bends over and tries to catch hold of his case
some people like snails better than anything
the native driver was waiting in the breeze
we always hope to be really normal

The Parthenon horse shivered in the north wind
what has the horde of field mice not devoured?
we were as cold as if naked on the pack-ice
not everyone is given to liking verbal shocks

From the Ganges to the Malabar coast lisps the English lord
you salt shark eat it smoked with shallots
the country lane is fed on dung

South America seduces ambiguities
you wore without hesitation your worst rags
Are Beaune and Chianti the same wine)

While the shifts between lines may seem fairly tenuous, it is interesting to
see on the one hand how easy it is to read some of them continuously or to
find links between them and, on the other, to note how little difference
there is in this respect from the poems of Apollinaire and Cendrars which
do not allow the reader to suppose or deny any continuous syntax but
demand that the line be given primacy. As François Le Lionnais has
commented, Queneau's technique here is comparable to that of Mozart,
since it allows the same phrase to find many different meanings according
to the context in which it is placed. It does not dehumanize or attempt to
dehumanize language or poetry since it operates on the basis of permutat-
ing phrases entirely composed by Queneau.[4]

Queneau's poetry like his prose works displays his determination to find
popular expression for any subject or idea. At the threshold of the 1930s
it seemed to him that the French language was threatened with a schism
between its written and spoken forms as radical as that which had split
the literary language of the Greeks from the demotic. And while his
attempts to create a *néo-français* which would be the written form of
the spoken language, lead as much to humour as to the transcription of
twentieth-century *parigot*, in all his writing he retained the central notion

that great ideas can be stated in simple language, even if that simple
language is susceptible of multiple readings. What marks his poetry in this
regard is its ludic qualities:

> Un train qui siffle dans la nuit
> C'est un sujet de poésie
> Un train qui siffle en Bohême
> C'est là le sujet d'un poème
>
> Un train qui siffle mélod'
> Ieusement c'est pour une ode
> Un train qui siffle comme un sansonnet
> C'est bien un sujet de sonnet   (Q, 110)
>
> (A train whistling in the night
> That's a subject for poesy
> A train whistling in Bohemia
> Now that's a subject for poetry
>
> A train whistling melod'
> Iously that makes an ode
> A train with a starling's whistle
> That makes a good epistle)
>   *[Note – unlicenced translator's licence!]*

This often gives his poetry the characteristics of nursery rhymes, but most
of his verse stems from a source which oscillates between the erudition
of the editor of the Pléiade encyclopaedia, which Queneau was, and an
everyman/Pierrot figure,[5] simple observer of great and general truths – the
banalities of wisdom:

> Je crains pas ça tellement la mort de mes entrailles
> et la mort de mon nez et celle de mes os
> Je crains pas ça tellement moi cette moustiquaille
> qu'on baptisa Raymond d'un père dit Queneau
>
> Je crains pas ça tellement où va la bouquinaille
> les quais les cabinets la poussière et l'ennui
> Je crains pas ça tellement moi qui tant écrivaille
> et distille la mort en quelques poésies   (Q, 123)
>
> (I'm not so scared of that the dying of my guts
> and the dying of my nose and that of my bones
> I'm not so scared of that me this little bug
> they baptised Raymond father's name Queneau

I'm not so scared of that the way of all bookishness
the seller's stalls the reading-rooms the dust and boredom
I'm not so scared of that me the busy scribbler
and distiller of death into a few lines)

The poems of the second section of Queneau's *Chêne et chien* record his self-analysis and transition through psychoanalysis, which he had undertaken as a result of his interest in the Surrealists' ideas. They mark his violent break with (Surrealist) ideas that suggest certain ways of knowing and ordering the coming together of internal and external worlds, and thereafter his poetry seldom looks inward unless by looking outward. He declared in 1938 that the poet was not the slave of the association of ideas, but knew the forces of rhythm and language, and knew, above all, what he was doing.

Both Apollinaire's 'Zone' and Cendrars's 'Les Pâques à New York' centre on the crisis caused by the loss of faith – religious faith that is – which clearly places at the heart of each poem a loss of that which gave unity and purpose to the life of the artist. The poet's consciousness is now adrift in a world which assails his senses with a fragmentary experience. Despite the optimism with which 'Les Collines' ends (and the poem, like 'Zone' in *Alcools*, is placed near the beginning of *Calligrammes* while belonging chronologically near the end) all that follows in *Calligrammes* is just as much a struggle for style, for expression as these lines from 'La Victoire' reveal:

Et ces vieilles langues sont tellement près de mourir
Que c'est vraiment par habitude et manque d'audace
Qu'on les fait encore servir à la poésie   (A, 310)

(And these old tongues are so close to death
That it's really from habit and lack of boldness
That we still make use of them for poetry)

Thus the predicament of the poet is inescapable since language is a shared instrument and cannot be remade by the individual except at the risk of solipsistic exclusion. Hence the prevalence of the wanderer and the displaced figure. Each encounter between the poet and the world will take shape on a more or less contingent basis. It will be, moreover, successful to the degree that some part of the previous contract with the world can be discarded or lost:

A l'institut des jeunes aveugles on a demandé
N'avez-vous point de jeune aveugle ailé
O bouches l'homme est à la recherche d'un nouveau langage
Auquel le grammairien d'aucune langue n'aura rien à dire   (A, 309–10)

(At the institute for the young blind they asked
Don't you have a young blind winged man
Oh mouths man is looking for a new language
On which the grammarian of no tongue will have a say)

From the earliest years of the century to the end of his life in 1918, Apollinaire introduced into his poetry various figures – often compared to the characters of the blue and pink periods of Picasso's painting – whose associations are with the circus, street-entertaining and popular theatre: the acrobats, jugglers, harlequins and others who can trace a complex ancestry back through various nineteenth- and eighteenth-century art forms – the poetry of Laforgue, the painting of Watteau, to name but two – all the way to the *commedia dell'arte*. Through these figures we can see the evolution of Apollinaire's view of the artist as an essentially isolated figure able to touch an audience only occasionally and then more through a sense of what is not articulated than of what is.

Le second saltimbanque
N'était vêtu que de son ombre
Je le regardai longtemps
Son visage m'échappe entièrement
C'est un homme sans tête [...]

Le petit saltimbanque fit la roue
Avec tant d'harmonie
Que l'orgue cessa de jouer
Et que l'organiste se cacha le visage dans les mains
Aux doigts semblables aux descendants de son destin
Foetus minuscules qui lui sortaient de la barbe
Nouveaux cris de Peau-Rouge
Musique angélique des arbres
Disparition de l'enfant

Les saltimbanques soulevèrent les gros haltères à bout de bras
Ils jonglèrent avec les poids

Mais chaque spectateur cherchait en soi l'enfant miraculeux
Siècle ô siècle des nuages

(The second acrobat
Was dressed only in his shadow
I looked long at him
His face escapes me entirely
He's a headless man [...]

> The little acrobat cartwheeled
> With such harmony
> That the organ ceased to play
> And the organist hid his face in his hands
> With his fingers resembling the descendants of his destiny
> Minuscule foetuses which were coming out of his beard
> New redskin whoops
> Angelical music of the trees
> Disappearance of the child
>
> The acrobats lifted up the heavy weights to arm's length
> They juggled with the weights
>
> But each spectator was looking in himself for the miraculous child
> Century oh century of clouds)

These lines from 'Un fantôme de nuées', first published in 1913, show a much more complex treatment of the group of acrobats than that which Apollinaire had accorded them in the 1909 poem from *Alcools* 'Saltimbanques':

> Ils ont des poids ronds ou carrés
> Des tambours des cerceaux dorés
> L'ours et le singe animaux sages
> Quêtent des sous sur leur passage   (A, 90)
>
> (They have round or square weights
> Drums and golden hoops
> The bear and the monkey wise animals
> Beg for money as they pass)

This is really simply an evocation of a mood, whereas the later poem is a presentation of the artist as performer, belonging to a long tradition, but one which no longer automatically finds the common ground upon which it once supposedly rested. Between these two extracts lies the evolution away from the potentially symbolic power of the group of itinerant performers as representatives of the condition of the artist and the use of the tawdry magic of the street entertainer at the heart of a complex poem which refuses to yield its meaning on any such level. As the title indicates, 'Un fantôme de nuées' is a shifting figure not to be pinned down to any permanent way but not to be ignored either.

The same sense of language as being all we have, of poetry existing in a long, long line of performances, which are, like circus acts, variations upon each other, is found in Queneau's poetry as, in many of his poems, he introduces lines that are variations upon well-known lines from other poets, or of proverbs and sayings. A glance at any of his volumes produces echoes of most of the best known French poets and he often wittily conflates references to more than one:

> Enfin vint un fourreur qui le premier en France
> Donnant un sens plus pur au beau mot de vison   (Q, 272)

> (At last came a furrier who the first in France
> Giving a purer meaning to the good word mink)

Here the first line alludes to Boileau's famous salute to Malherbe in his *Art poétique* while the second alludes to Mallarmé's celebrated 'Donner un sens plus pur aux mots de la tribu'. It is impossible to escape this aspect of Queneau's poetry; clearly, for him the artist is no more and no less than performer, but the rare word, the erudite term and the lexicon of the mid-century street-wise Parisian bear the same relationship to the phenomena of the universe. Each time the poet takes up one or the other he takes the world in his hands:

> Un poème c'est bien peu de chose
> à peine plus qu'un cyclone aux Antilles
> qu'un typhon dans la mer de Chine
> un tremblement de terre à Formose   (Q, 105)

> (A poem's only a little thing
> barely more than a cyclone in the West Indies
> than a typhoon in the China sea
> an earthquake in Formosa)

13

High Formal Poetry

GRAHAM DUNSTAN MARTIN

In twentieth-century poetry in English, elevated diction has become rare. In France it is still common, but has adopted two very different forms: on the one hand the tight, perfectionist scansion of traditional verse; on the other, the *verset*, echoing the loose rhythms of Biblical verse.

The great prophet of the former manner was Paul Valéry who, to judge by his own statements, viewed the writing of a poem rather as a climber views Mount Everest – as a challenge whose very difficulty is its attraction. 'Shoes that are too tight', he writes, 'would make us invent new dances' (I, 1305; cf. Voltaire's position, described in Chapter 8).[1] He was suspicious, even condemnatory of inspiration. 'It is not a poet's function to experience the poetic state: that is a private matter. His business is to create it in others' (I, 1321). Despite the fact that he recognizes the impossibility of completing a work by conscious means alone (I, 1328), the emphasis is on the maximum of conscious craftsmanship (I, 640). A word should be chosen because it fulfils the multiple requirements of the context as to sound, metrics, meaning, etc. Poetry resembles music: it is a matter of rhythm, resonance, syllabic count, and the interaction of multiple meanings (I, 1334). The highest poetry, like the highest music (which he ascribes to J.S. Bach), evokes 'a feeling like no other' (I, 676), a purely *aesthetic* emotion. This emotion is ineffable: 'What can be expressed in other words is prose' (II, 555), and 'what cannot be summarized is poetry' (II, 638).

Valéry claimed that it was not poetry as such which was the centre of his interests. 'I'll grant that Mallarmé may be obscure, sterile and precious; but to have made me [...] prize above all the conscious possession of *the function of language* [... – this] remains for me an incomparable boon' (My italics: I, 660). What interests Valéry essentially is the poem as evidence of the power of language and of the nature of the human mind. Poetry should therefore be difficult for the reader too.

> Dormeuse, amas doré d'ombres et d'abandons,
> Ton repos redoutable est chargé de tels dons,
> O biche avec langueur longue auprès d'une grappe,
>
> Que malgré l'âme absente, occupée aux enfers,
> Ta forme au ventre pur qu'un bras fluide drape,
> Veille; ta forme veille, et mes yeux sont ouverts.
>
> 'La Dormeuse' (I, 122)

> (Sleeper, golden mass of shadows and abandons,
> Your redoubtable repose is loaded with such gifts,
> O doe stretched out with langour under the grapes,
> That despite the absence of your soul, busy in the underworld,
> Your form with its pure flank draped by a liquid arm,
> Is on watch; your form watches, and my eyes are open.)

In Valéry's poetry, a spade (e.g. the presumably sexual 'grappe') is not called a spade, but lifted (as in the eighteenth century) on to a euphemistic level. There is a taste for tenuous metaphor (i.e. metaphor justified only by one link): thus the woman's repose is 'redoubtable' only in the one sense that the poet is reluctant to waken her; and her soul is in Hell only in the sense that while she sleeps it is busy in the unconscious. The sleeper is replaced (in l. 1) by a description of the light and shade in a painting. (See also l. 5.) She has, like a painting, 'form' rather than a 'body'. We wonder if the poem is after all about a sleeping woman; perhaps it is about poetry. The imagery is recherché, fanciful and far-fetched: precious, in a word.

None the less the musical, visual and emotional qualities are strong. Line 1 is a charming alliterative pattern, which charges vision and sound with the emotions of 'viewing a nude' and with sexual 'abandon'. And the 'message' at the end is more than abstract Bachian music: the poet's mind and the physical and unconscious depths of reality 'observe' each other. The world, for this very intellectual poet, is not after all pure intellect – and a sense of wonder illuminates the world's – and the woman's – physical surfaces.

As our example of the *verset*, let us take St-John Perse. Valéry may use a lofty tone, but he does not get 'carried away' – whereas the younger poet, read aloud, sounds like an orator in a passion:

> Etroits sont les vaisseaux, étroite notre couche.
> Immense l'étendue des eaux, plus vaste notre empire
> Aux chambres closes du désir.

Entre l'Eté, qui vient de mer. A la mer seule, nous dirons
Quels étrangers nous fûmes aux fêtes de la ville, et quel astre montant des fêtes
  sous-marines
S'en vint un soir, sur notre couche, flairer la couche du divin.

En vain la terre proche nous trace sa frontière. Une même vague par le monde,
  une même vague depuis Troie
Roule sa hanche jusqu'à nous. Au très grand large loin de nous fut imprimé
  jadis ce souffle . . .
Et la rumeur un soir fut grande dans les chambres: la mort elle-même, à son de
  conques, ne s'y ferait point entendre!   (*Amers*)[2]

(Strait are the vessels, strait our couch.
Immense the spread of the waters, vaster still our empire
In the closed chambers of desire.

Enter Summer, fresh from the sea. To the sea alone, we shall tell
What strangers we were at the feasts of the Town, and what star mounting
  from feasts beneath the sea
Came one evening, on our couch, to scent out the couch of the divine.

In vain the earth nearby traces its frontier. The same wave across the world,
  the same wave since Troy
Rolls its hips unto us. In the ocean deeps far from us once this breath was
  born . . .
And the murmur one evening was great in the chambers: there death itself, to
  the sound of conches, could not make itself heard!)

These rhythms stem from Claudel, and his in turn from Whitman and
from the binary structure of the biblical Psalms, in which there is no rhyme
and no regular rhythm, but a system of syntactic balances and parallelisms.
Thus, Psalm 19 begins:

The heavens declare the glory of God; and the firmament sheweth his
  handwork.
Day unto day uttereth speech; and night unto night sheweth knowledge.

Each verse divides into two halves, and each half echoes, supports or
contrasts with the other. Claudel had initiated the use of the psalm-like
verset because, in rhymed verse, 'It is not always easy to produce hypnosis,
but it is very easy to provoke sleep'.[3]

Unlike Claudel, St-John Perse is a pantheist, not a Christian. Sea and
Summer, Death and the Town, are personified, and often capitalized.
The physical world is alive with spirit – and, in compensation, personal
experience disappears into timeless myth (except for his delightful early
Eloges). The rather grotesquely described wave connects the couple to a
legend outside history, that of Paris and Helen. The couch is an altar.

Love-making is a rite, timeless and placeless, those who engage in it are gods. But then, all activity in St-John Perse is heavy with ritual, and the acts of man within time reflect a divine and eternal world rather like that of Plato's ideal forms. *Amour* and *mer* are echoed against each other: they are manifestations of the life-force. For mankind is on its grand march through time and eternity, perhaps as in Bergson or Teilhard de Chardin (*Œuvres*, 445).

In exile in America, St-John Perse was attacked by certain critics for his 'rhetoric' (a *bête noire* of the New Criticism, then at its apogee). He took up the cudgels in *The Berkeley Review*. These 'larges déroulements poétiques français' were actually, he said, 'a sum of contractions, omissions and ellipses'. Taking the war into the enemy camp, he went on to attack the very nature of English as a poetic language. English poetry was

> a poetry of idea, therefore of definition and elucidation, always explicit and logical, because rational in origin. [...] English poetry always seems to spring from a meditation, not from a trance; to follow the line of a modulation, not the genuine complexity of an incantation.

We must note here that St-John Perse believes in trance, and in incantation.

As for French poetry, it is capable of

> Integrating itself, alive, with its living object; fully incorporating itself and confounding its substance with it, to the point of a perfect identity and unity between subject and object, poet and poem. (*Œuvres*, 565–6)

The poem 'becomes' and 'is' the object, 'in its movement and its duration'. Whereas English poetry is 'dualistic' – it separates language from referent, and regards the two as different from each other. (And indeed, how could the two not be different? We here touch the roots of the mutual incomprehension of two neighbouring and related languages!) We shall find Emmanuel expressing the same sort of hope. We are in the presence of a persistent French myth: that of the concrete reality of language.

English seems to be accused here of not being ambiguous. Certainly French is more ambiguous than English, on account of its 'long evolution towards the abstract', which has produced 'ambiguity or polyvalence' (*Œuvres*, 567). St-John Perse welcomes this as a positive poetic value. I am more sceptical: is his 'ambiguity' not really more abstract than polyvalent? The danger in *Amers* is that love may be abstracted from its many-faceted particularity, and reduced to mere generality.

English poetry, says Perse, permits public performance, for it is less ambiguous than French poetry. This is because, when reading aloud, one has to impose a single interpretation on a poem. French poetry does not permit a single interpretation, 'whence the extreme repugnance of the

French poet for any spoken reading' (*Œuvres*, 567). French poetry should be read, not aloud, but silently, 'for the inner ear', as Beethoven in his deafness apprehended music (*Œuvres*, 568). Might we speculate that (according to Perse) this activity may produce a special type of concentration – which puts one in touch with the rhythms of nature hidden within one's own unconscious?

The English-speaking reader will quite rightly recoil from this distortion of his own native poetic experience. But we are not in the business of discussing the rights or wrongs of the Frenchman's view of English poetry, but rather French poetry's picture of itself. The difficulty here is that Perse's suggestion raises more problems than it solves. For example, don't we readers of English usually read poetry in precisely the way Perse recommends? And isn't it on the basis of such silent readings *also* that the accusation of 'rhetoric' is based? Then again, can non-poetic writings of an oratorical kind be treated in the same way and to the same effect? And if not, why not? Besides, many French poets would entirely reject the suggestion that their poetry is 'for the inner ear alone'. It would have been more convincing to be told that the line between acceptable and unacceptable 'rhetoric' is drawn in a different place by French and English readers.

Some of the same problems are encountered with Pierre Emmanuel. He echoes the very accents of Hugo himself, beginning, as the earlier poet did so often, with a dramatic apostrophe. One wonders if the picture which the reader of such lines has of himself is not that of a passive witness of a play, a sermon or a speech: he is being 'taken out of himself', he is being manipulated, elevated and inspired, he is being asked to echo and applaud:

> Consolateur! quand j'allais ramener le soir
> sur mon visage pour m'éteindre avec ma race
> une musique m'éveilla: c'était le vent
> qui chantait dans mes os, – ou peut-être la terre
> ôtée du four et que pénètre le serein
> craquelant la chaleur du sol. Ainsi des siècles
> se plaignent-ils quand on défourne des tombeaux
> couvés par les déserts d'une brûlante Asie
> les vases des Empires morts. Si je suspends
> la harpe de David dans les saules, je vois
> le roi danser autour de l'arche: et quand le livre
> s'ouvre aux commandements du vent, voici gémir
> Jérémie sur Moab comme une flûte.   ('Veni Creator')[4]

> (Consoler! When I was about to draw the evening
> over my face to die with my race
> a music woke me: it was the wind
> singing in my bones, or perhaps the earth
> drawn from the kiln and penetrated by the evening dew

crackling with the heat of the soil. Thus centuries
lament when one draws from tombs
hatched by the deserts of a burning Asia
the vases of dead Empires. If I hang
the harp of David in the willows, I see
the king dancing around the Ark: and when the book
opens to the commandments of the wind, here is Jeremiah
mourning over Moab like a flute.)

Along with the inflated dignity of this language, there is a curious vague-
ness. True, 'drawing the evening over one's face' is a concrete and vivid
image of the sleep which is death. But when the poet writes 'C'était le
vent / qui chantait dans mes os', what are we to imagine? The image is
absurd ... and remains so even if the bones are not his own, but belong
to the dead lying about him (following the apocalyptic vision of death
glimpsed in 'Plus que la Sentinelle', a previous section of the poem). But
then there is an uncomfortable staginess in calling them 'my bones'. For
this is old-fashioned poetic diction, signifying 'the bones belonging to my
people'. Now the use of such a lofty register may work where it wrenches
us away from the modern, and keeps the poetry apart from bathos ... but
it is a miscalculation where it fails to do so.

A somewhat Hugolian metre. But one can glimpse Emmanuel's biblical
rhythms too: the binary rhythm of 'Si je suspends ...' is balanced against
'et quand le livre ...'; a complex binary rhythm, for *within* each phrase
there is again a binary contrast, which we can tabulate like this:

A. 1. Si je suspends / la harpe de David dans les saules,
   2. je vois / le roi danser autour de l'arche:

B. 1. et quand le livre / s'ouvre aux commandements du vent,
   2. voici gémir / Jérémie sur Moab comme une flute.

The metrical skill here is amazing, as Emmanuel syncopates the rhythms of
the Bible against those of Hugo; but I am too Anglo-Saxon a spirit to find
Emmanuel's melodramatic and excitable manner appealing. Still, it is a
manner which a certain tradition of French poetry finds perfectly accept-
able – or even to be the true mark of poetry. Moreover, the poet's theory
has considerable interest, for it continues one of the most venerable
traditions in French (and indeed European) poetry – the belief that poetry
is a matter of inspiration (see above, Chapter 5), that its words have a reality
above the words of ordinary language, and that some central spiritual
truth can be communicated through them.

For instance, Emmanuel experiences the poetic trance. By his own
account, when he wrote his early *Christ au Tombeau*, 'I was beside myself,
almost an automaton. [...] Re-reading [the poem] the next day, I was

scandalized to discover that I could not understand it'.[5] For the material of poetry comes from deeper down in the mind than does normal language. These depths are spiritual depths, where the unity of humankind and the immanence of God are to be found. Like Perse and Bonnefoy, he is suspicious of the concept or 'abstract idea', and regards *le sens* (meaning/ sense) of words as superficial. He wants to attain to 'not the sense [of a phrase], but its soul' (*A*, 432).

> Speech seems to me like a fifth element, as natural as the four others – the spiritual element which concretizes them and establishes the human space. Now the most concrete language is poetry, for the words it uses are indivisible from the things it names: it substitutes for abstract ideas those living relationships, those correspondences, those analogies which are like the nervous system of our universal presence. [...] Thus it reveals to us the profundity of our incarnation: we are the heart of matter, in principle and for a purpose. (*A*, 443)

As in St-John Perse, words have a Platonic reality – are the incarnation of the things they name. He compares the action of poetry to that of contemplation (*A*, 433), and writes: 'I would wish to love words so deeply that every one becomes a prayer' (*A*, 477).

Now there has often been a substitution, in the nineteenth and twentieth centuries, of artistic for religious experience. Not that Emmanuel is an 'idolater' of poetry: he has not substituted it for God – or, as he says some atheist poets such as Jacques Dupin have, for the absence of God.[6] One must not remain in static worship of a poem, for he recognizes that one must not remain fixated on any single object, each object being merely a stage in an endless spiritual progress: 'For every man who is truly alive is on a quest' (*FH*, 281).

None the less, it is certain that the function of the poet in Emmanuel in part replaces that of priest and prophet: 'No matter how unworthy the poet is, some trace remains in him of his prophetic calling' (*A*, 473). The very name 'Pierre Emmanuel' is a pseudonym with evident religious over-tones (*A*, 197). We should note that 'St-John Perse' is also a nom-de-plume. For, whether he is a Christian or a mystical pantheist, the poet as prophet is not to be identified with the social exterior of the citizen whose body he inhabits. He is a different and more exalted being.

It is not surprising therefore that the prophetic manner, the high rhetorical tone, is Emmanuel's favoured style. This prophetic manner remains one of the French Catholic poetry reader's most common expectations. It causes no discomfort, and is to him a sign of 'the poetic'. Nor is this at all surprising from another point of view. For the solemn and portentous rhythms of the French Bible – and, before it, of the Latin Bible – carry for the believer the high seriousness of the Christian message.

Such rhythms act as the vehicle which allows the message to 'pass' – all the more so when they are blended with the traditional metre of serious French poetry, from the alexandrine of Racine to the (at times partially liberated) alexandrine of Victor Hugo's 'visionary' works. Such rhythms are associated with the notion that poetry marks a specially privileged mode of consciousness, a state of inspiration in the poet, and exaltation in the reader.

The poet whom Emmanuel hero-worshipped, and from whom as a tyro poet he sought advice, was Pierre Jean Jouve. His work however seeks eloquent expansion less often than compressed intensity. This sonnet is hermetic, almost Mallarméan:

Rêve du livre

Un petit livre ouvert dont je cherche l'abord
Est-il à le manger un abîme discord
Un livre avec du feu dans les plis et les lettres
Humides de sang rouge et comme veine ouverte

Où réconciliés sont amour et son manque
Et Dieu! et les baisers du pli et l'épuisante
Ascèse qui mélancolique bat la grève
De mourir et les cheveux langoureux et les lèvres

Le livre (est-ce le pli dévoré) s'ouvrira
Sur le massacre des amants par le poème
Et j'aurai toujours lu sa lettre avec fracas

Le livre de la chair et de Dieu abolis
En leur amour orgasme et seul esprit béni
L'unité d'un seul don dans les cuisses de femme.[7]

(Dream of the Book

I seek the way in to a little open book
Is there to eat it a tuneless abyss
A book with fire in its folds and the letters
Wet with red blood and like an open vein

Where reconciled are love and its lack
And God! and the kisses of the fold and the exhausting
Ascesis that mournfully beats against the shore
Of dying and the languorous hair and the lips

The book (is it the fold devoured) will open
On the massacre of lovers by the poem
And I shall always have read its letter with commotion

> The book of the flesh and of God both killed
> In their love orgasm and single blessed spirit
> The unity of a single gift between woman's thighs.)

The book, though open, is at the start of the poem uncut. It, and its uncut folds, are feminine symbols, and the paper-knife is of course phallic. As often in Jouve, the act of sex is also seen in terms of a mutual suicide or a knifing to death. For the forces of Eros and of Thanatos (the death-wish) are the two sides of the secret of life – which is also the same secret as that act of love known as the crucifixion. The book, as well as being poem and woman's body, is also the Bible. For Jouve was at once a Freudian and a Christian.

The assonances and false rhymes assist the sense of agonized intensity. So acute is the compression that, one feels, Jouve's syntax has been wedged into a box too tight for it. Others of these sonnets are so compressed that they are of less than fourteen lines.

'Poetry is the expression of the heights of language', writes Jouve.[8] According to Pierre Emmanuel's *Autobiographies*, Jouve's demand for perfection was so intense that

> A speck of dust on a table was for him a spiritual stumbling block: he staked the whole of beauty on the placing of a word in the universe of a white page; and probably he was afraid of his own handwriting, for he had drilled and cramped it until its rhythm and proportions resembled print on the published page.

Here we have again the Mallarméan mystique of the white page. Jouve worked 'to the point of making the pain of writing atrocious, and the mutism of words almost insurmountable' (*A*, 185).

With such ascetic ideals, one might suspect that Jouve might be Mallarméan also in this, that he regards poetry as designed for an elite. And indeed he declares:

> There can be no question of [poetry's] being understood by the majority, the masses transfixed by well-defined 'artistic and sporting' amusements. [...] Readers who seek to enjoy themselves are irrelevant to us, and we are irrelevant to them. (*EM*, 15, 155)

To Emmanuel he gave this advice:

> Language is not truly necessary, he told me, except when an inner experience informs each word from within; words are not the small change of the idea, but the idea itself, lived in the singular, carrier of an entirely personal energy [...] No one is a poet unless his experience transforms itself into language. (*A*, 185–6)

Here we have, not so much poetry as an expression of the individual, but rather the individual training himself like an anchorite to become the voice of his own intimate depths. Jouve tells us that he had sought 'revelation', but until his discovery of Freud had not been able to guess at the nature of the unconscious darkness from which such revelation comes. (*EM*, 35). After his Freudian 'conversion', these depths are seen at once in terms of the unconscious and of the soul.

More interesting still, perhaps, is the notion of poetry as a reality, not a symbolic system, and of the poet as directly transmuting experience into language. Other forms of discourse are symbolic systems, but poetry is of a different nature. Psychic and spiritual reality 'fill' each poetic word as water fills a goblet. Like his disciple Emmanuel, Jouve believes that 'Poetry is founded [. . .] on the occult power of the word to create the object' (*EM*, 10). Again there is a suspicion of the abstract concept, a tendency to see poetic language as non-conceptual, as providing a non-mediated contact with a spiritual reality. Again there is something akin to Platonism.

Many of these concerns reappear in Yves Bonnefoy:

L'Ecume, le récif

Solitude à ne pas gravir, que de chemins!
Robe rouge, que d'heures proches sous les arbres!
Mais adieu, dans cette aube froide, mon eau pure,
Adieu malgré le cri, l'épaule, le sommeil.

Ecoute, il ne faut plus ces mains qui se reprennent
Comme éternellement l'écume et le rocher,
Et même plus ces yeux qui se tournent vers l'ombre,
Aimant mieux le sommeil encore partagé.

Il ne faut plus tenter d'unir voix et prière,
Espoir et nuit, désirs de l'abîme et du port.
Vois, ce n'est pas Mozart qui lutte dans ton âme,
Mais le gong, contre l'arme informe de la mort.

Adieu, visage en mai.
Le bleu du ciel est morne aujourd'hui, ici.
Le glaive de l'indifférence de l'étoile
Blesse une fois de plus la terre du dormeur.[9]

(Foam on the reef

Solitude beyond scaling, countless the paths.
Scarlet skirt, uncounted the time together under the trees.
Yet farewell, in this cold dawn, my clear water,
Farewell despite the agony, shoulder, slumber.

You hear: an end to hands seeking to clasp
Like foam slipping eternally from its rock,
An end even to sight closing on shadows
In preference of sleep while still sleep's shared.

An end to wishing voice and prayer were one,
Hope and darkness one, the lure of precipice and homestead.
It is not Mozart battles in your heart
But the gong, against the formless instrument of death.

Farewell the lips of spring.
Here, today, the sky is desolate with blue.
The sword-blade of a planet's high indifference
Bloodies once more the sleeper's earth.)

No luxuriance here. A grey, silver, black, and sombre world, whose only other colours are a cold sky-blue, and the ambiguous red of passion or of blood. This accords with Bonnefoy's description of the nature of the French language ('excluding instead of describing') and of the central tradition of French poetry – where the poet 'locks himself away in a closed and simpler world among a few privileged objects'.[10]

He too defines himself by contrast with English poetry (he is a notable translator of Shakespeare). Unlike St-John Perse, he writes, 'Who has ever doubted that there is an English poetry?'[11] But he uses his deep sympathy for English so as better to write in an un-English way.

The temptation of French, he says, is to suppose itself a language of Platonic essences. Though this is a fallacy, the poet may write 'as if', and may sometimes make it seem to be 'really so'. Bonnefoy's practice in fact is similar to that of other poets discussed in their chapter (particularly Jouve). None the less, the poetry in Bonnefoy is sometimes in the failure of the essence to be evoked; which is perhaps why his poetry is so often tragic.

The particular experience therefore dims, as it becomes transparent to the general human truth. (This is what happens when poets listen to the dictum of critics that 'the poet's mistress is but a fiction: she is "the beloved" in general'.) Everything moves onto the plane of the eternal. There is a persistent use of 'le', 'la', to indicate both a precise reference and a general one (for the article in French may indicate (1) a particular event or object in the outside world (e.g. 'le cri'), (2) a unique identity (the sky) and (3) generality (the foam, i.e. foam in general). The occasional unusual word or reference stands out with all the more force – Mozart, the gong.

Everything depends on a great precision of tone. Bonnefoy's rhythms are traditional, but inlaid with deliberate flaws (as in ll. 13–14). As he explains in one of his essays, faults must appear in perfection, otherwise a veil of pretence will conceal the world's tragic reality. This is also one of his safeguards against abstraction. Hence the poem celebrating the destruction of 'Beauty'.[12]

Bonnefoy, like St-John Perse and Jouve, is hostile to the abstract concept. As in Perse, because French words are more general, they risk becoming abstract. On the other hand, for the same reason, they can be poetically ambiguous. Thus, it is not clear in l. 4 whether orgasm or pain or grief at the coming parting is meant by 'le cri'. Generality in Bonnefoy is not the usual generality of conceptual language – it is *much wider* – so wide indeed that I am tempted to say it is bound to carry with it mystical suppositions – for the wider the extension of a word, the more contradictions it subsumes. Both French and English poetry reject the abstract, but in doing so the French poet takes an opposite direction to the English one: away from sensory experience, towards experience perceived as mystical.

Like Bonnefoy, René Char adopts the stance of an atheistic mysticism. Unlike him, his poetry shows an immense variety of manner and tone, ranging from the nature lyric full of verve, directness and precise observation ('Complainte du lézard amoureux') through the lyric in prose ('Congé au vent') and the eloquent love-poem ('Le Visage nuptial') to a well-nigh impenetrable intellectual compression (e.g. 'Les Dentelles de Montmirail', which is simply a sequence of aphorisms). Char is a metaphysical poet in Eliot's sense of the word: sensibility is not dissociated from intellect.

A single exemplary poem from this great poet cannot therefore be found. I am reduced to fragments. Here is an aphorism from the *Feuillets d'Hypnos*, a 'diary' of his time in the Maquis:

> Le fruit est aveugle. C'est l'arbre qui voit.   (no. 165)

> (The fruit is blind. It is the tree that sees,)

Such Heraclitean inscrutability produces different senses when applied to different contexts. It is a vehicle awaiting a tenor, an actor awaiting a play, a metaphor awaiting a multitude of referents. Char's theory seems to be this: *Compress an abstract thought enough, and it becomes poetry.*

As for observation, what could be more cruel, more penetrating, than:

> Il en va de certaines femmes comme des vagues de la mer. En s'élançant de toute leur jeunesse elles franchissent un rocher trop élevé pour leur retour. Cette flaque désormais croupira là, prisonnière, belle par éclair, à cause des cristaux de sel qu'elle renferme et qui lentement se substituent à son vivant.   (*Feuillets d'Hypnos*, no. 173)

> (It's the same with some women as with waves of the sea. Surging up with all the pride of their youth they reach a rock too high to return from. Like a pool henceforth she crouches there, a prisoner, beautiful by flashes, because of the salt crystals which she contains and which slowly replace her life.)

Some critics have objected to the elitist over-intellectualism which they detect in his work. And it is true that (as we saw with Valéry) metaphysical poetry runs the danger of preciosity, as in these lines:

> A présent disparais, mon escorte, debout dans la distance;
> La douceur du nombre vient de se détruire.
> Congé à vous, mes alliés, mes violents, mes indices.
> Tout vous entraîne, tristesse obséquieuse.
> J'aime.   ('Le Visage nuptial')[13]

> (Now disappear, my escort, standing in distance;
> The sweetness of number has been destroyed.
> Farewell to you, my allies, my hard men, my signposts.
> Everything draws you away, obsequious sadness.
> I love.)

Is this not over-dignified? For he means simply: 'I am in love; so I am saying farewell to my male friends.' He has inflated a simple thought into a lofty cortège of words. This is not to deny that there are felicities on the way: 'indices' is splendid; so is 'debout dans la distance'. But there is a pretentiousness, due (could it be?) to the unease the poet feels, quitting his male comrades for a woman. Besides, what does 'tristesse obséquieuse' mean? He transfers his own sadness at the parting into his friends' obedient departure – or should we suppose that it is *he* who is obedient to the call of love? Unfortunately 'obséquieuse' suggests slavishness, an overdone obedience; but is this not to distort the emotion? For this is the danger of metaphysical poetry; instead of the intellect engaging with the emotions, it may stand back from them and obscure them. When the proportion between mind and emotion is not rightly balanced, we fall into preciosity. However, this magnificent poet falters rarely, and

> Aucun oiseau n'a le coeur de chanter dans un buisson de questions.

> (No bird has the heart to sing in a bush of questions.)[14]

I cannot conclude these pages on high formal poetry without mentioning the work of Jean-Claude Renard, who describes his own spiritual progress in the early pages of *Quand le poème devient prière*.[15] Poetry is, for him, a quest for truth which he constantly compares and contrasts with that of the mystic; the poet is akin to the magus or visionary (*QP*, 65). Renard too may appear to come close to asserting that words are realities; but it seems to me that, unlike Emmanuel, he does not really take this final step. For the further reality with which he is concerned is quite avowedly ineffable, and 'goes beyond both speech and silence'.[16] Poetry is rather, in him, a *means* of conveying a further reality (*NP*, 75–6), on account of its ability to go beyond ordinary meanings into the paradoxical. Besides, just as in Valéry, interpretation is the reader's affair: 'Everyone sees what he wants in the poem' (*QP*, 25). Thus, just as mysticism is fundamentally undoctrinal – on account of the paradoxical and tolerant nature of its message – so poetry is fundamentally anti-dogmatic – it is 'une idéologie de l'anti-idéologie', a system against all ideological systems.[17]

The formal progress of this poet is interesting. The search for certainties in his life, culminating in the traditional versification of *Père, voici que l'homme* (which was greeted as orthodox Catholicism by his readers), was succeeded by 'the return of questioning' (*QP*, 38). He abandoned classical verse forms, adopted those of free verse, and along with them obtained a different readership, interested not in having found, but in searching, for God. Since then, he too has on occasion written aphoristic poetry, as in 'Oracles' and 'Dire' (*Toutes les îles sont secrètes*):

> L'autre est-il l'infini de l'un?
> (Is the other the infinite of the one?)

His normal poetic manner is, however, sensory – or almost more sensual than sensory:

> Si tu sais où dort Jeanne,
> vêts-toi de laine verte,
> monte dans la forêt où s'ouvre la caverne
> et sur le premier chêne luisant comme un lingam
> pose un moment la bouche.[18]

> (if you know where Jeanne sleeps,
> dress in woollen green,
> climb through the forest to the cave mouth
> and on the first oak shining like a lingam
> set for a moment your lips.)

The vocabulary here is the usual French language of essences, yet the attention to sensory experience gives perhaps a more concrete impression. As for the rhythms, there is some resemblance to Bonnefoy's practice: a closeness to the formal alexandrine, along with some deliberate 'imperfection'.

All this raises fundamental questions. Is there, in French poetry, a connexion between the certainties of belief and the use of formal metre? Is there a connection between the uncertainties of a mystical quest and the use of free modern forms? Or is the opposition more complex than that? It looks as if a belief in certainty, even a certainty not yet found, expresses itself in formal rhythms, such as those of Valéry (the sceptical intellect, comfortable in its scepticism) and Emmanuel (the spokesman of God). As if the prophetic soul (St-John Perse) bursts out of these rhythms into so high a rhetoric that credence breaks. As if a belief in uncertainty, even the certainty-within-uncertainty of mystical experience, expresses itself in a free but unrhetorical verse. Has rhythm something to do with belief, and with the nature of that belief? As we have seen, Bonnefoy asks this sort of question. He identifies the certainties of classical French perfection with the rhythm of the alexandrine, he identifies the honest bewilderment of our struggles with experience with metres that are less 'perfect'. Is the key to all this the phrase 'certainty-within-uncertainty'? Is this expressed rhythmically by form emerging from an appearance of formlessness?

In all this, it seems, Valéry (in whom the word is merely a linguistic entity, not a vehicle for spiritual 'presence') is the odd man out. Scepticism, like certainty, and like formal verse, is out of fashion. And indeed, few contemporary poets can be found who say a good word for Valéry. Renard is the great exception.

And how does modern French poetry look in the context of other European poetic traditions? It begins to seem that it constitutes the irrational or super-rational dimension in European poetry, the European language in which the mystical dimension is most readily expressed. Whereas poetry in English and Scots 'begins with a flea, and ends with God' (which is doubtless true of many other European poetries) — in French, the poet is drawn immediately towards the primal, the ultimate, the universal, and believes that language can deliver him to that destination.

Surrealism: The Assault on Meaning and the Cult of the Image

KEITH ASPLEY

If Surrealism were a racehorse, one might be able to say that it was by Lautréamont out of Alice in Wonderland; or perhaps by Rimbaud out of revulsion at the seemingly mindless carnage of the Great War. Its emergence as a movement was really confirmed, however, by the publication in October 1924 of the *Manifeste du surréalisme* by André Breton. Many people nowadays would probably be surprised to learn that a few weeks later one of the group, Max Morise, writing in the first number of their new review *La Révolution surréaliste*, was still pleading for the extension of Surrealism to the plastic arts. Yet anyone who has read the *Manifeste* will be familiar with Breton's indication that initially Surrealism was understood in terms of automatic writing and arose out of investigations into the process, even the mystery, of poetic creation, which I discussed in Chapter 10. In the 1924 *Manifeste* the word 'surrealism' is defined as 'pure psychic automatism by which it is intended to express either verbally or in writing or in any other manner the real way in which thought functions. Thought's dictation, in the absence of any rational check and without regard for any aesthetic or moral preoccupation' (*M*, 36).[1] Breton goes on to claim that 'Surrealism depends on a belief in the superior reality of certain forms of association neglected hitherto, in the omnipotence of dream and in the disinterested play of thought'. These words clearly bear witness to the influence of psychoanalysis; and indeed Breton, who had worked during the war in a psychiatric centre, freely acknowledged his debt to Freud.

A few months after the appearance of that first manifesto, however, a collective tract emanating from the newly established *Bureau de recherches surréalistes* made it plain that the concept could be taken in a much broader context. The twenty-six signatories of the Declaration of 27 January 1925 argued forcefully that '*Surrealism* is not a new or easier means of expression, nor even a metaphysics of poetry. It is a cry from the mind turning back on itself and it is desperately determined to break free from its fetters, if need be by using material hammers'.[2] There are many facets to the Surrealist movement. None the less, its members continued to set great store by poetry: Philippe Soupault, the co-author with Breton of the first Surrealist text, *Les Champs magnétiques*, individual chapters of which were published in 1919, was quite adamant that 'Surrealism is first and foremost poetry' (*PR*, 112).

One of its central concerns was always language. Breton's manifesto in miniature entitled 'Du surréalisme en ses œuvres vives', dating from 1953, begins with the reminder that 'Surrealism as an organized movement had its origins in a large-scale operation focussing on language' (*M*, 165). He disclosed that it had been a question of 'nothing less than rediscovering the secret of a language whose elements might stop behaving like flotsam on the surface of a dead sea. With that in view it was important to take away their strictly practical use; this was the only way of emancipating them and of giving them back all their power' (*M*, 165). At the same time he recalled the desire for an insurrection against the tyranny of a debased language. All this was a consequence of his dissatisfaction, voiced in the opening pages of the 1924 *Manifeste*, with what he saw as the reign of logic, rationalism and reason.

For Breton, 'realist attitudes' seemed to be 'hostile to intellectual and moral flowering' (*M*, 16) and he expressed his loathing of their 'mediocrity, hatred and unimaginative bumptiousness'. A few years earlier, when Dada was all the rage,[3] its driving-force, Tristan Tzara, went so far as to proclaim with characteristic vehemence: 'Logic is always wrong ... Married to logic, art would live in incest, engulfing, swallowing its own tail ... fornicating in itself'.[4]

One symptom of the reign of logic, rationalism and these 'realist attitudes' was, and no doubt still is, the desire, on the part of certain critics and the general public alike, to seek the 'meaning' of a poem. A recent review of John Ashbery's *April Galleons*[5] began with the admonition: 'For too long, too many schoolteachers and academics have instilled in their pupils the idea that poetry is a matter of paraphrasable meaning. It does not take much wit to see that, in the case of true poetry, this is insufficient'.[6] Over sixty years earlier Breton took great delight in pouring scorn on a particular application of such an approach, when he lashed out at one of the leading *fin de siècle* critics, Remy de Gourmont:

> There was once someone sufficiently dishonest to draw up, in the preface of an anthology, a list of some of the images found in the work of one of the greatest living poets: you could read

> *Caterpillar's tomorrow in ball dress* means: butterfly.
> *Crystal breast* means: a carafe.
> Etc. No, sir, *does not mean.* Stuff your butterfly in your carafe. You can
> rest assured that Saint-Pol-Roux said exactly what he meant.   (*PJ*, 23)

One of the most direct indications that Breton knew that a poet's use of words is not determined merely by their sense is provided at the start of an early essay, 'Les mots sans rides', where he explains that some writers at least were ready to liberate them from their role of 'little auxiliaries', or 'little helpers' (*PP*, 167). Bearing in mind Rimbaud's concept of 'the alchemy of the verb', he presents this process in terms of a veritable chemistry 'which first of all had devoted itself to the release of properties of words, only one of which, their meaning, is specified in the dictionary'.

Of course, Breton is here merely touching on potentially vast topics, not just that of semantics, which have fascinated philosophers and linguists through the ages. In *The Meaning of Meaning* by C.K. Ogden and I.A. Richards,[7] 'the other words annexed to a word in the Dictionary' is just one of the sixteen main definitions of 'Meaning' they catalogue (p. 186), coming in between 'a unique unanalysable Relation to other things' and 'the Connotation of a word'. John Lyons defines the *sense* of a word as 'its place in a system of relationships which it contrasts with other words in the vocabulary'.[8] Although Saussure's first principle was 'the arbitrariness of the sign', he added the important rider that the word 'arbitrary' must 'not give the idea that a signifier depends on the free choice of the speaking subject [...] it is not in the power of the individual to change anything in a sign once it is established in a linguistic group'.[9] Saussure would therefore not have accepted the blunt championing of the totally personal nature of meaning by Humpty Dumpty in *Through the Looking Glass*, when he declared to Alice: 'When *I* use a word [...] it means just what I choose it to mean – neither more nor less'.[10]

So what did Breton have in mind in 'Les mots sans rides'? In that essay, the French poem to which Breton attaches the greatest importance in this field is Rimbaud's 'Voyelles': 'It was by assigning a colour to the vowels that for the first time, *en connaissance de cause* and accepting the consequences, the word was deflected from its duty of signifying' (*PP*, 168). He also mentions Paulhan, Eluard, Picabia, Ducasse (or Lautréamont), Mallarmé's *Un Coup de Dés*, together with Apollinaire's 'La Victoire' and some of his 'calligrammes', to illustrate his thesis. Breton's theoretical frontal assault was thus merely the culmination of a gradual erosion of the tyranny of meaning in French poetry. Baudelaire's notion of poetic language as a 'sorcellerie évocatoire'[11] and the lauding of suggestion, by Mallarmé and others, had also paved the way.

Louis Aragon too was to challenge the simple equation of meaning with dictionary-definitions, in one of the subtler moments of his *Traité du style*,

a text that in many other areas pulls no punches: 'The sense of words is not
a simple definition in a dictionary. It is known, or it should be known, that
there is meaning in every syllable, in every letter, and it is quite obvious
that spelling out, that leads from the heard word to the written word, is
a particular mode of thought, the analysis of which should be fruitful'
(*TS*, 191–2). When Aragon wrote these words in 1928, he would have
been aware of some of the linguistic experiments of Desnos and others,
discussed later in this chapter.

For the Surrealist poets, however, it was the second feature of the
notion of verbal chemistry, 'the way in which words interact', that was of
greatest import, for it raised the whole question of imagery. Soupault's
little-known 'Essai sur la poésie', written in 1950 and re-issued at the end of
the quaintly titled *Poèmes retrouvés 1918–1981* (pp. 97–119), lucidly recalls not
only the feverish cerebral activity in which he and his associates were
engaged at the end of the First World War but also the importance that the
poetic image was taking on in their eyes (p. 112). Before writing *Les
Champs magnétiques*, its two authors, in the course of daily conversations
over a period of several months in 1919, had sought to pinpoint, as many
others have tried to do, particularly in our time, the nature of poetry.
Looking at examples above all from the work of Rimbaud, Apollinaire,
and then, after their discovery of *Les Chants de Maldoror*, Lautréamont,
and remembering certain of Reverdy's investigations, Breton and
Soupault recognized the prime importance of the imagery: 'It was the
images, their construction, their constitution, their appearance, their
radiance, their duration, their "life" that held the attention' (*PR*, 112).
Images such as Lautréamont's famous 'beautiful [...] like the chance
encounter, on a dissecting-table, of a sewing-machine and an umbrella'
seemed to Breton to elucidate the phenomenon of 'lyricism' in poetry, that
subsequently he was to present in terms of a 'spasmodic surpassing of
controlled expression' (*E*, 43).

In 1918 Breton had been struck by something Reverdy had written in
Nord-Sud:

> The image is a pure creation of the mind.
> It cannot be born from a comparison but from the juxtaposition of two
> more or less distant realities.
> The more the relationship of the two juxtaposed realities is distant and
> just, the more powerful the image will be – the greater its emotive force
> and its poetic reality (or truth?).

The sticking-point for Breton was the idea of the 'justness' of the rela-
tionship between the two juxtaposed 'realities' or terms. The experience,
or the gift, of the strange phase, something like 'Il y a un homme coupé
en deux par la fenêtre' (There's a man cut in two by the window),

convinced Breton that such images arise spontaneously, arbitrarily, without premeditation. Although Breton in the *Manifeste* compiled a brief list of 'Surrealist images' (categories such as 'apparent contradiction' and 'the negation of an elementary physical property'), they all shared this particular form of 'arbitrariness', that is, they are as far removed as possible from 'practical language' or from mere mimesis. This separation of 'practical language' from 'poetic discourse' depends heavily, in the context of Surrealism, on surprise, a criterion Breton recognized as a legacy of Apollinaire (see *PP*, 41). Indeed the most enduring Surrealist images at times provoked not just surprise but shock. Very often what lingers most strongly in the mind after reading a Surrealist poem is one single image, just as the part of Dali's *The Persistence of Memory* that leaves the deepest impression on most people is the flaccid watches, rather than the tree, the platform, or the semi-amorphous head. In 'L'Evidence poétique' Paul Eluard wrote of the supreme attraction that inexplicable images held for him, 'the absolutely new relationships of which so-called surrealist poetry affords us a glimpse'[12] and went on to claim that 'images exist, they live and everything becomes imagery. For a long time they have been taken for illusions, for they were limited and subjected to the test of reality, an insensitive, dead reality, instead of putting reality to the test of its interdependence'. Eluard even made a collection of striking verbal images, images that obsessed him, beginning with Lautréamont's 'beau comme ...' and ending with Pierre Unik's 'Les forêts boivent le marbre' (The forests are drinking marble (ibid, p. 105)).

With such images we are beginning to see how the theory was translated into practice, but let me now preface an over-brief survey of Surrealist poets and poetry with a couple of recipes, the first one, by Tzara, being Dada rather than Surrealist proper:

> To Make a Dadaist Poem
> Take a newspaper
> Take a pair of scissors
> Select an article of the length you intend to give your poem
> Cut out the article
> Then cut out carefully each of the words in that article and
> put them in a bag
> Shake gently
> Then take out all the cuttings one by one in the order in which
> they left the bag
> Copy conscientiously
> The poem will resemble you

And lo and behold you are a writer; infinitely original and endowed with a sensibility that is charming, though beyond the comprehension of the vulgar[13]

Whereas in a collage poem there could well be some conscious arrange-
ment of the cuttings, here the distribution of the words is random, so
much so that this Dadaist recipe is almost a recipe for chaos. Its Surrealist
successor, supplied in the 1924 *Manifeste*, is the recipe for automatic
writing that commences: 'Have writing materials brought to you, after
settling down in a place as conducive as possible to concentration. Put
yourself in the most passive, most receptive state you can. Disregard
your genius, your talents and those of everybody else [...] Write quickly
with no preconceived subject, sufficiently quickly to avoid remembering
and being tempted to read over what you have written' (*M*, 41).

The greater part of *Les Champs magnétiques* is the record of the first
sessions of Surrealist automatic writing. It consists mainly of pages of only
somewhat disjointed prose in which normal conventions of syntax are
by and large respected. However, one chapter, 'Eclipses', contains a few
'sentences', apparently written at maximum speed, which raise, in an
extreme manner, the questions of sense, nonsense and the relationships
between words: 'Suintement cathédrale vertébré supérieur' (Oozing
cathedral higher vertebrate); 'Pneus pattes de velours' (Tyres velvet paws);
'Raide tige de Suzanne inutilité surtout village de saveurs avec une église
de homard' (Suzanne's stiff stalk uselessness especially village of flavours
with a lobster church).

Similarly, a later use of automatic writing by Breton and Eluard to
simulate *dementia praecox*, or schizophrenia, ends not just in a series of
neologisms but also in an invented tongue: 'U quaïon purlo ouam gacirog
olaïama oual, u feaïva zuaïaïlo, gaci zulo. Gaci zulo plef. U feaïva oradar-
fonsedarca nic olp figilê. U elaïaïpi mouco drer hôdarca hualica-siptur.
Oradar-gacirog vraïlim ... u feaïva drer kurmaca ribag nic javli' (*IC*, 49).
The mere presence of anaphora and other repetition is inadequate to
rescue for poetry a text where sound is totally divorced from sense, even
though logically (!) we have here Surrealism's most extreme, if not
supreme, assault on meaning.

Aragon's 'Au Café du Commerce', one of nine such texts that 'survived
the years, removals, police searches, waste paper baskets' to be published
for the first time in 1970, begins and ends as follows:

> La beauté de la femme m'émeut davantage que le loup garou l'explosion
> de grisou le chant du coucou hibou pou genou Je regrette de ne trouver
> d'autre point de contact avec la réalité ou plutôt des points de com-
> paraison si médiocres Les larmes coulent dans tous les sens sur les joues
> des dialecticiens les plus éclairés Je ne crois pas que cette forme liquide de
> la douleur ait une grande valeur aux yeux de la divinité Elle en a assez des
> Jérémies des Brunetières et de tous les danseurs de corde La corde de
> pendu dit-on préserve de la petite vérole On ne supprimera jamais la
> peine de mort Présage sombre Demain jè ferai mon marché moi-même et

je rapporterai la laitue-à-chanter [...] Un beau jour toutes les caresses se sont confondues et les compagnons ne se sont plus compris Danseuse cambodgienne Comment dit-on la bouche en langue barbare Les abîmes poussent toujours entre les glaciers Ce sont des sortes d'edelweiss Un autre edelweiss c'est le baiser dans l'oreille J'ai un petit enfant dans mon sein gauche Ecoute-le   (*MP*, 147–8)

(The beauty of woman moves me more than the werewolf the fire-damp explosion the call of the cuckoo owl louse knee I regret not finding any other point of contact with reality or rather such mediocre points of comparison Tears flow in every direction on the cheeks of the most enlightened dialecticians I do not believe that this liquid form of grief has great value in the eyes of the deity It has had enough of the Jeremiahs the Brunetières and all the tight-rope walkers The hanged man's noose it is said offers protection against smallpox Capital punishment will never be abolished Gloomy omen Tomorrow I'll go to market myself and bring back the singable-lettuce [...] One fine day all the caresses were confused and the companions no longer got on together Cambodian dancing-girl How does one say mouth in barbarian language Chasms still grow between the glaciers They are sorts of edelweiss Another edelweiss is the kiss on the ear I have a small child in my left breast Listen to it)

Even these brief extracts reveal the rather desultory nature of the discourse. The retention of upper case to mark the beginnings of 'sentences' – the sole vestige of punctuation apart from the recourse to dashes elsewhere in the text – facilitates the reading, even though conventional syntax is at times assailed, as in the listing of 'coucou hibou pou genou', words brought together in this grammarian's jingle by their rhyme plus the initial semantic link between the two bird-names. By the simple process of juxtaposition, if not by some association of ideas as well, there is the suggestion that the nineteenth-century critic Brunetière is one of life's Jeremiahs. Words themselves can generate other words. Semantically it is quite a long leap from 'tight-rope walkers' to 'capital punishment': they are 'distant realities', but the transition is smoothed by the intermediary phrase, 'La corde de pendu', which operates tangentially. At the end of the text alliteration (of the 'c') is at first the most prominent feature, but then there is a series of blatantly Surrealist images: the presentation of the chasms as 'sorts of edelweiss'; the merging of the concrete and the abstract in the metaphor 'Un autre edelweiss c'est le baiser dans l'oreille'; and then possibly a 'negation of an elementary physical property' in the thought of a small child in the male author's left breast. Arguably the most eye-catching (or ear-catching) image in this text, the veritable stroke of inspiration is the neologism of the 'laitue-à-chanter', left poised by Aragon at the far frontier of intelligibility.

Despite Breton's claim at the end of 'Les mots sans rides' ('Words have stopped playing. Words are making love', *PP*, 171), word-play and word-games were deemed very important by the Surrealists. For a systematic exploitation of all kinds of word-play in poetry one may turn to Robert Desnos, whose aim has been described as 'bringing language to the point where meaning is perpetually vanishing and where the words weave amongst themselves unforeseeable and peremptory associations'.[14] The texts of the 1923 collections *L'Aumonyme* and *Langage cuit* contain fundamental attacks on preordained conceptions of both linguistic usage and of poetry itself. Some of these verbal experiments are impossible to translate adequately: the poem-manifesto 'P'oasis' (*CB*, 64–5) is built around the initial homonymy of 'pensée' (the word for both 'thought' and the flower, the pansy) and proceeds not only to re-open the perennial debate over the primacy of thought or language but also to explore a rudimentary *lettrisme*[15] that relies on the French pronunciation of certain letters of the alphabet. For example,

> – Je vois les Pan C
> – Je vois les crânes KC
> – Je vois les mains DCD

which could also be written

> – Je vois les pensées
> – Je vois les crânes cassés
> – Je vois les mains décédées
>
> (– I see the thoughts/pansies
> – I see the smashed skulls
> – I see the deceased hands)

On the other hand an attempt can be made to render into English a 'prose poem' such as 'Idéal maîtresse' (Governing ideal) (*CB*, 75)

> Je m'étais attardé ce matin-là à brosser les dents d'un joli animal que, patiemment, j'apprivoise. C'est un caméléon. Cette aimable bête fuma, comme à l'ordinaire, quelques cigarettes, puis je partis.
> Dans l'escalier je la rencontrai, 'Je mauve', me dit-elle et tandis que moi-même je cristal à pleine ciel-je à son regard qui fleuve vers moi.
> Or il serrure et, maîtresse! Tu pitchpin qu'à joli vase je me chaise si les chemins tombeaux.
> L'escalier, toujours l'escalier qui bibliothèque et la foule au bas plus abîme que le soleil ne cloche.
> Remontons! mais en vain, les souvenirs se sardine! à peine, à peine un bouton tirelire-t-il. Tombez, tombez! En voici le verdict: 'La danseuse sera fusillee à l'aube en tenue de danse avec ses bijoux immolés au feu de son corps. Le sang des bijoux, soldats!'

Eh quoi, déjà je miroir. Maîtresse tu carré noir et si les nuages de tout à l'heure myosotis, ils moulins dans la toujours présente éternité.

(I had tarried that morning cleaning the teeth of a pretty creature I am patiently taming. It's a chameleon. As usual, this amiable animal smoke a few cigarettes and then I left.

I met her on the stairs. 'I mauve', she said whilst I myself crystal high sky at her glance rivering in my direction.

Now it locks and, mistress! You pitch pine that the pretty vase has I chair myself if the paths tomb.

The staircase, still the staircase that library and the crowd down below more abyss than the sun bells.

Let's go back up again! but in vain, the memories sardine! scarcely scarcely a button money-boxes. Fall down, fall down! And here is the verdict: 'The dancer will be shot at dawn in her ball-gown with her jewels sacrificed to the fire of her body. The blood of jewels, soldiers!'

What! already I mirror. Mistress you dark square and if the clouds of just now forget-me-not, they mills in the ever present eternity.)

In 'Idéal maîtresse' Desnos at his most clever-clever (or crazy or inventive) uses the idea of the pet chameleon learning to talk as his pretext for confusing different parts of speech. Although it slips into nonsense at times, this is a shade less pronounced in the original than in the translation for the simple reason that French verbs are more highly inflected than their English counterparts.

Near the end of his life Desnos expressed the desire to make 'Poetics' a chapter, or branch, of mathematics, asking the rhetorical question, 'Isn't Poetry also a science of numbers?'[16] This ambition had been anticipated literally by Benjamin Péret in '26 points à préciser' (*GJ*, 83–6), one of the most hermetic of all Surrealist poems. It consists of a succession of phrases or sentences all coupled with algebraic formulae of seemingly ever-increasing complexity. Whether or not the latter have meaning for the mathematician, they signify next to nothing to the reader of average literacy. The text begins

> Ma vie finira par a
> Je suis $b - a$
> Je demande $cb - a$
>
> (My life will end in a
> I am $b - a$
> I ask for $cb - a$)

and ends with the offputting formula for his date of birth

ma date de naissance

$$\left(\frac{\frac{m}{n}\left(\sqrt{\frac{de}{(cb-a)f}}+k-i\right)^{j}+kl+o}{\sqrt{(pq+r)\,s}}-uv-w\right)^{x}-\frac{y}{z}$$

On this kind of evidence one might think that the Surrealists were half-demented scientists *manqué*, who spent their days devising weird if not always wonderful experiments with words and numbers and anything else that might have come to hand; but the whole truth is very different. We saw in Chapter 10 that Desnos could write sublime love-poems. Most of the time Péret's revolt took on more orthodox forms. In his political and political-cum-scatological poems, in his tirades against God, the Church and religion the meaning could hardly be more plain, even if the modern reader may not always be too familiar with some of the allusions. Their directness is illustrated by the last section of '6 février', a poem that celebrates the infiltration (by some 5000 Communists) of the right-wing demonstrations that day in Paris in 1934:

> Vive le 6 février
> et vive le 7
> J'ai hurlé pendant deux jours
> A mort Cachin A mort Blum
> et j'ai volé tout ce que j'ai pu dans les magasins
> dont je brisais les vitres
> J'ai même volé une poupée que j'enverrai à Maurras
> pour qu'il essaie de la violer
> en criant A bas les voleurs[17]

> (Long live the sixth of February
> and long live the seventh
> I howled for two whole days
> Death to Cachin Death to Blum
> and I stole all I could from the big stores
> whose windows I smashed
> I even stole a doll I'll send to Maurras
> so he can try to rape it
> shouting Down with the thieves)

It may help marginally to know that 'A bas les voleurs' was the slogan the Communists were ordered to shout, that Cachin was to become the first Communist senator, that Blum was the Socialist leader and that Maurras was one of the mainstays of the semi-Fascist *Action française*; but even without this information the reader (or hearer) of the text could hardly fail to notice the vim, the venom and the violence engendered by the alliteration of the 'v' above all.

As for Breton, his best known poem is probably his *blason* of the female body, 'L'Union libre' (*CT*, 93–5), the quality of which is evident right from the opening sequences:

> Ma femme à la chevelure de feu de bois
> Aux pensées d'éclair de chaleur
> A la taille de sablier
> Ma femme à la taille de loutre entre les dents du tigre
> Ma femme à la bouche de cocarde et de bouquet d'étoiles de
> dernière grandeur
> Aux dents d'empreintes de souris blanche sur la terre
> blanche
> A la langue d'ambre et de verre frottés
> Ma femme à la langue d'hostie poignardée
> A la langue de poupée qui ouvre et ferme les yeux
> A la langue de pierre incroyable
>
> (My wife with woodfire hair
> With thoughts of summer lightning
> And a sand-glass waist
> My wife with the waist of an otter trapped in the tiger's
> teeth
> My wife with a mouth of cockade and a cluster of stars of
> the greatest magnitude
> With teeth of white mouse footprints on white ground
> And tongue of polished glass and amber
> With a stabbed host tongue
> The tongue of a doll whose eyes open and close
> A tongue of incredible stone)

The reader is bombarded with images. Just a few are almost clichés, e.g. the 'taille de sablier', but the great majority look like gifts from the gods. In a few words 'la chevelure de feu de bois' evokes colour, texture, fragrance; in l. 6, the repetition of the adjective not only makes the teeth seem whiter than white but also sets up an almost Mallarméan purity; and all the time the anaphora creates an insistent incantatory effect.

This poem also highlights another problem, however: the extent to which context can be a guide to comprehension, when ambiguity is involved. The feet are evoked in two lines near the middle: 'Ma femme aux pieds d'initiales/Aux pieds de trousseaux de clés aux pieds de calfats qui boivent.' Kenneth White's translation runs as follows: 'My wife with the feet of initials/With the feet of key-bunches with the feet of drinking caulkers.'[18] Admittedly in a Surrealist poem the reader is conditioned to expect the presence in a metaphor of 'distant realities' and it is not completely out of the question that Breton, when he wrote these lines, employed 'calfats' in the sense of 'caulkers'. My own preference, in what is basically a love-poem about the essence of Woman, would be for the alternative meaning, 'Java sparrows', not only because these cage-birds would have been readily available and visible in Paris in the 1930s but also because they would make Her more petite and exotic.

The consensus is that Paul Eluard is the finest of the Surrealist poets and the following text may be regarded as the epitome of his art:

> La terre est bleue comme une orange
> Jamais une erreur les mots ne mentent pas
> Ils ne vous donnent plus à chanter
> Au tour des baisers de s'entendre
> Les fous et les amours
> Elle sa bouche d'alliance
> Tous les secrets tous les sourires
> Et quels vêtements d'indulgence
> A la croire toute nue
>
> Les guêpes fleurissent vert
> L'aube se passe autour du cou
> Un collier de fenêtres
> Des ailes couvrent les feuilles
> Tu as toutes les joies solaires
> Tout le soleil sur la terre
> Sur les chemins de ta beauté   (*CD*, 153)
>
> (The earth is blue like an orange
> Never an error words do not lie
> They no more make you sing
> It's the turn of kisses to be heard
> Lunatics and loves
> She and her wedding lips
> All secrets all smiles
> And what garments of indulgence
> To believe her stark naked
>
> The wasps blossom green
> The dawn slips on around her neck
> A window-pane necklace
> Wings cover the leaves
> You have every solar joy
> All the sun on earth
> On the paths of your beauty)

This lovely poem begins with one of the most famous of all Surrealist images. The average reader is probably struck first of all by the apparent contradiction of colour in the incipit. Yet, somewhat paradoxically, this image, on analysis, stands up to rational examination, when due allowance is made for its elliptical quality. We are now familiar with photographs taken of the Earth from space that show both its bluish hue and the fact that it is shaped like an orange: slightly flattened at the poles, it is not a perfect sphere. In a sense the opening line coalesces two distinct points: a) the earth is blue; b) it resembles an orange; but it becomes a superb example of poetic vision and indeed of poetic knowledge, a case of a strange image happening to hit on the truth. If l. 1 gives us the illustration, l. 2 provides the theory – Eluard's total trust in words – and, with its combination of positive affirmation and negative form, raises anew the basic problem of poetry, truth and language. Though he refers here to 'les mots' rather than 'les images', he has written a poem that is perhaps primarily about imagery in general and Surrealist imagery in particular.

These first two lines form the introduction; after the *tour de force* of the initial image and then the theoretical statement, Eluard gives the impression of settling down to his poem, one that clearly belongs to the collection *L'Amour la Poésie*. Line 3 in part anticipates his later title *Donner à Voir* but it also suggests that words by themselves do not suffice. So the next lines seem to imply that beyond the words there is need for some genuine emotion. The verbal harmony should ideally be accompanied by, for instance, the harmony of the lovers, with their wordless communication. In the cryptic expression of l. 4 Eluard penetrates to the heart of the matter, but in addition the abstract terms give the line a pleasing quality of half-vagueness, half-precision. In the strange coupling of 'les fous' (concrete) and 'les amours' (abstract) that this time heralds Breton's celebrated concept, 'l'amour fou', the surprise is generated by the choice, if choice it be, of the word 'amours' rather than 'amants'. Lines 4 to 6 are linked phonically by the recurrent 'ou' sound but at the semantic level the themes of the kiss and the union of lovers are picked up again with the clever transformation of 'anneau d'alliance' (wedding-ring) into the new image of the 'bouche d'alliance'. It is in ways like this that words are allowed to 'make love'. With its lyrical alliteration and assonance, l. 7 evokes lovers' secrets and the smiles they have for each other, but the repetition of 'tous' and the division of this octosyllabic line into two equal hemistichs create further balance and harmony. Then, in l. 8, the poet's surprise, evinced by the exclamation, is matched by the surprise in the form of the words, the preference for the nominal construction, 'quels vêtements d'indulgence'; and the opening section ends with the subtle transition from 'vêtements' to 'A la croire toute nue', the nakedness that makes possible the complete physical harmony of the lovers. Thus in these first nine lines there is a movement from the initial focussing on word and image to an evocation of love and the beloved.

The second section too opens with an astonishing image, 'Les guêpes fleurissent vert', where there appears to be some fusion of wasps and flowers, but the reader is left with the feeling that it is one of those strange phrases like 'Il y a un homme coupé en deux par la fenêtre'. With such an image the initial shock-effect is crucial, but one can begin to dissect l. 10 rationally, by recognizing that the word 'fleurissent' possesses both literal and metaphorical connotations (it could have been translated as 'flourish' instead of 'blossom'). Moreover both the verb and the adjective-cum-adverb 'vert' connote vitality. As with the incipit, Eluard hit, wittingly or no, on a 'scientific' fact: there are wasps such as cuckoo-wasps that are a brilliant metallic green. The dawn-motif adds further suggestions of freshness and, as the sun shines on the 'collier de fenêtres', transforming in the poet's imagination the presumably identical windows into a string of pearls, the poem is suddenly bathed in light. The impressionistic image of the wings (rather than the birds themselves) brings a momentary implication of shadow as well as the more important ideas here of protection, warmth and security. This dynamism serves to introduce the poem's final unit, the last three lines, which become an alliterative apostrophe to the beloved who is merged with both the sun and the Earth. These concluding lines are filled with, and characterized by, light, the light that is almost invariably the most positive note in Eluard's verse and universe.

This poem, as is so often the case with him, contains a pleasing blend of form and freedom. Written in free verse, there is a naturalness about the diction: though no constraints are imposed by regular rhyme and metre, there is a fundamental but by no means facile symmetry in the structure of its two sections and a balance in individual lines and images. Yet however many times you read and reflect on this text, you keep coming back to the famous opening line, a line that still eclipses everything else.

From the middle of the 1920s onwards, the Surrealists' assault on meaning and their cult of the image had been threatened, at least potentially, by the political commitment of some of their number. The five Surrealists who joined the Communist party in 1927 (Aragon, Breton, Eluard, Péret and Unik) hoped that their political activity could complement their poetic activity. Breton, for one, was quickly disillusioned by their reception within the Party. He cited the way in which one of them was greeted with the declaration: 'If you are a Marxist, you have no need to be a Surrealist' (*M*, 92).

Aragon's two journeys to the Soviet Union in 1930 and 1932 were to contribute to his decision to opt in favour of Communism and to embark on his series of Socialist Realist novels. Yet early in the 1930s he came to believe that in a future war, whatever the precise circumstances might be, poetry could be a means of addressing the multitude, if only poets returned to traditional modes, those to which the man in the street is accustomed. When the Second World War did break out, Aragon started writing the poems that were to be published in 1941 with the title *Le Crève-Coeur (Heartbreak)*. The fact that this volume was not immediately banned illustrates the success of another idea that he had conceived, 'contraband poetry'. With this, the intention was to hoodwink the censors by concealing a subversive message beneath superficially acceptable themes and heavy reliance on allusion to myth and legend, to the Bible, to history.

A number of the erstwhile Surrealists (e.g. Aragon, Char, Desnos) played an active role in the Resistance. Eluard's most famous wartime poem, 'Liberté' (Freedom), could hardly be clearer in its message, even though the title-word is held back until the very end as an isolated line after 21 quatrains. The first twenty all end with the same line and all depend on a hypnotic deployment of anaphora, after the model of the first:

> Sur mes cahiers d'écolier
> Sur mon pupitre et les arbres
> Sur le sable sur la neige
> J'écris ton nom[19]

> (On my schoolboy jotters
> On my desk and the trees
> On the sand on the snow
> I write your name)

Breton's most important wartime poems ('Pleine marge', 'Fata morgana', 'Les Etats généraux', 'Ode à Charles Fourier') were much more esoteric, much more surreal. If anything, their difficulty is increased by their length. If his mood when he wrote the first two, in the months immediately after the Fall of France, was of confusion and despair, some of this was dispelled when he made the acquaintance in Martinique of Aimé Cesaire. When Césaire presented him with an offprint of his most celebrated poem, *Cahier d'un retour au pays natal* (usually translated as *Return to My Native Land*), Breton saw it as 'the greatest lyrical monument of that time'.[20] He drew attention not only to Césaire's militant spirit but, even more importantly, to the fact that in the *Cahier* 'there comes to the fore in bold characters what has always been the first article in the programme of Surrealism: the clear-cut intention to deal the fatal blow to the so-called "common sense" that has impudently usurped the title of "reason"'.[21]

No brief extract could do justice to this vehement and passionate poem, seventy or eighty pages in length. To show how Césaire's language and imagination can operate, I prefer to quote the last few lines from a more recent poem, his tribute to the writer from Guatemala, 'Quand Miguel Angel Asturias disparut':

> quand les flèches de la mort atteignirent Miguel Angel
> on ne le vit point couché
> mais bien plutôt déplier sa grande taille
> au fond du lac qui s'illumina
>
> Miguel Angel immergea sa peau d'homme
>   et revêtit sa peau de dauphin
>
> Miguel Angel dévêtit sa peau de dauphin
>   et se changea en arc-en-ciel
>
> Miguel Angel rejetant sa peau d'eau bleue
>   revêtit sa peau de volcan
>
> et s'installa montagne toujours verte
>   à l'horizon de tous les hommes   *(ML, 79)*
>
> (when the arrows of death struck Miguel Angel
> one saw him not lying down
> but rather unfolding his great stature
> in the depths of the illumined lake
>
> Miguel Angel immersed his human skin
>   and donned his dolphin skin
>
> Miguel Angel doffed his dolphin skin
>   and changed into a rainbow
>
> Miguel Angel discarding his blue water skin
>   donned his volcano skin
>
> and installed himself an ever green mountain
>   on the horizon of all mankind)

In the space of a few lines we see Césaire's characteristic anaphora that lends his poetry a seemingly relentless power. More interestingly, we see how his imagination transformed the circumstances of the death and made it truly heroic: in reality Asturias was taken ill in Spain and died there in June 1974. Césaire makes his fellow-writer the subject both of the metamorphoses that were striking features of the Guatemalan's magic realism and of the donning of the skin that calls to mind certain Aztec rituals.[22] Furthermore, something like the 'prose of fire' cited by the Swedish Academy when it awarded Asturias the Nobel Prize in 1967 is a quality of Césaire's verse, here as elsewhere.[23]

Although Surrealism died in a sense with Breton in 1966, its shock waves are still being felt, perhaps less in poetry than in many other walks of life, in pop videos and advertising, for example, just as they were felt on the streets of Paris in the heady days of May 1968, when students daubed quotations from Breton, Péret, *et al.* on the walls.

In poetry iconoclasm for iconoclasm's sake is almost certainly not enough. For this reason Breton could see as early as 1920 that a Dada masterpiece was impossible (see *PP*, 76). Yet when Surrealist poets could come up with spell-binding *trouvailles* or could succeed in translating into practice in some way Rimbaud's concept of the alchemy of the verb or Breton's desire to let words 'make love', they were able to give a new meaning and a fresh impulse to poetry and to show that the image was not necessarily a false god.

Eleven Post-War Directions

GRAHAM DUNSTAN MARTIN

What then is the modern idea of poetry? Is it the product of thought, of inspiration, of trance, of overpowering emotion, of toil, or of chance? Does it appertain to the intellect, to the immortal soul, or to the Freudian unconscious? Is it concerned with eternal truths, or with the contemporary world? Is it Valéry's formally accomplished, polished work of art, or is it just precisely (as the Surrealists thought) the opposite of that? Has it still anything at all to do with verse? As we have seen in the last few chapters, many different sorts of writing have been dubbed 'poetry'. As we contemplate the second half of the century, we may well wonder if the term continues to have much meaning. Do we still know how to define it? In some cases it seems as if the word 'poetry' is applied to anything which is aware of the problem of its own definition! In others, it is perhaps the critics' fault: they call 'poetry' anything which they cannot readily classify. It is as if the word 'poetry' has ceased to indicate a genre at all; as if it stands for an essential bewilderment, and applies merely to anything that falls into no other accepted genre.

But Modernism is always, by its nature, experimental; one of its basic features is its love of the notion of 'genre' – as a challenge which it aggressively takes up. Show Modernism a boundary, and it will transgress it.

Let us look first at Henri Michaux. In him the disintegration of genre has gone a long way. He has a whole assortment of manners, ranging from the more poetic to the more prosaic. This enables him to move from one manner to another comfortably, just as his material dictates. This reminds one of the reason given for free verse back in the nineteenth century, by Laforgue – namely that free verse allowed one to select exactly the right words and rhythm for one's meaning. But Michaux's tendency to slip from one manner into another also gives a strong impression of the improvised, of the rough and unfinished. We shall see this phenomenon again with other poets. A sense of the unfinished is in fact a requirement of the modern reader, who is used when, for example, looking at the paintings of Cézanne, to appreciate the sense of the artist at work, actively exploring and struggling with his material. (It is no accident that this is the century in which improvised music has once again become of the first importance.)

When he is writing what is more recognizably 'poetry', Michaux tends to introduce inarticulate noises and compulsive rhythms. 'L'Avenir' (which is about the horrors of contemplating the void) opens thus:

> Quand les mah,
> Quand les mah,
> Les marécages,
> Les malédictions,
> Quand les mahahahahas,
> Quand les mahahaborras, ...[1]

> (When the mah,
> When the mah,
> The marshes,
> The maledictions,
> When the mahahahaha
> When the mahahaborrors, ...)

and so on for some lines which include a number of grotesque-sounding invented words. The sense of the improvised is strong here: immediate emotional reaction issues in inarticulate sounds which are, as it were, prior to language.

This improvisatory quality reminds one of the Surrealists. Michaux's material is of similar nature to theirs: from deep down within the least admissible of human impulses. One of his most famous prose poems describes a group of people who amuse themselves by tearing off other people's heads. Another describes a fictitious tribe called the Emanglons who, when one of their number has difficulty in breathing, have him stifled. As executioner they select a beautiful young virgin who weeps tears of joy when she has completed the operation. These scraps of imaginary anthropology cast an unusually intelligent light on the nature of human behaviour.

Michaux's descent into the human mind does not, however, stop at Freud's physicalistic unconscious, seen in sexual terms by Freud, in terms of aggression by Michaux. Behind and beneath all this lie the surging energies of the Ground of All Being, and beneath that the ultimate stillness of Nirvana. Hence his Aldous Huxley-like investigations into the function of drugs in producing altered states of consciousness.

But what counts as 'poetry' in Michaux's 'Projection'?

> Cela se passait sur la jetée de Honfleur, le ciel était pur. On voyait très clairement le phare du Havre. Je restai là en tout bien dix heures. A midi, j'allai déjeuner, mais je revins aussitôt après.
>
> . . .
>
> Et tout d'un coup vers huit heures, je m'aperçus que tout ce spectacle que j'avais contemplé pendant cette journée, ça avait été seulement une émanation de mon esprit. Et j'en fus fort satisfait car justement je m'étais reproché un peu avant de passer mes journées à ne rien faire.
>
> . . .
>
> Et [. . .] ainsi arrivai-je pour dîner à l'hôtel d'Angleterre et là il fut bien évident *que j'étais réellement à Honfleur*, mais cela n'arrangeait rien.
>
> . . .
>
> Au milieu de la nuit, [l'horizon] a disparu tout d'un coup, faisant si subitement place au néant que je le regrettai presque.   (p. 173)

> (It happened on the jetty at Honfleur, under a clear sky. You could distinctly see the lighthouse at le Havre. I stayed there for a good ten hours in all. At twelve I went for lunch, but I came back straight after.
>
> . . .
>
> And suddenly about eight o'clock, I saw that the whole of the scene I'd been looking at all day long, was simply a projection from my mind. And I was delighted – because I'd just been reproaching myself for spending my days doing nothing.
>
> . . .
>
> And so [. . .] I went to dinner at the Hotel d'Angleterre and there it became quite obvious *that I was really at Honfleur*, but that solved nothing.
>
> . . .
>
> In the middle of the night, [the horizon] vanished without warning, giving way so suddenly to nothingness that I very nearly missed it.)

Is this a joke or is it deadly serious (it relates the Buddhist experience of *perceiving* the world to be a projection of consciousness)? In fact irony and seriousness do not, in Michaux's world (or the Buddhist's for that matter) exclude each other. In what way, however, is this 'poetry'? We may define poetry as a mode of language in which rhythm, meaning and sound are unusually dense and complex. The language of this text is however no more compressed than 'normal prose'. Is 'Projection' merely a very short short story? I am forced to the conclusion that *the only thing which defines this as poetry is its brevity*.

Francis Ponge's case is very different from Michaux's for, though he too usually writes prose poetry, there is no doubt about the density of the language he uses. None the less, it equally crosses the boundaries of genre, for he compares his work to a scientific activity providing a form of knowledge,[2] and in some ways it resembles the taxonomic descriptions of zoologists, botanists, etc. Of course not only can it be compared, it can also be contrasted, with theirs.

The source and subject of Ponge's work is the indescribability of the simplest and most commonplace of objects. He spent his whole writing career struggling to describe such things as a pebble, a bar of soap, a snail, bread, water, moss ... Here is a part of his 'Guêpe' (Wasp):

> Hyménoptère au vol félin, souple, – d'ailleurs d'apparence tigrée –, dont le corps est beaucoup plus lourd que celui du moustique et les ailes pourtant relativement plus petites mais vibrantes et sans doute très démultipliées, la guêpe vibre à chaque instant des vibrations nécessaires à la mouche dans une position ultracritique [...] Elle semble vivre dans un état de crise continuelle qui la rend dangereuse. Une sorte de frénésie ou de forcènerie – qui la rend aussi brillante, bourdonnante, musicale qu'une corde fort tendue, fort vibrante et dès lors brûlante ou piquante, ce qui rend son contact dangereux. [...][3]

> (Hymenopteron with a supple feline flight – tigerish-looking – its body much heavier than the mosquito's though its wings relatively smaller but vibrant and doubtless in a lower gear, the wasp throbs at every moment with the vibrations needed by a fly in urgent peril [...] It seems to live in a state of continual crisis which makes it dangerous. A sort of mania or frenzy – which makes it also brilliant, buzzing, musical as a string stretched taut, ultra-vibrant and so burning or stinging, which makes its contact dangerous. [...])

Like all of Ponge's work, this poem demonstrates two points quite clearly – how many things had never been said about a wasp – and how many more remain to say! As he says, 'Fix your attention on the first thing that catches your eye: you'll see at once that nobody has ever looked at it properly, and that the most elementary things remain to be said about it'.[4] As he tells us, his early writing faced a succession of problems:

> 1st: I grasped the impossibility of expressing myself;
> 2nd: I fell back on attempting to describe things [...];
> 3rd: I recognized [...] the impossibility not only of expressing
>   but also of describing things.
> That's the point I've reached. I could either decide to be silent,
>   but this doesn't suit me: one can't face being a dullard.
> Or publish descriptions or accounts of *failures to describe*.   (PPC, 181–2)

Consequently, Ponge's *La Rage de l'expression* contains many repeated efforts – all of them self-confessedly 'failures' – to describe a wasp, mimosa, a pine-wood, a threatening Provençal sky ... For it's the object that matters, not the poem. We must cease to look at things without seeing them – which we do by simply putting them in the conventional category or by applying the conventional qualities to them. 'If you can manage to elicit from a stone qualities other than hardness, you can get off the merry-go-round.' (Or maybe we should translate it 'sorry-go-round'.) 'Never give in to an arrangement of qualities which seem harmonious. [...] It's likely they seem so because they correspond to something automatic in us. [...] It's not a matter of arranging things, [...] they have to disarrange you. They have to get you off the treadmill.' And then perhaps when we've looked at the object afresh, seen more of its reality – which is inscrutable because non-human – will come the orgasmic moment of truth – 'the moment when truth "comes", [...] when the object jubilates'.[5]

All this implies a craftsman's way with language, and indeed Ponge's language is wonderfully colourful and unexpected. None the less, he complains that the moment you publish your jottings, society 'treats you as a poet'.[6] As if to be called a poet was an insult! Ponge no more wants to be categorized as a poet – for that would put him in a box, and blind his readers to his purposes – than he wishes his wasp, his oyster, or his pine-wood to be categorized.

But what expectations in his readership does this reflect? Oddly enough, I should link this attitude of Ponge's with Valéry's assertion that 'la poésie ne m'intéresse pas' and that what does interest him is the investigation of the power of the human mind through the evidence of language. Ponge and Valéry are never mentioned in the same breath. Yet, surprisingly, Ponge ends up in a similar position: for the whole truth can never be said about even the simplest object. And so he ends up engaging in verbal exercises which are in principle uncompletable – just like Valéry.

Both he and Valéry are interested in the activity rather than its completion. Both assert that perfection is not available. Thus Ponge sometimes gives repeated versions of the 'same' description, to give the impression of the effort of observing, and the labour of writing. We may even compare this with Bonnefoy's demand for some degree of imperfection in the poem (see above, p. 214), and it is not even certain that his rationale for this is in the end so different from Ponge's. For Bonnefoy believes that imperfections in the texture of poetry remind us of the rough edges of everyday reality.

Could it be after all that the 'non-poet', Ponge, is still insisting on being a seer? For Ponge is laying claim (as poets always have) to a specially valuable message, and to a special perceptiveness. This message is the wondrous otherness of the phenomenal world, which, if we see it aright, can provide us with 'reasons for living happily'. He was for some time a Communist, and he expresses a desire to see his poetry as revolutionary (just as revolutionary, he says, as Communism) (*PPC*, 218). What is at issue is nothing less than the ability to perceive non-human reality, so that

(a) it can be understood to some degree in human terms, and (b) it can to some degree extend our all too human understanding.

Just as Ponge's manner of writing elicits the unexpected from his subject-matter, so his manner in public lectures was unexpected: it was direct, colloquial, natural. It was not the heavy intellectual manner so common among French writers. But this is entirely Pongian: he sought – and triumphantly achieves – the apotheosis of the ordinary, by revealing that it is the ordinary above all which is wonderful, amazing, baffling.

How different this is from Michel Deguy, who tells us in *Actes*[7] that the poem 'is a calligram, not of some "imitated" outline like a bottle or a fig, but rather of the secret configuration of our existence'. It would seem, again, that the poet is a seer, one who possesses an almost occult knowledge. 'Poetic writing is licentious; it is the form of writing which busies itself with dislocation'.[8] This disruption goes very deep; in *Jumelages*[9] Deguy suggests that poetry may disturb the basic mechanism of verbal meaning – that it may confuse the relationship between word, concept and referent (*signifiant, signifié* and *référent*).

What results does this theory produce? The conventional boundaries of poetry break down. It develops an immense hunger – to assimilate and swallow other modes of writing. In *Reliefs* (p. 38) he writes:

> *purpose:* to bring together hyperdistant registers; to fling into the dance dead codes (e.g. the language of justice, advocates, solicitors, ushers) or codes which are hermetic through their functional univocity (the medical code).

He then draws a diagram, figuring a clash of such codes. Now, Deguy claims that poetry is a quite different discourse from prose. How does he manage at the same time to swallow other registers and to assert the difference of poetry? The answer must be, that what he seeks is *to define poetry as the internecine clash of all literary and linguistic genres.* This is an immense ambition: though Deguy does not draw this parallel, it can be compared to Valéry's longing to see poetry as the measure of the potential of the human mind.

Yet this is not to throw away anything more conventionally poetic. It is merely to add to it. A small prose poem called 'Interlude' appears in *Reliefs*. It reappears several times in *Jumelages* in fragmentary, rewritten form; most notably as part of the last section of that 'poetic collection', i.e. a 'poem' entitled 'Table des matières'. Dividing this (somewhat artificially) into sections, we find:

1. a section of prose poetry, where the punctuation is expressed as gaps, thus:

De l'autre côté de l'arche qui passait l'an   le mur alunissait ta
chambre   O tendre souef précieux corps l'odeur de rose animait ta
statue   j'étais un collier de ton cou d'encens   mais anonyme pour
toi toujours   puisque tu ne m'appelais pas

(On the other side of the ark that traversed the year   the wall
enmooned your bedroom   O tender douce precious body the odour
of roses animated your statue   I was a necklace on your neck of
incense   but nameless for you always   since you did not call me)

2. an even more passionate outburst in free verse, though the language
is at times that of sexual handbook or medical textbook;

3. A reversion to poetic prose;

4. A descent, after a mention of Tanzania, into inarticulate noises
in capital letters, followed by a set of fragmentary experiences between
which no evident connexion can be found – the words here often suffer
amputation: thus, 'pological', 'veloped'.

Let me comment first that, as with Ponge, the repetition and rewriting
of texts suggests their unfinished, provisional nature. More importantly,
however, we have here an intense clash of registers, an encroachment on
other registers' territory, the inclusion of learned and obscure words (so
that even you and I, learned though we are, dear reader, will have to look
some of them up in Liddell & Scott's *Ancient Greek Lexicon*), annexation,
infringement, disruption. Disruption of emotion too. Thus, Deguy's
description of the sexual act in rowing terms goes like this:

'yole mallarméenne ou trirème servile: plongée à l'unisson en l'abîme,
ahan du corps ramassé qui propulse l'aviron, pause, concentration qui
replie les muscles et la rémige, silence, ahan ... *ratis* pour *navis* "en
poésie"...'

((Mallarméan yawl or slavish trireme: plunged in unison into the abyss,
panting of the body keyed up to propel the oar, pause, concentration
tensing the muscles and the oar-wing, silence, panting ... *ratis* for *navis*
"in poetry"...))

or, in other words, 'in poetic diction one writes "raft", not "ship"'.

What does this do to the sexual emotions? It lends them a twentieth-
century cynicism (conveyed by the use of a Virgilian conceit!). There is a
mixture of detachment and conviction. A lesser poet would have descended
into bathos. Now, this is not bathos. It is a serious undermining of
emotion, made serious by the splendidly physical imagery of the rowing
boat, and by the obscurity of the comment. The bathos is avoided by the
reader's need at this point to consult a dictionary! If Latin were not a dead
language, Deguy could not have achieved this *tour de force*.

Deguy's mixing of emotional and learned registers may thus work emotionally. In *Jumelages* (p. 161) he points out that, when reading philosophy, you often have the same experience as in poetry: you slip down the biggest of the snakes in the snakes and ladders game, and find yourself 'back in the pit'. This is quite simply *because you don't understand*. Poetry, he says, treasures such moments, loves to extend them and draw them out.

Well, we may agree that poetry is sometimes as difficult as philosophy. But that does not mean that poetry and philosophy are difficult *in the same way* as each other. If Deguy supposes them to be so, it is perhaps for this reason: that he knows what poetry is about too clearly, too abstractly. Has he misunderstood the balance between the writer's necessary passion, and that same writer's equally necessary dispassion? Tempted by the devil of abstract theory, is he not now too passionately detached? To this, but with deep unhappiness, I reply Yes. Deguy is a writer of magnificent gifts. I wish he was still building on the achievements of *Ouï dire* – one of the collections which will survive from the twentieth century.

There coexist with such experiments a range of much more traditionally poetic manners. Arthur Koestler's *Act of Creation* suggested that the secret of laughter is connected with the secret of both artistic and scientific creation. With scores of fascinating examples he sought (in my view, successfully) to prove that humour depends on the sudden and unexpected intermeshing of two (or more) systems of expectation, or 'matrices', as he calls them. Thus the tedious old joke of referring to Christmas and New Year as 'the alcoholidays' works because the disparate matrices of 'alcohol' and of 'holidays' are caught up together and illuminated with a new light by their pivoting upon the shared syllable, 'hol'. Koestler argues that scientific discoveries like that of Archimedes depend on similar unexpected associations of things that previously had seemed unconnected.

As a theory of the poetic image Koestler's view fits remarkably with the poems of Jean Follain – which work by the intersecting of non-humorous matrices. Here is a typical illustration:

Les Siècles

Regardant la marque du sabot
de son cheval de sang
le cavalier dans cette empreinte contournée
où déjà les insectes préparaient leur ouvroir
devina la future imprimerie
puis pour lui demander sa route
il s'approcha du charpentier
qui près d'une rose
en repos contemplait la vallée
et ne lirait jamais de livres.[10]

(The Centuries
Gazing at a hoofmark
left by his thoroughbred
the horseman in the curving print
where insects were already at their needlework
divined the future printing-press
then to ask his way
went up to a carpenter
resting by a rose
looking out across the valley
and who would never read a book.)

Almost the whole effect depends on one central association of two separate ideas: namely (1) the horse's hoofmark, (2) the shaping of wood, via (3) the imagined printing press. An unexpected connexion has appeared between distant, causally unconnected, events. The human mind is strangely fascinated by this. In short, the poem is a simplification, an exemplification (we may say), of the nature of poetry. It offers nothing more than one essential thing. The language is studiedly literal. There is apparently only a single metaphor to be found in it, namely the insects busy at their needlework (though this is decoration and therefore a prosaic, not a poetic, metaphor). What sobriety!

It is not quite true that there are no images here except the central one. 'Contournée' is also a term in heraldry; and so fits the world of the medieval knight. There is a further complication, for the poem is even more Koestlerian than I have said. For this particular association isn't merely poetic: it is also an instance of how ideas come together to create a technological invention – the printing press.

Nor are the rhythms of the poem notably 'poetic'. The lines end where the breath ends. They correspond to natural segments of meaning, and in no way disturb that meaning. The poetry therefore is not 'in' the language: it is permitted by the language's standing aside, allowing meaning to enter. The poetry is in our sense of ineffable strangeness, and no longer in the words, which merely enable it. A poem such as this moves in a direction totally at odds with Deguy: an absolute simplification of technique, so as to reach the essential – which is a single powerful image.

The image – as opposed to verbal dislocation – is the secret also for Guillevic and Jaccottet. The latter especially prizes the day he discovered the *haïku*. For, 'far from pursuing delirium and rupture, it succeeded [. . .] in illuminating the infinite in day-to-day moments and day-to-day existences'.[11]

But what of the metrical problem? The contemporary poet who has agonized over it most is Jacques Réda:

Le Prix de l'heure dans l'Ile St-Germain
Les ombres des passants s'allongent à vue d'oeil,
Marquant l'heure cosmique en travers des pelouses.
Aussi chaque brin d'herbe a son ombre qui bouge
Comme l'aiguille d'un trop sensible appareil.
Mais d'en haut, au sommet du large monticule,
Cette agitation demeure imperceptible. Un grand
Arbre déjà rougi par l'automne spécule
Solitaire au milieu de son vaste cadran.
De l'or pulvérisé tombe sur la colline:
A mesure que le soleil pâle décline,
Ce brouillard triomphal auréole Meudon
Puis un jeune passant qui répète: 'Pardon,
Monsieur, n'auriez-vous pas deux francs, deux francs cinquante?'
Tenant de l'autre main sa valise à brocante,
Il attend. Et je m'exécute. Encore un franc.
Je pense qu'il ira les fumer ou les boire.
Si l'on nous aperçoit depuis l'Observatoire,
Nous devons avoir l'air, dans le soir de safran,
D'un groupe antique sur le point de faire un pacte.
En échange en effet: 'Avez-vous l'heure exacte?'
Ai-je cru devoir dire alors qu'il s'éloignait.
D'un geste las il a découvert son poignet:
Rien. Mais sur la pelouse en bas son ombre oblique
Donnait l'heure (elle était juste et mélancolique).[12]

(The Price of Time on the Ile St-Germain
The shadows of the passers-by visibly lengthen
Marking the cosmic hour across the lawns.
And every grass-stem casts its shadow, quaking
Like the needle of a too sensitive machine.
But high up, at the top of the topmost rise,
This quivering is imperceptible. A tall
Tree already red with autumn speculates
Alone in the midst of its vast sun-dial.
Powdered gold scatters across the hillside:
By degrees as the pale sun declines,
The triumphal fog encircles, haloes Meudon,
Embraces a young passerby who keeps repeating:
'Excuse me, sir, would you happen
To have 2 francs, 2 and a ½ francs?'
His other hand clutches his peddler's case.
He waits ... I hastily ... Another franc.
I expect he'll drink them, smoke them.
If someone watches us from the Observatory,
We surely look, in evening's saffron glow,
Like Ancient Greeks about to make a pact.

> And yes, in exchange: 'Do you have the right time?'
> I tried to say as he slunk off.
> Exhaustedly he bared his wrist.
> Nothing. But on the lawn beside him his slant shadow
> Was registering the time (it was correct and mournful).)

Réda believes that poetry should 'capture in writing the energy of speech',[13] It is the rhythms of speech made to 'swing', and indeed it is this that distinguishes poetry from prose (*CQVPL*, 58). For he is a notable jazz critic. He writes that 'The ideal would be [...] a sort of dynamic super-regularity' (*CQVPL*, 88). For swing may be defined as the notes being struck at the ideally precise moment. One should add to this that – as I said in my *Language, Truth and Poetry* (Edinburgh, 1975) – poetic rhythm has a fundamental syncopatory character: the actual words of a poem operate cross-rhythms across a basic rhythmic framework. The mute 'e' is vitally important here, since it forces some syllables to be lengthened, producing a tension and release comparable to jazz (*CQVPL*, 65).

But this is not the most important thing about Réda. In 'The Price of Time' many levels of experience are present. Here we have rational causality, implicit in the fluttering of every grass-blade in the wind. Here we have the experiential real: the grass, the glow of the sinking sun upon the hilltop; – and the social dimension: the young tramp with his servile plea, the rite of exchange between humans. We have the frightening intuition of some supernatural wheel, silently turning. This is a true metaphysical poetry: it connects many dimensions of experience into a whole.

Yet another poetic manner is adopted (at least much of the time) by Queneau, Tardieu and of course the very popular Prévert. I shall illustrate it from Tardieu's *Monsieur Monsieur*:

> Les Catégories de l'entendement, ou Les Idées innées
>
> 1.–   L'eau qui gémit dans les tuyaux d'étage
>   est triste énormément et m'a donné l'image de l'Infini.
>
> 2.–   Je vais de ma table au bureau
>   et de mon bureau à ma table
>   et de ma table dans mon lit.
>   C'est pour les pas c'est pour la vue
>   ce que je nomme l'Etendue.
>
> 3.–   J'ai contemplé dans l'ombre des Musées
>   des Apollon sans bras, des torses mutilés
>   et c'était ça l'Eternité.[14]
>
> (The Categories of Understanding, or, Innate Ideas
>
> 1.–   The water gurgling in the pipes
>   is terribly sad and has given me the image of the Infinite.

2.– I go from my table to the desk
       and from the desk to my table
       and from my table to my bed.
       Walking and seeing
       is what Extension's for.

3.– In the shade of the Museums I looked
       at armless Apollos, mutilated torsos.
       So that was Eternity.)

Like much of the rest of this collection, this has so flat a tone that it sounds naïve, fatuous, baffled. Some of these poems have stage-instructions, telling us how they should be read (e.g. 'magnificently erudite' or 'peremptory and stupid, bureaucratic and pompous'). In this context, portentous abstractions such as 'infinity' and 'extension' sound nakedly absurd, and human knowledge is presented as no more than a useless set of tautologies – as in 'Je m'embrouille' where Tardieu solemnly explains that what separates two villages is the space between them. Vast capitalized abstractions and forces such as 'Space' know no more than we do, and we are (in 'Le Traquenard' (The Pitfall)) the victims of the great 'ON' who wants to make us look ridiculous, lets us talk nonsense, and never answers our questions. The world is a series of absurd misunder-standings, as in 'Les Erreurs' (The Mistakes), which is reminiscent of Lewis Carroll's lines: 'He thought he saw a railway clerk descending from a bus / He looked again and saw it was a hippopotamus'. The universe is not merely indifferent to us, but insultingly indifferent. In 'La Môme Néant' (The Zero Kid), the language is so childish that it is as if the world has been created by a congenital idiot, who is now speaking to us.

Philosophical questions are jeered at in nonsense verse, and shown to be quite pointless; yet the absence of answers is at the same time curiously disquieting, as in 'Le Syllogisme', which offers the dreadful thought that the poet is the only mortal soul in an otherwise immortal world.

Such anti-poetry is thus at the same time essentially poetic. The trivial and nonsensical are being used as the mark of our discomfort, as exiles in the world. One is reminded of Ionesco, and of the *koans* or nonsense-like riddles of Zen Buddhism. The message of Ionesco and of Zen is that the world is not as it appears to the eyes of reason. Nonsense is the path towards grasping its most profound meaning. The world is a tragi-comic stage, where human courage declares that our last and best act is thumbing our noses at the supernatural powers that thumb their noses at us. However bitter this futile mockery, there is a bitter joy in it too. The world is seen as absurd because meaning is absent from it; but once it is seen as absurd, there is a partial restoration of meaning – a meaning which is inexpressible, but implicit in the laughter. And indeed a writer of this kind defines laughter as being close to tears and close to the essence of poetry.

Alain Bosquet's *Sonnets pour une fin de siècle* often present a similar message: hoots of almost masochistic derision, directed at the miseries and hypocrisies of the human condition. This collection contains the angriest and most tormented of Bosquet's poems. He turns his savage wit in all directions – against politics, commercialism, sexual athletes, philistines and above all against himself – gradually building a polemical picture of the contemporary world. This is social poetry with a vengeance. Here is one of the gentler poems:

> Portrait d'un peuple heureux
>
> Ils ont conquis la Lune, et nous on se demande
> à quoi ça sert, cet astre nu comme un fromage.
> Ils se sont massacrés pour être un peu plus libres,
> au Bangla Desh: à deux poignées de riz par jour,
>
> vous parlez d'une affaire! Et ça coûte combien,
> cette sonde envoyée sur Mars et sur Vénus
> où de toute façon il fait trop chaud pour vivre?
> Ils ouvrent des musées: c'est à n'y rien comprendre,
>
> ces ronds qui sont carrés, ou ces taches trop rouges.
> Ils font des plans pour l'avenir; et le présent
> alors? Ils ont, c'est entendu, plus de pétrole
>
> que nous, et cependant pour la douceur de vivre,
> ils devront repasser: le bistrot où l'on cause,
> les copains, le tiercé, le beaujolais tout jeune . . .[15]

> (Portrait of a Happy Race
>
> They've set foot on the Moon – so what?
> That satellite as bald and bare as a Gruyère.
> They've slaughtered each other for freedom's sake
> in Bangla Desh. At two handfuls of rice a day,
>
> Big deal! The probes they sent to Mars and Venus,
> Whatever did they cost? It's far too hot
> to live there anyway. They keep on opening
> art galleries: who can make head or tail
>
> Of all those reddish splotches and square circles?
> They draw up plans for the future: what about
> the present? I know they have more oil than us,
>
> But as for the good life – pardon me while I laugh.
> They'll have to try harder than that. The bistro on the corner,
> your mates, the betting-shop, the *beaujolais nouveau* . . .)

Bosquet is usually a man of glittering images. Here he is a man of biting ironies. One supposes at first that 'the happy race' is the Americans, but this is immediately demolished by line 3. Then the poem veers to the opposite of a happy people – with a touch of sarcasm at the expense of Western wealth. We return to the Americans, sending space-probes to Mars and Venus – an activity again demolished by vulgarian common sense. Modern art is sneered at – a philistine is speaking apparently, but when he lauds the value of oil-wealth, this too is turned on its head, and 'la douceur de vivre', the great French value, is praised in its turn. The French, it seems, are a happier people than the Americans or the oil-rich Sheiks of Araby. But to identify 'the happy race' is to uncover a further irony, for the very phrase is an invitation to mockery. Bosquet is attacking French chauvinist self-satisfaction, and accusing his fellow-countrymen of philistinism.

What definition of 'poetry' do we deduce from these 'sonnets'? As poetry should, this works by compression, by continual surprise – in this case, not of images so often as of ironies: each irony is overturned by the next; and the deepest irony of all is not stated, but left for those who can see it to congratulate themselves upon. It is in accord with modern definitions of 'poetry' too in the sense that it is formally surprising: if these are sonnets, they are decadent *fin-de-siècle* sonnets which don't rhyme, and yet have fourteen lines of strictly twelve syllables each; and, though the satire is an ancient poetic genre (e.g. the Romans' savage and scatological Juvenal), Bosquet wants to amaze us by using the romantic-erotic, or at all events usually passionate, sonnet for the purposes of social comment.

Modern France has many other poetries to offer. There is OULIPO, a movement with which Queneau was associated, where mathematical games with letters were regarded as the secret of poetry. Thus, a pre-existent text might have applied to it the Method $M\pm7$, whereby every seventh word is replaced by the seventh word after or before it in the dictionary. Or a text might be produced under the constraint that it contains no letter *e* (as in Georges Perec's novel *La Disparition*). There is nothing *in principle* that is new in such exercises, for is the rationale behind them not thoroughly Valéryan? It is a clear case of 'If your shoes are too tight, you'll invent new dances', i.e. of the theory that poetry either 'is', or is the result of, formal constraints. The question, however, is not whether the dance is new, but whether anyone wants to watch it. OULIPO is as interesting as a parlour game, that is to say: it is also as boring as a parlour game.

Is Denis Roche's *Eros énergumène* more rewarding? Certainly there are tantalizing erotic images which constantly (but fleetingly) emerge and disappear from the page. A member of the committee of the avant-garde review *Tel Quel*, Denis Roche is prone to statements such as 'Poetry is inadmissible; besides, it doesn't exist'. An extreme anti-poetry, this, in which the typical *Tel Quel* procedure is adopted: i.e. you claim to be destroying something very old hat; however you are actually parasitic upon it. Parasites of course do sometimes kill their hosts – but only at the cost of dying themselves.

This anti-poetry has the ambition of seeking out the essence of poetry if only so as to throttle it. Roche speaks of 'bringing poetic production to its point of extremist *misculture*, the zero point [. . .] of poeticity'.[16] Once again we see the French taste for 'essences':

> mes phrases malgré la vitesse se
> détériorent comme ta lettre me faisait tout à
> l'heure comme une petite balle d'avoine issue
> de celle qui tire si adroitement par le traver
> s de mon torse que la douleur entre à pas comp
> tés, comptez dix mille, j'suis loin, et elle n'   (*M*, 113)

> (my phrases despite the speed fall
> off as your letter made me just
> now like a little bullet of oats fired out
> of her who shoots so dexterously acros
> s my torso that pain enters in meas
> ured steps, measure ten thousand, I'm far away, and she isn')

An anti-poetry of this kind is the simplest possible activity. Fit together a number of phrases which, à la Burroughs, might be drawn from the sentences of quite different books; cut words off in mid-syllable; disrupt language in as many ways as you can. Yet how can this debunk the emotional power or the significance of poetry, when it contains nothing that is either emotional or significant? Roche seems to suppose that 'poetry' is a category which exists only by social convention. His attack on it, however, gives it more content than this, for he depicts poetry as being defined by (1) the disposition of words on the page, (2) the space around the words, (3) disruption of meaning. Ironically, such works thus prove that that is *not* what (essentially) defines poetry. I assume that they also prove that poetry is not merely a social convention (though it is that too). Philippe Sollers's final phrase in his preface to *Le Mécrit* can be quoted ironically: '*Merde!* The blighter's got away!'

French poetry tends to seek out the ultimate – which it usually defines as either the essence of Being or the essence of language. Where the poet in question is sceptical about such ineffable entities as Being, it is poetry about poetry. Roche's poetry is of this kind. Like others of the *Tel Quel* group, he tends to suppose literary language to be a kind of cripple which has suffered the amputation of its referents: i.e., whereas ordinary language is referential, and relates to events in the real world, literature is self-referential, and exists in a circular and purely linguistic universe. It is a delusion to suppose that fiction, and therefore still less poetry, relates to reality. Alternatively, there is the view popularized by Derrida (who was also associated with *Tel Quel*) that our relationship to reality is fundamentally linguistic, so that we human beings are totally enwrapped, or enrapt, in words, locked within the reflecting mirrors of our own language systems. The writer is left therefore narcissistically contemplating his own writing, and, if he is of the avant-garde, subverting it. Now this too is an ancient doctrine dressed up in new and gladder rags: art for art's sake and anti-art for anti-art's sake both equally turn their backs on reality.

This kind of theory is also usually applied to the work of Edmond Jabès, which tends to be read through the distorting glass of Blanchot and Derrida. Thus, in the poet's interviews with Marcel Cohen, the latter remarks that 'your work situates itself as an empty container showing the impossibility of literature', and that it is 'properly speaking *illisible*, i.e. *irrécupérable*'(unreadable, i.e. intractable).[17] These literary buzz-words are the great and most modernist compliment of all, and suggest that Jabès's work offers so many contradictory interpretations that one cannot 'restore the text to the known' (as Cohen puts it). This shows how an influential group of readers and critics wish to define 'poetry': namely as a mode of writing so exemplarily resistant to interpretation that it ends up whirling in a void, bearing no relation to the world.

Is this however an accurate view of Jabès? Is it not due to the blinkers worn by these particular critics and philosophers? Jabès is of Egyptian Jewish origin, and his works are intensely Judaic. They read like fragments of the Talmud, or even the Kabbala. They are full of aphorisms and short anecdotes resembling parables. They frequently discuss the mysterious nature of God and the incapacity of human experience to grasp Him, and seethe with footnotes contributed by rabbis of whom I cannot say whether they are real or imaginary. Let me quote:

> You comment on your commentary and so on ad infinitum, until you're no more than the great-grandson of your son.[18]

> Burn your books, son. There's still time.   (*RL*, 83)

> Did not Rabbi Arwab write: 'The infinite opens like a book and, within it, all is blank.'[19]

In *Le Soupçon le Désert* there is a parable of a book which contains only blank pages, and in *El* there are a number of pages which are actually blank. When the author is brought to trial in *Le Livre des ressemblances* it is not merely treachery to literature he is charged with, but also treachery to Jewry, to religion and (by an equal and opposite irony) to atheism. His answer to these charges is inaudible to his judges. It can be seen why readers have taken this work to be an attack on the referentiality of language. However,

> Every written work conforms in the end with the unpronounceability of
> the name of Yahweh: such is the lesson of Judaism.[20]
>
> (And, remembering that 'we are made in God's image',)
> 'Can one resemble Him who, of his essence, has no likeness?' asked
> Rabbi Eliav. They answered him: 'Are we not the image of the void
> which has no image?'   (*LR*, 31)

Evidently Jabès has been misunderstood. This is all very much in the
Talmudic tradition, where the Bible – the word of God – is regarded as
being infinitely ambiguous. He is a mystical writer, whose message is, not
the irrelevance of language and the meaninglessness of experience, but the
reality (though He is inscrutable) of God, and the meaningfulness
(though it is ineffable) of ultimate reality. It is odd that he has been
misunderstood, however, since these concerns are not at all strange in the
modern French context. He is not engaged in the destruction of meaning,
but in the raising of it into a paradoxical dimension. He writes in
aphorisms like Char. He is busy (in his own way) with the same sort of
intense experience as Renard and Bonnefoy.

Whether Jabès's work is 'poetry' depends upon definition, which
depends in turn upon fashions in definition. Anthony Rudolf is in accord
with contemporary French intellectual life in calling him 'this great
poet'.[21] He is happy to be talked of under that heading, it seems. But then,
writers don't mind the heading so long as they are talked of. Jabès is
another illustration of Ponge's remark: if your writing belongs to no
familiar genre, you will be treated (or maltreated) as a 'poet'.

As we saw in Chapter 13, the over-riding flavour of modern French
poetry is mystical. Bonnefoy asks, not 'What is the nature of poetry?' but
'What is the nature of French poetry?' In short, the poetry is dictated by
the nature of the language. If we suppose that poets can best discern that
nature, then French oddly enough is no longer, in the twentieth century,
the tongue of the revolutionary Goddess Reason, but has discovered its
true nature as the language of mystical experience.

In reply to the question: 'What is the nature of poetry?', Guillevic starts
(but does not end) with concrete experience: 'Poetry is the awareness of
our relationships with the most humble things as well as with the most
important things.' Ideally, this is a rule of life, a way of being at home in
the world: 'The role of both poet and poem is to help others to find their
own poetry, to live their own lives, and perform the most everyday
actions, in the state of "presence" to oneself and to things: making coffee,
alone in the morning in the kitchen, going to work, watching a passing
pigeon, a falling stone . . .'[22] This is a state akin to contemplation. Poetry
replaces faith, and rightly so, because poetry is 'at the basis of all religions

[...] One might say that every religion is a poetry which has succeeded too well and has thereby become frozen and sclerotic' (*VP*, 34–6).

The shape of his poems on the page is meaningful: it tends towards the perpendicular, for the direction of words on a page of prose – and therefore of their movement through time – is horizontal: 'The poet sets up the poem *vertically* like a dam across time, the poem stands upright, and upright in its brevity as far as concerns those modern texts in which an awareness of the *arrested instant* is very intense.'[23] The Guillevic poem is both vertical and brief, for it is a moment of intense, almost mystical, concentration, during which time stops. We should not, says Guillevic, be surprised by the sight of old peasants sitting in motionless silence, for they are experiencing the sense of Being, 'they are living themselves, they have come to be in possession of themselves, of silence and of the moment. [...] Silence is the vase in which to collect the moment' (*CP*, 86–7). He speaks of the state in which the poet prepares to write his poem ('le pré-poème') in terms of communion with the nameless, impersonal universe (*VP*, 190–1).

Even André Frénaud, who says 'I believe that at death everything is finished,' could be thought to be conveying mystical experience. Such an experience is in fact described in his prose piece 'Cette nuit-là, à Florence'.[24] And many of his poems relate the excited creation of a wonderful castle, the poem, which struggles to communicate a mystical vision. He terms this 'the passage of the visitation'. Unfortunately, the vision always fades, and is succeeded by a state of disenchantment. At the very least he is another example of the modern French poet's search for the ultimate.

Now no one could be more sympathetic to mysticism than myself. Modern French poetry explores this experience wonderfully. One has the impression of a set of gifted experimenters, continuously perfecting their research instrument – language – and consistently confirming each other's findings. But it must be remembered that there is a venerable form of mysticism which regards the manifestation of the ultimate as no more and no less than *the real world*. Why is there no social poetry, or poetry of the everyday experience in contemporary France?

The truth is that there is such a poetry. I have not talked about it here because I have talked mainly about what is at present deemed important. We all know that poetry is a matter of fashion, and that Scève and Théophile de Viau – and for that matter John Donne – were out of fashion for two hundred years or more. To what extent is fashion dictated by 'authorities'? Who are these authorities, and how are they appointed? Am I one of them? And if I say the things I am saying now, will anyone listen to me?

It is true that there is a great deal of poetic activity in France, and that it is of many styles. However, the 'market-stall' most readily available to French readers of poetry is dominated by a few famous publishers. A poet accepted by one of them has 'arrived'. It is striking how many reputable poets are themselves editors in these same publishing houses – a situation which entails all the dangers of the self-perpetuating clique. Taste is dictated by these houses, by certain critics and by the intellectual elite. It will be argued that among the members of this elite, controversy is often cut-throat. True, but even the members of opposing coteries would in general agree about the *parameters* of the discussion. However 'orthodox' they take themselves to be, however fiercely they anathematize each other as 'heretics', all the competing churches of poetry agree at least as to who are the heathen, i.e. what kinds of poetry are outside the pale.

But what will French poetry look like in a hundred years? Will the great-great-grandchildren of Bonnefoy, Du Bouchet, Tardieu and Jaccottet still be reading them? Might they perhaps prefer the savage social comment of Bosquet, or Jean Pérol's wonderful *Le Cœur véhément* for its sense of life (in a Japanese sexual context)? Might they be reading Armen Lubin for the terrifying humanness of his experiences in hospital? Could they be reading Géo Norge for the very accessible wit and humanity of his view of human beings, organized into skilful and humorous metres? Will they be reading women poets, who seem to be rare among the current high-priesthood?

At present, however, the definitions are different. They are also various. Poetry may be defined by density, or by mere uncompressed brevity, or by the presence of white space on the page; by the sense it gives of a struggle with intractable material, lending it an improvised quality; by difficulty of interpretation, by disruption of linguistic forms, or by an imperialist desire to ingest all other forms of discourse. It may even be defined in more traditional ways, in terms of the image, or in terms of rhythm. But in any case the French poet wants always to know exactly what he is doing. He is fascinated by ultimates (whether in language or in Being), is drawn towards lofty peaks (of mysticism or of abstract theory). Perfection of form – or any way to define such a thing! – has vanished in this modern age, but by a curious irony it has been replaced by the search for perfection of thought.

Notes

Chapter 1

1 P. Zumthor, *Essai de poétique médiévale* (Paris, 1972), p. 98.
2 Jean Bodel. *La Chanson des Saxons*, ed. F. Michel (Paris, 1832, repr. Geneva, 1969).
3 Albert B. Lord, *The Singer of Tales* (Cambridge, Mass., 1960). The title reflects the notion that the epic singer recreates the story as he produces it in performance.
4 *La Chanson de Ste Foy*, ed. A. Fabre (Rodez, 1940).
5 *Parataxis* is a form of sentence construction in which the logical links provided by subordinating conjunctions are suppressed leaving a series of juxtaposed statements whose relationships must be inferred by the hearer. The syntactic system of fully articulated subordination is called *hypotaxis*.
6 *La Vie de Saint Alexis*, ed. C. Storey (Oxford, 1946).
7 A.G. Hatcher, 'The Old French Poem of Saint Alexis: A Mathematical Demonstration', *Traditio*, 8 (1952), 111–58.
8 P. Zumthor, 'Les Planctus épiques', *Romania*, 89 (1963), 61–9.
9 *La Chanson de Roland*, ed. F. Whitehead (Oxford, 1942).
10 The normal French name for Old French epic poetry is *chanson de geste*, in which *geste* means 'heroic act'. As used in the texts themselves the word comes to mean the tradition (oral or written) by which such 'deeds' were preserved and the family or community in which they were preserved.
11 *Tmesis* is the artificial separation of the elements of a word to emphasize some significant feature.
12 Marie de France, *Lais*, ed. K. Warnke, translated by L. Harf-Lancner (Paris, 1990), p. 14.
13 Chrétien de Troyes, *Le Conte du Graal*, ed. W. Roach (Geneva, 1959).
14 Chrétien de Troyes, *Yvain*, ed. M. Roques (Paris, n.d.).

15 Jean Renart, *Le Roman de la Rose ou de Guillaume de Dole*, ed. R. Lejeune (Paris, 1936); *Le Lai de l'ombre*, ed. J. Orr (Edinburgh, 1948).

16 M. Zink, 'Chrétien et ses contemporains', in *The Legacy of Chrétien de Troyes*, ed. N.J. Lacy, D. Kelly and K. Busby, Vol. 1 (Amsterdam, 1987, p. 8) traces this phenomenon back to Chrétien. This may be true with regard to his *Yvain*, the text on which Zink bases his claim, but it is not true of any other romance by Chrétien. Indeed, even in *Yvain*, the truth claim depends in part on the contemporary perception of Arthur as a historical figure.

Chapter 2

1 Roger Boase, *The Origin and Meaning of Courtly Love, a Critical Study of European Scholarship* (Manchester, 1977).

2 Costanzo de Girolamo, *I Trovatori* (Turin, 1989), p. 6; Henri Davenson, *Les Troubadours* (Paris, 1961), p. 10.

3 Frank R. Hamlin, Peter T. Ricketts and John Hathaway, *Introduction à l'étude de l'ancien provençal; textes d'étude* (Geneva, 1967), p. 99.

4 Paul Zumthor, *Essai de poétique médiévale* (Paris, 1973), pp. 205–19.

5 Hamlin, Ricketts and Hathaway, op. cit., p. 57.

6 Cesare de Lollis, *Vita e poesie di Sordello di Goïto* (Halle, 1896), pp. 180–1.

7 Hamlin, Ricketts and Hathaway, op. cit., p. 189.

8 Ibid., pp. 114–16.

9 Albert Pauphilet, *Poètes et romanciers du Moyen Age* (Paris, 1952), pp. 902–3.

10 I.M. Cluzel and L. Pressouyre, *La Poésie lyrique d'oïl, les origines et les premiers trouvères; textes d'étude*, 2nd edn (Paris, 1969), pp. 109–10.

11 Eustache Deschamps, *L'Art de dictier*, in *Œuvres complètes*, Vol. VII, ed. Gaston Raynaud (Paris, 1891), p. 269.

12 John Fox, *The Rhetorical Tradition in French Literature of the Later Middle Ages* (Exeter, 1969).

13 *Anthologie poétique française: Moyen Age*, ed. A. Mary (Paris, 1967), II, 145–6.

14 On the concept of subtlety as a compositional principle see Jacqueline Cerquiglini, *'Un engin si sutil': Guillaume de Machaut et l'écriture au XIVᵉ siècle* (Geneva, 1985).

15 Guillaume de Machaut, *La Louange des dames*, ed. Nigel Wilkins (Edinburgh, 1972), p. 88.

16 Ibid., p. 89.

17 On this group, and on the inappropriateness of the name traditionally given to them in critical writings, see Paul Zumthor, *Le Masque et la lumière* (Paris, 1978) and *Anthologie des grands rhétoriqueurs* (Paris, 1978), p. 7.

18 Christine de Pisan, *Ballades, rondeaux and virelais*, ed. Kenneth Varty (Leicester, 1965), p. 5. In Varty's text the penultimate line

reads 'En dur estat ma fortune embatue'. The editor does not take Fortune as the inimical goddess so frequent in the poetry of this period. In this respect Varty follows the Maurice Roy edition (*SATF*, I, 148). However, Roy links the past participle syntactically to the auxiliary 'est' of the previous line, leaving the refrain totally isolated. I prefer Varty's reading which links the last line of the stanza structurally to the refrain. The spelling 'Pizan', used in the rest of this chapter, was established as correct in 1961 by Elena Picolini, Christine's father being from Pizzano.

19 Charles d'Orléans, *Poésies*, ed. Pierre Champion, 2 vols (Paris, n.d.), II, 449.

Chapter 3

1 François Villon, *Œuvres*, ed. A. Longnon and L. Foulet, 4th edn (Paris, n.d.), p. 33. Laundry was traditionally done by beating the cloth with sticks or stones at the river's edge; similarly the bride and groom had to 'run the gauntlet' of the guests at their wedding. In other words Noel gave Villon a good drubbing when he caught him with Katherine de Vausselles. I have corrected the readings of l. 6 and 8 in accordance with the edition of J. Rychner and A. Henry (Geneva, 1974).

2 François Villon, *Selected Poems*, tr. Peter Dale (Harmondsworth, 1978), p. 235 (n. 22).

3 I. Siciliano, *François Villon et les thèmes poétiques du Moyen Age* (Paris, 1934).

4 *Les Chansons de Colin Muset*, ed. J. Bédier, 2nd edn (Paris, n.d.), pp. 7–9.

5 P. Zumthor, *Essai de poétique médiévale* (Paris, 1973), pp. 251–2.

6 *Les Chansons de Guillaume IX, duc d'Aquitaine*, ed. A. Jeanroy (Paris, n.d.), pp. 8–13.

7 For instance in 'Les Contredits de Franc Gontier', in Villon's *Testament* (*Œuvres* ed. cit., pp. 59–60). Villon contrasts the traditionally idyllic, 'Arcadian', view of the peasant's lot, which he considers in its harsh reality, with the luxury of a canon's life. He spies his canon through a keyhole:

> Sur mol duvet assis . . .
> Lez un brasier, en chambre bien natee,
> A son costé gisant dame Sidoine . . .
> Boire ypocras a jour et a nuytee . . .
>
> (Sitting on a soft eiderdown . . .
> Near a stove, in a soft-draped room,
> Beside him lying Lady Sidoine . . .
> Drinking mulled wine all day and all night long . . .)

8 Colin Muset, ed. cit., pp. 1–3.

9 *Œuvres complètes de Rutebeuf*, ed. E. Faral and J. Bastin, 2 vols (Paris, 1969), I, 526–30.

10 Ibid., I, 531.

11 The *Roman de la Rose* was started by Guillaume de Lorris as an allegorical poem dealing with the quest of an I-narrator for his lady's love (symbolized by a rose bud). The underlying ideology of the poem is that of the *trouvère* lyric. The poem was interrupted by Guillaume's death (*c.* 1230) and taken up by Jean de Meun (*c.* 1270), who transformed it into an encyclopaedic discussion of Naturalism, creation and sexuality, the nature of language and of human relationships, and the nature of women and their place in the natural and social order. It remained a controversial work, fuelling proto-feminist debate and setting the agenda for literary works dealing with love well into the sixteenth century.

12 A. Pauphilet, *Poètes et romanciers du Moyen Age* (Paris, 1952), pp. 971–2.

13 *The Penguin Book of French Verse: 1 – To the Fifteenth Century*, ed. B. Woledge (Harmondsworth, 1961), pp. 241–2.

14 Villon, *Œuvres*, p. 73.

Chapter 4

1 Pierre de Ronsard, *Les Amours*, ed. H. and C. Weber (Paris, 1963), p. 108. References to Ronsard's poems in this chapter are to this edition.

2 It is not always easy to distinguish the influence of Petrarch from that of his Italian followers of the fifteenth and sixteenth centuries, but French poets were often more familiar with his witty imitators, such as Serafino, Tebaldeo and Cariteo, whose manner was frivolous and more worldly, as well as with the more classical and more earnest later poets, Bembo, Ariosto and Tasso.

3 Maurice Scève, *Délie*, ed. I.D. McFarlane (Cambridge, 1966).

4 The name 'rhétoriqueur' is given to those poets who wrote at the end of the fifteenth century and the beginning of the sixteenth, who were associated with the court and noted for sophisticated verbal play. See Chapter 2, p. 27 and n. 17.

5 On Du Bellay, see below, Chapter 5, pp. 64–6.

6 In France, apart from Marguerite de Navarre, the author of courtly and religious love-poetry, as well as other spiritual poems, and Pernette du Guillet, of the Lyon school, there are no others of any standing at all.

7 Louise Labé, *Œuvres complètes*, ed. François Rigolot (Paris, 1986), sonnet 14.

8 See above, Chapter 3, n. 11.

9 See above, Chapter 1, pp. 1, 13.

10 Mariann Sanders Regan, *Love Words. The Self and the Text in Medieval and Renaissance Poetry* (Cornell, 1982), p. 51.

11 Doranne Fenoaltea, *'Si haulte architecture'. The Design of Scève's Délie'* (Lexington, Kentucky, 1982).

12 T.S. Eliot, 'Tradition and the Individual Talent' in *Selected Essays* (1919, 3rd edn, 1951), p. 22.

13 'Petrarchism and the quest for beauty in the *Amours* of Cassandre and the *Sonets pour Helene*' in *Ronsard the Poet*, ed. Terence Cave (London, 1973), pp. 79–120.

14 Donald Stone, Jr., *Ronsard's Sonnet Cycles: A Study in Tone and Vision* (Newhaven and London, 1966).

15 Fenoaltea, op. cit., p. 11.

Chapter 5

1 On sixteenth-century understanding of the imagination, see G. Castor, *Pléiade Poetics: A Study in Sixteenth Century Thought and Terminology* (Cambridge, 1964), pp. 143–67.

2 For poems by Ronsard, references are to *Œuvres complètes*, ed. G. Cohen, 2 vols, Bibliothèque de la Pléïade (Paris, 1950). (Abbreviated as 'Pl.' hereafter). Cohen gives the 1584 text, the last revised by Ronsard himself. In the case of this sonnet, I have preferred to use the text of the first edition (1552); see Ronsard, *Les Amours*, ed. H. and C. Weber, p. 20. For the 1584 version, see Pl. I, 14.

3 Rémy Belleau, *La Bergerie divisée en une première et seconde journée* (Paris, 1572). See also *La Bergerie*, edited by D. Delacourcelle (Geneva, 1954).

4 J. Du Bellay, *Les Regrets et autres œuvres poétiques*, ed. J. Jolliffe and M.A. Screech, Geneva, 1966, p. 104.

5 See D.B. Wilson, *Descriptive Poetry in France from Blason to Baroque* (Manchester, 1967).

6 See Castor, op. cit., pp. 37–50.

7 See E. Armstrong, *Ronsard and the Age of Gold* (Cambridge, 1968). On the 'language of the gods', see also above, Chapter 7.

8 Pl. II, p. 973. See also D.B. Wilson, *Ronsard Poet of Nature* (Manchester, 1961).

9 The *Antiquitez* are included in the edition by Jolliffe and Screech (see n. 4 above).

10 See 'Ronsard's Mythological Universe' in *Ronsard the Poet* (London, 1973), and *The Cornucopian Text: Problems of Writing in the French Renaissance* (Oxford, 1979), which includes an extended analysis of the sequence of Seasonal Hymns.

11 B. Aneau, *Imagination poëtique, traduicte en vers François des Latins et Grecs, par l'auteur mesme d'iceux* (Lyon, 1552).

12 See *The 'Délie' of Maurice Scève*, ed. (with an introduction and notes) I.D. McFarlane (Cambridge, 1966).

13 Pl. II, 321–31. See also Cave, *The Cornucopian Text*, pp. 256–68.

14 Pl. I, 515–21.

15 Pl. II, 64–72.

Chapter 6

1   See among others J.-P. Chauveau in the introduction to his *Anthologie poétique du XVIIe siècle* (Paris, 1987).

2   Quotations from Théophile's poetry are from the edition by G. Saba, *Œuvres complètes*, 3 vols (Paris, 1978–85). As this is the only modern critical edition now available, I have preserved the spelling. In the case of Tristan, there being no complete edition of his works, I have modernized the spelling rather than oscillate between conventions; all page references are to his *Poésies*, edited by P.A. Wadsworth (Paris, 1962). Quotations from Saint-Amant are taken from a variety of editions, mainly *Œuvres poétiques de Saint-Amant*, ed. L. Vérane (Paris, 1930). [N.B. At the time of going to press G. Saba has issued the authoritative modernized version of Théophile's poetry, *Œuvres poétiques* (Paris, 1990).]

3   See J. Marmier, 'La Poésie de Théophile de Viau, théâtre du moi', in *Papers in French Seventeenth-Century Literature*, 9 (1978), 50–65.

4   See Théophile, *Œuvres poétiques*, ed. J. Streicher (Geneva, 1951–8).

5   There is some dispute about the precise dates of composition, and therefore place of composition (prison, Chantilly, etc.), for several of these odes.

6   This may well be 'orfraye' (osprey), but the context suggests 'effraie' as the better reading.

7   From his *Les Plaintes d'Acante* (Antwerp, 1633).

8   The last of his volumes of verse (Paris, 1648).

9   Ed. C. Grise (Geneva, 1972).

Chapter 7

1   Page numbers for quotations from La Fontaine in this chapter refer to his *Œuvres diverses*, ed. P. Clarac (Paris, 1958).

2   Racine, *Œuvres*, ed. R. Picard, vol. II (Paris, 1952), p. 417.

3   See P. France, 'Between Prose and Verse', in *The Classical Tradition in French Literature*, ed. H.T. Barnwell and others (London, 1977), pp. 145–55.

4   Bernard Lamy, *La Rhétorique ou l'art de parler*, 4th edn (Amsterdam, 1699), p. 284.

5   Dominique Bouhours, *Entretiens d'Ariste et d'Eugène* (1671), ed. F. Brunot (Paris, 1962), p. 35.

6   Molière, *Le Bourgeois gentilhomme*, Act II, Scene 6.

7   T.S. Eliot, Introduction to Ezra Pound, *Selected Poems* (London, 1928).

8   Quoted by M. Gilman, *The Idea of Poetry in France* (Cambridge, Mass., 1958), p. 15.

9   Fénelon, *Œuvres*, ed. J. Le Brun (Paris, 1983), pp. 35–6.

10 *The Poetry of France*, ed. Alan Boase, Vol. II, 1600–1800 (London, 1973), p. 271.

11 Quoted in *Les Poétiques du classicisme*, ed. A. Kibédi-Varga (Paris, 1990), pp. 95–6.
12 Quoted by Gilman, op. cit., p. 109.
13 See Descartes, *Correspondance*, ed. C. Adam and G. Milhaud (Paris, 1936–63), VI, 133, and d'Alembert, *Œuvres* (Paris, 1821–2), I, 78.
14 Diderot, *Lettre sur les sourds et muets*, in his *Œuvres*, ed. H. Dieckman, J. Proust and J. Varloot, Vol. IV (Paris, 1978), pp. 169ff.
15 Molière, *La Princesse d'Elide*, Act II, Scene 1.
16 Racine, *Œuvres*, ed. R. Picard, Vol. I (Paris, 1950), pp. 965–9.
17 Abbé Desfontaines, Preface to Virgile, *Œuvres complètes*, Vol. I (Paris, 1743).
18 See P. France, 'The French Pope', in *Alexander Pope, Essays for the Centenary*, ed. C. Nicholson (Aberdeen, 1988), pp. 117–29.
19 See R. Finch, *The Sixth Sense, Individualism in French Poetry, 1686–1760* (Toronto, 1966) and his anthology *French Individualist Poetry, 1686–1760* (Toronto, 1971). For a full-scale study of French poetry in the first half of the eighteenth century, see S. Menant, *La Chute d'Icare: la crise de la poésie française, 1700–1750* (Geneva, 1981).
20 *Œuvres de Madame et de Mademoiselle Deshoulières* (Paris, 1753), I, 25.
21 References to Chénier are to André Chénier, *Œuvres complètes*, ed. G. Walter (Paris, 1958).

Chapter 8

1 Page numbers for quotations from La Fontaine's *Fables* refer to the edition by G. Couton (Paris, 1962).
2 On the thirteenth-century debate see above, Chapter 1.
3 N. Rapin, *Réflexions sur la poétique de ce temps*, quoted in *Les Poétiques du classicisme*, ed. A. Kibédi-Varga (Paris, 1990), pp. 156–8.
4 References to *Clovis* are to the facsimile edition published by Félix R. Freudmann (Louvain and Paris, 1972).
5 D. Maskell, *The Historical French Epic, 1500–1700* (Oxford, 1973), p. 19. On the biblical epic see R. A. Sayce, *The French Biblical Epic in the Seventeenth Century* (Oxford, 1955).
6 H.G. Hall, *Richelieu's Desmarets and the Century of Louis XIV* (Oxford, 1990), p. 307.
7 For *La Henriade*, see in particular the edition of O.R. Taylor in *The Complete Works of Voltaire*, ed. T. Besterman *et al.*, Vol. IV (Geneva, 1970).
8 Voltaire, *Mélanges*, ed. J. van den Heuvel (Paris, 1965), p. 235.
9 Thomas Traherne, *Century II*, quoted by B. Vickers in 'The *Songs and Sonnets* and the Rhetoric of Hyperbole', in *John Donne: Essays in Celebration*, ed. A.J. Smith (London, 1972), p. 148.
10 Quoted by R. Finch in *French Individualist Poetry, 1686–1760* (Toronto, 1971), pp. 136–7.
11 Finch, op. cit., p. 144.

12   P.-D. Ecouchard-Lebrun, *La Nature, ou le bonheur philosophique*, quoted by J. Roudaut in his interesting anthology *Poètes et grammairiens au XVIIIe siècle* (Paris, 1971).

13   Page numbers for quotations from Delille refer to the 10-volume *Œuvres* (Paris, 1833). On Delille, see *Delille, est-il mort?*, ed. P. Auserve (Clermont-Ferrand, 1967) and E. Guitton, *Jacques Delille et le poème de la nature en France de 1750 à 1820* (Paris, 1974).

14   Page numbers for quotations from Boileau's *Satires* refer to the rich edition of C.-H. Boudhors (Paris, 1936; new edn, 1966).

15   See P. France, *Rhetoric and Truth in France: Descartes to Diderot* (Oxford, 1972), pp. 3–4.

16   Jean-Jacques Rousseau, *Emile*, ed. F. and P. Richard (Paris, 1962), p. 115.

Chapter 9

1   Victor Hugo, *Hernani*, I, i.

2   A.G. Swinburne, *A Study of Victor Hugo* (London, 1886), p. 13.

3   Théodore de Banville, *Petit Traité de poésie française* (Editions de la Bibliothèque de l'Echo de la Sorbonne, Paris, 1872; repr. by Editions d'Aujourd'hui, Plan de la Tour, 1978), p. 91. All references will be to this edition.

4   André Chénier, *Œuvres complètes*, ed. G. Walter (Paris, 1958), p. 195. See also above, pp. 118–20.

5   Victor Hugo, 'Réponse à un acte d'accusation', *Poésie*, ed. B. Leuilliot (Paris, 1972), I, 642. The second hemistich of the second line consists of just one word, 'révolutionnaire', which Hugo counts as six syllables.

6   Preface to *Odes et Ballades* (1826), *Poésie*, I, 86.

7   Théophile Gautier, *Histoire du romantisme* (Paris, 1911; 1st edn, 1874), p. 2.

8   Charles Baudelaire, 'Marceline Desbordes-Valmore', *Curiosités esthétiques – L'Art romantique*, ed. H. Lemaitre (Paris, 1962), p. 746.

9   Marceline Desbordes-Valmore, *Œuvres poétiques*, ed. M. Bertrand (Grenoble, 1973), I, 109.

10   Gérard de Nerval, *Œuvres*, ed. H. Lemaitre (Paris, 1966), pp. 705–8.

11   The word 'orbite', though it is, like the English 'orbit', ambiguous, more normally has the sense of 'eye-socket'.

12   Baudelaire, *Les Fleurs du Mal*, ed. A. Adam (Paris, 1961), p. 38.

13   Stéphane Mallarmé, *Œuvres complètes*, ed. H. Mondor and G. Jean-Aubry (Paris, 1945), p. 74.

Chapter 10

1   The following abbreviations are used (in all cases the place of publication is Paris and, unless stated otherwise, the publisher is Gallimard): *PSI* Rimbaud, *Poésies, Une Saison en enfer, Illuminations*

(1973); *LP* Lamartine, *Poésies*, Hachette (1957); *LC* Hugo, *Les Contemplations* (1965); *MP* Musset, *Poésies*, Hachette (1949); *CB* Desnos, *Corps et Biens* (1968).

2   Letter to his friend Virieu, 25 January 1821; in *La Chute d'un ange: Fragment du Livre Primitif*, ed. M.-F. Guyard (Geneva – Lille, 1954), p. 13.

3   By N. Araujo, *In Search of Eden: Lamartine's Symbols of Despair and Deliverance* (Brookline – Leyden, 1976), p. 177.

4   By M.-F. Guyard, op. cit., p. 36.

5   See, for example, P. Lejeune, *L'Ombre et la lumière dans 'Les Contemplations' de Victor Hugo* (Paris, 1968), p. 38; or S. Nash, *'Les Contemplations' of Victor Hugo: An Allegory of the Creative Process* (Princeton, 1976), pp. 179–89.

6   In P. Berret, *La Légende des Siècles de Victor Hugo* (Paris, 1957), p. 56.

7   See L.S. Senghor, *Liberté I: Négritude et humanisme* (Paris, 1964), p. 128.

8   See R. Bourgeois, *L'Ironie romantique* (Grenoble, 1974), p. 16.

9   See P. Gastinel, *Le Romantisme d'Alfred de Musset* (Paris, 1933), pp. 484–5.

10 See A. de Musset, *Poésies complètes*, ed. M. Allem (Paris, 1962), p. 738.

11 The French word *dérèglement* is ambiguous.

12 Yves Bonnefoy, for instance, relates the reference to Leviathan in l. 50 to Hugo's 'Pleine Mer' rather than to Job or Hobbes (PSI, 259); S. Bernard sees in l. 15 a possible allusion to 'Oceano Nox' (Rimbaud, *Œuvres*, ed. S. Bernard (Paris, 1960, p. 423)).

13 Jean Richer, *L'Alchimie du verbe de Rimbaud* (Paris – Brussels – Montreal, 1972), pp. 169–94.

14 (Paris, 1972), pp. 40–1.

15 See C.A. Hackett, *Rimbaud: A Critical Introduction* (Cambridge, 1981), p. 116.

16 A. Breton, *Anthologie de l'humour noir* (Paris, 1966), p. 266.

17 C. Cros, T. Corbière, *Œuvres complètes*, ed. L. Forestier, P.-O. Walzer and F.F. Burch (Paris, 1970), p. 722.

18 Ibid., pp. 681–4.

19 A. Breton, *Manifestes du surréalisme* (Paris, 1985), pp. 110–11.

20 Published in *Domaine public* (Paris, 1953), pp. 346–53.

21 Ibid., p. 347.

22 Ibid., p. 348.

23 In 'La Vision hallucinatoire chez Victor Hugo', *Modern Language Notes*, 78 (1963), 225–41 (p. 227).

24 Baudelaire, *Œuvres complètes*, ed. Y.-G. Le Dantec (Paris, 1954), p. 946.

Chapter II

1   Théodore de Banville, *Petit traité de poésie française* (Paris, 1872; repr. Editions d'aujourd'hui, Plan de la Tour, 1978), p. 6.

2   Baudelaire, *Petits Poèmes en prose*, ed. R. Kopp (Paris, 1973), p. 22. All
     references will be to this edition.
3   Aloysius Bertrand, *Gaspard de la Nuit*, ed. M. Milner (Paris, 1980),
     pp. 217–18. All references will be to this edition.
4   'Enfance V', in Rimbaud, *Œuvres complètes*, ed. A. Adam (Paris,
     1972), pp. 124–5. All references will be to this edition.
5   The French verb 'louer' can mean either 'rent' or 'praise'. If one takes
     the latter sense, the beginning of this sentence might be translated:
     'It is high time I heard sung the praises of this tomb.'
6   Comte de Lautréamont, *Œuvres* (Paris, 1987), p. 372. All references
     will be to this edition.
7   Stéphane Mallarmé, *Œuvres complètes*, ed. H. Mondor and G. Jean-
     Aubry (Paris, 1945), p. 869. All references will be to this edition.
8   Free verse ('vers libres') has referred to various things at various
     times in the history of French poetry, including La Fontaine's use
     of rhyming lines of assorted lengths in his fables, written in the
     seventeenth century. Mallarmé, however, has in mind here a specific
     movement. From the time of Hugo until about 1870, all serious
     French poets (including Mallarmé and Baudelaire) stuck to the rules
     governing French versification, more or less as laid down by
     Banville; every line had to have a precise syllable count, and if all the
     lines in a poem were not of the same length, then they had to be in
     stanzas with a recognizable pattern. But after that, particularly under
     the influence of Verlaine, lines of uneven length began to be used
     occasionally; and in 1887 came what was felt to be a decisive break.
     Gustave Kahn, in his *Palais nomades*, used lines whose length
     conformed to no consistent pattern. Mallarmé, like most poets, felt
     that French verse had reached a historic crisis point. Even in verse,
     the features that traditionally defined poetry were henceforth to be
     considered not as obligatory, but as optional. One could ignore
     them, and still be counted a poet.
9   Pages from *Un Coup de dés* are reproduced on the endpapers to the
     present volume.

Chapter 12

1   Guillaume Apollinaire, *Œuvres poétiques*, ed. M. Adéma and M.
     Décaudin (Paris, 1965). All references to Apollinaire's poetry (A) are
     to this edition. References to Cendrars's poetry (C) are to Blaise
     Cendrars, *Œuvres complètes*, Vol. I (Paris, 1963). References to
     Queneau's poetry (Q) are to Raymond Queneau, *Œuvres complètes*,
     ed. C. Debon, Vol. I (Paris, 1989).
2   In *Anthologie de la poésie française du XXe siècle*, ed. M. Décaudin,
     Vol. I (Paris, 1983), p. 226.
3   Revised and enlarged edition (Paris, 1965).
4   See his 'A propos de la littérature expérimentale' (Q, 347).
5   See also Queneau's *Pierrot mon ami* (Paris, 1943).

Chapter 13

1   Paul Valéry, *Œuvres*, ed. J. Hytier, 2 vols (Paris, 1957–60).

2   St-John Perse, *Œuvres complètes* (Paris, 1972), p. 326.

3   Paul Claudel, *Positions et propositions* (Paris, 1928–34), I, 17.

4   Pierre Emmanuel, *Babel* (Paris, 1951), p. 293.

5   Emmanuel, *Autobiographies: Qui est cet homme? L'Ouvrier de la onzième heure* (Paris, 1947 and 1953), p. 187. (Henceforth *A*.)

6   Emmanuel, *La Face humaine* (Paris, 1963), p. 189. (Henceforth *FH*.)

7   Pierre Jean Jouve, *Diadème* (Paris, 1966), p. 39.

8   Jouve, *En Miroir*, 2nd edn (Paris, 1970), p. 9. (Henceforth *EM*.)

9   Yves Bonnefoy, *Pierre écrite* (Paris), 1969), p. 23.

10 Bonnefoy, *Hamlet* (Paris, 1962), p. 237–9.

11 Bonnefoy, *L'Improbable, suivi d'Un Rêve fait à Mantoue* (Paris, 1980), p. 259.

12 Bonnefoy, *Du mouvement et de l'immobilité de Douve, suivi de Hier régnant désert* (Paris, 1970), p. 153.

13 René Char, *Fureur et mystère* (Paris, p. 58).

14 Char, *Recherche de la base et du sommet* (Paris, p. 123).

15 Jean-Claude Renard, *Quand le poème devient prière* (Paris, 1987). (Henceforth *QP*.)

16 Renard, *Notes sur la poésie* (Paris, 1970), p. 152. (Henceforth *NP*.)

17 Renard, *Une autre parole* (Paris, 1981), p. 154.

18 Renard, *La Lumière du silence* (Paris, 1978), p. 36.

Chapter 14

1   The following abbreviations are used (in all cases the place of publication is Paris and, unless stated otherwise, the publisher is Gallimard): *M* Breton, *Manifestes du surréalisme*, 1985; *PP* Breton, *Les Pas perdus*, 1924; *PJ* Breton, *Point du jour*, 1970; *E* Breton, *Entretiens*, 1952; *CT* Breton, *Clair de terre*, 1966; *IC* Breton & Eluard, *L'Immaculée Conception*, Seghers, 1961; *PR* Soupault, *Poèmes retrouvés 1918–1981*, Lachenal & Ritter, 1982; *TS* Aragon, *Traité du style*, 1928; *MP* Aragon, *Le Mouvement perpétuel*, 1970; *GJ* Péret, *Le Grand Jeu*, 1969; *CB* Desnos, *Corps et biens*, 1968; *CD* Eluard, *Capitale de la douleur*, 1966; *ML* Césaire, *Moi, laminaire . . .*, Seuil, 1982.

2   In M. Nadeau, *Histoire du surréalisme*, suivie de *Documents surréalistes* (Paris, 1964), p. 219.

3   The Dada movement is often regarded as a precursor of Surrealism. It may even be considered as its first, more negative phase. Breton, who was not a totally impartial observer, preferred to present the two movements as 'two waves, each of which in turn covered the other' (*E*, 57).

4   Tristan Tzara, *Sept Manifestes Dada. Lampisteries* (Paris, 1963), p. 31.

5   Manchester, 1988.

6   Lachlan Mackinnon, *The Independent*, 30 June 1988, p. 14.

7 London, 1923; new edn, 1949.

8 John Lyons, *Introduction to Theoretical Linguistics* (Cambridge, 1969), p. 427.

9 Saussure, *Cours de linguistique générale* (Paris, 1979), p. 101.

10 *The Complete Works of Lewis Carroll*, with an introduction by Alexander Woollcott (London – New York, 1939).

11 Baudelaire, 'Théophile Gautier', in *Œuvres complètes*, ed. C. Pichois, 2 vols (Paris, 1975–6), II, 118.

12 Eluard, *Le Poète et son ombre*, ed. Robert D. Valette (Paris, 1963), p. 104.

13 Tzara, op. cit., p. 64.

14 By M.-C. Dumas, *Robert Desnos ou l'exploration des limites* (Paris, 1980), p. 300.

15 At the end of the Second World War Isidore Isou led a group of so-called *Lettristes* whose poetry was based on the central idea that 'nothing exists in the mind that is not, or can not, become a letter'; in Isou, 'Bilan lettriste 1947', *Fontaine*, October 1947; quoted in J. Rousselot, *Les Nouveaux Poètes français: panorama critique* (Paris, 1959), p. 112.

16 Desnos, *Fortunes* (Paris, 1969), p. 162.

17 Péret, *Œuvres complètes*, 2 vols (Paris, 1969), I, 281.

18 *André Breton: Selected Poems* (London, 1969), p. 33.

19 Eluard, *Choix de poèmes* (Paris, 1951), p. 273.

20 A. Césaire, *Cahier d'un retour au pays natal* (Paris, 1971), p. 20.

21 Ibid., p. 24.

22 See R. Callan, *Miguel Angel Asturias* (New York, 1970), pp. 120, 162; and C. Couffon, *Miguel Angel Asturias* (Paris, 1970), p. 45.

23 See Callan, p. 162.

Chapter 15

1 Henri Michaux, *Mes propriétés* (Paris, 1929); repr. in René Bertelé, *Henri Michaux* (Paris, 1957), p. 118.

2 Francis Ponge, *Nioque de l'avant-printemps* (Paris, 1983), pp. 61–2.

3 Ponge, *La Rage de l'expression* (Paris, 1976), p. 15.

4 Ponge, *Le Parti pris des choses* (Paris, 1967), p. 173. (Henceforth *PPC*.)

5 Ponge, *Le Grand Recueil: Méthodes* (Paris, 1961), pp. 255–7.

6 *Entretiens de F. Ponge avec Philippe Sollers* (Paris, 1970), p. 15.

7 Michel Deguy, *Actes* (Paris, 1966), p. 73.

8 Deguy, *Reliefs* (Paris, 1975), p. 22.

9 Deguy, *Jumelages, suivi de Made in U.S.A.* (Paris, 1978), p. 165.

10 Jean Follain, *Territoires* (Paris, 1953).

11 Philippe Jaccottet, *Transaction secrète* (Paris, 1987), p. 312.

12 Jacques Réda, *Retour au calme* (Paris, 1989).

13 Réda, *Celle qui vient à pas légers* (Paris, 1985), p. 64. (Henceforth *CQVPL*.)

14 Jean Tardieu, *Le Fleuve caché, Poésies 1938–61* (Paris, 1968), p. 136.
15 Alain Bosquet, *Sonnets pour une fin de siècle* (Paris, 1980), p. 62.
16 Denis Roche, *Le Mécrit* (Paris, 1972), p. 139. (Henceforth *M.*)
17 Edmond Jabès, *Du Désert au livre, entretiens avec Marcel Cohen* (Paris, 1980), pp. 155, 158.
18 Jabès, *Le Retour au livre* (Paris, 1965), p. 21. (Henceforth *RL.*)
19 Jabès, *L'Ineffaçable L'Inaperçu* (Paris, 1980), p. 21.
20 Jabès, *Le Livre des ressemblances* (Paris, 1976), p. 140. (Henceforth *LR.*)
21 *Modern Poetry in Translation*, 16, ed. Anthony Rudolf (London, 1973), p. 5.
22 Eugène Guillevic, *Vivre en poésie, Entretiens* (Paris, 1980), p. 11. (Henceforth *VP.*)
23 Guillevic, *Choses parlées, Entretiens avec Raymond Jean* (Seyssel, 1982), p. 79. (Henceforth *CP.*)
24 André Frénaud, *Haeres* (Paris, 1982), pp. 63–6.

Select Bibliography

The inclusion of studies of individual poets would have made this bibliography excessively long. It is therefore confined essentially to anthologies and general studies.

General Anthologies

Boase, Alan M., *The Poetry of France*, 4 vols (London, 1964–73)
The Penguin Book of French Verse, 4 vols (Harmondsworth, 1957–9): I Woledge, Brian (ed.), *To the Fifteenth Century*, 1957; II Brereton, Geoffrey (ed.), *The Sixteenth to the Eighteenth Century*, 1958; III Hartley, Anthony (ed.), *The Nineteenth Century*, 1957; IV Hartley, Anthony (ed.), *The Twentieth Century*, 1959

General Studies

Gilman, Margaret, *The Idea of Poetry in France from Houdar de la Motte to Baudelaire* (Cambridge, Mass., 1958)
Lewis, Roy, *On Reading French Verse: A Study of Poetic Form* (Oxford, 1982)
Martin, Graham Dunstan, *Language, Truth and Poetry* (Edinburgh, 1975)
Mazaleyrat, Jean, *Eléments de métrique française* (Paris, 1974)
Sabatier, R., *Histoire de la poésie française*, 9 vols (Paris, 1975–88)
Scott, Clive, *The Riches of Rhyme: Studies in French Verse* (Oxford, 1988)
Scott, Clive, *French Verse-Art: A Study* (Cambridge, 1980)

Anthologies – Medieval

Pauphilet, Albert (ed.), *Poètes et romanciers du moyen âge*, revised by Régine Pernaud and A.-M. Schmidt (Paris, 1967)

Critical Studies – Medieval

Cerquiglini, Jacqueline, *'Un engin si soutil': Guillaume de Machaut et l'écriture au XIVe siècle* (Paris, 1985)

Dragonetti, Roger, *La Technique poétique des trouvères dans la chanson courtoise* (Bruges, 1960)

Freeman-Regalado, Nancy, *Poetic Patterns in Rutebeuf: A Study in Non-Courtly Poetic Modes of the Thirteenth Century* (New Haven, Conn., 1970)

Paterson, L.M., *Troubadours and Eloquence* (Oxford, 1975)

Poirion, Daniel, *Le Poète et le prince: l'évolution du lyrisme courtois de Guillaume de Machaut à Charles d'Orléans* (Paris, 1965)

Rychner, Jean, *La Chanson de geste, essai sur l'art poétique des jongleurs* (Geneva, 1955)

Stevens, John, *Medieval Romance* (London, 1973)

Stevens, John, *Words and Music in the Middle Ages: Song, Narrative, Dance and Drama, 1050–1350* (Cambridge, 1986)

Topsfield, Leslie T., *Chrétien de Troyes: A Study of the Arthurian Romances* (Cambridge, 1981)

Uitti, Karl D., *Story, Myth and Celebration in Old French Narrative Poetry 1050–1200* (Princeton, N.J., 1973)

Zumthor, Paul, *Essai de poétique médiévale* (Paris, 1972)

Anthologies – Sixteenth to Eighteenth Centuries

Picard, Raymond (ed.), *La Poésie française de 1640 à 1680*, 2 vols (Paris, 1964–9)

Roudaut, Jean (ed.), *Poètes et grammairiens du XVIIIe siècle: Anthologie* (Paris, 1971)

Rousset, Jean (ed.), *Anthologie de la poésie baroque française*, 2 vols (Paris, 1961)

Schmidt, Albert-Marie (ed.), *Poètes du XVIe siècle*, 2nd edn (Paris, 1964)

Steele, Alan J. (ed.), *Three Centuries of French Verse, 1511–1819*, 2nd edn, rev. (Edinburgh, 1961)

Critical Studies – Sixteenth to Eighteenth Centuries

Castor, Grahame, *Pléiade Poetics* (Cambridge, 1964)

Cave, Terence, *The Cornucopian Text: Problems of Writing in the French Renaissance* (Oxford, 1979)

Demerson, Guy, *La Mythologie classique dans l'œuvre lyrique de la 'Pléiade'* (Geneva, 1972)

Finch, Robert, *The Sixth Sense: Individualism in French Poetry, 1686–1760* (Toronto, 1966)

McFarlane, Ian D., *A Literary History of France. Renaissance France, 1470–1589* (London & Tonbridge – New York, 1974)

Menant, Sylvain, *La Chute d'Icare: la crise de la poésie française, 1700–1750* (Geneva, 1981)

Moss, Ann, *Poetry and Fable: Studies in Mythological Narrative in Sixteenth-Century France* (Cambridge, 1984)

Mourgues, Odette de, *Metaphysical, Baroque and Précieux Poetry* (Oxford, 1953)

Raymond, Marcel, *Baroque et renaissance poétique: préalable à l'examen du baroque littéraire* (Paris, 1955)
Raymond, Marcel, *La Poésie française et le maniérisme* (Geneva, 1971)
Rousset, Jean, *La Littérature de l'âge baroque en France* (Paris, 1960)
Weber, Henri, *La Création poétique au XVIe siècle en France* (Paris, 1956)

Anthologies – Nineteenth and Twentieth Centuries

Bédouin, Jean-Louis (ed.), *La Poésie surréaliste*, 2nd edn (Paris, 1983)
Berton, Jean (ed.), *Nouvelle Poésie contemporaine: une anthologie* (Paris, 1985)
Bosquet, Alain (ed.), *La Poésie française depuis 1950: une anthologie* (Paris, 1979)
Broome, Peter, and Graham Chesters (eds), *An Anthology of Modern French Poetry 1850–1950* (Cambridge, 1976)
Décaudin, Michel (ed.), *Anthologie de la poésie française du XXe siècle* (Paris, 1983)
Hackett, C.A. (ed.), *Anthology of Modern French Poetry from Baudelaire to the Present Day* (Oxford, 1964)
Higgins, Ian (ed.), *Anthology of Second World War French Poetry* (London, 1982)
Martin, Graham Dunstan (ed. and tr.), *Anthology of Contemporary French Poetry* (Edinburgh, 1972)
Rees, William (ed.), *French Poetry 1820–1950* (Harmondsworth, 1990)
Watson-Taylor, Simon, and Edward Lucie-Smith (eds), *French Poetry Today: A Bilingual Anthology* (London, 1971)

Critical Studies – Nineteenth and Twentieth Centuries

Banville, Théodore de, *Petit Traité de poésie française* (Plan-de-la-Tour, 1978)
Beaumont, E.M., J.M. Cocking, and J. Cruickshank (eds), *Order and Adventure in Post-Romantic French Poetry: Essays Presented to C.A. Hackett* (Oxford, 1973)
Bernard, Suzanne, *Le Poème en prose de Baudelaire jusqu'à nos jours* (Paris, 1959)
Bishop, Michael, *The Contemporary Poetry of France: Eight Studies* (Amsterdam, 1985)
Bonnefoy, Yves, *Entretiens sur la poésie, 1972–90* (Paris, 1990)
Broome, Peter, and Graham Chesters, *The Appreciation of Modern French Poetry 1850–1950* (Cambridge, 1976)
Cardinal, Roger (ed.), *Sensibility and Creation: Studies in Twentieth Century French Poetry* (London – New York, 1977)
Caws, Mary Ann, and Hermine Riffaterre (eds), *The Prose-Poem in France: Theory and Practice* (New York, 1983)
Clancier, Georges-Emmanuel, *La Poésie française: panorama critique de Rimbaud au surréalisme* (Paris, 1959)
Cornulier, Benoît de, *Théorie du vers: Rimbaud, Verlaine, Mallarmé* (Paris, 1982)
Deguy, Michel, *Actes* (Paris, 1966)
Frénaud, André, *Notre inhabileté fatale: entretiens avec Bernard Pingaud* (Paris, 1979)
Gibson, Robert, *Modern French Poets on Poetry* (Cambridge, 1961)
Jabès, Edmond, *Du désert au livre: entretiens avec Marcel Cohen* (Paris, 1981)

Kristeva, Julia, *La Révolution du langage poétique: Lautréamont et Mallarmé* (Paris, 1976)

Lehmann, A.G., *The Symbolist Aesthetic in France 1885–1895* (Oxford, 1950)

Meschonnic, Henri, *Pour la poétique*, 3 vols (Paris, 1970–3)

Michaud, Guy, *Message poétique du symbolisme*, 2nd edn (Paris, 1966)

Onimus, Jean, *La Connaissance poétique* (Paris, 1966)

Onimus, Jean, *Expérience de la poésie* (Paris, 1973)

OULIPO, *La Littérature potentielle* (Paris, 1973)

Raymond, Marcel, *De Baudelaire au surréalisme*, 2nd edn, rev. (Paris, 1969)

Renard, Jean-Claude, *Une autre parole* (Paris, 1981)

Richard, Jean-Pierre, *Onze études sur la poésie moderne* (Paris, 1964)

Richard, Jean-Pierre, *Poésie et Profondeur*, 2nd edn (Paris, 1976)

Roubaut, Jacques, *La Vieillesse d'Alexandre* (Paris, 1978)

Index

COMME SI

Une insinuation

au silence

dans quelque proche

voltige